K3+

ERASMO ACOSTA

WITH GALA STEVENSON

ERASMIX BOOKS
PORTLAND, OR

This is a work of fiction. All names, characters, places, and incidents are either products of the author's imagination or are used fictitiously. No reference to any real person is intended or should be inferred.

ISBN: 978-0-9899987-9-6 (digital)
ISBN: 978-0-9961544-8-2 (audio)
ISBN: 979-8-5785865-8-3 (paperback)
ISBN: 979-8-8036211-4-0 (hardcover)

Copyright registration: TXu 2-115-168

Cover and notebook image (Chapter 5) by Adriana Ayala (adriayala@me.com)

Cover image and internal image 1 (Chapter 1) courtesy of: *NASA*, *ESA*, S. Beckwith (*STScI*),and The Hubble Heritage Team (STScI/*AURA*)

Erasmix Books Dyson Swarm logo by Vedexent at Wikipedia, GFDL, altered for scenebreak image

Internal images by Katie Byrne

> Image 2 (Chapter 2) A small Rotating Habitat interior. A green plant filled tube runs through the axis of rotation and human figures are visible working in the foreground.
>
> Image 3 (Chapter 3) Interior of a large rotating habitat. A children's playground is depicted in the foreground, with cities and residential areas along with rivers and lakes in the background.
>
> Image 4 (Chapter 4) A Partially Complete Statite shell with the sun visible on the left side of image.
>
> Image 5 (Chapter 4) A rung of rotating habitats orbiting a star.
>
> Image 6 (Chapter 5) A partially complete Dyson Swarm with around a star. The structure takes on the form of many rings of habitats orbiting the star.
>
> Image 7 (Chapter 6) A cylindrical space station with spokes and a central hub orbiting a moon.

Table of Contents

Dedication

No one is self-made. We all owe a part of our achievement to others. Civilization has brought all of us forward. I stand on the shoulders of the great people before me who imagined, discovered, or invented many of the wonders that made this story possible.

Although I've never met him in person, the wealth of knowledge I gained from American futurist Isaac Arthur was the fundamental motivator for me to write this story. I first came across one of the videos in his YouTube channel entitled, *"The Fermi Paradox: The Dyson Dilemma"* [1], which put me on a learning path culminating in this book.

Like a gateway drug, I was soon hooked into heavier stuff like rotating habitats, Dyson swarms, and Statites, which he did not invent but explains with the utmost clarity in his videos. His Facebook community, *Science & Futurism with Isaac Arthur* (SFIA)[2], has been so patient and forgiving with my sometimes stupid and impertinent questions; and their answers helped me fill in many of the gaps in the story.

I therefore dedicate this book to Isaac and his ragtag band of science junkies from SFIA for showing me what's possible and for all the help they gave me in writing this story.

In our obscurity—in all this vastness—there is no hint that help will come from elsewhere to save us from ourselves.

Carl Sagan

Preface

You might not even know or believe that we are already capable of addressing the most crucial challenges faced by our civilization. Not only can we avert a planetary scale catastrophe by solving climate change within a decade; but we can colonize our solar system and create a post-scarcity civilization for a quintillion souls–without making a dent in the resources available to us. We can travel to Alpha Centauri within the span of a human lifetime.

We live, instead, deadlocked in never-ending competition, longing for war, and squeezing the least fortunate in the process, because that's what we were taught.

While eighty percent of the world lives on less than ten dollars a day, the cosmos awaits with answers to all our terrestrial predicaments. All we lack is the will to unite and look outside the box into which we have put ourselves.

The Clarketech Myth

In 1962, British author Arthur Clarke wrote in *Profiles of the Future*, "Any sufficiently advanced technology is indistinguishable from magic."

Try to imagine what a plane or an automobile would look like to a Neanderthal, whose kind had not even invented the wheel.

Clarke's quote inspired the term "Clarketech": a qualifier for a technology so advanced, so miraculous, and so powerful that it would allow a civilization to build and achieve prodigies beyond our imagination.

Whenever Dyson swarms or interstellar travel are discussed, most people assume that Clarketech is a must to achieve such a feat when, in fact, many of the key technologies already exist today.

While a Dyson sphere is definitely Clarketech, a Dyson swarm is not. They are often confused with each other and used interchangeably, but they are fundamentally different. The first is to the second as Saint Peter's Basilica would be to a 15,000-square-meter tent settlement.

We might not be able to build a Dyson sphere, even a billion years in the future, as it defies the laws of physics as we currently understand them. But a Dyson swarm is well within reach of our means today. It is true that it will take over 1,000 years to complete, but humanity is no stranger to such long projects. The Great Wall of China was built in 2,000 years; Stonehenge in 1,600 Petra in the Jordan Desert took 850 years.

Although a sheer challenge of scale, we do have more technology and resources than any of those great civilizations predating us. Nevertheless, this will be the most challenging project humans have ever embarked upon, one that will be visible from hundreds of thousands of light-years away, making our solar system a beacon on the galactic map.

With a few exceptions like Ansible Communication, which requires new physics, many of the eye openers used in this story—such as neural interfaces, eternal life, and genetic enhancements—are either possible with today's technology or are within the realm of possibility within the span of a human life.

O'Neill cylinders, Statites, and star lifting are more a challenge of scale than technological achievement. Statites themselves are not super high-tech by 2016 standards. Building enough of them in space to mine construction materials from the sun is the real challenge.

I tried to stay away from swishing and flicking my magic wand when describing any of humankind's future achievements, but when caught playing prophet to a billion years in the future, one has to make some concessions.

Chapter 0: A Billionth Year Birthday

IMMENSITY DEVOURED HIS WHOLE, A SPECK OF DUST IN the limitless darkness. After being launched from the orbital station on the boundary with outer space, Fedrix and his friends continued gaining speed. Now in free fall[3], they would soon feel the adrenaline-surging pull of gravity.

The supercontinent below spread modestly over a third of the planet's surface, dashed by brown-purple shades and blurry white strokes. Anthocyanin[4]-rich vegetation had taken hold in this wrinkled and craggy world, forming a rudimentary tapestry in ruby hues of pomegranate.

As Fedrix contemplated the blend of weather systems drifting above the rugged terrain, a message materialized sharp and lucid inside his mind.

"Happy Birthday, buddy! Better early than never, in case you die on your little adventure!" joked Stralk, one of his closest friends.

Fedrix immediately sensed his friend's childlike laugh. Stralk's short, unruly, and bright copper hair contrasted sharply with the neatly trimmed, half goatee that surrounded his smile. And, just as salt flavors a dish, his rusty-freckled skin added a final touch to his quirky personality, which Fedrix found refreshing.

Like his own thoughts, the message in his mind crystallized in real time, but he clearly identified the sender. Each individual's thoughts had a unique signature, like faces and voices, scents and fingerprints. Thoughts and emotions traveled from brain to brain instantaneously and regardless of distance, making the crudity and inaccuracy of spoken language optional. Therefore, no words were heard inside or outside Fedrix's head. He replied with a grin back to Stralk, who chuckled 800,000 kilometers away in his living quarters.

Ahead of them, Planet D grew in size. Easy to summon, its full designation was a long and unpractical sequence of letters and numbers identifying its galaxy[5], the star it orbited, and finally the planet itself. As any kid was able to point out, Planet D orbited a yellow dwarf[6] at the edge of M87[7], a trillion-star elliptical galaxy five times larger than the Milky Way[8], on the fringe of the Virgo cluster[9].

Over 300 years before Fedrix and his friends decided to go for a space-diving escapade, humans found their way to the star orbited by Planet D. They began harvesting the star's resources to gradually build a swarm of rotating habitats around it, currently providing living space for a few trillion people. Many colonized stars were hosts to rocky worlds like Planet D, and gravitating into them at breakneck speeds was a great source of amusement.

As they approached the upper atmospheric layers, Stralk shared an image with the fifteen members of the space-diving party: a frail-looking, wrinkled man with a curved back, wearing thick glasses.

"Is this you?" Stralk asked incredulously.

Fedrix stared at it, but nothing happened. It was just a still image with no additional sensory information. The weathered face resembled him and had his own features, but it looked like a degraded version of himself. A pensive smile formed on Fedrix's lips, momentarily diverting his attention away from Planet D.

Eons ago human ingenuity won the battle against aging. Genetic manipulation and nanotechnology allowed people to live in their twenties-looking bodies for eternity. A few million people had already turned a billion years old, becoming some sort of celebrities, but Fedrix kept to himself. Most people who didn't know this fact were surprised upon realizing they'd met someone that old.

"From where in the universe did you dig up that image, Stralk?" an amused Fedrix asked.

The Universal Knowledge Bank answered this time. "Digital capture from a 2116 device, uploaded to the UKB in 2278..."

"From your personal archive," interrupted Stralk, with a chuckle. "What was wrong with your skin?"

"Before technology to stop dying of old age was developed, people's skin became creased with the passage of time," explained the UKB. "Age reversal was first achieved in 2110. Aging was classified as a disease in..."

"I still can't believe this was you almost a billion years ago, buddy!" interrupted Stralk again.

A vast quantum supercomputer with trillions of nodes distributed across colonized space, the UKB stored people's memories allowing them to relive and share them with others. It addressed each and every human need and ran civilization itself. Bias-free and always available, the non-sentient Artificial Intelligence (AI)[10] was humanity's omnipresent servant that never minded being interrupted.

"You even look...shorter!" Stralk continued. The space-diving party burst into laughter. "How's that possible?"

"Ha! I bet that image was made before the first wave of genetic enhancements became available," ventured SueLing.

"Uh...I'm not sure," said a confused Fedrix.

"The first generation of DNA improvements didn't become available until a century after the image was captured," said the UKB. "Furthermore, the natural wearing off of cartilage and bone-density loss reduced the height of people affected by age, which shortened and bent their spinal..."

"I've never seen an aged person before," said Stralk pensively. "SueLing, isn't it gross?" he asked, with a pinch of disgust.

"Gross is you putting silly thoughts in my mind. Just stop it, please," she said calmly.

"Alright, alright, SueLing. You're no fun," Stralk laughed. "Can you remember what that felt like?" he asked Fedrix.

Fedrix searched recollections in the UKB from when he was in his hundreds and shared one up. The group experienced a glimpse of the constant pain all over his body, the ominous terror for the next organ failure, the impaired hearing and vision, the fog in his brain that made it hard to concentrate, the loneliness and isolation that came along, and the different systems in his body breaking down and desperately needing to be repaired for his survival...then, a doctor trying hard to convince him to go through an aging reversal procedure.

Everyone was shaken. Not many had experienced so much unpleasantness before.

"That was so painful!" said SueLing full of pity. "Why didn't you want to go through the procedure?"

Because she was a biologist, Fedrix thought she might be the only person in the group that could grasp the meaning of aging.

"I was afraid it wasn't safe enough and, if my body got damaged, I would die. It was stupid...but I was less rational back then," said Fedrix.

"Interesting. Why was it all a bit fuzzy?" asked Celeste inquisitively.

"The memory was over ten years old and had slightly degraded when it was uploaded," intervened the UKB.

"How much content is there about him from that era?"

"There are 704,329 content items related to Fedrix," answered the UKB.

"Phew!" she said surprised.

"See you at the party," Stralk said, enjoying the stunning 360-degree view shared by the group. "Have fun; don't go too crazy."

"Wise advice from a loon, right, Fedrix?" added Celeste with laughter, while spreading out several meters away from Fedrix. Along came SueLing, Len, and the others, as gravity continued to seize them toward Planet D.

"Don't worry. You know me..." Fedrix started to say.

"Yes, I do. Reckless is what you are. It would be such a shame if you killed yourself before your billionth birthday," interrupted Celeste.

"Is that the reason you all came? To make sure I don't kill myself?" asked Fedrix, amused and a little bit touched.

Vague noncommittal statements of denial with varying levels of intensity from his friends ensued.

"Liars!" cackled Fedrix.

"I came for the fun!" exclaimed Len. "You know I love this stuff."

Fedrix had known Len the longest—all the way back to their days on Earth, when people were forced to work their asses off for a meager living—before interstellar travel, before humanity became a spacefaring civilization building Dyson swarms[11]. They went so far back Fedrix couldn't remember when they first met. Nor could Len.

As they continued falling towards the planet, Fedrix recognized the whitish, spiral shape of a storm, about ten degrees west of their path of descent. He wondered what it would feel like diving through it at full terminal velocity[12].

"You do understand the physics behind our shields, don't you?" Len reprimanded. "If you get caught in strong turbulence..."

An outer layer, an atomic-scale force field stronger than graphene[13], held a permanent coat of breathable air around their bodies, making pressurized suits unnecessary. Fedrix and his friends also wore a skinfit, a special garment that wrapped their bodies and, together with the force field, prevented their body heat from dissipating into space.

Made of a dark, paper-thin, unreflective metamaterial[14], skinfits had replaced the cumbersome space suits for a more enjoyable space-diving experience long ago. Revealing a strapping bone structure and toned muscles, the malleable and tensile material enveloped Fedrix tightly from head to toe, blocking cosmic rays and the star's radiation. On his back, the skinfit insensibly merged into a tiny backpack about the length of his forearm. Special goggles shielded his eyes and adapted the vision field, whether he faced the star or looked in any other direction.

"Can I keep Darwin if you die?" asked Celeste, half kidding and half concerned.

People with no filter on their thoughts and emotions were sometimes a bit annoying, but the majority were like that. Truth was, Fedrix wouldn't have it any other way and only befriended people with unfiltered minds. The advantages vastly outweighed the disadvantages. Fortunately, in a population of 3.5 times 10^{32} (350 nonillion), one could find a full spectrum of thinkers—from those with completely unfiltered thoughts to individuals who only communicated verbally. The same could be said about tastes in food, art, drugs, entertainment, and sex.

As the party of friends continued their ever-fast decent, piercing the upper atmospheric layers faster than sounds were transmitted on Planet D's atmosphere, friction heated their shields making them slightly warmer in their suits. They could now better appreciate details of the geography below. A horseshoe-shaped body of water embedded in a snow-capped mountain range caught Fedrix's attention. At first, Fedrix thought it was a river until it became clear it was a lake. He wondered why it wasn't frozen.

Following his thoughts, the UKB responded. "The snows on the mountain range are perpetual, but there's enough seasonal melt to replenish the lake. Precipitation maintains the water level, which overflows into nearby rivers. Close to 100,000 species are known to live..." The explanation stopped when Fedrix lost interest.

Friction had slowed their descent to subsonic speed, and the temperature cooled down to normal. It was now possible to steer by moving their limbs.

"Set force field to variable mode. Delta wing from shoulders to heels. Maintain progressive aerodynamics to the movement of my arms," Fedrix commanded the UKB.

"That isn't a bright idea," said Len.

"What do you mean? Delta wings are a fantastic idea for high-speed subsonic flight!" grinned Fedrix.

"That's not what Len...oh, forget it! Try not to hurt yourself," said Celeste with frustration and concern.

"Terminal velocity and atmospheric density will constrain your ability to steer. Avoid sharp turns," warned the UKB. "Follow a sweep angle of sixty degrees and attack angle of fifteen degrees for the wing design."

"Agreed. And please set bevel angle at thirty degrees, if you may?" Fedrix added with mock politeness and a broad smile.

Slowly spreading his arms, he restructured the shield to the agreed angles. As he glided into a diagonal trajectory to reduce the descent speed, his peripheral vision caught a glimpse of Celeste, Len, and the rest of the party turning into blurry dark bullets as they flew past him.

He first tried gliding in a simple wave pattern. Tiny movements of his arms altered the wing aerodynamics, allowing him to execute pirouettes in midair any bird would envy. The pressure on his shoulders mounted as he initiated tighter spirals to get acquainted with the new configuration. He couldn't help but whoop with delight as his friends careened closer to the planet beneath him.

He took a deep breath and went down in a long spiral. The recycled air he breathed came from a cylindrical pump in his tiny backpack that filtered CO_2 and noxious gasses. Together with the force-field emitter, they filled half the pack. The other half stored a chute and a set of instruments that included multiple imaging devices.

After a series of corkscrews, he emerged from a layer of clouds into a herd of balloon-like creatures drifting through the wind. Neither plant nor animal and the size of a three-story house, they produced methane to keep their plump bodies airborne.

"We call them bulbs," explained SueLing. "Bottom of the food chain, they feed on organic molecules from the air."

"A bit repulsive. And what are those hairy limbs sticking out?" he asked, zigzagging through the bulbs.

"That's how they harvest hydrocarbon molecules for nourishment," answered SueLing.

A flock of winged creatures the size of doves flew amongst the bulbs, clashing into them. "And those are remoras, the energy bars of the sky. All other flying species love to eat them."

Grossed out, Fedrix noticed their suction cup-like oral disks, allowing them to prey on the bulbs by feeding on fluids from their rounded, fleshy bodies.

A sudden thud on his back startled Fedrix. He accessed his rearview devices, but it was just one of the remoras that landed on his back. The rasping mouth fruitlessly tried to latch on to the force field and pierce it with a single, beak-like tooth. The stomach-churning sight lasted just a few seconds before giving up and moving on to more appetizing fare, amid a chorus of laughter from Fedrix's friends.

"Eew!" chortled Len.

Snorting at the futile attempt of the critter to turn him into a meal, Fedrix pushed towards a clearing, seeking a way out through sheets of clouds. As he left the feeding frenzy behind, a pack of enormous fliers soared through the air, their metallic-white backs shining at each twirl and turn of their twenty-meter wingspan.

"Pteranoraptors," the UKB announced, as Fedrix shared his visual perspective with the group.

He accessed the species profile. They were born, lived, and died in the air. The white top of their bodies, permanently exposed to the sun, was suspected to be a cooling mechanism. The large, diamond-shaped head hosted a brain that seemed too large for such a basic creature, but too small to expect intelligence. Extending outward from the broad base of the wings, the body was rather simple in shape and functions; a flattened short trunk, with no limbs or tail, was focused on digestion and methane production—their only secretion.

Cylindrical structures inserted in their sleek, delta wings puzzled Fedrix. "Magnificent!" he thought. "Like those ancient airplanes Stralk loves to pilot..."

"Are those reaction engines?"[15] Fedrix wondered in his shared thoughts.

"Similar to a reaction engine, yes," confirmed the UKB. "One of the oldest known propulsion..."

"What do they use for thrust?" Fedrix asked.

"These guys are propelled by methane combustion," replied SueLing. "Methane is produced internally and burned in those pod-like organs you see embedded into their wings. See how they maneuver by flexing their wings? They're also varying the amount of methane burned. Efficient, aren't they? But be careful. They're the apex predator of Planet D; try not to rattle them!" she urged.

Before the spark of another question had a chance to form in his brain, the alpha broke away from the pack, making a straight line for Fedrix.

"Remove delta wing conf..." he started to utter; but the UKB did so before the thought had formed in his mind.

Like dropping off a flight of stairs, Fedrix plummeted toward the surface. Panic and excitement competed for control of his body as he reached terminal velocity, the predator still gaining on him.

"And these fellows eat what, exactly?" he asked SueLing with gloomy sarcasm.

"Certainly not the bulbs; they don't pack enough energy. They prefer remoras and...other species with higher caloric content", she replied apprehensively.

"Gravity gradient is against you, and thrust-to-weight ratio favors your attacker," the UKB calmly informed. "Perform evasive maneuvers until interception."

"How long before..."

"Seconds," interrupted the UKB.

"We're all safe on the platform! You'll make it too," Celeste said in a brittle squeak.

He knew the energy shield around his body would protect him against those innate weapons, but the collision with the predator could easily knock him unconscious. The earlier warning from Len about personal shields replayed in his mind like a bad omen.

"Stop thinking about that shit, and focus on evading the pteranoraptor!" urged Len with the equivalent of an angry telepathic scream. Like everybody else, he was following him in real time. Fedrix also felt the distressing, watchful stare of SueLing.

Through his rearview imaging device, he saw the predator's approach in glorious detail: jaw open wide and showing its fearsome fangs, designed to dismember large prey while in flight.

Fedrix tucked into a barrel roll, speeding on a parallel vector to its approach and spinning against the white flat side of the beast just as the creature would have been upon him. Eyes flashing, the pteranoraptor sped past him and bellowed with fury, showing its powerful jaws bristling with parallel rows of razor-sharp teeth ready to slash, slice, and tear. It slightly bent its wings to turn into a tight V, pivoting over the tip of its wing as easily as swinging around a flagpole.

Fedrix couldn't help but marvel at the beast's flying skills. Hands on his buttocks brought wind resistance to an absolute minimum, plummeting in the direction of the platform. However, in a spectacular display of strategy, the pteranoraptor matched his own descent vector and charged diagonally from the side.

"Maybe not that small a brain..." he thought briefly as the predator rammed him at full speed.

Fedrix's left arm and half his ribs shattered, as he lost consciousness seconds before his spine snapped.

Feeling as if his head was swiveling like a spinning top, Fedrix began regaining consciousness. Simultaneous thoughts from Celeste, SueLing, Stralk, Len, and the rest of his space-diving buddies—and others who were not even in the room—began to enter his mind. He tried in vain to open his eyes. He was aware of himself but couldn't see, hear, or feel anything the usual way. It was as if his body was gone.

As his body started to wake up, the UKB came up gently in his mind. "Hello, Fedrix. You're coming around now."

He sensed feelings of...confusion, amusement, and concern? Yes, a mix of all three. It was so rare for someone to be hurt in an accident, some of his friends were just blown away. However, the jovial mood of Stralk and others told him all he wanted to know; he would be alright. As he regained his motor functions, Fedrix became aware of the rest of his body and was able to open his eyes.

"You were in a serious accident," continued the UKB from what seemed far away. "Your body is being repaired."

"How are you feeling?" inquired SueLing wearily. She hadn't slept much since the accident. Fedrix tried to move in search for an accurate reply.

"Don't try to pull yourself up," warned the UKB. "You suffered multiple spinal fractures, internal organ bleeding, and extreme trauma to your occipital lobe..."

"Is t-that it?" He was able to articulate the thought, but something was wrong in the transmission process. "W-what's wrong?" he asked.

"Everything is fine now. I'm recalibrating your Neural Interfaces (NIs)[16]. Try again," continued the UKB.

Fedrix was disappointed with himself. Here he was, a billion-year-old guy who specialized in risk assessment, and he nearly got himself killed!

"What a fool I am," lamented Fedrix. After a pause, he instructed the UKB to apprise damages.

"Twenty-one bone fractures, some of which are still being healed, but the most severe damage has been repaired. You were unconscious and under assisted ventilation for twelve hours while multiple surgeries were performed. Spontaneous breathing was regained two hours ago and the respirator removed. Your higher brain functions are entirely restored. You'll make a full recovery," reported the UKB.

He didn't feel any pain, but, surely, it was being managed.

"Pain is under control by your nanobots and drugs. It's imperative that you minimize all movement for the next six hours. It might be necessary to continue pain management after leaving the care unit. You'll be under observation until then," explained the UKB following his thoughts.

"That's in plenty of time for your birthday party!" said Len. "Cheer up, the worst is behind; he'll be okay."

"That was so reckless," said Celeste in her husky manner but with a hint of nervousness.

"C'mon, that didn't happen because he was being reckless..." Stralk started to argue.

"Of course, he was! Somehow he angered that bird; it saw him as some kind of territorial threat."

"They're not birds. Although they have wings, the pteranoraptor is actually a species of..." SueLing tried to explain in the same professorial demeanor she addressed her students, prompting Stralk and Len to exchange a quick smirk behind her back.

"You could have died, Fedrix!" interrupted Celeste again.

"Come on...," he tried to deflect. But he knew she was right.

"Here, see for yourself," interceded Stralk, excitement glinting through his pale, blue zephyr eyes. He shared a surveillance recording from the research station at the time of the accident.

Fedrix watched himself outsmart the pteranoraptor with that initial barrel roll, but then the beast interrupted its descent, transferred its momentum into a sharp ascent, and swung back to snatch Fedrix's body midair. When it couldn't crush him between its teeth—thanks to the force field—it shook his body like a rag doll, crushing his spine before drones stunned it and rushed Fedrix to the research station.

"It's a good thing I was unconscious through most of it!" joked Fedrix.

How naive of him to think that after such an encounter he would have walked away with only a few cracked ribs! He had barely survived the attack.

"Well, maybe you're a fool, Fedrix," SueLing added smiling. "But that was a cool bit of flying!" The girl read his mind better than anybody else and interjected with a wisecrack to cheer him up.

"Him?" asked Stralk, following her lead. "Or the pteranoraptor?" Everyone laughed heartily.

"Hey! We should play this at the party," added Stralk. "It'll be way more entertaining than another of his long-winded speeches!"

His comment truly brought down the house, lightening everyone's mood, except Fedrix's. Letting out a tired sigh, he forced a smile.

"Shield me from this set of memories," he ordered the UKB.

He allowed the recollections to remain in the UKB, but he wouldn't be able to access them. Others would be able to experience them but not share with him. No matter how advanced human beings had become, people were still susceptible to PTSD.

The long, sleek body of a feline approached Fedrix on the right side of the bed where his free arm was resting. Placing his large head on the bed—a pair of bright yellow eyes on Fedrix—Darwin meowed to get his attention. Through gentle stimuli, the UKB guided the cat, preventing him from going to the left side where Fedrix's arm was still inside a cylindrical surgical instrument. His torso was covered by a plate under which microscopic surgical devices were still at work.

The cat's gaze jumped from Fedrix to Celeste. The animal let out a pleading, almost silent meow. She rushed to lift the large cat (not without difficulty) and placed him on the bed.

Fedrix smiled cheerfully. Darwin could jump three meters in the air, chasing after a toy, without effort. Like all modern cats, he had been genetically engineered from an enhanced version of the original domestic cat. With a higher IQ than a chimpanzee, he was fully tailored to match Fedrix's personality. Darwin didn't need to be picked up; he just loved to be held and had plenty of tricks in his arsenal.

Celeste followed his train of thought. "You naughty beast!" she said, pulling on Darwin's fur affectionately.

Curling up its dark slate paws, the cat lay down, brushing Fedrix's hand, and began purring. The bluish tint of a dark autumn sky was shining on his smooth and fluffy coat. Fedrix experienced a rush of love and compassion through the NIs implanted in Darwin; the animal understood he wasn't well and pitied him. Fedrix petted his head, and the cat gently nibbled and licked his fingers. He experienced waves of profound affection and gratitude towards his cat that made him feel better.

"...part of what used to be called the placebo effect," Len was saying, and Fedrix realized he had been distracted from the thought exchange.

"Placebo?" asked Celeste.

"Yep. It was discovered back on the home planet, before the space era. Basically, if you're in good spirits, you heal faster," said Len.

"Total bullshit!" exclaimed Celeste, wondering if Len was serious.

"The Placebo effect was..." began to clarify the UKB.

"No, really! It was an early human trait. The genes that enable it were identified and tweaked to amplify the effect. Today, we all carry that genetic enhancement. I'm pretty sure that's why you were asked to bring Darwin," explained Len.

"Back on the home planet," repeated Celeste, "And you know this without even consulting the UKB. Really? You guys are living fossils!" she said, provoking another hearty laugh from the group.

Early the next morning, Celeste accompanied Fedrix for a walk. He had lived onboard The Eternity for the last 700,000 years, going from star to star in the M87 galaxy, building Dyson swarms. As they strolled along a beach, Fedrix enjoyed the familiar architecture of the ship. It was the paradigm of a rotating habitat optimized for space travel—with its 200 kilometers radius by 3,000 kilometers length, providing a living surface of 3.8 million square kilometers. Larger than the old country of India, it was designed to comfortably house a billion people for hundreds or thousands of years. With plenty of room and amenities to ease boredom and prevent overcrowding, it was still able to decelerate fast enough with the minimum amount of fuel.

Upgraded so many times, only the hull remained from the original ship. The current engines were the latest generation of antimatter reactors for maneuvering, slowing down at its destination, and supplying power to all the ship's systems while in deep space.

Upon reaching its destination, machines woke up from their long sleep and began mining elements from the star's atmosphere to build rotating habitats, quantum processors, laser-beam generators, and every other component necessary for a self-sufficient Dyson swarm.

As soon as the first rotating habitats were completed, people started moving out, drawing the ship's population down to a skeleton crew of less than a million. However, it would replenish back to capacity while traveling to its next destination, as people continued to be born. After a few hundred years, depending on their host star's metallicity[17], the swarm would reach critical mass and the colony ship would be slowly accelerated towards its next destination.

"Do you ever miss home?" Celeste suddenly asked.

"Uh...I don't know. Do you?" he said, confused, after mulling over the question for a few seconds, trying to figure out what she was getting at.

Eons ago, Earth ceased being Fedrix's home. Born centuries before the space era, he had been among the many pioneers of space colonization since the first ship left the solar system for Alpha Centauri[18], and he hadn't been back since.

Very early in history, humans realized they did not need to colonize planets to expand throughout the universe. Stars were gargantuan fusion generators of extraordinary power, releasing vast amounts of free energy. Building trillions of rotating habitats around a star allowed them to sustain quintillions of inhabitants, capturing every single watt of power.

"I was born here, silly! For me, The Eternity is home," she chuckled.

Currently, in intergalactic space just outside M87 in the Virgo cluster, which included over 2,000 galaxies about sixty-five million light-years away from Earth, The Eternity's next destination was VCC1281, a dwarf galaxy satellite of the M87 massive ellipse. Over 30 percent of the stars in this colossus were already dysoned.

Gazing at her scrutinizing, deep jade eyes, Fedrix ventured. "I've been jumping from one ship to another most of my life. I was born on the home planet but lived there less than a hundred years before moving to the first rotating habitat in space," he replied.

"Where did you go next?" asked Celeste.

"I joined the first interstellar voyage soon after turning 500. And after that...what can I say? The time I've not spent in a ship is negligible—a few millennia in total. I lived in regular habitats after our ship was decommissioned while waiting for the next one to be built."

Based on elementary Newtonian physics, a rotating habitat was a cylindrical megastructure made of a rectangular section bent until the two longer sides met, forming a tube and topped by two circular sections acting as lids on both ends. Earth's gravity (aka 1G)[19] was simulated inside the rectangular section, or drum, by spinning the cylinder along the imaginary line connecting the centers of the two circular sections. Objects inside were accelerated outward pushing against the drum by the effect of artificial gravity.

"So, which of those habitats do you call home, then?" she continued to question.

"I suppose the answer to your question is that home is where my friends are, where you are, where I feel the happiest. My heart is here," Fedrix concluded.

This was the right answer, and she rewarded him with a radiant smile and a kiss.

"You've traveled and seen so much. At times I wonder, how much have we extended through the universe?" she asked, still in his arms.

The answer from the UKB was as immediate as non-intrusive.

"The Milky Way, with its 200 billion stars is the second largest of fifty galaxies, including Andromeda[20], Triangulum[21], and a few dwarfs in the Local Group[22], one of the 500 galactic clusters[23] inside the Laniakea supercluster[24] which encompasses over 100,000 galaxies spread across 520 million light-years..."

"It took only 1,000 years to completely dyson the home star and a little over a million to colonize every viable star in the Milky Way. Now after a billion years of space exploration, humanity has dysoned every viable star and galaxy inside the Local Group," interrupted Fedrix.

"Every single one?" Celeste raised her forehead to look him, amazed.

"There are billions of ships, like The Eternity, colonizing stars inside galaxies in all neighboring clusters, creating an expansion wave that can be seen nearly a billion light-years away across the universe," explained the UKB.

"As you know, a single Dyson swarm blocks all visible light from a star. To the naked eye, it would appear as if all stars and galaxies inside the Local Group have vanished—swallowed by humanity's expansion wave as it continues its slow but nonstop progress throughout the universe," explained Fedrix.

Celeste bit half her lower lip, nodding pensively. "I see!"

Contemplating the sea arching above their heads, they rested in each other's arms on the warm sand, enjoying the mellow breeze. A few hours later, they called for a transport to the rotation axis to spend some time in a microgravity[25] chamber before the birthday celebration. Fedrix chose one with a large window to enjoy the views, while floating and playing for hours. There were thousands of these rooms available and getting a reservation was never too much trouble.

A plush, cushy material covering all surfaces allowed the occupants to bounce against them. Plenty of fluffy toys and pillows made it a very amusing activity. Fedrix armed himself with a long pillow and a fake scowl and attacked Celeste. In turn, she grappled the pillow and wrestled his good arm, both of them bursting into laughter.

A pillow fight in zero gravity was not an easy thing to pull off. The exhausting, short-lived experience paced them down, as they drifted towards the window to catch their breaths. Still recovering from his multiple surgeries, Fedrix felt weak and in need of a good nap.

Unfazed by the grueling exercise, Celeste cuddled against his battered body while he slept, enjoying the magnificent view of the jet streams from M87's supermassive black hole. Fedrix's last scars and bruises slowly receded before her eyes, as the couple floated randomly across the room. She ended up instructing her own body to sleep.

Humanity's 350 nonillion souls—and growing—lived in a single time zone. They referred to it as the universal clock or just time. When humans started colonizing space in the twenty-first century, it was decided to follow a universally coordinated time based on a clock set to London time and later to entrust it to the UKB.

Even if Fedrix could remember, there wasn't anything left of Earth where he grew up. Neither London, nor any of the other cities, existed anymore; erased—not by war but by plate tectonics[26]. Two hundred thousand years—a mere blink of an eye in geologic terms—saw the dawn of the *Homo sapiens* and its conquest of space. However, Earth didn't stand still. The tectonic engine took millions of years to shape geography, but it never stopped. In over a billion years, all of Earth's land masses had merged back into a supercontinent and broke apart again into new mainlands that resembled nothing of the Earth on which Fedrix had grown up.

Birth records, uploaded to the UKB prior to the last war, proved that Fedrix had been born in Colombia on the old South American continent, five hours behind London time, so he decided to start the party at 1900 hours on the day before his birthday and celebrate right at midnight. There would be plenty of daylight by the time the party started since ships, as habitats, kept a sixteen-to-eight-hour balance between day and night all year round.

The party was held at the Asimov tower, Fedrix's favorite building in Science City. Like a titanic spoke, the gigantic structure spanned the 400 kilometer diameter of the ship. Multicolored facades flowed seamlessly from every edge and curve, thanks to sleek construction materials, featuring different designs and shades every few kilometers.

Distributed along its 5,500 floors were research and engineering facilities, party venues, parks, headquarters and facilities of the Space Colonization Initiative (SCI), residential space, sports centers, zero-gravity rooms, and other recreational areas—integrating dynamic urban designs without constraints to human imagination.

On the 400th floor, a magnificent hall was placed in the middle of a green oasis. The clean-cut, fragmented geometry of the exterior contrasted with the smooth contours and ultra-luxurious space inside. Five-to-fifteen-meter-high ceilings highlighted a sense of freedom and grandeur. Overflowing into a massive wraparound outdoor terrace, breathtaking day and night views of the city and the rest of the ship sneaked in through the transparent alloy of outer wall.

The cylindrical architecture of The Eternity made it possible to admire neighboring cities set throughout the curved wall of the ship, along with the surrounding mountains and lakes. Farther away, the deep-blue waters of the small sea gradually shifted into lighter hues of blue and green in the shallow waters around the islands and sandy beaches.

Hosting a variety of resting areas, spas, pub-like zones, and cozy lounges for every taste, the high-tech building also had enough temporary bedrooms to accommodate all the guests. But they would be used sparingly. Genetic enhancements, combined with nanobots in their bloodstreams, allowed them to party for weeks without sleep.

Designed to entertain a few thousand guests, the hall offered a diversity of chambers and living levels featuring different types of ambiance and food, making it the ideal place for a week-long celebration.

The tiny transport, carrying them across the 300 kilometers separating the zero-gravity room from the Asimov tower, docked into one of the many ports on the building. There, a high-speed elevator delivered them 2,600 floors down to the party.

A few minutes after 1900 hours, the couple walked hand in hand into the party. Towering images and videos featuring ancient Earth's cities, landscapes, and works of art—from the time he lived on the home planet—played randomly in the air above the chamber.

Celeste walked a few steps ahead, skimming through the levitating icons. She turned her head searching for Fedrix, her jet-black hair with golden highlights fluttering graciously at every move.

"This is completely unnecessary!" she said, amused. "Anyone can just access this content directly from the UKB and appreciate it in far greater detail. You're such a softie!" she added but squeezed his hand affectionately at the same time.

Leaping down a wide staircase from one of the many food and drink bars, Stralk jumped effortlessly over the smooth curved railing with the agility of a circus acrobat and reached the couple in seconds. Following Stralk, SueLing calmly walked down the stairs to reach them. Rimmed in a deep cobalt blue liner, her angular black eyes extended softly toward her temples. It created a subtle edge to her large, monolid eyes, the most alluring focal point on her face. The whole was framed by silky, dark burgundy hair down to her waistline.

"There you are! Happy billionth, my friend! How does it feel being a living fossil?" said Stralk, giving him a hug while holding a glass loaded with a dark purple liquid. "Hey, don't roll your eyes; it's Celeste who came up with the expression!" he giggled.

"He's so mean!" laughed SueLing, while giving Fedrix a prolonged hug. She raised her straight eyebrows and looked Fedrix in the eye. "Ignore, ignore, ignore the silly boy."

"No worries, sweetheart. The name doesn't suit me, by definition. A fossil implies that no change has taken place, but I have changed. By the way, Stralk, she called us all living fossils," Fedrix chortled.

As SueLing broke from the embrace, she accidentally bumped into Stralk's arm, almost knocking his drink. With a fast twist from his wrist, he prevented the liquid spilling out of the glass, saving Celeste's polished backless dress—not that it needed saving. The metamaterial fabric of all their garments repelled dirt and other foreign bodies, but the drink would have gotten on her skin and hair.

"Oops, sorry! That was close," said SueLing, moving away clumsily and bumping this time against Celeste. "Oops!" she said again with a guilty smile, revealing a line of utterly perfect teeth.

"No harm done, sweetie," replied Stralk, laughing. "We all love you just as you are!"

The couple was the living proof that opposites do attract. Fit and agile, Stralk had the feline stance and figure of a gymnast. A head taller, SueLing's curvy body and small waist seemed to somehow challenge her center of gravity to find balance.

Born on The Eternity during the last 350 years, they shared an insatiable, almost insane, intellectual curiosity. Stralk was a brilliant space colonization engineer, and SueLing was an astrobiologist[27] and passionate researcher, who also taught advanced classes in her subject. She was considering visiting the different planets and moons around the current star to study the native life, while Stralk would remain on the ship as it moved towards VCC1281. But that didn't necessarily mean the end of them as a couple; long-distance relationships were common through Ansible[28]. Couples were able to interact and have sex using their NIs while millions of light-years apart. Fedrix himself had tried it with old flames and had to confess there was no difference from the physical act. The touch, smell, sensations— everything was indistinguishable from being with the other person. However, he preferred the real and messy experience over the high-resolution one.

"Time for snacks and drinks?" Fedrix asked his friends.

Lavish food stations loaded with culinary delights from across colonized space, including most of Fedrix's favorites, were strategically placed throughout the hall. In over a billion years, humanity had created a myriad of palatable foods and inebriating beverages, producing a wide gamut of sensations and safe sense-bewitching concoctions.

Man first became a gregarious animal when our ancestors began gathering around the fire to cook, but food evolved beyond the fundamentals, eons ago. Genetic enhancements allowed humans to perceive a much wider variety of flavors, textures, and scents than the original *Homo sapiens*. Nutrition was now a social and gastronomical experience, engineered at the molecular level to please a beast of infinite mouths.

Delicate morsels of subtle superficial tension would liquefy instantly from the warmth inside the mouth or fuse into changing textures as they were chewed. Some would make each bite taste different, while others exploited the olfactory system to communicate a particular sensation or delivered the flavor directly into the brain through the smell receptors. And there were the ineluctable drug bars designed to satisfy people to the maximum. Drinks had become equally creative, producing a wide gamut of sensations and the enchantment of the senses.

Fedrix pulled a bottle of wine from a nearby drink station.

"Sh...Chateau Mon...Mount..."

He looked up surprised, as did everyone around him. SueLing had uttered actual words from her mouth. She held an identical bottle and was trying to read the label.

"Chateau Montelena," the UKB corrected, allowing them to hear the actual words in their minds.

Only an infinitesimal fraction of the population could read at all. Written language became unnecessary eons ago, and even the spoken language had lost popularity as a way of communication. People these days hardly ever troubled themselves with putting thoughts into words; thought exchange was much easier, faster, and more efficient.

"It was one of the many places on Earth where they made wine. They were called wineries," Fedrix added.

"Why the odd shape and heaviness? Seems impractical. And is this number, 2109, the actual year it was made? The monochromatic image...I don't know why, but I find the whole object so lovely! What does it all mean?" SueLing inquired, switching back to thought exchange.

"It was called a bottle," explained Fedrix. "Wine was originally bottled and sealed to age, using a cylindrical piece of wood. The shape is just to help trap the excess of sediment right before the neck of the bottle as you pour the liquid. Sediment was a solid residue in suspension that precipitated at the bottom of the bottle; edible but not pleasant. Very old wines needed to be filtered and aired before drinking."

"Really? Sounds complicated. What's in the liquid?" SueLing asked with curiosity.

"Grapes, a fruit native to the home planet; 2109 is the year the fruit was originally harvested. The juice went through a fermentation process and aging to develop the alcohol and flavors. Its molecular composition was recorded in 2120. Because the taste of the wine evolves with the passage of time, this is how the 2109 wine tasted in 2120," he explained, sipping the wine with delight.

"Fruit juice turns into this? Even though I understand the chemistry of the fermentation process, I'm still amazed," confessed SueLing.

"No need to wait for it to age and no sediments either. I had the bottles printed and filled...unnecessary, of course, but I just love to observe the old traditions."

SueLing held the fragile stem glass precariously, uncertain if to use the left or the right hand.

"The whole ceremony is just charming," she said.

Fedrix swirled the wine in his glass, revealing reddish legs that slowly returned to the pool of liquid below it. SueLing followed the movement, mesmerized. The wine in her glass tilted dangerously.

"I think it tastes delicious," said Stralk. He raised his glass, holding it by the round base in perfect balance between the tips of his fingers.

"Me, too!" added SueLing, hugging and kissing Fedrix again.

Fedrix moved on to the food, choosing a dim sum piece based on an ancient 1920s Earth recipe, uploaded to the UKB in 2240. The energy field extending from his fingertips allowed him to levitate, slice, or scoop food without touching it with his hands. Scents from different spices and condiments invaded his senses, as meat juices mixed with aromatic vegetables inside the dumpling spilled over his tongue when he crushed it between his teeth. Followed by a generous gulp of wine, swirled inside his mouth for a few seconds, made it a singular experience.

"HAPPY BIRTHDAY, BUDDY!" yelled Len at the top of his lungs with his typical vitality, turning heads as he walked waving toward them.

No need to wave after such a scream; he was the tallest person nearby. No one could have missed his large, muscular frame and handsome looks. Outgoing and energetic, he shared a craving for adventure and a natural ability for high-adrenaline sports with Fedrix.

With a splendid white smile, he wrapped Fedrix in a suffocating embrace that lifted him off the ground.

"Welcome to the club, Fedrix!" Having two billionarians onboard The Eternity was incredibly rare. Len had celebrated his billionth birthday just a few years earlier.

Putting his friend down, Len turned around and introduced his date.

"Hey, everybody! This is Sharon. And these are Fedrix and Celeste, Stralk and SueLing," he said, gently hugging the voluptuous girl by her waist.

Just like him, she was a stunning individual, impossible to miss even among a large crowd. Her deep emerald-green hair was as brilliant and vivid as one, lying in copious wavy strands over her bare shoulders. Intense blue cat eyes, with delicate epicanthal folds enhanced by her winged smoky makeup, contributed to her sultry and sexy look.

Accessing her profile in the UKB, Fedrix learned she had been born twenty-five years ago and had already completed advanced studies in culinary science, psychotropic drug design, and art. Her Intelligence Quotient stood out very high on the standard chart.

Vulnerability wasn't a thing individuals averaging 200 IQ points suffered from in a Clarketech post-scarcity society, where everyone sported an early-twenties physique. With NIs making it possible to look into a person's mind, there was no such thing as taking advantage of someone in a romantic relationship. Both men and women chose freely based on chemistry, temper, attractiveness, smarts, goals, accomplishments, and many other characteristics they cared about.

"That's impressive!" Fedrix said.

"That she has so many degrees, or that she's so young?" asked SueLing, who was looking at her UKB profile too.

"Both! Young people don't usually develop interest in a specialty until they're over 200 years old, by and large, and in just one field of study."

"She's one of the developers of Death Shrouds!" said Len excitedly.

The latest rage in mind-altering drugs, Death Shrouds induced an out-of-body experience, enhanced creativity, and produced a strong amusement sensation by increasing dopamine levels in the cerebral cortex. A lightning bolt of sheer pleasure shot right through the brain, while nanobots in the visual cortex randomly projected kaleidoscopic supernovae-cloud remnant images from the UKB database. Simultaneously, it created a euphoric zero-gravity sensation while keeping the subject aware of their surroundings. Users felt immersed in the psychedelic kinetic energy of the star explosions. Nanobots stimulated the nerve endings and the pressure receptors on the skin to finish the experience in a holistic orgasm.

Fedrix had tried mind-altering drugs many times before, but, for some reason, the habit never caught on. He preferred the modest buzz from wine or, better, the pleasure of pairing beverages with food.

"Wow! I had no idea! I guess we're trying it before the party ends?"

His friends cheered.

"Very well, Shrouds and fireworks it is!" he declared.

Someone thought of launching antimatter fireworks from the ample space in front of the hall, and the idea spread like wildfire among the guests. Fedrix agreed, hoping the party wouldn't be too disturbing to the neighborhood.

"It's better as a shared experience," Sharon explained. "The more the better! And someplace fun—like the beach rather than alone in a room—as your surroundings become part of the adventure, with the supernovae clouds as a backdrop."

"Does the subject have control over the drug? How long does it last?" inquired SueLing, visibly excited.

"Depends on the amount you take, but you can stop it at any time by simply instructing your nanobots to cancel the reprogramming and by clearing the drug molecules from your system."

"If I take it before my speech tomorrow, will it be less boring?" Fedrix joked.

Loaded with antimatter dots, drones drifted lazily in the air close to midnight. A tiny force field generator, each dot held matter and antimatter particles close together. While in storage, the field was kept powered, but, once launched, it was remotely deactivated to allow the particles to interact, annihilating each other in spectacular displays. By controlling when to disable the field generator, it was possible to draw all sorts of patterns and images, and, by varying the type and number of particles inside the dots, to produce any color in the visible spectrum.

Right at midnight, the drones started firing. The detonations produced a dazzling extravaganza with no other waste than light and sound. A simple display of 3D geometric figures in the beginning, it soon progressed toward increasingly complex drawings of plants and animals, old Earth's pre-spatial era icons (like cars, planes, and boats), the Eiffel Tower and the Taj Mahal, and an astronaut inside an old space suit. Then, an ancient image of the Earth's first rise ever photographed from the moon in the twentieth century and the first actual picture of the Milky Way from above the galactic plane were followed by pictures of the most beautiful galaxies dysoned by humankind. The twenty-five-minute show culminated in a slow-dissolving picture of the known universe.

In high spirits, the group went for a night walk around the parks below, away from the crowd and the raging party. Wide lawns of lush grass and moss gardens sprawled among ponds and canals connected by bridges, walkways, and stepping-stones—all illuminated by a profusion of colors and textures designed to make the night appealing. Wandering through the blooming landscaped gardens, peppered with woodlands and bushes, defied any preconception of nature's beauty.

"That was the most amazing display of fireworks I've ever seen!" said Celeste with awe and excitement.

"Have you seen many fireworks?" Fedrix asked, piqued by curiosity.

"It was my first," she smirked.

"Can you believe the original fireworks were made by igniting a powder fashioned from a mixture of sulfur, charcoal, and potassium nitrate?" asked Stralk, with his never-ending intellectual curiosity.

"Really?" asked Sharon. "It probably smelled awful!"

"Eew!" echoed SueLing.

"Did you ever witness one of those?" inquired Celeste.

"I'm pretty sure I did when I lived on Earth," replied Fedrix. Then, addressing the UKB, "Did I upload any content with fireworks?"

Within a fraction of a second, video from nearly a billion years earlier was shared with the group. Accustomed to the rich sensory input that accompanied regular memories, it took them a few seconds to comprehend what they were looking at.

The footing was unstable; it had been made from a boat, anchored a short distance away from a conglomerate of buildings. The archaic looking structures, roads, and surfaces were eroded, and, even at that distance, appeared dirty. A clock tower emerged from a low-rise building running along the waterfront, with all its windows illuminated. Sculpted in thick, glowing red letters were the words: Port of San Francisco. High above the crowds massed on the streets, the hands of the clock met at the top.

Bright, multicolored fireworks overlapping one another suddenly lit the sky above the city, followed a split second later by the sound of detonations. The stunning polychromatic display splashed random tones and patterns over the battered buildings.

Although not comparable to the antimatter fireworks they had just witnessed, the home planet fireworks were beautiful and bold in a primitive kind of way.

The grayish and smoky sky left behind by the fireworks didn't seem to bother the audience, who hugged and kissed with happiness in scattered groups and couples throughout the deck.

"Happy New Year!" they repeated cheerfully, while "Auld Lang Syne" [29] played in the background. The UKB translated to words in the standard language: an amalgam of English, Chinese, Spanish, and others.

A silken female voice was heard, a few moments later. "Happy New Year, darling. May all your dreams this year come true," she said lovingly.

She must had been very close to the recording device because, although softly spoken, her words carried above everything else. Then with the smacking sound of a kiss and a blurred view of the deck, the video ended.

Even though it was just a flat recording with no thoughts or emotional content, Fedrix and his friends were profoundly touched by the experience. Such an intimate moment from nearly a billion years in the past! Everyone asked Fedrix at the same time who the girl was.

"I...sorry...I don't know. That was centuries before the UKB came into existence. I have no recollection whatsoever of the events depicted," said Fedrix, suddenly saddened. He then instructed the UKB to provide some context.

"The metadata attached to the content indicates it was recorded on January 1, 2016. Location: San Francisco, a city in the state of California, on the old North American continent, the United States."

No one interrupted it this time. Accustomed to detailed answers, they felt this explanation was inadequate and beyond lacking, but the UKB couldn't produce what it didn't have.

Celeste gave him a hug.

"That was beautiful! That woman sounded like she loved you—called you 'darling'! How does it feel not being able to remember a part of your life?"

"We all forget," answered Fedrix dismissively. "Anything you didn't save to the UKB in the last 300 years is forever gone."

"Of course! But those are relatively meaningless things I do while my mind is somewhere else—stuff not worth remembering. I can't imagine forgetting key moments and people of my existence, seeing them like this and not being able to remember...I find it a little overwhelming," Celeste said with sadness engraved on her face.

"I know. Unfortunately, there's nothing I can do. Please, don't pity me; I don't deserve it," said Fedrix holding her between his arms, trying to cheer her up. He hated being the cause of someone's sorrow.

Celeste embraced him tighter.

"I understand; it's silly of me," she said with an apologetic half smile.

"Let's not make too much of this. Even when you relive one of your own memories stored in the UKB, the transition is so smooth it feels like it was actually stored in your brain, but it's not! Humans have a tiny storage capacity, for beings who live eternally," said Fedrix, trying to cheer them up.

However, the video had gotten them all a bit emotional. Len, a few years older than Fedrix and who surely had similar experiences, felt deeply affected. Stralk, always with a sly joke at hand, was unable to articulate a thought; he limited himself to hold an almost tearful SueLing in his arms. And even the extroverted brainy Sharon, with her sky-high IQ, was contemplative.

After a short while, Stralk finally managed to utter. "It amazes me that after a billion years we still get all excited making things burn and explode," in a feeble attempt at a joke to lighten the solemn mood.

"Aren't we going to try the Shrouds?" suggested Len, changing the subject.

And, with everybody in favor, the three couples lay down for some mind-altering fun to cheer them up.

Seven days later, the party continued to go strong, and there was even talk of extending it. Somehow, it reminded Fedrix of Louis Wu's 200th year birthday celebration in *Ringworld*[30]. Being a fan of the novel, as well, Len started reminiscing about their favorite parts, to the amusement of the others. Sharon found Teela Brown fascinating and teased them both about whether a callow fictional character from a twentieth century sci-fi novel was their ideal woman.

Fedrix spent a great deal of time answering as many messages as he could from friends and family all over colonized space. He had only two daughters but millions of descendants and relatives from them and from his own siblings. In nearly a billion years, he had helped settle millions of stars and made billions of acquaintances, friends, coworkers, and lovers.

He had also donated a digital clone of his mind to the Matrioshka Brain[31] Project. Although that copy of himself had diverted into a fully differentiated individual over hundreds of millions of years, they kept in touch, often having long Ansible exchanges. Always interested in finding out stories of life in the Big Brain, as it was often referred to, Fedrix was glad to see his digital self celebrating with an equally entertaining party, joined by millions of friends.

On the last morning of his birthday celebration, Fedrix and his friends chose a nice spot by a pond in the gardens to have lunch, and he summoned Darwin to join them. Prowling along the garden paths changed his stance from a purring and cuddly pet to a hunter. Fedrix was always amazed such a large animal could step on leaves and branches without making a sound. Darwin loved to stalk and chase fish in the ponds, but his favorite activity was to climb up a tree and lie on a branch, lurking and flicking his tail, ready to leap on his victim—a butterfly, most of the time.

Losing interest in the elusive prey made the cat switch from hunting to grooming. He finally curled into a ball, his upper half resting on Celeste's lap. She pulled and scratched his fur, and the animal turned his large head face up, lazily. He blinked slowly at her a few times, eyes half-closed and purring loudly in utter delight. He rubbed his mouth against her arm as she stroked his tummy.

Fedrix felt almost jealous. Although his cat's responses were tailored to him, Celeste had a natural rapport with Darwin. Cats would be cats, genetically enhanced or not, he said to himself.

Perhaps, Celeste became the cat's new favorite person when Fedrix met her at that same park, hundreds of years before. In the beginning, she behaved almost as independently—keen and aloof as his cat—but noticeably warmed up to Fedrix after getting to know him better.

Born onboard The Eternity nearly 500 years ago, Celeste specialized in agriculture. All food was grown along the rotation axis of the ship in the microgravity section. With everything fully automated and all the work done in the normal gravity zone, nobody was allowed inside the area. But she loved to visit and peek from outside the glass with her own eyes. It wasn't rare for her to instruct the drones inside to bring her samples of her favorites.

"...already have enough laser generators in place to accelerate the ship to cruise speed," Stralk was saying.

The conversation had moved to future plans. Colony ships were accelerated by targeting an array of laser beams against their rear shield. Sustained for long periods, it produced a tiny acceleration, allowing a vessel to reach 0.6c—sixty percent of the speed of light[32]. At such speed, a voyage from star to star could take anything from tens to hundreds, or even thousands, of years when in intergalactic space.

"Well, it makes sense for me to stay, but I would miss you guys too much," said SueLing. "I'm pretty sure the SCI will still have use for me if I decide to remain onboard."

"What about you, Cel? Will you stay here or continue towards VCC1281?"

Even though most people on the ship had been born with the purpose of colonizing the current star, no one was required to stay. Many would choose to continue on the ship from one destination to the next, for millions of years before settling down—if ever.

Fedrix hoped Celeste would remain on The Eternity, but it wouldn't dishearten him if she decided to stay behind like others in his past. A billion years of existence created lots of scar tissue. But he had to admit just one devastating breakup could harden a person for eternity. He was permanently inoculated against the aches of love, something Celeste—at her short age—had never experienced. He hoped not to be her first.

"If I stay, I'm keeping Darwin," smirked Celeste, following his train of thought.

"Traitor!" said Fedrix gruffly.

Celeste was being facetious; they both knew it. He would never have to give up his pet; she could easily get an exact clone from Darwin's DNA in the UKB database. Or she could start from scratch from the base DNA of the species—like Fedrix did—and tweak looks and responses to her liking, perfectly matching her personality. There was no shortage of options.

"Whatever you guys decide, we'll have many more birthdays and other celebrations together," said Celeste, grabbing SueLing's hand.

"I promise," said SueLing, who was a fan of the huge parties that took place throughout the year.

"The Eternity is not scheduled to depart toward its next destination for another thirty-three years," Fedrix added. "However, it'll be up to the SCI to change our departure. As you know, the swarm is ahead of schedule. What's the rush, kiddo?"

"Doesn't it bother you that, after colonizing trillions of stars in hundreds of galaxies, we still haven't found one single alien civilization?" asked Stralk getting to the subject he wanted to discuss.

"There he goes again," laughed SueLing, shaking her head. "He's obsessed!"

"When we lived on Earth, most people believed—or hoped—for alien civilizations to be all over the Milky Way. Some even declared that aliens had either visited us in the past or were living among the population, disguised as humans..." blurted Len.

"But that's mental!" interrupted Sharon. "What about Fermi's law?"

She was fascinated with the pre-space-era culture.

"Back then, it was known just as the Fermi Paradox[33]. Most people didn't even know about it, and the few who did ignored it subconsciously, speculating that aliens had some sort of advanced technology that somehow prevented us from detecting them," said Len.

"What kind of technology?" inquired Sharon.

Len laughed heartily.

"They were never specific! But most took for granted that aliens were more advanced and had Faster Than Light[34] travel capability. Even with FTL travel, however, you'd still need to build Dyson swarms. If we could travel faster than the speed of light, it would have taken us a fraction of the time to dyson all viable stars in the home galaxy."

"Because humans evolved on a planet, they dreamed of colonizing and terraforming other planets and moons. The idea of building swarms wasn't on anyone's mind," added Fedrix.

"Completely mad! Imagine traveling so many light years just to colonize a planet, leaving all that space to waste..." snorted Sharon.

"And all that energy!" added Stralk.

"That's not the only consideration..." Fedrix started to say.

"You can't be serious!" interrupted SueLing. "Accommodating humans implies a huge terraforming effort! It would doom the native life if we deployed our own chemistry and microorganisms to make a planet habitable for people."

"That's the point I was trying to make," smiled Fedrix. "Back on the home planet, the atmosphere where we evolved was shaped by Cyanobacteria[35]. We've found very few planets where single cell organisms produced an oxygen-based atmosphere, and they were all based on a different chemistry."

"Don't be too hard on our fellow ancestors. Although reined in by reason, a few human biases still exist today. For those who grew up in a rotating habitat, it's unnatural to live on a planet; that's why living on a research station for a while is seen as adventurous. People who grew up on the home planet felt the same way about rotating habitats in space," explained Len.

"I understand your point," replied SueLing. "However, I still find it hard to grasp such a waste of stellar resources; besides, after nearly a billion years of space colonization, we haven't found another rocky planet suitable for human life without terraforming. The destruction of countless ecosystems would have been inevitable if humans had established colonies on planets. What were they thinking!" she finished, aghast.

Absentmindedly, Fedrix gazed at the half-kilometer-wide Asimov tower ascending in front of them, becoming thinner with distance until it narrowed to a needle. Gone from their sight hundreds of kilometers high above their heads, it landed on the opposite side of The Eternity.

"A corollary to Fermi's law is that life must cross a series of filters to go from organic chemistry to civilization. It's a slow process. Not all intelligent species are capable of building a civilization. For the *Homo sapiens*, however, once we figured out agriculture and started settling down in villages, our future was pretty much set," Fedrix said.

"Not if they self-destructed with weapons of mass destruction!" exclaimed Celeste.

"Would a war with WMDs annihilate the entire population? What about the survivors? It would have taken longer, that's all. Civilization would reboot after a few centuries. You'd have to exterminate everybody—no exceptions—in order to stop the spread of civilization," said Fedrix.

"You talk about it like it's a virus," Celeste pointed out with a smile.

Stralk continued with eagerness. "We expect any rising civilization to follow a similar path to ours. First, dyson their home star and then grab neighboring ones, even before their first swarm is complete. Once neighboring stars are colonized, they'll launch ships to grab their neighbors—and so on and so forth—until all the stars in their home galaxy disappear from the visible spectrum under their expansion wave. If that were happening on M87 or in any of the galaxies ahead of us, we'd know it already! The only expansion wave we can see is our own!" he said, shaking his head and rubbing the back of his ear.

"And this is a problem because...?" asked Celeste.

"It just drives me crazy!" replied Stralk. "The universe is fifteen billion years old, and we still haven't found another civilization! We have millions of automated telescopes searching nonstop five billion light-years in all directions for alien Dyson swarms. All we see is raw wilderness," he said in dismay.

"Maybe our telescopes aren't good enough," joked Celeste.

"Actually, they're pretty good. A star's gravity bends light, focusing it more efficiently than any instrument we can manufacture. We've placed optical devices in orbit around stars at a distance where light focuses, turning them into gravitational lensing telescopes[36]. We have them on millions of stars, strategically chosen throughout the colonized space, dedicated to pure research and also to look for alien civilizations ahead of our own expansion," explained Len. "As Stralk said, we haven't found anything, so far."

"Don't forget that a telescope sees back in time at the speed of light. A billion light-years away is also a billion years in the past. Anything further than two billion light-years away is probably too early for a civilization to have emerged, as the universe was a lot more turbulent back then. We'll have to wait, I guess," said Fedrix.

He didn't want to kill Stralk's enthusiasm, but, in fact, he was terrified of what the contact between two technologically advanced civilizations would bring. They would be able to see each other's expansion waves millions of light-years away. How would they react? Would they meet, and what would be the result? Would they stay away from each other's region of space? What if both civilizations needed the same stellar resources to continue growing? Would they create WMDs of incalculable power that would inflict serious damage upon each other? Could two intergalactic civilizations coexist peacefully?

These were not questions the UKB could answer; but SueLing, who had followed his musings, put a soothing hand on his shoulder and said, "I find that terrifying, too!"

"It's silly to worry about it, because our cosmic neighborhood is empty. There's no real threat my dear. I'm just being a silly caveman."

"So, this keeps Stralk awake at night?" Sharon asked SueLing.

"Oh, we've had this same conversation so many times!" she chuckled, rolling her eyes.

Darwin farted loudly, sending waves of laughter throughout the group of friends.

Chapter 1: Fiftieth Year Birthday

HE WAS BORN FEDEERICO TARIFA IN PAIPA, A SMALL town in Colombia on the old South American continent, in 1966. Originally from Spain, his grandparents emigrated to Colombia, where his father was born, during the second World War.

About a century earlier, men were being recruited in alphabetical order from a lineup in his great-great-grandfather's hometown. These were the times of the Spanish-American war, and, among the reluctant candidates, a lanky young man smoked under the scorching Spanish sun, shifting his weight nervously from one foot to the other in the conscription line. Deeply sucking in the smoke, the man stared at the cigarette between his bony fingers. *Tarifa* read the brand, inscribed in tiny letters. "Alvarez!" cried out a guy ahead of him. Startled, he changed his last name on a whim, from Amaya to Tarifa, to avoid being drafted. The recruiting was going up to the letter "M" that day. It was a story his grandfather had told him many times in a fit of laughter. Of course, he had no way of knowing if the origin of his family name was true. According to Federico's father, there were no records. For better or for worse, they were stuck with it.

Federico grew up on a farm near an oil boomtown, not far from his birthplace. Fascinated with American TV and movies, he fell in love with the country's culture and the middle-class way of life. He finally got a taste of the American dream at the age of twelve when his father, an oil-industry worker, was sent to Tulsa, Oklahoma, for a six-month training. The company covered the expenses for the family to join him for the Christmas holiday.

Those were the three most amazing weeks of his childhood, better than in those movies he watched over and over again. People worked, paid their taxes, and made a decent living. Regardless of their type of job, everyone seemed able to effortlessly reach the middle class. Poverty was hard to find, and no one appeared to be struggling to make ends meet. It was so different from his homeland, where the stagnating life of hard-working people with no other choice but to work much harder and dream of a far distant lifestyle prevailed.

Right then and there, he decided he would have that lifestyle for himself, and achieving it became his goal. A few years later, he pursued a degree in computer sciences at a college in Bogotá, hoping it would help him find a job with an American company. His dream came true in 1995. Years of hard work and study had finally paid off. He landed a job at a small software company in Silicon Valley that sponsored him into the US with an H1-B visa[37]. The day he got the news was the happiest of his life, so far. A few weeks later he packed his bags and prepared to move to California.

A few crucial moments in our existence appear to be frozen in time. For Federico, one of these was his last New Year's Eve in Colombia, when he realized his life was about to change. Already with a plane ticket, a starting date to show up at work in early January, and all the arrangements carefully made by the company, he couldn't remember where he was when the clock struck midnight, except that it heralded the New Year and, with it, the promise of a glorious new beginning.

But he remembered saying goodbye. He drove his loud, worn-out '74 VW Beetle from house to house, visiting his closest friends and their families before his departure. He would miss the old *carcacha* he had for a car, with its greasy, and simple engine mechanics, that he could fix with a Swiss-Army knife whenever it broke down.

Where had he read, "Friends you make in college will accompany you for the rest of your life"? A known author or urban knowledge? The words rang loud in his ears as he drove until dawn. But Federico wouldn't look back; he had made it! His long, most-cherished childhood dream was about to come true, though the cost was high: leaving friendships of over ten years and his family behind. Some, he would never see again.

Embracing the American dream in all its glory, he was determined to succeed and move upward through hard work. With a house in Silicon Valley, a roadster in the garage, and a comfortable lifestyle in the San Francisco Bay Area, he became a fan of most good things the middle class was so fond of. He made lots of friends and developed an interest in a variety of hobbies and activities, including a true passion for the wine country.

Over the years, on a winning streak, the small software company became bigger, merged, and grew some more, until it was acquired by a larger Fortune 500 corporation. Things continued to run more or less smoothly for years, until one morning in March 2016, just a few days short of his fiftieth birthday, he was called to his manager's office.

"These are difficult times for our company, Federico," the manager began, and then gave him the same platitude-filled talk given to millions before him.

In shock from this sudden turn of events, Federico began rethinking his life. Looking back, he realized how increasingly miserable and isolated he had felt for the past eight years, while struggling to fit into a corporate culture that valued growth at all costs and profits over people. He was stressed from being forced into overdrive 24/7 and tired of avoiding the daily politicking and posturing, which led to being defined and measured against his peers, as well as the resulting betrayals and backstabbing. Pushed to bend the rules by unattainable goals, he was threatened with punishment, if caught. For a long time, he'd been fed up with spouting the corporate line to push worthless and pricey technology onto his employer's customers who, in turn, acted like they owned him.

The constant drive for short-term profits at the expense of the worker's quality of life made him feel that he was losing value as an employee and as a human being. More than anything, he hated being forced to work harder every year for less money—running faster and longer to accomplish more but still getting nowhere, like a hamster in a spinning wheel.

And God forbid he dropped the ball! Slip-ups were vindictively punished. Federico was once bullied to speak at a conference on a highly specialized topic in front of a large audience. Pondering the situation, he tried to explain the subject was not his area of expertise and that in the company there were better qualified people for the engagement. As a result, he was admonished by his manager, who criticized his social media posts and eating habits as the root cause of his "negative attitude."

And now, after all the abuse and sacrifice, he was laid off from his job in some kind of final soul-defeating ritual—just in time for his fiftieth birthday.

During the Great Recession of 2008, he had learned about the heart-wrenching stories of families whose livelihoods were taken away and their struggles to endure. Paranoia put Federico in their shoes, triggering an unsettling dream in which he dropped the keys to his house on the breakfast bar of his beautiful kitchen before walking out forever because he couldn't afford it anymore.

Although Federico rarely remembered his dreams, he couldn't forget this one nor the sensation of despair that continued to haunt him for the following months. Now at a new crossroads in his life, that nightmare had all of a sudden become one of the possible paths ahead of him.

What happened to the land of opportunity? He no longer recognized the country he visited in his teenage years. The elusive American dream was now ephemeral—a much harder to achieve membership, an enormous sacrifice at the end of a treacherous road fraught with disappointment and tears.

Under a cloak of corporate responsibility and lies, American corporations were in the business of fucking the American people, sweeping their sins under the rug with a philanthropy broom. Ruthless, predatory, and driven solely by the profit motive, they achieved record earnings by exploiting customers and workers equally. Four decades of union busting, monopolies, and automation had pounded the middle class, precipitating the collapse of the American mobility structure. No wonder a household in which both parents worked two jobs needed food stamps to get by. What kind of society praised the remarks of a famous CEO who stated it wasn't profitable to cure sick people?

Wiping out the competition by lobbying Congress to bury antitrust laws, the never-ending mergers and acquisitions process led corporations to become mighty behemoths to the cheers of Wall Street. Consumers were constantly tricked, cheated, trapped, and ripped off by fees, bullshit services, term contracts, and other questionable business practices hidden in fine print—all chipping away at the American way of life.

The labor market wasn't tight, but he could sense the strong bias against individuals his age who were not executives or management. More than a rejection from prospective employers, Federico felt rejected by society, as if the shadow cast by his age prompted doors to shut. The thought of starting from scratch this late in his life obsessively haunted him.

Being laid off started a clock that inexorably undermined his self-confidence like a treacherous and unexpected low blow. After fruitless months of sending his resumé out, desperation was creeping in. His unemployment benefits exhausted, questioning his skills, and burning through his savings, his short lease on the American dream was coming to an end. The clock had run out for him.

Getting a glimpse of the emotional train wreck that led so many to take their own lives, he analyzed the crude examples of others in similar situations. If they were unable to find an equivalent job, they either sold their house and got a small apartment, moved in with family, or made some other drastic lifestyle change to continue getting by. Federico never felt more defeated.

In a flooding rush of anxiety, he came up with the idea of buying a cheaper house—somewhere, anywhere—to retire early. It didn't take long to find an affordable place on the Oregon coast. Being sold by her children due to her terminal illness, the property belonged to an old lady. Feeling worse than a vulture, he took advantage of the opportunity by offering a lower price. His offer was accepted.

It wasn't easy to hide his situation, but he kept his family and friends in the dark. They had no means to help him financially, and they were too far away. Most importantly, there was no point in worrying the people he loved.

Even harder was keeping the secret from his Persian girlfriend, Yasmin, who had emigrated to the United States with her parents and worked in the glamorous San Francisco financial district. But with his Silicon Valley house already on the market and his moving date just days away, he couldn't put things off any longer.

They had dinner at a tiny French bistro in the Sunset district of San Francisco. A waiter poured the remaining wine from a bottle Federico bought for her in Napa Valley during a wine tasting trip together. Quite a few years younger than he, she exuded youthfulness and seductiveness. Looking at him with those disarming hazel eyes and drinking the last sips, she was saying something. Her words brought him back to reality:

"...you have so many qualities that I value in a man. None of them ever treated me like a lady, the way you do...the way you've always done," she confessed bashfully, in a whisper.

He reached out and grabbed her small hand between his, overwhelmed by this sudden revelation. He caressed the smooth skin on her cheek, and she tilted her head into his hand kissing it lightly with her soft, heart-shaped lips.

Federico managed to articulate. "How could anybody not treat you with kindness?"

"You would be surprised, Fedri joon. The guy I dated before you was an Italian soccer player...a beautiful model type. To make a long story short, he told me he was separated from his wife—and many other lines—to take advantage of me in more than one way," she confessed.

"I'm really sorry, Yasmin," he said.

"Please, don't be! You've won me over with your manners, your sweetness, and kindness."

"Too young, too beautiful. Too lucky a man I've been," he told himself.

Federico never thought himself eye-catching. Skeptical and pragmatic, he didn't believe in such things as leagues, but it was clear Yasmin was well out of his.

He had asked her out that evening to open up and tell her the whole truth.

"I'm so sorry to hear that," she said in shock. "You deserve so much better. Life can be so unfair! You must have been through hell these past few months."

After a long pause Yasmin added hesitantly, "I understand why you didn't tell me sooner, but...I hope you understand I cannot leave my job, family, and friends to move with you to Oregon."

He wasn't even asking. He understood the hard reality beforehand and knew she couldn't come with him, but he was grateful she even considered the possibility. They spent one last night together. The next morning, she gave him a very passionate goodbye kiss before leaving.

"I love you Fedri joon and will never forget you. I hope you find happiness in Oregon," she said wiping her eyes.

And that was the end of it—a relationship that started as a dream, cut short before having a chance to bloom.

They had met on a plane from New York to San Francisco. Their flights having been canceled due to bad weather, they registered for the next one available, a red eye leaving at 10:00 p.m. and arriving at 1:30 a.m. Chance placed their seats next to each other. After take-off, the poor girl held both armrests of her seat with a tight grip. She let out little squeaks every time they hit a rough patch. Captivated by the lovely stranger, Federico couldn't help starting a conversation; it would help time go faster for both of them. It was a week before Christmas, and he promptly asked her out. Although he had a hunch she was settling for him, he did everything possible to move things forward between them.

They spent New Year's Eve together on a private steamboat cruising along the bay, carrying only twenty guests and a superb chef, where they enjoyed an unforgettable romantic dinner. Not far from the Ferry Building, they were treated to a front-row view of the fireworks. As midnight came, Federico pulled out his iPhone and started recording a video. Yasmin approached from behind and stood very close to him, peeping occasionally. Without warning, she placed her arms around his waist and hugged him loosely from behind. He could smell her perfume and feel the heat emanating from her mouth. Turning slightly, he was struck by her gaze.

She approached even closer and said, "Happy New Year, darling. May all your dreams this year come true."

Pressing her lips against his cheek, she kissed him with adoration. He stopped recording and turned around. They hugged and kissed with passion, suddenly oblivious of the world around them. His heart bursting with happiness, Federico was convinced a new page in his life was turning.

After that night, he saw himself differently, nursing hopes of a long-term relationship, maybe even marriage. The few wonderful months they spent together filled him with sheer exhilaration. But that was before becoming a casualty of corporate America, when he was a gainfully employed member of the ever-diminishing middle class and not being forced into early retirement like an old shoe. Whatever the future held in store for him, Federico would always remember Yasmin as the beautiful girl who gave him butterflies in his stomach.

He decided to meet with his friends to say goodbye in small groups, one or two at a time. They took him out for dinner and drinks; his closest friends knew he preferred getting together like this, rather than all of them at once. "If America is the land of installments, why not say my goodbyes the same way?" he joked. Truth was, he'd rather spend quality time talking with each person dear to him, reminiscing about the good times they had together.

Over the last twenty years, Federico had done reasonably well with his finances for a software engineer. He had saved, just not quite enough to retire yet; but, adding the proceeds from selling his house, he wouldn't wither away in poverty.

"Oregon is the only state where I can be nearly as happy as in California for half the price," he repeated to himself.

His new place in Oregon wasn't half the size of his house in Silicon Valley. Time to decide what to keep and what to cast aside. His Le Corbusier living-room furniture was too big for his new home. 'But no way I'm leaving my LC4 chaise lounge!' he thought.

As memories of wonderful occasions flooded his mind, he felt his world getting smaller with each item he was forced to abandon. The living room came alive with memories of noisy parties and stimulating conversations with friends, of cooking with Yasmin in the ample kitchen that opened to the living room, of those intimate evenings sharing a bottle of wine. Or simply sitting on his couch in front of the fire with Darwin resting on his lap. The wonderful life he had taken for granted was inexorably retreating away.

Then, reliving that unsettling dream of years ago, he dropped the keys on the breakfast counter and walked out of the dark, silent house. He felt a lump in his throat as he glanced at the For Sale sign. The small trailer, stuffed with all he could carry, was hooked to his convertible. With Darwin in his carrier on the passenger's seat, Federico got behind the wheel and, leaving the last twenty years behind, drove north to start the next chapter of his life.

Countless days of blue skies during his first summer in Oregon almost made him believe the word overcast didn't apply to the region. Cloudy mornings and rainy days later on were just as magical. The misty fog rising from the lake—framed by the nearby snowy peaks—uplifted his spirits.

A short walk from the beach, his cozy 1950s cottage had been a lucky choice. Fetching even more than the realtor predicted, the sale of his Silicon Valley house went well. So, his budget wasn't too tight and even allowed him a once-a-month dinner with a glass of wine at a decent restaurant.

Throughout the seasons, Federico hiked miles of the nearby trails and went kayaking often. Long walks along the beach allowed him to meditate about the rights and wrongs in his life. He was filled with a peace and tranquility he had never experienced as a pawn of corporate America. Even Darwin rewarded him with the unconditional love only a pet was capable of giving. Every day he found new reasons to be grateful and had plenty of time for his favorite pastimes: reading and learning about science, space, and futurism.

On one of those quiet mornings, while flipping through content on YouTube, Federico came across a video titled *The Fermi Paradox: The Dyson Dilemma*. The Fermi paradox was somewhat familiar to him: an idea put forward by physicist Enrico Fermi[38], speculating that humans could be the only civilization in the cosmos.

"The Dyson dilemma? No clue what that is about, but it must be related to Dyson spheres[39], like in *Ringworld*."

Ringworld was one of his favorite sci-fi novels. Larry Niven briefly explained Freeman Dyson's[40] conjecture that an advanced alien civilization might build a massive spherical shell around their home star, achieving two objectives: capture the entire energy output from the star, providing them with virtually unlimited energy to power their civilization, and give them billions of times the surface of their home planet to grow and multiply. But Federico had also learned long ago such a megastructure was impossible to build.

'Quacks and charlatans post so much junk on social media!' he thought, reluctant to watch the video.

But curiosity won. It turned out to be more of a podcast with poor graphics, but the content gave him goosebumps all over his body as the flood of ideas overran his brain. With the technology available in 2017, it would take humankind just a thousand years to completely surround the sun with rotating habitats, a.k.a. a Dyson swarm. It would take a million years to achieve the same for every viable star in the Milky Way.

It made a profound impact, a crossroad that reshaped his way of thinking and very existence to unimaginable extents; it was the most profound defining moment of his existence. He replayed the last few minutes of the video.

"...because the universe is 13.8 billion years old, there has been enough time for a single alien civilization to have done the same already. Had that been the case, we would not be able to see stars in the night sky. There must be no such thing as alien civilizations in the Milky Way or its neighboring galaxies," concluded the narrator.

Discouraged, Federico shook his head. The idea made sense.

A vast power generator releasing insane amounts of free energy, a star had millions of times the space of all its planets and moons put together. Faced with formidable power and room constraints, a burgeoning civilization at our current technological stage would be able to tap into both by building a swarm of rotating habitats around their home star in order to continue growing.

"Yeah, sure. Easy breezy!" he snorted, sarcastically speaking to the narrator in the video. But his dismissal could not disprove the argument.

Furthermore, galaxies were spaced between tens of thousands and millions of light-years from each other. If an alien civilization could traverse their home galaxy, which typically spanned a few hundred thousand light-years, it could also engage in intergalactic colonization, and this would happen in a blink of an eye on the cosmic scale.

"Therefore, vast regions of the universe should be colonized already," a reluctant Federico was forced to admit, again out loud.

He refilled his coffee mug, sat down heavily on his LC4 chaise lounge, and sighed.

"If there were alien civilizations currently building Dyson swarms in the Milky Way, or any of its neighbors, we would see them as expanding voids made by stars going dark." Pensively, he reviewed his understanding of the issue. "The fact that we don't see a single swarm means there probably isn't a civilization capable of building them yet," he concluded.

He had grown up watching *Star Trek* and avidly reading loads of sci-fi novels, and the belief that humans were not alone in the cosmos was as deeply rooted in him as faith in religion. He dreamed of the day aliens would arrive to lift earthlings from the shadows of their own brutality. He cherished the thought that the mere existence of an alien civilization would, finally, unite humankind and put an end to war, poverty, and hunger. At the least, he hoped it would usher in a new era of scientific cooperation and betterment for humanity.

"This can't be!" he muttered to an invisible audience.

Leaving one of his core beliefs behind was incredibly challenging, but the arguments in the video appeared incontrovertible, making him feel lightheaded and disappointed. To add insult to injury, if the Fermi paradox was still around after nearly seventy years of contentious scrutiny, it had to be that nobody had come up with a good solution yet.

The emotional flattening haunted him for weeks, and Federico took refuge in research. During a lunch at Los Alamos National Laboratory in 1950, Fermi brought the idea to some of his colleagues, but he died of cancer a few years later, never having the opportunity to publish a paper on the subject. The account of that fateful conversation by his colleagues was the only one on record. However, Fermi's argument was so powerful that, instead of fading away, it strengthened over time and was still known as the Fermi paradox.

Image by Hubble Heritage Team, modified by Adriana Ayala

In 1975, astronomer Michael Hart[41] published the first paper building on Fermi's argument. Hart proposed that if an alien civilization had evolved in our galaxy, it would have developed interstellar travel, colonizing its neighboring stars. These colonies would, in turn, launch colonizing expeditions to their neighboring stars, and so on, occupying the entire Milky Way within two million years.

Ringing in Federico's brain like a fire alarm was a memory of his overexcited coworkers hushing each other as he walked into the cafeteria on a hot afternoon in October 1995. Gathered around a large CRT television on full volume, they watched the announcement of the first confirmed exoplanet[42] discovered around another regular star. The massive Jupiter-sized gas giant orbited 51 Pegasi b, some fifty light-years away from Earth.

Until that day, nobody knew for sure if the sun was the only star with planets in the universe. Now, there was scientific evidence that other stars had planets too! The dream of alien civilizations became less science fiction that day and bathed him in overwhelming humility.

It was the start of the golden age of exoplanet discovery. Twenty years later, scientists had found close to 3,000 additional exoplanets. Even amateur astronomers were discovering exoplanets from their backyards. As better instruments allowed them to detect Earth-sized rocky worlds in the habitable zones[43] of their stars, it became clear that 25 percent of all the planets discovered were similar to Earth.

'Wow! That means there could be forty billion Earth-like worlds just in the Milky Way alone, capable of hosting life,' thought Federico.

But this fact only supported the argument that our galaxy should have been colonized already. Yet, in the words of Fermi himself, "Where is everybody?"

Months went by. The more he researched, the more convinced he became. Dropping his ballast of preconceived ideas, Federico embraced the Fermi paradox at last. Certain that humanity's future lay in space, building a swarm of rotating habitats around the sun, now made a lot more sense than trying to colonize and terraform planets.

Browsing the internet regularly, he searched for recent news and publications. "... speed of 0.2c, SpaceChip... journey to Alpha Centauri star system 4.3 light-years away." What? A little cry of amusement escaped his lips.

Awestruck, he discovered that humans already knew a way to accelerate a prototype for a tiny spacecraft to a decent fraction of the speed of light! Focusing a large ground-based array of laser beams would give it a push without burning fuel.

The Breakthrough Starshot[44] project planned to speed up a probe, the size of a postage stamp, to 20 percent of light-speed towards Alpha Centauri. But Federico immediately reasoned that a much larger laser array in space, with virtually unlimited energy from the sun, would be able to accelerate a bigger ship to any fraction of light speed. It was just a matter of scale.

"Are Dyson swarms inevitable? Are they the only way an advanced civilization can colonize space?" he asked himself.

He combed the internet for references to Dyson swarms. Every article he found described them as immense power collectors around a star with the purpose of beaming power to the planets. There was no mention about a swarm of rotating habitats! However, space and energy went hand in hand; a civilization needed room to grow, otherwise they wouldn't have use for all that energy.

'We can fit more people in a single Dyson swarm, made of rotating habitats, around the sun than on all planets and moons (habitable or not) in our entire galaxy, and today we already have the technology to start building one!' he thought excitedly.

Paddling on the lake during one of those cloudless summer nights, Federico looked up at the starry sky. It reminded him of Carl Sagan's old *Cosmos* episode, *The Shores of the Cosmic Ocean,* that inspired him so much as a teenager. Setting the paddle inside, he turned off the little green light that allowed others to see him in the dark. Only the tiny waves gently lapping against the side of his kayak broke the silence. In total darkness, he looked up. The expansive sky seemed to swallow everything around him.

'Could we actually be alone in the universe?' he wondered.

Hammering at the same subject, again and again, had him trapped in a vicious loop frying his brain, but he couldn't help it. What could possibly prevent an alien civilization from colonizing the galaxy? It was logical to assume a civilization would grow and expand if it had access to resources. Could the aliens be hiding on purpose? From what? A large civilization could not hide from any of the few things capable of threatening it: a natural phenomenon like a gamma ray burst[45] or a nearby black hole[46]. And even these couldn't destroy an entire interstellar civilization, except for one or two of their Dyson swarms; the rest would go on and continue expanding.

He had read about the Great Filters[47] hypothesis just a few days earlier and was fascinated by it. Hanson argued that life needed to overcome a progression of milestones or filters, in order to reach different levels, culminating in the colonization of the cosmos: organic chemistry single cell life multicellular life intelligence civilization.

Federico shifted in the kayak, continuing this line of thought. 'If our cosmic neighborhood looks empty, either we are the only advanced civilization in this part of the universe, or there's another great filter still ahead of us—one we haven't thought of and no other civilization has yet crossed.'

A shiver crawled down his back, making the tiny boat wiggle. If that was the case, humanity was doomed.

Prey to the shallowness of our basic instincts and obsessed with celebrities, pop culture, greed, and war, we failed to see the universe was a wondrous realm and pursue the bigger plan. In the meantime, the cosmos lay empty, its doors wide open, just waiting for its first tenant.

'Isn't being alone in the universe a more attractive proposition than being one of many, just another pebble on one of the many shores of this vast cosmic ocean?' he asked himself. 'And if so, is it not our destiny, our duty, and even our birthright to spread throughout the cosmos and colonize it, to make it our playground, like a species of gods? And what does it mean to be a god?'

For eons, human beings gazed at the stars wondering if they were supreme beings charting their destinies. Even the brightest scientists, such as Newton and Galileo, invoked the divine when faced with the limits of their knowledge. But as science continued to outstrip God's signature achievements, pushing humanity's Perimeter of Ignorance[48] further away, would people still continue worshiping the almighty?

Federico turned the dim green light back on and headed home. The night enveloped him in its gigantic shroud of the unknown.

A famed astronomer, Joshua Gordon was followed by millions and loved for sparking the light of science in people's minds. In a mad era of irrationality, conspiracy theories, internet junk, and fake news that swayed a recent presidential election, he was a beacon of sanity, one of the few voices of reason—an Isaac Asimov[49] to the millennial generation, according to some—and a brilliant communicator who reached out and connected with people. He hosted a science, pop culture, and comedy radio talk show with Ronald Shock, a stand-up comedian and good friend.

"Today! Alien Abductions, with Joshua Gordon!" said Ron. "No, we're not discussing the coincidence of your husband being abducted at the same time as his secretary! [A pause] You know what happened, and so do I." (Background laughs in the studio)

With Darwin dozing on his lap, Federico listened to Joshua deflate conspiracy theories with the patience and determination of a kindergarten teacher potty training a bunch of misbehaved toddlers. Unable to move and having nothing better to do, he called into the show and amusedly waited for his turn.

"And now, we have Fed-ah-rrrree-coh from Lincoln City, Oregon! Is that a cool name or what, buddy? What's your question?" asked Ronald, enjoying rolling his Rs.

"I have a Fermi paradox question for Dr. Gordon," Federico said. "An alien civilization at our current technological level would be able to entirely surround their sun with a cloud of rotating habitats in about a thousand years, then do the same with every star in the Milky Way within a million years. The universe, being fourteen billion years old, isn't the fact that we can see stars in the night sky the best indication that we are alone?"

"Wait a second!" said Ronald. "If a star is covered by a cloud and you can't see it, how can you say it isn't there?"

"Such a cloud would glow like a Christmas tree on the infrared telescope," interjected Joshua. "Our friend on the phone is referring to a Dyson sphere. What I find interesting is that he's using our apparent ability to build a Dyson sphere today as an argument in favor of the Fermi paradox. I believe we avoid the subject because the prospect of being alone in the cosmos is unbearable for most of us. But if the Fermi paradox doesn't bother you at an existential level, it's because you haven't thought about it hard enough."

Federico was about to object that a Dyson sphere was not what he was proposing, but Ronald jumped in first.

"Hold on! Let me be the devil's advocate here. What if aliens shared the destructive nature of humans and annihilated themselves in a war? Then, they existed for a brief moment in time and then disappeared."

"They would have had to kill every single individual. If only a few survive, they would be able to reboot civilization after a few hundred or thousand years," said Joshua.

"And if they evolved the way we did, they had to fight to survive. Expansion will be second nature to them. Even if they've become a highly evolved and humane society, their desire to grow and expand will drive them to spread throughout the universe," added Federico.

"What if they create an artificial super-duper intelligence that wipes out every single dude?" Ronald joked.

"That would count as one species taking over another, just like we took over the Neanderthals. An AI would still dyson—if I may use Dyson as a verb—its own star and grab neighboring ones. Even faster, because it wouldn't need cushy rotating habitats with gravity and atmosphere; it would be much happier in solar powered data centers orbiting the sun. That's why I don't buy the argument of *The Matrix*," replied Federico.

"Ohhh!" said the other two men at the same time.

"Are you a physicist, a philosopher?" asked Joshua.

"Software engineer. Retired. Curious..." replied Federico.

"I see," replied Joshua. "I agree with your argument. If just one civilization in a million survived, our galaxy would already be dysoned. Mind you, the Milky Way is very old, and our solar system is quite new in comparison."

"Come on, guys! I want to believe in aliens; there must be *someone* out there," Ronald emphasized. "Okay. What if they had a source of energy so powerful and cheap that they didn't depend on their sun? Therefore, no need to dyson anything, and the stars would look just like they are," he added.

"Of course, that's a possibility, but I won't speculate on something that requires new physics," said Joshua. "Based on what we know today, there are very few hints such a thing would be possible any time soon. We are stuck with the laws of thermodynamics for the foreseeable future."

A thought exploded in Federico's brain.

"That's it!" he screamed, jumping off his lounge chair and startling Darwin off his lap. "If we are bound by the laws of thermodynamics, Dyson swarms are inevitable! A growing civilization that has depleted its planetary resources and has a desperate need of room to grow will have no other option than to build rotating habitats around their home star to avoid choking to death! And once they've harnessed their home star, spreading across the galaxy will only require persistence and a pinch of cosmic time!" he finished, provoking a few laughs in the studio.

"I wouldn't go that far, but it's definitely more likely than we thought," cautioned Joshua. "The fact we haven't found one yet does seem to support your argument."

"I still have my doubts. You are speculating on how a civilization will evolve. For all we know they're perfectly happy to stay home. No need to go out, conquering the universe," added Ronald dramatically. "Why can't they be a nonviolent, sedentary kind of 'episcop*alien* mamm*alien*'?" he finished with a giggle.

After the outburst of laughter simmered down, Federico's time on the phone was over; the call was put on hold; and the show went to commercials. He was about to hang up when someone picked up the call again and spoke to him.

"Hello, Federico? This is Joshua. It's very nice to meet you."

"It's nice to meet you too!" he responded with mounting excitement.

"That was a very interesting exchange! I was wondering if you'd like to stay in touch and bounce a few ideas off each other from time to time?" asked Joshua.

"It w-w-would b-b-be a pleasure!" he stuttered, almost choking with emotion, and they exchanged email addresses.

Foolishly and in disbelief, Federico stared at his phone for a few seconds after the call ended. He didn't expect anything out of that call, but it was exciting, nonetheless.

He got an email a few weeks later.

B I U S ⚫ 🖼 🔗 ⚫ 📋 ⬚ ⬚ ⬚

Dear Federico,
I'll be in Berkeley on the thirteenth of next month, having dinner with some friends in the scientific community. I know it's not exactly close to you, but we would be delighted if you could make the trip to join us.
With kind regards,
Joshua Gordon.

Carefully analyzing his budget for the adventure, Federico realized flying would save him time, but he would still need a car in California. However, time wasn't something he was short on, and he would save money if he drove. Comparing the miles he needed to drive to the wear and tear on his car—which still needed to last him a few more years—he decided the cheapest alternative would be to rent a car and drive all the way back to the Bay Area. There, he could stay with friends in Silicon Valley within a half hour from Berkeley. He would even take the Pacific Coast Highway, a longer but much more enjoyable drive.

Placing enough water containers throughout the house for Darwin, he secured the doors so the cat wouldn't lock himself in a room by accident. Then he opened a bag of dry food.

"I might end up eating this too, buddy," he joked, filling up a large kitchen pot.

He might not be going out to dinner any time soon, but the adventure was worth it.

In the Thousand Oaks neighborhood, the party was held at a handsome Mediterranean Revival-style mansion with weeping willows planted in the front corners of the lush garden. Federico crossed the wide stone path, rang the bell, introduced himself, and was ushered into a large room full of people. Joshua advanced forward to greet him, stretching out his hand.

"And you must be Federrrrico! Very nice to meet you in person," he said, in his booming radio voice. "Allow me to introduce you."

A few names here and there were familiar, but Seth Shostak[50] stood out among others, as Federico had listened to many of his podcasts over the years. Soon, Joshua got pulled away to talk to other guests, and Federico was left on his own.

With a sublime view of the Bay Bridge diving into San Francisco amid the chilly summer night weather, he found a smörgåsbord and a hot food table in the backyard. Starting with a hot beef bouillon to warm up, Federico helped himself to serving after serving of delicious and mouth-watering food from beautiful platters and vessels. Although Oregon wines were excellent, the cherry on top was pairing the food with some of his favorite California wines that he missed so much.

A small group of people approached the wine table, and Federico somehow got dragged into the conversation. Within just a few minutes, he was being challenged by one of the other guests.

"What do you have against colonizing Mars?"

Federico was now at the center of it. He pondered his reply cautiously; he was a bit tipsy and didn't want to embarrass himself.

"I just think it's a pretty hostile environment: low gravity, an almost nonexistent magnetic field, and no breathable atmosphere. We would even have to grow our own microorganisms. It would take centuries to terraform, during which people would have to live underground. Not to mention, we have no near-future technology that can hope to replenish Mars's atmosphere. Plus, we haven't terraformed anything before. We don't even know the long-term effects of low gravity on the human body because nobody has spent more than twenty-four hours on the Moon. Just look at the dramatic changes a little bit of extra sugar produces in our bodies. Living and breeding in low gravity is bound to have a distinctive impact on human physiology," he finished.

"We will adapt," replied the man.

"Please tell me you don't mean bioforming," said Federico scandalized.

"Possibly, yes."

Federico, who strongly opposed the idea of genetically altering people to survive in low gravity or to breathe in the nitrogen atmosphere of Titan, threw caution to the wind.

"Do you realize that, even if we had the capability to bioform ourselves, the human DNA changes might very well cast the subjects off the *Homo sapiens* genus, creating a new species that will be unable to interbreed with regular humans, possibly leading to wars between both species in the future?"

"Nah, you're making too much of it," said one of the guy's friends.

"Throughout history, we've used technology for shaping the environment to suit us, not the other way around. With all due respect, the idea of reshaping our bodies, possibly becoming a different species to fit an alien environment, is just unacceptable," Federico said in a more passionate and instructive tone than he wished.

"The technology will be there when we need it. Within a couple of generations, we'll have terraformed Mars, and people will be living on the red planet as happy as on Earth," the guy insisted with an acerbic dry smile.

'I'm pretty sure the FDA will say differently,' thought Federico, but decided to keep it to himself.

Federico pictured the guy as dead set in his beliefs, someone who did extensive research and had ready answers to all objections, and he wasn't in the mood to proselytize. Nevertheless, an idea suddenly crystallized in his alcohol-impaired brain.

"Earth is humanity's womb! Once it gives birth to a spacefaring civilization, the umbilical cord will be cut. That's why Mars can't be a replacement for Earth. Our future lies in space with virtually unlimited energy and room to grow. We just need the *cojones* to take the first steps!"

Surprised, the guy frowned and squinted, unable to reply.

Overconfident now, Federico ratcheted the pressure. "Given the Herculean effort required to free ourselves from Earth's gravity well, why drive ourselves into a ditch and become captives to another gravity well on Mars?" he added, certain of having the winning hand.

The guy tightened his jaw and fidgeted with his wine glass. It took him a few seconds to articulate with a beaver-toothed grin. "You're delusional my friend. How long do you think it'll take to build a rotating habitat?"

With an unexpected turn of the tables, Federico was trapped, and he knew it. Here was the killer argument. Inhospitable and hostile to Earth's life, Mars was, at least, already there and waiting to be settled. Rotating habitats would need to be built from scratch in space. With no space-bound infrastructure, it would take many decades to build the first cylinder. Although things would progress faster afterward, it was a tough sell because humans were hardwired for instant gratification. Given the option, most people would rather settle for Mars today than wait.

"Well, it'll be a bit before we can build anything like an O'Neill cylinder[51]..." Federico started, in full retreat, trying to sidestep the issue.

"A bit? A bit! You're so full of shit, dude!" the guy interrupted with a loud, derisive laugh. Obviously, Federico wasn't the only one impaired by the wine.

"Listen, we didn't have all the technology when we started building the James Web Space Telescope[52], but we developed it as the project went on. It'll be similar but on a much larger scale.

Rotating habitats are our best option for long-term space habitation. We can have perfect gravity, atmosphere, and weather. No storms, climate change, earthquakes, tsunamis, or volcanoes. Nor mosquitoes!" Federico argued.

A few laughs behind him made Federico turn around, surprised. A small group of people had congregated behind him. How long had they been listening to the discussion?

"Great job embarrassing yourself. Idiot!" he told himself.

Swiftly pushing his thick-framed glasses up with a mechanical gesture, Federico peered at the bystanders and tried to smile. His deep-set eyes and thin face seemed buried under the heavy frame.

"Our friend Kyle here is a devout supporter of the Mars First community," said Joshua, coming to his rescue from behind the crowd. "The biggest challenge we face today is that putting a pound in space costs $10,000. Until we can bring that down, both your arguments are moot."

His heart was still racing. While he hated drawing attention, Federico realized he had placed himself right under the spotlight, and it was too late to back out.

"Shouldn't we research other technologies in addition to rockets?" he asked, scuttling away from the wreckage.

In a regular rocket, less than 3 percent of the total mass was actual payload. The rest was fuel and engines, necessary to escape Earth's gravity, and was left behind before reaching orbit.

"Like what?" inquired Joshua, interested.

"Launch assist megastructures! Space elevators[53], star trams[54], skyhooks[55], even balloons!"

"Well...yes..." admitted Joshua, reluctantly. "The problem is that everybody is in a race to make rockets more efficient and not paying attention to anything else."

"Lowering the cost of getting to space to become a spacefaring civilization is a mega challenge. It requires a planetary scale commitment. It will take the collaboration of private industry, rival governments, and wealthy individuals. The *entire* human race needs to join forces to make this a reality," answered Federico

"Wishful thinking!" snorted Kyle contemptuously.

"Our turbulent evolutionary past predisposes us to compete against each other, to fight to the death. We've seen this in every aspect of our civilization, past and present. A hundred years ago, a single individual was able to make breakthrough discoveries; today it takes teams of people. It will take even larger teams to make new developments and discoveries in the future. We must learn to put aside our egos and collaborate to move humanity forward. Those who don't recognize this fact are living in the past!" proclaimed Federico.

"So, what is it that you propose?" asked Joshua, smiling.

"The scientific community—you, in particular—needs to take the lead in raising public awareness and even get the players together and convince them to join forces for the betterment of the human race," replied Federico.

"Me? Why don't you do it?" challenged Joshua, amused.

"You're the rockstar, oozing star power! Do you seriously believe they're going to listen to Mr. Unknown from Oregon with the hard-to-understand Latino accent? Oliver Twist would stand a better chance!"

A raucous wave of laughter broke from behind, and the weight of dismissive glances landed heavily on him. An uneasy tension spread out; the crowd lost interest and dispersed. Kyle laughed dryly, looked down on Federico for an instant, and approached the wine table for another glass.

Federico grabbed a small bottle of sparkling water from a table, twisted the cap open, and drank unceremoniously.

At the end of the green lawn to his left, a tantalizing mound of red caught Federico's attention. He decided to take a stroll to investigate; nature always had a soothing effect on him. The colorful plant was a butterfly bush, arched by exploding red-purple blooms on its branches. He circled around the bush and walked down a few limestone steps to the next terraced level of the garden. The outline of a man stood out from the landscape. Behind him and far in the distance, the view opened to the bay, fog spilling silently over the harbor and the city.

Recognizing the silvery white hair, as they had been briefly introduced earlier in the evening, Federico sat on the limestone ledge with Seth Shostak. A few feet away, Joshua played fetch with the family's golden retriever.

"That was an interesting argument back there," said Seth, with a friendly smile. "I think you made a compelling case for living in rotating habitats rather than on the moon or Mars."

Curious, Federico asked him, "What's your position on the matter?"

"I'm an alien seeker; my interests are with SETI, and I think we should keep all options on the table."

Ever since the invention of radio, there had been an ongoing effort to listen for possible transmissions of extraterrestrial origin. Founded in 1984, Search for Extraterrestrial Intelligence scoured the skies looking for radio and laser signals in search of intelligent life in the universe. It had been argued that alien civilizations would have different methods of communication—superior to anything humans had–which was the reason why alien transmissions went undetected.

"We've been searching for a long time, although meaningful progress has been achieved only in the last ten years as a result of Moore's law. I'm inclined to think alien civilizations might be just too far away," said Federico.

"If you think we're alone in the universe, then why should we keep SETI around?" asked Seth.

"I can't help wondering why an advanced alien civilization would still use radio communications. A hundred and twenty years after Marconi, we use it a lot less. But science must remain objective, and I think we should expand the program to find out for sure if we are really alone," Federico replied.

"Did you hear that, Josh? I still have hope for keeping my job!" chortled Seth.

"But I believe the best way to find an alien civilization is by detecting their megastructures, like Dyson swarms. I think it's the natural outcome when a civilization becomes as advanced as we are," clarified Federico.

"But you personally don't believe there's life, do you?" pressed Seth.

"I actually do. I think it's quite common in the universe. We know life started early on Earth; I think the same likely happened on countless other planets across the universe. But did they reach civilization? We have other intelligent species on this planet, but none of them are capable of developing technology." He paused and took a long sip from the water bottle. "Think of the tribes that have never been in contact with the outside world. They have not developed a hint of advanced technology; they haven't even invented the wheel! In fact, the number of advanced civilizations on Earth that rose and spread might have been only one. This leads me to speculate that not even big brains—and I mean intelligence—result in advanced civilizations a hundred percent of the time," Federico added.

"Hmm... not a bad conjecture, Mr. Unknown from Oregon," smiled Seth.

"The Neanderthal didn't develop technology in 400,000 years, and they had fire at their disposal," Federico continued. "Maybe the spark they lacked was the right genetic makeup. Perhaps civilization needs to close the loop: technology makes it easier to survive and reproduce in greater numbers. More individuals increase the chances technology will improve, leading to even greater numbers of individuals who make better technology. Either this circle never closed for the Neanderthals, or we exterminated them before it happened."

Federico wondered if he would live long enough to see the improvements in the next loop of his own civilization. Primates steered their own evolution from the moment they manufactured stone tools; fire and agriculture followed. Genetic engineering with new tools, like CRISPR[56], could soon enable humankind to take the next step by allowing the creation of super humans. What would they be like? Smarter people, multitasking brains, stronger and faster bodies?

Seth brought him back from his thoughts.

"What makes you say we exterminated the Neanderthals? The evidence points at us interbreeding with them."

"The evidence can also be interpreted as the *Homo sapiens* exterminating all their males and taking the females as slaves. They would have mixed with them as well. I believe that explains why we carry Neanderthal DNA," retorted Federico.

"But there must be alien civilizations somewhere!" exclaimed Seth. "There's so much room in the universe; I just find it hard to believe that everything interesting is happening here on Earth. I never found this to be a reasonable point of view."

"That's a fair point, and it's hard to argue against. Until recently, I was of the same opinion. But to me, the absence of Dyson swarms appears to indicate that we are the only civilization in this part of the cosmos! If there are others, they're so far away that the light from their civilizations haven't had time to reach us yet," said Federico.

"I think we shouldn't be prejudiced and keep looking for whatever our current instruments allow us to detect."

"Agreed!" said Federico. "I wish I could give NASA more than a penny. I'd give them at least twenty cents of every tax dollar!"

"You're dreaming!" said Joshua, who gave up playing with the dog and walked over to join the conversation. "Anyway, where will you get the materials to build a Dyson swarm? Obviously, we can't haul them from the ground."

He sat down and waited for Federico's reply with a curious expression.

Federico's first thought was Earth's moon, so large that many considered the pair a double planet. But the satellite was already receding away, and removing enough mass from it would make it do so even faster, affecting the climate, tides, and even tectonic plates.

"I'd love to mine the moon, but I don't know the threshold at which it will begin to affect our planet. What about mining Near Earth Asteroids (NEAs)[57] and use them to develop the kind of infrastructure that will allow us to mine Mercury? Then we can build the first O'Neill cylinders. But that's just a stepping-stone. The ultimate goal is to develop the technology to extract heavier elements from the sun," said Federico.

"Star lifting?" [58] A creaky sound escaped from Seth's throat as he nodded, eyes brightening up.

"I believe that's what it's called, yes," said Federico.

"That's only a concept; it's never been tested," said Joshua.

"We don't know a lot about how star lifting will work," said Federico. "However, the fact is there are obscene amounts of gold, platinum, and rare earth metals in the sun, thousands of times the weight of the entire planet Earth in carbon, and less valuable metals like iron—enough to build our Dyson swarm many times over. We also know they're not sunk down to the core but floating around, carried by the sun's convective process. All we need is to figure out how to extract them. Whether we call it star lifting or something else is irrelevant. If it works, we'll get virtually unlimited construction materials and decrease the sun's mass, so it won't become a red giant. Hypothetically, it will shine for a trillion years instead of a few billion!"

Joshua raised his eyebrows and turned to look at Seth, who broke the silence.

"Where did you dig up this guy, Josh? This is too much fun!"

"What you want is quite ambitious, Federico. How do you propose to start something that large...if you have a proposal?" asked Joshua.

Federico smiled shyly. "First, we need a foothold in space to manufacture things, but we're hostages to Earth's gravity well. Rockets are terribly inefficient, but we don't have anything else. We start by mining NEA's to build our initial infrastructure. Once we start mining Mercury, things will move much faster, and we'll be able to build O'Neill cylinders, solar panels, and laser generators in space," said Federico.

"Whoa! Wait! You want to put lasers in space?" asked Seth.

"For protection against comets and asteroids headed our way. Also, to accelerate interstellar ships to a fraction of light-speed. We will start colonizing neighboring stars long before we finish building our first Dyson swarm. Humanity will become an interstellar civilization before reaching K2 status," said Federico, enthusiastically.

"K2!" said Seth, laughing and shaking his head in disbelief. "That's it. I throw in the towel with this guy."

Federico was nine years old when he read about the Kardashev scale[59] in a dusty astronomy volume. The book had been misplaced in the geography section of the library where troublemakers did detention at his elementary school.

Developed by Soviet astronomer Nikolai Kardashev in 1964, the scale offered a glimpse of the unrelenting technological advancements of a civilization based on its energy consumption and expansion. Capturing all the energy falling on their home planet, or 10^{16} watts in the case of Earth, a K1 civilization would have an estimated population of ten billion, or 10^{10}. Harnessing all the energy of their home star, or 10^{26} watts in the case of the sun, a K2 civilization would surround their star with a population of 10^{20} in a Dyson swarm. Masters of their home galaxy with a population of 10^{30} in swarms around all viable stars in their home galaxy, a K3 civilization would be immune to extinction with access to 10^{36} watts of power—in the case of the Milky Way.

"The scale is imprecise as planets, stars, and galaxies come in many different sizes. But I do agree with you. Our species is destined to become an interstellar civilization in the distant future," said Joshua, sitting down.

Seeing Federico's face light up with excitement, he raised an objecting hand. "Emphasis on the word *distant*! And that, only if we don't perish or turn Earth into a wasteland before reaching K1."

"I find it fascinating," commented Seth. "There are many speculations about the next level. Would a K4 utilize the energy of the entire universe or, perhaps, just their entire galactic cluster or supercluster?"

"All seems possible with such immense power, don't you think? I'm certain humanity will go on to become a K3+ civilization," said Federico.

"We will need to raise awareness with the public," commented Seth, inspired. "Right now, Mars and the moon are the only things on people's minds. A Dyson sphere is nowhere in people's radar."

"By the way, could we call it a Dyson swarm or cloud? A sphere is impossible to build, as you both know, and the name will create so much confusion," said Federico.

There wasn't a material strong enough to withstand the stress of such a large megastructure, not even theoretical ones that material scientists were dreaming about. Plus, the sphere would have no gravity itself; everything inside would just fall into the sun.

"That's unavoidable. I just did it myself, involuntarily," chuckled Seth. "As soon as we mention Dyson, someone will mistakenly switch it to a Dyson sphere. I'm afraid that's something we'll have to live with."

"Don't encourage him, Seth! Or are you being serious about this?" asked Joshua staring at him in awe.

"Why not? We do have a lot of the technology. And we don't need to come up with new physics! I'm just trying to keep all options open," Seth answered pensively.

"It will be like providing housing for a billion people. You don't do it all at once! You start small and increase capacity to meet demand as resources become available. Nevertheless, it will be a tough first step. But imagine what we can build in space with virtually unlimited resources!" added Federico with growing excitement.

The fog now sat as a mysterious thick blanket, revealing the tips of the San Francisco skyline and the bridge. The three men kept quiet for a while, admiring the view. A cool breeze carried a fragrance of freshly cut grass. Joshua took a deep breath, enjoying the open air.

"Have you thought about the economic implications of what you're proposing?"

"The gold and precious metals in some NEAs are worth tens of trillions! It is a very profitable venture capable of attracting wealthy investors." answered Federico.

"Do you realize many of those 'wealthy investors' you refer to are ultra-conservative?" asked Seth. "They won't listen to us."

"If they see the potential for making a hundred times their investment, they might go for it," responded Federico confidently.

"This is all so far-fetched. I agree with Joshua; you're dreaming," said Seth skeptically.

"Listen guys...," Federico started to say.

"I'm still trying to understand what exactly you are asking of us. What is your plan?" interrupted Joshua.

"I have no idea; I have no plan. At least, not until this very minute. I came to this party to meet interesting people. But now I realize only you guys can do this. You reach billions, you shape people's minds. Right now, a bunch of billionaires with fat personal egos are toying around with rockets in a wasteful race to satisfy their delusions of grandeur. The grown-ups must step in and push things in a different direction."

They both smirked, but briefly.

"You make science cool. Younger generations listen to you. Spread the word to create the rotating habitats mindset; it will produce a change, I'm sure of it. I can't possibly predict how this will play out. But I'm sure we'll have no chance to galvanize the public's attention and resources if we don't first coalesce around a message that can be delivered through your talking points," said Federico.

"Our talking points?" said Joshua with a dry laugh. "You want us to put the word out about Dyson swarms, when we know there isn't a cost-feasible way to put stuff in orbit. It will take many decades, if not centuries, to build the space-bound infrastructure."

An uncomfortable long silence followed. They were back at the main stumbling block: the insurmountable obstacle and the main reason would-be colonists were willing to live inside a lava tube under the surface of the moon or Mars. Federico knew there was no easy way around it. He felt his head was about to burst.

How to start? That was the big question. On the cusp of becoming a spacefaring civilization, humanity needed a push in the right direction.

Federico suddenly felt lost, defeated, and ridiculous. He was not up to the task. With a bunch of tycoons using their power and influence to make their voices heard, pushing towards Mars and the moon, what chance did he stand? What the hell was he thinking?

"Wine is such a bad influence," he told himself.

This was not his call. Someone else, in the future, might eventually rise to the challenge. He regretted having spent his scarce money on the trip, and for what? What was he doing here—a place where he didn't fit at all—talking nonsense about technologies of which his knowledge could barely scratch the surface? All he could think of now was to rush back home and forget the whole damned thing!

Having just turned fifty-two, his savings should last him another twenty to thirty years. Perhaps, he would write a book or get dead drunk every day on his kayak—anything—but he would stop wasting his time on futile research leading nowhere. He was done with futurism.

"You're right. I got carried away. It's getting late; I should be heading home now. It was a pleasure meeting you both."

Stiff and tense, Federico managed to stand up. Hands at his sides and gazing at the ground, he managed to bow his head courteously. But before turning around to leave, he couldn't help but add to his departing words.

"Have you ever seen the Banaue rice terraces, built by people from the Ifugao mountains in the Philippines? Consider the grueling transformation they went through by leaving their nomadic lifestyle...to settle down, carving those magnificent structures with almost nothing but their bare hands, to feed themselves. As leaders of the scientific community, it's now your turn to do something equally transformative. Help shape the vision that will lead our species in the right direction to take the first step in becoming a K2 civilization! This could be the most important thing you'll ever do in your lives: a legacy the two of you, and others, will leave for humankind and, perhaps, be remembered for eternity."

Chapter 2: First Steps

Walking behind the security guard through a long corridor flanked by endless rows of cubicles, Federico witnessed the bustling fast-paced activity, as employees worked feverishly in their assigned spaces and fish-tank meeting rooms.

'A cubicle farm!' The furtive thought sketched a prelude to a smile on his thin lips.

As they went by, some glanced at Federico without stopping the frenetic tapping on their keyboards then quickly turned back to their screens. Occupants of a half-empty section, near the end of the hall, gave him a more open and appraising look in a quieter and relaxed atmosphere devoid of the madness he just left behind.

'This must be the workspace of the Space Initiative,' Federico thought, smiling at them.

Stopping by an indistinct door, the guard led Federico into a small office. Motion sensors turned the lights on when he walked in. The shabby little room was part of a subdivision in the vast office complex owned by a large pharmaceutical conglomerate. Expecting much larger returns than trying to cure the sick, they invested a large chunk of their profits in the Space Initiative, rather than in the traditional research and development of new drugs.

"He'll be with you in a few minutes," said the guard, signaling vaguely at two chairs in front of a solitary desk pushed against the wall. Closing the door behind him, the man left.

Federico couldn't decide if the fabric of the large acoustic panels on the walls was plain ugly, dirty, or both. He chose to sit on the chair farthest away from the door. Judging by the dented bookshelves, it seemed the safest place to avoid being hit when it swung open. A battered, old laptop was the only item on an equally worn desk.

A few years earlier, Joshua Gordon began to raise awareness on his radio show and speaking engagements, making the case for building rotating habitats instead of colonizing the moon or Mars and brought to light some of the technologies required.

A group of ex-NASA scientists, engineers, and private industry leaders coalesced around the idea of taking space exploration in a different direction. A few years later, they became the Space Initiative: a non-profit organization aimed at making humanity a spacefaring civilization.

The biggest challenge was signing up investors to fund Phase 1 of the project. Neither the United States nor any other nation wanted to join, nor did any of the major space-race players. The idea of living in a rotating habitat didn't even register in their minds. So, rather than joining the Initiative, they continued with their plans to terraform Mars or colonize the moon.

Regardless, by 2021 they had finally signed a few investors, bringing in enough funding to start mining NEAs, but they were cash-strapped for anything else. Federico had to spend money from his precious savings that had been earmarked for emergencies for a cross-country plane ticket to attend the interview.

The door squeaked, and Federico rushed to stand up as a man walked in.

"Very nice to meet you, Federico!" he said, with a welcoming pearly-white smile. He shook Federico's hand with assertive enthusiasm.

"Likewise, sir," he responded.

As they both sat, Federico glanced at the clean-shaven, two meters (6 feet 5 inches) tall man and thought he would look great on a ballot for political office, like so many of his astronaut peers. It amused Federico to wonder what led to the stereotype. Now in his late fifties, the chairman of the Space Initiative was still a natural charmer. The blond, broad-shouldered, still-athletic washout from NASA's astronaut program was a handsome man by any standard.

Federico's 1.7 meters (5 feet 6 inches) height and scrawny build were quite a dramatic contrast. He had chosen a vegan, calorie-restricted lifestyle after learning how it significantly slowed down aging and reduced the risks of cardiovascular disease, cancer, and diabetes. According to his physician, his health checkup never looked so good, despite his age.

As an added benefit, he saved a bundle in healthcare and food. It also allowed him to comfortably fit in the new extra-small seats, designed by the airlines to cram even more people into their oversized planes.

Flipping the laptop open, the chairman pulled out a keyring from his pocket and selected a digital authentication key. At his thumb's contact, the little device read his fingerprint and unlocked his workstation. He then started reading through his notes on Federico's resumé.

"Great performance at Future Worlds. Very thorough," he said, lifting his eyes from the screen. "I watched the exchange on the same day it was uploaded."

A month earlier, Federico had been invited as a panelist to a discussion about space colonization at the Future Worlds Conference. Wearing a goofy tee shirt inscribed with "A Star is a Terrible Thing to Waste", he passionately argued for building rotating habitats in space in lieu of trying to settle and terraform celestial bodies. However, the Q&A turned into a heated exchange.

"I was amused by the way you handled the guy in the audience who started attacking you by making him contradict himself. The crowd had a good laugh!" the chairman said, smirking.

"He didn't take that too well, though. Fool, stupid, reckless— what else did he call me?" smiled Federico.

"Narrow minded!" said the chairman with a hearty laugh. "It was clear his biases were doing the talking. You disarmed each of his points with logic. But the guy struggling with the usher over the microphone...seriously!"

"Well-intentioned people don't realize that believing what they believe, without willing to reason, lays the foundation for imposing those beliefs on others. Even so, I didn't expect it to get so bad until security showed up soon after," said Federico.

"Calling him a Planetary Chauvinist[60] probably had something to do with it!"

It was Isaac Asimov who coined the term back in the 1970s. During a joint TV interview[61] with Gerard O'Neill[62], carried by WNET's *Round Table* in New York, he described the bias against living in rotating habitats. Born and raised on Earth, inhabiting another spherical body was too deeply ingrained in people's psyche.

"Still, I suppose that being the only person on the panel who wasn't an accredited scientist made me the target," said Federico.

Friends made at that party in California helped him develop a network of acquaintances throughout the scientific community. This led to a few invitations to appear as a guest on futurism channels, culminating with the panel on space exploration at the recent conference.

"I was impressed by your arguments, however, because we didn't train you. Only a handful of people understands what the Space Initiative is trying to accomplish. I couldn't have done a better job myself."

"Thank you, sir. That's quite a compliment."

"As a matter of fact, I've watched some of your other social media appearances and posts. Very exciting stuff; they say more about you than your resumé. For example, listen to this."

The chairman played a video segment. Federico recognized it as one of his conversations about star lifting with the host of a futurism channel a few weeks earlier.

> An economy is an exchange system designed to manage and distribute limited resources across a population. But if a civilization has free access to more energy and raw materials than it can use, those resources will be virtually unlimited. Would such a society still need an economy to satisfy the needs of its population, or will economics become an extinct science? I'm not talking about an upper-middle class lifestyle. Even if new forms of currencies and exchanges emerged in such a utopia, everybody would be rich! It would be a true post-scarcity society where people...

"Interesting proposition," said the chairman, pausing the video. "But imagine, instead, a few plutocrats establishing mega-empires, thousands of times bigger than anything that ever existed on Earth."

A chill rolled down Federico's spine. The image of a bunch of ruthless and impulsive alpha males, backed by mercenary armies incessantly competing against each other, materialized in his mind. Almighty in their individual kingdoms, the oppression of their citizens would reach unprecedented levels. With virtually unlimited energy, devising WMDs of inconceivable power would lead to an arms race of catastrophic proportions.

"These oligarchs will go to war over stupid stuff, killing trillions and spreading slavery, misery, and destruction. It's scary!" Federico shuddered. "I fail to understand, with unlimited resources and a fully automated workforce, what they could possibly gain from oppressing their fellow human beings. How likely, do you think, is such a dystopia to materialize?"

"I can't even guess the probability. The idea just came to me when I first watched this video. I'm surprised you didn't consider it before. It's obvious, given human nature."

Throughout history, humanity had tried one oppressive system after another. Invariably, the ones at the top enjoyed most of the benefits, while standing on the shoulders of the exploited and oppressed masses. Benign as some of those might have started, in the long run people became prisoners as they tightened their grip. Democracy was a noble idea until it got hijacked by capitalism.

"A terrifying prospect!" said Federico, still shaken. "...a gilded era of space feudalism where people are born and die in bondage, perpetuated for millennia by an abundance of resources."

"Exactly my thinking," said the chairman.

"It must not be allowed to happen! Cultural deification of wealth, broadcasted by the corporate media, gaslights the public to believe plutocrats are brilliant thought leaders, rather than a parasitic cancer on civilization. Space must be open and free to humankind, no exceptions. The greed and tyranny of a few cannot prevent us from building a spacefaring civilization where the well-being of every single human soul is guaranteed. We can't be ruled by another czar aristocracy; egalitarianism must be the founding principle of the space era."

"I'm afraid I don't have a solution at the moment."

"Our chaotic economic system perpetuates a moral swamp, creating a fertile ground for inequality and bigotry. No matter how we reform it, people will always be left behind. But in a true post-scarcity society, inequality can be eradicated forever," responded Federico.

The chairman smiled. In spite of the passionate discourse, Federico's tone remained deep and calm. Turning back to his computer, he continued the interview.

"You come to us very highly recommended by a few of our associates in the scientific community."

Building rotating habitats wasn't in the minds of the most brilliant scientists of the time, who had the attention of the public. Therefore, the Space Initiative worked hard to create awareness in the scientific community for them to get the word out. Posts and articles about rotating habitats began appearing more and more often. Seth and many others followed Josh's lead, and, little by little, several effective communicators spontaneously sprouted within the related fields of science.

"Are you a futurist?" the chairman asked.

"I've been called that on a number of occasions," said Federico. "However, my studies in college were focused on computer sciences. In my last job, I did a lot of project and technical account management for a Fortune 500 company."

"Right...and this position will be a mixture of both. We need you to manage a few ongoing projects that will require interfacing with some of our vendors. I also want someone who understands what the Space Initiative is trying to achieve and will stand by our objectives. In a nutshell, I want *one of us* in this role," said the chairman.

"Yes, sir."

"Let me ask you something. What are your motivations for wanting this job?" the chairman asked, leaning back in his chair.

"Humanity's future is in space, but the public doesn't grasp this yet. Not their fault; they were born on Earth and expect to colonize another celestial body. In the coming years, they will try—and fail—to establish colonies on Mars or the moon. When that happens, the Space Initiative needs to be ready with a viable alternative. Once we get a consensus, they will embrace the Dyson Swarm Project, especially as our population continues to grow. To answer your question, I want to help make that future a reality."

Humans were fast approaching the carrying capacity[63] of Earth. This was the maximum population the planet could sustain, given its energy and resource constraints. Estimates varied, but the average put that number at about ten billion people. Exceeding it could make life on Earth unsustainable, which contributed to the motivation for finding additional living space on Mars, the moon, and even Titan.

"What would you do differently?"

"Nothing! Human confirmation bias will take a lot of resources to overcome, and right now, building a space-bound infrastructure is a better use for our limited funding than winning hearts and minds. I do pity the lab rats who will become the first settlers, but let them try and fail. Maybe they'll start to listen. I wish we could get a piece of the space-program budget, though," answered Federico.

The general population didn't know what was in their best interests. Didn't 52 percent of the public believe that GMOs were less healthy than their organic counterparts? Homeopathy continued to be a growing three-billion-dollar-a-year industry. Close to 30 percent of the population believed the condensation on airplane wings that left those white trails across the sky was a secret government plot to make people sick. Millions without celiac disease unnecessarily followed a gluten-free diet to their own detriment. And about 20 percent of individuals believed aliens had already visited Earth or lived disguised among us, despite an absolute lack of evidence.

"People don't like being wrong, especially those who believe they've critically analyzed a subject but live in an echo chamber filled with their own beliefs. Shielded by selective perception, they don't verify the accuracy of the information fed to them, as long as it reinforces their beliefs. We can't reengineer humankind into an evidence-based society overnight," smiled the chairman.

"Precisely my thinking, sir."

The background check indicated that Federico was retired and living off a fixed income after having been laid off from his previous job five years earlier. So, he probably expected to get paid. Therefore, he decided to make things clear.

"You're aware none of us is being paid yet, although we get health insurance through one of our investors, who also owns this facility. Currently, all funding is dedicated to building our space-based infrastructure, and, when we finally start mining asteroids, most of our cash flow will be committed to pay back our loans. We're a long way from being debt-free," explained the chairman.

Based on their proximity to Earth's orbit and an abundance of metals, the Space Initiative had identified a few NEAs as mining targets for developing construction and manufacturing equipment in space, along with the first experimental rotating habitat. Because they were rich in gold and rare earth metals, they would also allow them to repay their investors.

"Yes, that was explained to me, and I'm fine with it, sir."

Health insurance was the biggest item, by far, in Federico's limited budget, and Medicare was still over ten years away.

"And what are your career expectations?"

"The Space Initiative should start construction of the first rotating habitat in a few decades. I've seen the published specs; it'll house a modest-size colony. I would like to be one of them. The sooner we establish a foothold in space, the sooner we'll be able to develop the infrastructure to begin mining Mercury."

Based on the expected availability of raw materials, the first rotating habitat would be 225 meters in radius by 200 meters long, yielding a living surface of 283,000 square meters—about the size of the Burj Khalifa[64] building in Dubai—and capable of housing in the vicinity of 2,000 people.

"Why would you want to do that? The first settlers will be guinea pigs for studying human physiology inside a rotating habitat in space. Besides, you'll be in your mid-eighties by then."

"I'm beginning to find life on Earth...burdensome," said Federico. "Pandemics, air pollution, groundwater contamination...Did you know that caffeine, antibiotics, and even birth-control hormones are finding their way into our drinking water? And now there's circumstantial evidence that CO_2 could be making our food less nutritious! As our numbers continue to approach carrying capacity, life will become less safe. Finally, either a solar flare will fry the electric grid sending civilization back to the 19th century, or the Kessler syndrome[65] will strand humanity on a dying planet for millennia. I'll gladly leave Earth if presented with the opportunity."

The chairman had grown up in a well-to-do family from the South, enshrouded in privilege and entitlement, with access to the best schools. Combined with his great looks and personality, it opened many doors and created amazing opportunities, from leadership positions in student bodies and sports teams to the space program.

In contrast, Federico was quite an oddball. The disproportionately large nose, skinny frame, prematurely wrinkled skin, and those extra-large thick-framed glasses against his yellow-brown face all conspired to create his frail, librarian looks.

Truth be told, the chairman would have preferred someone more mainstream and marketable—someone more like himself. 'But what the heck! We are like-minded to no small extent,' the chairman thought.

In spite of Federico's thick accent that often made him hard to understand, the chairman couldn't think of anyone with better qualifications and enthusiasm. After meeting him in person, he regarded Federico not just for the job but as an asset to the Space

Initiative—someone who really believed in and understood what they were trying to achieve.

"Fair enough, Federico! You'll work remotely and use your own resources until we can provide you with a workstation. If we need to fly you around, we'll pay for the plane ticket and hotel. The meal allowance will be frugal, and we ask that you use public transportation."

"I understand, sir. I'm in for the long haul."

"Don't worry. A bunch of those guys out there are getting new workstations soon, and we'll get their old equipment," said the Chairman pointing outside. "I made good friends in Facilities, and they will select the best assets for our people."

Our people echoed in Federico's thoughts.

"Great! I'll send you an email with your contract and other forms to sign. Welcome aboard," said the chairman sincerely.

Dubbed Terminus in honor of the great Isaac Asimov, the first rotating habitat was completed in the year 2050. Orbiting at 40,000 kilometers from the ground, it was safe from the cloud of space debris that raced above the atmosphere at speeds close to 28,000 kilometers per hour. With a diameter over twice as long as its length, it looked like a fat disk floating in space.

Facing the sun twenty-four hours a day, Terminus followed a polar orbit avoiding Earth's shadow, allowing the ultra-high efficiency latest generation solar panels to generate eight times more power than on Earth's surface—enough to sustain the colony and run its research operations.

An artificially generated magnetic field around the cylinder, using an electromagnet made from coils of superconducting wire, shielded Terminus from the solar wind and cosmic rays. In the cold temperatures of space, electromagnets didn't need to be cooled down to become superconducting. Wires had no electrical resistance and conducted much stronger electrical currents, generating an intense magnetic field.

It took decades to painstakingly pull the asteroids into Earth's orbit. Each diverted at the point where its orbit was closest to the planet, using robotic ships. Once in orbit, they were mined to extract precious metals, which were anonymously sold in small chunks to avoid saturating the world's markets—keeping prices up—to repay their investors. Lesser value elements such as iron, aluminum, carbon, and silicon were entirely dedicated to construction. Most of the manufacturing infrastructure continued to be developed on the ground and sent into orbit using rockets, whose price had come down to $1,000 per pound.

Of the very few pioneers interested in leaving Earth, most dreamed of settling Mars and calling themselves Martians. There weren't a lot of takers to live in the first rotating habitat, so Federico's wish was granted. He sold his house in Oregon and, bringing a few personal objects that were very dear to him, joined the tiny space-bound community of over 1,800 scientists and engineers from dozens of nations and disciplines.

Meanwhile, the oligarchs lobbied Congress to defund Social Security and Medicare to a large extent by raising the age of eligibility to eighty-five. With his savings nearly depleted, Federico's livelihood was modestly improved by moving to space.

However, he became notorious for being the oldest person in Terminus, where the average age was twenty-five and the oldest person after Federico was forty-five. Nevertheless, his amiable disposition and enduring willingness to help in any situation gained him lots of friends in the small space community.

Image by Katie Lane

Promoted a number of times, Federico had not received a salary yet, although his responsibilities had evolved and increased. Early in his new career, it became clear that his enthusiasm, communication skills, and vision of space colonization were much more valuable than his project-management skills. In his current role as Colony Administrator, he oversaw the day-to-day operations of Terminus.

At eighty-four years of age, the aggressive calorie restriction diet, combined with intermittent fasting and new technologies, kept him in decent health. He ate well and exercised daily. He started his day with a bowl of fruit—grown in the zero-gravity section of the habitat—in his minuscule quarters, standing up in front of the screen and watching the news. A reporter standing on the White House lawn was saying,

> *You might be watching right now a first draft in the space program's death sentence. After a week filled with bad news, the United States is considering pulling the plug on the Mars colony. It's official. There are life-threatening conditions, drugs, and scandals on what was supposed to be a safe environment on the red planet. Stay with us for the full coverage...*

Federico's mobile device started ringing.

It was Patrice Waithera, the Space Initiative's Director of Operations.

"Transfer it to my TV," Federico instructed the device.

A waist-up image of a woman in her late forties replaced the newscast. Her hazel eyes pleasantly harmonized with a smooth-skinned ebony face.

"Hello, Patrice!"

"Great to see you, Federico! How's life in space?"

"I can't complain; I'm very happy and well taken care of."

"I'm glad to hear! You look great! Did I catch you at a bad time?"

"Not at all!" he said, putting the bowl down. "What can I do for you?"

"How do you feel about being interviewed by Alice Kelvin?"

His morning enthusiasm instantly evaporated.

"Not that much?" she asked, sensing his mood change.

"C'mon, Patrice! There's 1,823 people living on Terminus! Why me? Any of them will make a more interesting interview subject," he nagged.

Alice Kelvin was a well-known investigative reporter with a reputation for being incisive, cunning, and armed with hard-dug facts that often led to the shame and ridicule of her victims.

"I'm sure you're aware of what's happening on Mars," she said.

"It's impossible to avoid in the news."

"Kelvin has been digging around and is now pushing for a visit to Terminus to have a closer look and interview some people."

"Why doesn't the chairman or you come with her and do the interview here?" Federico suggested hopefully.

"She traveled to Mars to interview people living in the colony, exposing the widespread substance abuse and other stuff going on right under the noses of the colony administrators! It's only fair she does the same with us...unless we have something to hide. Do we?"

"Of course not," he replied through his teeth.

"We need to demonstrate the Space Initiative isn't another failure in order to attract more investors and public attention," she explained.

Kelvin's recent piece on Mars blew the lid on a spectacular can of worms. Supported by scientific facts and expert opinions and well documented by emails and video recordings from the colonists—released by their families on Earth—it portrayed the bleak and depressing life on the red planet. Calling into question the job of the administrators, the candidate selection criteria, their training procedures, and even the wisdom in establishing a Mars colony at all, it created a PR nightmare by galvanizing public opinion against space colonization.

Although protected from radiation inside underground lava tubes, the deleterious effects of low gravity and isolation had taken a toll on human health that led to the colony's collapse. After decades, it proved to be a failure of epic proportions with an astronomical cost in national treasure and personal fortunes.

Many lost their jobs in the wake of the report, including the congressman from a district which benefited most from building the colony's infrastructure. There was also the matter of how much it would cost to bring over 600 people back home. Although a venture between government and private industry, Washington was shouldering most of the economic burden, and it would be taxpayers who got stuck with the bill.

"Is the chairman in on this?" Federico asked, in a last-ditch attempt to avoid the impending train wreck.

"He recommended you for the task!" she said with a winning smile and a wink.

"I'll be happy to." Federico gave up with a forbearing expression.

Patrice lifted her shoulders, opened her slender arms for an instant, and let them fall back in her lap in an exaggerated gesture of powerlessness, while feeling a bit of pity for Federico.

"Listen, we regret putting you in this situation. However, do this right and you'll get us out of a though spot. We cannot allow the failure of Mars to rub off on us, nor can we be perceived to have an unfair advantage. We need our best on this one. Nobody's better qualified than you to withstand this storm."

Patrice was sugar coating it but was right on a couple of points. An outspoken opponent of the Mars settlement from the beginning, the Space Initiative faced similar scrutiny now that their dire predictions had been proven right by the imminent collapse of the colony. They needed to show that, although claustrophobic, Terminus wasn't a failure; that its residents were fit and thriving. That's why the interview needed to be at the rotating habitat and his performance had to be nothing less than outstanding.

Resigned to his fate, Federico asked. "When is she arriving?"

"You have seven days to prepare," she said. "Please reach out if you need anything. Good luck, Federico, and thanks."

The reporter came back on the screen.

> *... as the low gravity led to birth defects, muscle and bone tissue degeneration, immune system deficiencies, vision impairment, cognitive decay, high blood pressure, and other illnesses. Circadian rhythm sleep disorders made it harder for people to concentrate, triggering a tenfold increase in the rate of accidents. To cap it all off, depression, alcoholism, and other substance abuse flourished unbeknownst to the colony administrators. It was made public by concerned family members here on Earth that breakouts of drug abuse and binging habits erupt during the*

*periodic communication blackouts, when Earth
and Mars are on opposite sides of the sun...*

"Phew," Federico whistled. "I'm not surprised. Lucky us!"

Close enough to Earth for regular delivery of supplies, Terminus had no communication blackouts or time delays, so people could have regular video conferences with their families on Earth. They hadn't had any births yet. But their newborns were expected to be as healthy as any child on Earth.

Numbers were in their favor, too. With the exception of Federico, no one else at Terminus had met everybody in the colony personally. With less than a third of the population, Mars had fewer people to interact with, meaning fewer people with whom to develop relationships and support groups. It also meant more difficulty in avoiding people one disliked.

They had alcohol onboard, as well as locally grown cannabis. There was plenty of room in the microgravity section for marijuana, along with all the other crops whose DNA they were tinkering with in order to increase their yields in microgravity. Although, the researchers seemed quite a bit more enthusiastic about this crop than the others.

Nevertheless, Federico was certain there wasn't a substance abuse problem onboard. Productivity remained high as people became more and more proficient at their jobs, so accident rates actually trended down over time.

There was no acceptable excuse to miss the monthly physical exams, which included psychological evaluations of all residents. The very few who got homesick had the option of returning to Earth on the next empty supply capsule.

If there was an addiction to anything at all on Terminus, it was sex. With so many young people locked in such close quarters working long hours and not enough entertainment options available, gossip of sexual exploits ran wild, abetted by the naive indiscretions of their young and outgoing population. But normal sex drives were only possible if people remained mentally and physically healthy. Furthermore, sex made people happier, increasing their productivity. 'This wouldn't be a bad thing to leak out,' thought Federico.

However, Terminus didn't have a perfect record. Their worst accident happened six months earlier but wasn't work related. A couple of daredevils were goofing around in the zero-gravity section without a safety line and got pulled away by the air flow. They didn't realize they had lost control until it was too late. As the air current continued to push them farther away from the rotation axis, their speed increased, precipitating to their deaths when they hit the ground at nearly 170 kilometers per hour.

Federico had ordered hand grips to be added all over both circular sections, as well as safety lines to the outside of the food production area along the rotation axis. He was criticized for not restricting access to the zero-gravity zone. But with so few entertainment opportunities available on Terminus, he didn't want to add to the problem by forbidding zero-gravity play.

Seven days after his talk with Patrice, he went to greet Alice Kelvin at the arrivals area. Incoming ships from Earth docked at the center of the circular section that faced away from the sun. Newcomers entered the structure through an access port in the zero-gravity section next to the food production area where an elevator carried them down to the normal gravity zone.

A spicy, mischievous-looking Hispanic of Dominican descent, Alice was in her late twenties. Her caramel skin, spellbinding brown eyes, and warm gaze conveyed a false air of kindness to her persona, as her victims were often too late to discover. With dyed auburn-red hair, she wore the customary one-piece garment designed for space travelers. A snug fit to her shapely Latina figure, the suit left nothing to guess about the curvy anatomy underneath.

"Very nice to meet you!" she said, exuding self-confidence in an almost flirty demeanor.

"It's a pleasure, Miss Kelvin," he said with professional courtesy, as alarm bells started to go off in his brain. Lowering his guard around this woman would land him in a lot of trouble.

"May we walk around?" Alice asked.

Without waiting for his answer, she stepped forward from the elevator area, followed by her recording engineer, who placed a large suitcase on the floor with a loud thump. The man opened it, releasing six flying camera drones which immediately started recording footage of Alice and the low-rise buildings around her.

The drones were preprogrammed with basic directives to avoid getting into each other's footage, bumping into people or obstacles, etc. But the engineer was still able to feed them additional instructions from a mobile console. All the feeds were sent live to the news station on Earth, where their production crew would assemble the final footage of the interview.

Federico rushed his pace to keep up.

"Can you give people on Earth an account of life on Terminus?" she asked.

Two of the drones realigned to record him from different angles.

"Our environment is optimum for human habitation, replicating Earth's conditions; some of our residents even have pets. This allows us to work as hard and efficiently as in any town back home."

"You call this Earth conditions?" Alice said with a patronizing smile. "It feels cramped, like I'm going to be crushed. I just got here, and it's rather claustrophobic to me."

"I was referring to Earth's gravity and atmosphere, which are crucial to human physiology," he rushed to explain, bothered by the blatant exaggeration. "There's no environment-related condition or disease among our population. Our residents remain in top health, and their productivity is on par. However, while most people on Earth spend quite a lot of their lives indoors, I agree the current setting is not ideal."

"What kind of work are you doing here?" Alice asked.

"Our population is made of researchers and engineers. We develop, test, and improve existing technologies for construction of rotating habitats and for mining Mercury."

"Why Mercury? Isn't that a very difficult planet to reach?"

"Reaching Mercury is very hard from Earth. But, in space, we don't need all that fuel to break off our planet's gravity well. From Terminus, the amount of propellant to reach Mercury and land is minuscule. Besides, Mercury is the leftover rocky core of a past collision that stripped the planet's mantle away, which means we won't have to dig very deep to reach the ore we need. So the mining component of our infrastructure will be hugely simplified. Furthermore, Mercury's proximity to the sun makes it the ideal location to build our star lifting infrastructure," answered Federico.

"Star lifting is a technique for extracting metals from the sun. It has recently captured a lot of attention in scientific journals," she said looking at the camera behind him. "Can you tell us more about it?"

Federico was surprised she knew about star lifting. It was clear she had done her homework before the interview.

"We plan to use Static Satellites[66], Statites, if I may. Hovering above the sun in a balance between gravity and solar wind, each Statite is an ultralight hexagonal sail over a kilometer across that reflects light back to the sun. Millions of Statites working together will form a giant curved mirror, focusing light at a specific spot on the surface—like a magnifying glass, heating it up. The solar wind will carry up the elements we need, including carbon and metals. We'll then capture and sort them using mass-spectrometer discriminators to feed into 3D printers and other construction devices."

"Have you been able to capture a single atom from the sun yet?" she asked.

"At this stage, we are still testing design and maneuverability of the Statites themselves."

"So, it's easier said than done. I see." Without further ado, she shot the next question. "Can you describe the mining operation for us?"

"Our infrastructure will consist of fully automated mining and refining equipment on the planet's surface. The bulk of the work will be the refining of raw materials. Batteries will allow machines to continue working throughout the long Mercurian night. The close proximity to the sun will allow us to harvest vast amounts of power to keep the operation going around the clock. We will use a

Mass Driver[67] to ship the refined ore to Earth's orbit, where we'll start building larger rotating habitats that will house millions."

"A Mass Driver? Who on Earth—pun intended—knows what a Mass Driver is?" she asked with a hint of arrogance in her cute smile.

"It's a long rail capable of accelerating ships and cargo away from the surface...like one of those catapults used on the old aircraft carriers to launch fighter planes. The low gravity of Mercury makes it the most practical way of delivery," said Federico.

"What about deployment? Will it also be automated? Or is there some assembly required?"

"Because of the communications lag, we need a small crew that will direct the robots doing the assembly. They will stay on Mercury for a few months getting the operation started."

"A small crew to be deployed, you say, like the colony on Mars? I see!" She turned and walked swiftly.

"As you know, we have a small moon base from which we extract water. Not only was it put together in the same way, but we send maintenance crews for short periods, and this has never been a problem..." Federico attempted to interject.

But Alice continued to walk toward a nearby building plainly identified as #10. There was no security; the doors slid open as soon as Alice approached. The Space Initiative had cut costs by sparing everything that wasn't indispensable.

Federico caught up with her.

"May I?" she asked.

He nodded. She wandered inside, followed by Federico and with her engineer in tow. She then chose a door and gave him an inquisitive look. Federico didn't like the idea of cameras in that room at all but had committed to full access. He responded with an acquiescing expression but also raised a hand in a gesture of warning.

"Okay. But be very quiet, and, whatever happens, do not bump into anyone or anything inside. This is very important! Understood?" he emphasized.

When they both nodded, he turned to the engineer.

"Even more important, keep the cameras at least 1.5 meters away from the people inside. Is that clear?"

The engineer agreed again and made the necessary adjustments on his console. Alice then stepped in front of the door which slid open to let them inside.

Wide, curved displays were set alongside the walls with wireless keyboards on the height-adjustable desks. People sat or stood in front of their workstations. Despite never having had a visitor before, none of the occupants diverted their attention to the newcomers or the cameras.

Away from the walls, a variety of sitting options furnished the area, from ergonomic couches to yoga mats. Individuals wearing Virtual Reality[68] gear reached out into the air, a few working in pairs or trios. Some of them were lying comfortably on a sort of large beanbag, set in a 360-degree swiveling metal structure. They appeared to be manipulating complex invisible machinery. Remotely controlling robots and equipment, their hands sketched random shapes in the void in front of them.

If it wasn't for the VR gear, the slow deep breaths would fool anyone into believing a cathartic workout therapy was taking place. The room was as quiet as a grave, and everyone inside it seemed engaged in activities that required their most absolute concentration.

"People at this facility are assembling and testing mining equipment to be deployed on Mercury," said Federico in an undertone. "The equipment they're working on is in space or being loaded into a cargo ship."

"May I speak to them?" Alice asked.

Federico was afraid of this but had no room to maneuver.

"Hello everybody," he said in a calm subtle voice, barely louder than a whisper. "We are joined by Miss Alice Kelvin from Earth, who's working on a news piece about life on Terminus. Anyone who can spare a few minutes to speak to her please come forward."

On a regular day, he would not have entered the facility, much less dared to interrupt their work. But given everything riding on the outcome of the interview, they were fair game. Later, he would have to find ways to make it up to them for this intrusion.

"I will," said one of the women in an equally quiet tone, standing in front of a workstation a few meters away.

Followed by all six cameras, Alice approached her. Federico decided to stay a few steps behind to avoid overcrowding the engineer's workspace. As the team leader, she ran and managed multiple interconnected tasks simultaneously, and others in the room depended upon her orchestration. Because a mistake would have caused a costly accident in space, she remained somewhat distant and was only able to respond with short sentences and monosyllables. The viciously dull interview was brief.

"You should be able to interview any of them after work or anybody you find on the street. I'm sure they'll be more forthcoming when not engaged in work. Most of our residents congregate at the six recreational facilities throughout Terminus," volunteered Federico, who was relieved to be leaving the building.

"Earlier, you mentioned larger rotating habitats. Are those the O'Neill cylinders we've been hearing and reading so much about?" Alice inquired, moving on to a new subject.

"That is correct."

The first reference design for a rotating habitat was proposed by physicist Gerard O'Neill in the 1970s. With a 4-kilometer-radius-by-32-kilometer length, it had a surface over 800 squared kilometers (about the size of all five boroughs of New York City) and was capable of housing ten million people, assuming steel as the construction material. Although more modern twenty-first century materials would allow them to push the original design further, it was still referred to as the O'Neill cylinder.

"When are you starting construction?"

"Within a few years, it will take some time to..."

"Pay your investors? Isn't that what's really preventing you from building an O'Neill cylinder?" she interrupted with a cynical smile.

"...gather enough refined ore," he finished loudly, annoyed by her attitude. "What's stopping us is additional infrastructure and availability of raw materials. There's just not enough matter in these asteroids to build a megastructure that size. For questions about our investors you need to reach out to our..."

"My sources reveal that proceeds from what you currently mine are all funneled to your investors, who are making spectacular returns," interrupted Alice again. She turned to face the closest drone camera beside her and added, "I'm talking trillions in profit, while so many people on Earth can't even afford one meal a day."

"We are here to build a future for the human race, but we must also pay our bills," said Federico in a tone of finality.

"Isn't it true that some very rich individuals are getting paid over 520 times their original investments?"

"I can't comment on...What?"

Federico was stunned out of his wits. No wonder why, after thirty years, they still didn't have enough money to pay salaries or provide adequate working conditions to their employees on Earth!

'So, this is the real purpose of the interview,' he thought enraged, '...To bring those numbers to light (if there was any truth to it) and embarrass the Space Initiative!' Federico suspected, however, it was a fact-checked statement. Kelvin would not risk her well-earned reputation if she wasn't sure. Her team must have really dug deeply to uncover this information.

"I can't comment on what I don't know," he said, promptly recovering. "All I can tell you is that we are making great progress in star lifting and deploying a mining infrastructure on Mercury in order to build O'Neill cylinders. Anything else is outside my purview."

"Will your O'Neill cylinders orbit Earth like Terminus?"

"No. They will be laid next to each other forming a ring around the sun, in the same orbit as Earth, starting at twice the distance from the moon. A system of tunnels, with rails inside them, will facilitate travel between the habitats. After many centuries, billions of these rotating colonies will completely surround the sun, harnessing its entire energy output—what we call a Dyson swarm."

"But even when you build the first O'Neill cylinder, will people come? I've seen some of the simulations, and, as nice as they look, do you think people will give up life on Earth to live in a rotating habitat in space?" she pressed.

Federico was ready with the answer. "Human population has already crossed the eleven billion mark. We are already at or beyond the carrying capacity of Earth. Moving to space is the only way to continue growing. Besides, at some point in the future, we'll be able to build McKendree cylinders[69] with much more room allowing for bigger landscapes," Federico answered, confident the worst of the interview was already behind.

"Earlier you said there are no health problems caused by your Earth-like conditions."

Wondering what she was getting at, he gave a quick and firm answer. "That is correct."

"What about motion sickness? I hear some people are getting dizzy," she ventured.

Federico almost tripped, caught by surprise again. Some people had reported experiencing occasional motion sickness but nothing serious. How the hell did she find out?

"Research done before construction indicated a radius of 225 meters was the minimum to avoid motion sickness, and this has proven true for the most part. However, one or two individuals appear to experience motion sickness once in a blue moon, and our physicians have not yet been able to identify the cause. Speculation is they must have more sensitive vestibular systems in their inner ear. It's only a minor discomfort, and we'll get to the bottom of it. I can assure you this won't be an issue with the O'Neill..."

"But, as you said, the research was done before construction. Besides, these aren't single isolated incidents. I hear that at least ten people have reported this condition happening more than once a week. In fact, aren't you one of them yourself?" she interrupted with an acidulous smile.

Patrice and the chairman were watching the interview back on Earth. Except for a poster of Terminus pinned to the padded wall and a different second-hand workstation, nothing in the chairman's austere office had changed since interviewing Federico over thirty years before.

They exchanged looks, feeling a bit guilty for throwing Federico under the bus.

"Letting her into the assembly facility was a ballsy move!" said Patrice, pausing the interview. "There can be no better testimony to our people's fitness than multitasking under the additional stress of an on-camera interview."

The chairman nodded. "Yes, I agree. However, I can't help wondering where she's getting her information?"

"It's tough to keep secrets these days. She and her team are famous for doing extensive research before their interviews. But I doubt it's coming from us; our operation is tiny. Only four people are in possession of the data related to our investors, and I can't imagine any of them leaking it. Must be coming from someone working for them. It's impossible to know how many on their side have access to the information."

"Speaking of which," said the chairman. "I met with the Big Three yesterday," informally referring to their three largest investors, who jointly negotiated a deal that would return 521 times their original investments over thirty years.

"How did it go?"

"They are looking for creative ways to reduce their tax burden…"

At already historic lows, taxation for the super-rich was also riddled with loopholes. Patrice rolled her eyes, appalled by the greed of some people.

"I know exactly how you feel," said the chairman. "But I also see an opportunity. If we become a sovereign nation, it'll cut their taxes to zero. It will also allow us to be free of laws and regulations from the United States or any other nation."

"It's a win-win idea!" exclaimed Patrice. "The current administration made foreign profits tax-free to encourage capital repatriation. And although we're a non-profit and already free from taxes, if we also become an independent nation, we can set the rules to help our own people and attract immigrants."

Even after the first O'Neill cylinders were finally built, Patrice often worried about how to entice people to move to space. However, if life continued to get harder on Earth, they might be compelled to move if offered decent living conditions without having to kill themselves working eighty-plus hours a week.

"I thought you'd like it," smiled the chairman.

"I love it! We'll have to start by having the United States and other major countries recognize the Space Initiative as an independent nation."

"Then others will follow suit, and the road will be paved. We will also apply for our own seat at the United Nations," continued the chairman.

"If our investors here are willing to lobby Congress to recognize us as a nation, it should be a cakewalk," said Patrice, ready for action.

"Happy New Year!"

The collective chant echoed amidst the sounds of party crackers and loud music, as Federico glanced from the balcony. Streaming down the streets below was a crowd of thousands, dancing and strolling or just standing, half-intoxicated.

Hovering high above, volumetric animated figures morphed into different shapes, created by tens of thousands of perfectly coordinated drones, replacing traditional fireworks. The 3D figures varied from several meters high and across to a square kilometer in size. Displayed right at midnight, a stunning garden of sparkling diamonds meandered in the cylindrical sky. Glittering in all directions, it felt as grandiose as a New Year's Eve anywhere on Earth.

It was the year 2080 and the first O'Neill cylinder was near completion. Replacing steel with Kevlar had made it possible to build a six-kilometer-radius-by-fifty-kilometer-long megastructure with a living surface of 1,885 squared kilometers. About the size of Maui, it was capable of supporting over twenty million people with no space constraints.

After decades of backbreaking work, the Space Initiative finally deployed a planetary scale mining operation on Mercury and now had an assembly line manufacturing the rotating habitats to form the first ring around the sun.

Made of 70 percent metals and 30 percent silicates, Mercury was rich in gold, platinum, and rare-earth metals, which they not only used for their own manufacturing needs but also for trading. The Space Initiative had paid all their loans, and a colossal influx of wealth allowed them to invest in the research and development of advanced materials, space travel, human life extension, and launch-assist megastructures to replace rockets.

After successfully harvesting elements from the sun with their Statite cloud, their star lifting infrastructure continued to grow towards deploying enough Statites to mine raw materials on a scale that would, someday, allow them to replace Mercury.

"Happy New Year, my friend!" said Patrice, embracing Federico in a tight hug.

She and the chairman, along with most of the Space Initiative's leadership, had made the long trip from Earth to join Federico in ushering in the new year. Gathered in an unfinished party hall, they were joined by a few hundred others.

Although the rotating habitat had been operational for some time, less than one percent of the housing and infrastructure inside was finished. Walls were unpainted, most windows were empty holes without glass panes or frames, and half the hall was cordoned off to prevent partygoers from wandering into construction areas.

All over the colony, the story was repeated. Parks didn't have grass, and the many young trees recently planted displayed a skeletal trunk and a few naked branches. Ponds were empty, and to find scattered construction equipment as part of the landscape was the rule. But that didn't deter anyone; thousands were out celebrating and going crazy.

Shifting through the ample streets, the crowd exchanged enthusiastic greetings, hugs, and handshakes. Soft melodies intertwined with the babble of conversations in multiple languages filled the atmosphere. Everyone understood this was the first page of the new space era. A collective sense of accomplishment filled the air with an incredible amount of excitement.

"Happy New Year!" said the chairman to both of them for the third time now, raising his glass.

Standing on a less-crowded corner by the balcony, the chairman pointed to the street outside.

"Look at that! You'd think there's...twice as many people!"

They cracked up, but Federico turned his head and glanced at the crowd.

"Hmm...shouldn't we have a lot more people already?" he asked, concerned.

There was room for 20,000 inhabitants already, but less than 5,000 were living in the cylinder. The very first group came straight from Terminus—whose population had increased close to 2,500 between births and arrivals—as soon as the first apartments were completed. Although they were joined by a few people escaping war, rising sea levels, famine, ethnic cleansing, etc., the fact remained that people from Earth weren't coming fast enough.

The new habitat felt enormous to former Terminus residents, who didn't mind multiple roommates until enough homes were completed for everybody. During the day period, it was possible to see multiple towns under construction 360 degrees around. Motion sickness had become a thing of the past for Federico and the few unlucky others who had been getting Dramamine shots for decades.

Terminus had been set to Eastern Standard Time. But with the Initiative now being an independent nation, the first O'Neill Cylinder was set to London time without the so-hated daylight savings. They also had sixteen hours of daytime followed by eight hours of nighttime, mimicking summer conditions all year round.

"Well, I expect we'll have waves of refugees in the coming years," said Patrice.

"Be patient, old friend," said the chairman cheerfully, placing a heavy hand on Federico's shoulder. He slurred his words mildly and a scent of scotch escaped his mouth. "We need to start health screenings and background checks before people can start coming in volume. It will happen; no worries."

"Funny how we always end up talking about work, isn't it?" chortled Federico. "Cheers to that!"

Lifting his glass, he added, "A toast to the Space Initiative. In Mr. Spock's words, 'May it live long and prosper!'"

They all raised and clinked their glasses, shaking with laughter.

"I need a refill," said the chairman, heading inside.

"We need to establish an immigration checkpoint," explained Patrice, returning back to the subject.

Their investors in the United States were successful in lobbying Congress to recognize the Space Initiative as a sovereign nation and, as predicted, acknowledgment from other countries followed. They even managed to have their profits retroactively recognized as foreign and get reimbursed for taxes paid before the Initiative's becoming a nation.

But a minority of Democrats in Congress pushed back. It took the chairman's meeting with the progressive caucus to explain they would ensure the basic needs of their citizens, without demanding paid work, to calm them down. But the most dogmatic members were unyielding and, although outnumbered, vowed to keep the fight going.

"How would that be implemented?" Federico inquired.

"In the coming years, more cylinders will come online to start the first ring around the sun," explained Patrice. "We plan to designate this as the official Port of Entry, although it will be just a formality because all the document checks will happen on Earth..."

Suddenly, a blinding flash flooded the room, and the thundering explosion that followed prevented her from finishing the sentence. For a fraction of a second, an eerie calm preceded the shock wave that blew Federico forward, knocking him down to the floor.

Lying on his stomach, in darkness for an undetermined lapse until the lights came back on, Federico was disoriented. His ears were buzzing, and muffled screams were all he could hear.

As he searched for his companions, Federico noticed a purplish incandescence from beyond the balcony. An unpleasant acrid smoke began to fill the air as alarms went off. He struggled to lift his head and look around. Patrice was holding onto the ledge of the balcony, trying to stand up. The chairman, a few meters away, was already on his feet and running toward her.

Although he could now distinguish some words through the chaotic and hoarse noises, mixed with screams of terror coming from the street, Federico's senses were still dulled. Dragging a hand through debris on the ground, he checked his own body: pain, though he couldn't really pinpoint the origin. One of his wrists shifted to a funny, unnatural position; the base of the thumb was very tender. He tried to move it, but that only increased the pain.

As people screamed and the sounds of footsteps rushing by were becoming clearer, columns of dark smoke continued to rise from the street.

"I can't just lie down on the floor doing nothing," he told himself, both frustrated and angry. He propped himself up using one hand and tried to use his legs to stand, but it made him howl in pain.

He spotted the chairman rushing to his side; he seemed only ruffled by the explosion. A limping Patrice lagged behind. She had lost the frameless glasses she depended on so much, and a large bloodstain ran from her waist all the way down to her ankle. But a smile of relief appeared on her face when their eyes met.

"Go out...to help!" cried Federico. "I'll be f...fine!"

Others came in from the hall and helped the chairman lift Federico onto a nearby couch. His skin turned chalky; his eyes widened from the excruciating pain.

"Go now!" he urged.

After the hall emptied, as its occupants rushed out to help and try to assess the damage, Federico lay alone in pain for what felt like hours. As the black smoke thickly billowed from the street, he racked his brain, wondering about the cause of the explosion. But the flawless design of the habitat made him realize it could only be an act of terror. He felt lightheaded and queasy, not sure if it was due to the horrible conclusion he had reached or the intense pain. Had the blast damaged the cylinder skin? They could be leaking atmosphere!

'No, don't panic! That would create strong winds and other side effects that would be unmistakable,' he thought through the haze of pain.

After what seemed an eternity, he heard the noise of voices in the hall.

"Federico! Are you there?" he heard someone call.

"In...h-here!" he cried.

Two emergency responders and a civilian carrying a stretcher came into view as they rushed towards the couch.

"What's hap...happened? How many...d-deaths?" Federico stuttered in pain.

"We don't know yet. Please try to calm down, sir, and don't move," said one of the guys assertively. He examined Federico's body and, simultaneously, placed a variety of wireless probes and electrodes on him.

The damage to the wrist was obvious. "Radius bone fracture; looks like a complete one," he said. "Where else are you hurt?"

"M-my knee..."

Propelled forward by the force of the blast, he had smashed a knee against the floor. The emergency responder quickly moved to open a case, pulled out a handheld device, and scanned him from head to toe.

"Comminuted fracture of the left patella. We have to take him straight to surgery."

As one of the paramedics began monitoring Federico's readings, his colleague pulled a hypospray from the case, ready to proceed.

"Wait," said the guy looking at the monitors. "There's a risk he could go into cardiac arrest."

"W-w-what? No! I can't. That's...n-not...p-poss..." Federico tried to protest, gasping for air. The pain was unbearable.

"He's having a vasovagal reaction to the pain."

His colleague pulled the hypospray away from him, removed the cartridge, and impatiently rummaged for a different drug in the med-kit.

"Does it hurt anywhere else?" he was asked again.

"Not sure..." replied Federico in a whisper, unable to hold back his tears.

The man nodded and his colleague gave him a shot with the hypospray at last. The pain began to dissipate right away. Federico started feeling lightheaded and was knocked unconscious a few seconds later.

It took weeks to sort out the chaos. The improvised explosive device killed twenty-five and injured over a hundred. The suicide bomber was a member of a cell affiliated with a terrorist group that claimed responsibility for his actions.

The material assessment was minor structural damage to the exterior of several buildings, and a few broken windows. The blast carved a large hole in the street but wasn't powerful enough to do extensive damage. Most importantly, the Kevlar composite that made the cylinder skin was untouched.

At the edge of the balcony, Federico and Patrice had faced the blast from an expanding shockwave. Most of Patrice's wounds came from small shrapnel that landed above her hip. But Federico underwent a kneecap replacement surgery, and his wrist took months to heal, forcing him to live on pain medication and physiotherapy for nearly a year.

As details continued trickling down, they learned the home-made device was assembled from commonly available parts and substances sold in stores. The IED contained small pieces of metal to maximize the amount of injuries and was detonated right in the middle of a crowd. The incident caused an extreme amount of panic, sending the message that even in space no one was safe.

A few months had passed, and, although his kneecap replacement operation was behind him, his ankle now got swollen and painful if he stood for long periods of time. Sitting in an armchair with his leg raised on a footstool, he pulled a side table closer, using his cane, and placed his coffee mug on it.

"Why are they targeting us? What have we done to them?" he asked, enraged.

"Security measures on Earth are tough to circumvent. They found it easier to make a statement here," responded Patrice. "The amount of money we paid our investors has contributed to make economic inequality worse, they say. They consider the Space Initiative responsible and made us a target."

"How can we be responsible?"

"We often think of ourselves as heroes engaged in a battle of good versus evil, but we fail to see the devil inside," lamented Patrice. "Anyway, this is a huge setback to our goal of attracting new immigrants!"

"Space is for the benefit of humanity as a whole. But we must safeguard ourselves from the self-destructive instincts harbored by some of our fellow human beings," said the chairman. "We must take decisive actions to address this challenge. I hate to say this, but we need better security measures."

"Meaning?" inquired Federico, not liking the sound of it.

"We engaged the top three security consulting firms. Each of them laid out a comprehensive plan, but their key points were pretty similar. There will be sensor arrays deployed throughout cities, including people's homes..."

"What? No way!" interrupted Patrice, aghast. "What about our people's right to privacy?"

"I'm afraid security will trump privacy, at least for the time being. The sensors will capture visual, audio, olfactory, temperature, and seismic data..."

"Seismic?" interrupted Federico, puzzled.

"Yes. On Earth they're used to detect anything from explosions to glass shattering," said the chairman. "In addition, people will be mandated to wear body cameras at all times..."

"That's...horrendous!" interrupted Patrice again. "There has to be another way."

"Guys, I dislike this as much as you do. But we need to ensure the safety and security of our citizens. I don't want to imagine what would have happened if they'd blown a hole through the skin of the cylinder!" the chairman responded. "That Kevlar composite is very strong—but nothing a well-designed explosive can't compromise."

"But sensors in people's homes? Body cameras? It'll turn us into a police state," argued Patrice.

"Please tell us there's a silver lining to this nightmare," begged Federico.

"There is." The chairman cleared his throat before answering. "A non-sentient AI will monitor the sensors and video feeds. Records will be sealed from human eyes without exception, unless the AI judges it necessary to prevent another incident like this. It will be able to alert our security teams in time. With our current technology, that's the best we can do," he finished.

As much as they hated it, nobody in the room could come up with a better solution.

Chapter 3: Refugees

AKIN TO AN OVERSIZED AIRPLANE'S FUSELAGE, THE ascension vehicle was a sleek cylinder lying between identical kilometer-long, dirigible hydrogen balloons. Offering a panoramic view from underneath, the gate's waiting area allowed passengers to appreciate the massive dimensions of the ship.

Looking through the towering window, Kristy tilted her head upward, taking in the gargantuan bottom that blocked most of the cloudless sky. Placing a hand on her conspicuous belly, she tapped it gently.

"Hush, hush," she whispered.

Wiping her glossy freckled forehead with the back of a hand, she lifted her hair, gathering it high on the head and held it in place with one hand. The AC never seemed to cool enough in that heat. She then expertly slid a bungee elastic from one of her wrists and wrapped the flocks of red hair into a ponytail, giving her already young face a childish flair. A wave of twitches rippled throughout her body when the baby kicked again, perhaps sensing her anxiety.

Located near Macapà, the spaceport was part of the operations center which housed training, medical, and administrative facilities. Immigrants went through rigorous physical examinations and decontamination procedures to ensure none of them were carrying communicable diseases into space.

Friendly to the Space Initiative, Brazil allowed them to rent this perfect location close to the equator. Earth's rotation made the equatorial line spin at 444 meters per second, and the ascension vehicles inherited this speed on takeoff without burning precious fuel.

The year was 2116, and the Space Initiative was now offering free living space to anyone who wanted it. There was already a line of five O'Neill cylinders in orbit around the sun with more under construction, forming the beginning of the first ring.

The warbled voice of the gate attendant spoke almost without pause through the PA system. Kristy walked away from the window and followed the others toward the gate.

A wide aisle, separating two sections of spacious seats inside the cabin, extended for a hundred meters. The windows and overhead bins made it look like a regular airplane cabin.

Sighing in relief, Kristy chose an aisle seat. The acceleration couch, which provided support to the occupant's entire body during the 72-hour-long voyage, resembled a wide thick-cushioned entertainment recliner with sockets for arms and legs.

Living in space had become more than reasonably comfortable to meet the needs of the average Joe. Yet, it wasn't the first choice for most: one had to be willing to give up sunsets, ocean, mountains, and blue sky. Even after the catastrophic failure of Mars sixty years earlier, they had not seen quite the immigrant influx they hoped. But with life becoming hellish for billions on the home planet, the gradual exodus had begun.

A category-six tropical megastorm along the US eastern seaboard produced the first multi-million immigrant influx when insurance companies filed for Chapter 11 to protect themselves, leaving countless without a roof over their heads. Numbers were trickling down but not enough to make a dent in Earth's population.

Unlike their tobacco-industry counterparts, the fossil-fuel industry had played their cards well. By lobbying Congress and hiring their own scientists to cloud public opinion to the perils of climate change, they avoided getting themselves isolated and shaken down by lawsuits and fines. The brilliant strategy allowed them to continue releasing greenhouse gasses into the atmosphere unchecked for centuries, triggering the largest human displacement in history.

The sea level rise created a refugee exodus of catastrophic proportions when hundreds of millions were forced to flee their homelands, as living became impossible in the most vulnerable coastal regions.

A thin woman stopped beside Kristy. Her dark clothes were modest and clean, though the edges of her pants and the cuffs of her long shirt had seen too many washes and were faded and frayed. A weathered olive hijab added a splash of color to her face. Hauling a rascal of a boy, she pointed at the two empty seats beside the girl.

"Seats taken? May we sit...please?"

Kristy smiled kindly and, with a waving gesture, said. "Yes, of course!"

"Thank you!"

Sitting in the middle seat, the woman urged her little boy in Arabic to take the seat next to the window. Loosening the headscarf revealed a thick jet-black strand of hair that curled around her cheek. Kristy noticed the woman's weathered and rough skin, despite her young twenties face.

"My name is Aaisha," said the woman. "And this is Omar," pointing at her boisterous little boy.

"I'm Claire," said Kristy.

Pregnant at fifteen, Kristy was running away to avoid being forcibly married to her child's father, a high-school classmate from their congregation. Kristy's father, a fundamentalist Christian pastor, had convinced the boy's parents and that was sufficient for their town's judge, regardless of the kids' opinions.

Kristy dreamt of becoming a teacher someday, sharing with others what she was never taught about life. But her father considered her pregnancy an embarrassment and removed her from school.

"You ungrateful child, get those selfish ideas out of your head," were her father's harsh words the evening before she escaped.

"Women were not made for work but to take care of their families. You would never be able to handle the stress, Kristy; a petty job is all you would get. Do you think that's enough to raise a child? This boy is God-sent to continue my legacy, to follow in my footsteps."

"We are from Iraq. You?" Aaisha asked, bringing Kristy back from her unsettling memories.

Having never recovered from the US invasion of over a century earlier, Iraq turned into a chaotic and failed state, allowing Iran to exert more and more influence until finally taking over fifty years before. Imposing a bloody regime that marginalized and brutalized the Sunni minority as payback for Saddam Hussein's rule which marginalized the Shiites, it forced tens of millions to flee the region.

"I'm from Chicago," said Kristy.

"When is your baby...?" Aaisha pronounced with difficulty.

"I am due in a few weeks," she smiled, with a hand on her belly. "It's a boy, I'm calling him Luke."

"In sha Allah! Omar and Luke to grow in better place," Aaisha said with a smile, pointing up to the sky.

Pulling a tissue from her handbag, Kristy dried her face with annoyance. Despite the pleasant temperature in the main cabin, drops of sweat ran down her temples. She felt for her passport through the rough outer fabric of her bag—for the fifth time. The girl had applied for immigration to space, using forged documentation that cost her all the money she had saved since running away from home. Except for a few clothes, she left everything behind, including her mobile device. Days before the wedding, her best friend helped her gather enough money for a one-way bus ticket to Chicago.

Leaving no trail to follow, she didn't keep in touch with her friend or anyone else back home. She simply vanished, lying low at homeless shelters for months, working low-paying temp jobs, and saving every penny. The money she gathered was spent to get the fake ID that would take her to freedom.

A calm voice through the PA system gave final instructions for take-off. On the back of all seats and at strategic locations throughout the ship, multilingual signs lit up on screens. The clicking of metallic buckles came and went throughout the cabin as passengers locked their safety belts. Aaisha fastened the waist and shoulder straps for her son and then secured her own. Kristy did the same.

On their way out, the flight crew closed overhead bins, secured latches, and completed final checks before sealing the cabin.

Ascending through the atmosphere for about two hours, the twin balloon cradle brought the ship to an altitude of fifty kilometers above the planet during the first leg of the trip. Hovering in place for a few minutes, with the seatbelt signs flashing and a countdown on all the screens, they waited in anticipation. With a quick jerk upwards when it reached zero, their bodies sank into their couches as the skyhook grabbed the ship. Although not unlike the simulations at all, a few gasps and cries were heard.

A 400-kilometer-long pivoting rod orbiting Earth, the first skyhook graced the upper atmosphere, snatching ships from their balloon cradles. Being swung upwards with enough velocity to be transferred to a longer skyhook at a higher altitude, they would continue speeding further up. After multiple transfers through longer skyhooks, orbiting at higher and higher altitudes, ships had enough momentum to escape from what little of Earth's gravity was left, requiring minimum fuel for course corrections to reach its destination. There, they would line up with a rail floating in space and use magnets to slow down.

Kristy met Aaisha's hazel green eyes; a worried frown joined the dark straight eyebrows and creased her forehead. Realizing the woman was as scared as she was, Kristy placed a hand on hers with a gentle, reassuring squeeze. Aaisha sighed but managed to smile back.

Chance placed them on the same habitat a few days later, and both women were delighted with the news. Over time, they became great friends. Kristy learned that Aaisha and her boy were the last survivors from her family escaping the Ayatollah's cleansing in Iraq. In turn, she told Aaisha her true story.

Two years later, a meeting of the Space Initiative's board gathered at their headquarters on Earth, except for Federico, who sat in his office at the Port of Entry. Having continued to climb his way up until getting promoted to the board some twenty years earlier, he was the only one of their members living in space.

"...we've reduced the time it takes to build an O'Neill cylinder to ten years," he was saying. "And, although the trend will continue, growing demand has finally caught up. We now face a waiting period of weeks that will continue to increase as more and more people want to come to space."

"With our mining operation running at full capacity, we risk being so far outpaced by demand in a few decades that the wait time will increase to years," said the chairman, concerned.

"Star lifting currently produces a negligible amount of construction materials but has the potential to produce a virtually unlimited influx," Federico volunteered.

"But in order to get there, we need to allocate more of the production from our Mercury mines to build more Statites and infrastructure, rather than to expand the mining equipment and build more O'Neill cylinders. It is a tough choice. Do you have a recommendation?" inquired the chairman.

"My instinct tells me to beef up star lifting, but our team of experts believes we shouldn't throw a monkey wrench into the system. They expect we'll reach stability in a few decades with minor adjustments. I know it's not much, but we should go with their recommendation," said Federico.

With no choice but for things to get worse before they got better, the chairman decided to drop the matter and move on to the next subject.

"What's the status of the new headquarters?"

"It'll be completed in six months. I strongly advise my fellow board members to start making living arrangements right now, as finding quarters of your liking might take longer than expected."

"I'm getting there next month," said Patrice Waithera. "Do you have an extra bedroom?"

Everybody in the room laughed, followed by Federico a little over five seconds later.

With radio signals traveling at light-speed, a message from Earth took about 2.6 seconds to reach the Port of Entry, at twice the distance from the Earth to the Moon. The response then needed to travel back another 2.6 seconds, assuming the receiver started answering immediately. Although the five-to-six-second delay seemed perfectly tolerable, it hinted of serious issues in the future.

There were only six rotating habitats, all close to Earth. But there would be trillions in the future when the Dyson swarm around the sun was completed. For two habitats located at the maximum distance from each other—a straight line on opposite sides of the sun—the signal would need to be relayed through a third habitat, placed in line of sight with the other two, increasing the delay to a whopping forty-eight minutes. Federico constantly wondered how they would keep a unified civilization without FTL communication.

Calling the room to order, the chairman continued with the agenda. "For those who are unaware of the new development, one of our start-ups has just discovered a way to mass produce carbyne[70], a carbon nanotubes-based material twice as strong as graphene..."

The excited babble of thrilled, but hushed, voices around him intensified a few decibels, and the chairman decided to wait a few seconds for it to quiet down.

"Yes, yes. At last, we'll be able to build megastructures even larger than a McKendree cylinder. With our experience building self-contained ecosystems, I have great expectations the next step will produce something beyond amazing, so grandiose that not a single person will miss Earth. Furthermore, the production process requires zero gravity which will work to our advantage, since we have easy access to it in space. It'll also give us a tremendous leverage in our trade with Earth, since we continue to have a strong dependence on the home planet for goods and services."

At the rate they had been injecting precious metals into the world markets for the last five decades, prices had gone down. It was imperative for them to find new goods for trading, or they would end up slaves to Earth's economy.

"Kudos to Federico!" said Patrice. "This was one of the many ventures he funded."

As everybody clapped, Federico started talking to gain 2.6 seconds while giving the applause time to subside.

"Thank you! In a few years, carbyne will become cheaper to produce than Kevlar, since carbon is one of the most abundant elements in the sun. It will also allow us to build longer skyhooks, maybe even space elevators that will shorten the trip from Earth down to hours!"

A little over five seconds later, people clapped again.

"But I'm concerned some on Earth might get nervous at the sight of a multi-billion people megastructure. I think, for the time being, we should conceal the first McKendree cylinder by building it at the L3 Lagrangian point[71], where it can't be detected or attacked, from Earth."

"Another terrorist attack?" asked one of the members with mild concern.

"No, no. But I think as their numbers begin to decline in the future, it'll become clear that countries will collapse due to underpopulation. Some world leaders are bound to get paranoid."

It was hard to grasp, but nobody argued the point. That scenario was so far in the future it didn't even seem worthy of their attention now.

After a long silence, the chairman continued.

"Finally, the topic we've all been avoiding: interstellar travel. Although carbyne may have a future role, we are no closer now to overcoming the biggest obstacles than twenty years ago."

Grunts and long faces all over the room made it clear that most of them considered the subject to be science fiction and would rather focus on more tangible issues of the present.

"As you know, two main technology gaps prevent us from building an interstellar ship: FTL communication and shielding," continued the chairman anyway. "There isn't good news on either front."

Over a hundred years earlier, they had solved the propulsion issue. A massive solar-powered array of lasers in space would slowly push the vessel to a fraction of light-speed. However, as it got farther away from the sun, it would be harder to keep the lasers aimed. The spacecraft could transmit its exact location, but, as the communications lag increased to months, it would become impractical. FTL communication would partially overcome that obstacle by making it possible to know the exact location of the ship in real time.

Friction caused by dust and loose particles produced tremendous amounts of heat traveling at a fraction of light-speed, making shielding even more critical. A small pebble a few grams in mass would impact with the force of a nuclear bomb.

"Sir, we don't even have a proof of concept in the works. Because none of these items is a crucial priority today, there's only one way to break out of the hole we are in. We have to put more resources in; I mean cash to fund new research. I believe carbyne will open new trading opportunities with Earth in the future, allowing us to increase funding in both areas," answered Federico.

Five seconds later, the chairman answered with a loud chuckle.

"It seems that throwing more money at it is always your answer!"

The mood in the room lightened.

"I agree with his assessment," said Patrice. "These are tough scientific problems to solve."

"Very well! Our current budget allows us to increase discretionary spending without compromising our social programs. I'll authorize doubling of the research budget for FTL communications and shielding only."

A few board members groaned. This budget increase would mostly benefit Federico, as he was the only one pursuing what they likened to *pie-in-the-sky* initiatives.

"Does anyone else have anything before we adjourn?" asked the chairman.

"Yes, sir." Federico raised his hand.

"Bring it on!"

"We've been funding Gravitational Lensing research at the University of Arizona for the last five years. They're now ready to test a practical application with a telescope. It will require placing an optical instrument about 550 Astronomical Units (AU)[72] away from the sun. Although it comes with a hefty price tag, the benefits will far outweigh the cost. Imagine a telescope the size of the sun! We'll be able to get high resolution images of all exoplanets and moons within a thousand light-years from Earth."

Back on Earth, board member Maiko Fujino raised her eyebrows.

"You just got your research budget doubled, and now you want a telescope?"

The memory of a reference to Oliver Twist made at a party a hundred years earlier crossed his subconscious mind but evaporated before Federico noticed, as he replied.

"Since we plan to start colonizing our cosmic neighborhood, we should be responsible and make sure it's actually uninhabited. In addition, this telescope will allow us to see so much deeper into the universe than any instrument in history. We must take advantage of this opportunity!"

"The Breakthrough Starshot project revealed no civilization on the planets around the Alpha Centauri stars or any others within a ten-light-year radius. We've detected no radio or laser signals from alien civilizations, no Dyson swarms, no bio or technosignatures of any kind," said Fujino. "Tell us again why you want this telescope?"

"It'll help us answer questions about our place in the cosmos and the future of the universe itself, even questions we've not yet formulated! Each time we build a new telescope, amazing new discoveries are made and preconceptions thrown away, allowing science and humanity to move forward."

"I'll take it under advisement," said the chairman breaking up the argument. "Send me your proposal. Meeting adjourned."

An upbeat Federico went back to work on the final touches to his Gravitational Lensing Telescope proposal. A few minutes later, a video call request popped in through his glasses' interface.

Neural Interfaces (NIs) were a thing, and many were having them implanted these days. Vastly superior to the original NIs that allowed the disabled to interact with wheelchairs or robotic limbs a century before, they now facilitated basic control over mobile devices and appliances. Federico, however, had become increasingly squeamish with the passage of time and hadn't had the guts to go through with the implants yet. He preferred sensors in his glasses for interfacing with his mobile. Audio was transmitted through vibration to his skull bones without the need for pods inside his ears.

It was the chairman. He instructed his glasses to send the call to the conferencing system so his assistant, Enzo, could listen.

"And now tell me, how are you, old friend?" the chairman asked.

"Old," chuckled Federico, "but great! Thank you for asking, sir."

Although he maintained a healthy lifestyle, new drugs and technologies had allowed him to extend his lifespan little by little over the past hundred years, shielding his body—currently 152 years old—from the ravages of aging. Now that producing any organ from a patient's own cells was commonplace, the predator had lost its teeth. An age-reversal procedure had just become available, but Federico's squeamishness prevented him from going through with it.

"I know exactly what you mean," said the chairman, who was a few years older than he. "Something important came up. You better sit down for this one. The Space Initiative is being accused of child kidnapping!"

Federico was stunned out of his wits. 'Never a dull moment with this job,' he thought with amusement.

"What's the root of the complaint?" he asked.

"I have no idea; I'll be sharing with you all the information I receive. But this is the kind of wrangling that could threaten our legal status. I want you to manage the situation personally; please make it your top priority."

"Of course. I'll find out if there's any merit to this claim," replied Federico.

"If there is, I want the kid sent back to Earth without delay. I also want you to determine what's wrong with our screening process. We need to respond to this ASAP. Keep me posted," said the chairman.

"Absolutely!" replied Federico, ending the call.

Enzo, sitting at a desk a few feet away, was already clearing out his schedule and gathering all the information available.

"Kristy Hamilton," read Enzo out loud. "The missing seventeen-year-old daughter of Luke Hamilton—a pastor from Columbia, Missouri—was identified off a promotional video for the Space Initiative!"

He zoomed a still from the video attached, showing a group of teenagers. Encircled in a red oval, a redheaded young woman held a toddler in her arms.

"A police report indicates Kristy ran away from home nearly three years ago while pregnant," the assistant said.

"What the fuck! Do we advertise now? Since when?" asked Federico, glaring at Enzo.

"For a few months now," said Enzo hesitating. "There have been a number of promotional videos made to entice people to the comforts of life in space. You should be able to find them in..."

"Yeah, it's irrelevant at this point. Give me the basics about the video related to this alleged kidnapping," Federico said gruffly.

Enzo's fingers danced over the keyboard, tapping at full speed.

"I'll look for the segment from which the still of this young woman was taken," he replied.

Enzo first queried "Kristy Hamilton," but it returned no results for any of the habitats. Several "Hamiltons" popped up, but none fit her description.

He then ran a face-matching query, using the last picture of Kristy before she disappeared, against the database of all people with any relationship to the Initiative. The algorithm produced a match in less than a second.

"Claire Jones from Chicago, Illinois," Enzo blurted out.

He quickly zoomed both images to about the same size and placed them side by side on the big screen.

There were similarities between the two faces, but they couldn't be absolutely sure. The glasses, hairdo, and makeup made the women look quite different; even the skin tones didn't match. Claire had a toddler and lived in the same cylinder where that segment of the video was recorded. The age of the child fit within the timeframe of the pregnancy.

"There is another discrepancy, sir. The file says Claire is twenty, but Kristy's age is seventeen," Enzo added.

"Unless Claire's ID is a fake."

"That must be it, sir. The search algorithm gives it a 100 percent match," said Enzo.

Federico looked at Kristy's picture again and felt sorry for her. She was barely fifteen when she ran away. Things must have been tough for her at home to make such a harsh choice.

They looked into Claire's background check; everything seemed to match.

"Better to be completely sure. Enzo, order a fingerprint match of both Claire and Kristy."

The result came back the next morning.

"There is no doubt. Kristy used fake documents to apply for immigration as Claire," confirmed his young assistant.

"She must be sent back promptly, or we risk landing the Space Initiative in trouble," concluded Federico.

If mishandled, the Hamilton incident could threaten the Space Initiative by forcing a review of their legal status as an independent nation. Many Democratic party senators in the United States were still unhappy due to the amount of lost tax revenue and were constantly pushing to revoke their autonomy. The fact that millions of US citizens lived in space and the overwhelming Republican majority in Congress—which was cozy with their former investors—kept the issue at bay.

With that whirlwind of ideas in mind, Federico arrived at the elevators to the south access port, where he was met by two security volunteers he had requested. Neither of them was armed; there were no firearms in space.

Aligned with Earth's poles, two vacuum tunnels linked each rotating habitat with its two neighbors. Not a single solid structure but connecting segments—each with multiple rails inside for different speeds and distances—they made travel convenient between habitats. Coated with a photo-voltaic pigment, the sun-facing side of the tunnels generated enough electricity to power the transports inside, which accelerated along the rails using a technology similar to Maglev[73]. Access ports at the center of the circular sections of each habitat allowed transports in the tunnel to enter and exit.

Carried up toward the access port where a small transport was docked, simplifying the transfer in zero gravity, they exited the Port of Entry through the access port and accelerated towards Kristy's habitat, the one before last in the line. There, a private transport delivered them from the access port in the direction of a suburban area, her place of residence, saving them time by skipping the elevator down.

After traversing a playground to reach her building, Federico instructed the guards to stay out of sight but to detain Kristy if she tried to leave the building alone.

With the pain in his knee and swelling of his ankle well in the past, Federico climbed two flights of stairs at a fast pace, enjoying the exercise. A few seconds after he rang her doorbell, footsteps approached, and the door slid open without hesitation. Kristy hadn't bothered to check who was on the other side.

The strict surveillance measures imposed after the terrorist incident over forty years before ensured the safety and privacy of all citizens. Only in the case of a serious crime—which hadn't occurred yet—would privacy be invaded, if necessary. People in space enjoyed unprecedented levels of freedom and security.

Kristy's smiling face changed to quizzical concern when she saw Federico.

"Oh...Hello! What can I do for you?" Kristy asked.

"Miss Jones, my name is Federico Tarifa. I'm a Space Initiative board member. Will you allow me to come in, or would you be more comfortable conversing outside?"

He didn't need to show any ID; he didn't even have one. Impersonating was a serious crime that would be easily caught by their security measures. Kristy had grown accustomed to the halcyonic lifestyle of space with no crime or police and without distrust.

"Oh, no. Please come in," she said with foreboding intuition and moved away from the door to let him in.

Spacious and comfortable with high ceilings and aesthetically pleasing areas, the standard dwellings were nothing less than opulent. Ample windows overlooking the city brought in plenty of daylight. Sculptures and paintings of Kristy's own making gave the place a warm touch, along with photographs of her and Luke, hanging on the walls.

She invited Federico into the broad living room where he chose an armchair, while she sat on the modern couch. Between them, an oval-shaped onyx coffee table rested over a polished metal base of avant-garde craftsmanship.

"Miss Jones, the Space Initiative is being sued by pastor Luke Hamilton for holding his daughter, Kristy Hamilton."

She remained motionless and as pale as the delicate statues decorating her home. Her bottom lip dropped and started to tremble. A moment later, her eyes filled with tears.

Federico remained silent with a lump in his throat.

"H...how...d...did they find me?" she asked, choking back her sobs.

"Your father saw you in a promotional video for the Space Initiative," he explained, instructing his mobile device to play the video on the coffee table.

Hidden beneath the surface, a 3D projection device requested Kristy's permission before allowing a stranger to play content on it. Kristy granted permission through her NIs.

After an unnoticeable sub-second delay, a high-resolution projection hovered half a meter above the table, replaying the video in full detail.

"Yes. That was a couple of months ago. I went out with a group of friends from school." Then, placing a hand on her forehead, "Gosh! I didn't realize someone was recording a video!"

She had been so meticulous in protecting her real identity. No one except Aaisha knew her true story, not even Omar. It was a wreck to be caught in such a foolish way after all that time.

"What will happen to me now? Are we to be deported back to Earth to be subject to their medieval laws? It is so unfair!" she cried in despair.

"May I call you Kristy?"

"Of course," she said gloomily, although a part of her felt relieved to take off the mask.

"Why did you leave, Kristy?"

"I was in high school and made a mistake with a boy I liked," she said, keeping her gaze to the floor and fidgeting with her fingers. "Father and the congregation...they only preach about abstinence. In school, not a word about safe sex practices. Contraception...it's practically illegal," she continued with a choppy voice. "I...didn't want to leave school, but Father forced me to and arranged for our marriage."

Federico was positive an abortion hadn't even been in the picture. Not only did schools teach it was a sinful abomination, but the Supreme Court had overturned Roe v. Wade[74] over a century earlier, making abortion illegal. The closing of the last remaining clinics turned the clock back to 1973, when back-alley abortions with improper sanitation and instruments often led to serious health complications and even death. Distributed illegally, the abortion pill came at huge risk. There was no way to ensure one was getting the actual drug, and both the buyer and the seller were prosecuted to the full extent of the law when caught.

Kristy collected herself a bit.

"Sex between unmarried Christians is severely punished...physical punishment. I couldn't bear it. I was so afraid of Father. I had no choice but to leave and cast off my real identity—to disappear. I ran away and worked until I saved enough to buy fake documents to apply for immigration. They even created an electronic paper trail that passed the scrutiny of the Space Initiative. I'll be of age in a few months; I was hoping they wouldn't find me before then," she finished, clearing her eyes.

"I do sympathize with your situation, Kristy, but we risk an international incident. There's close to 120 million people living in space, so it's imperative we have friendly relations with all nations. Picking a fight with the United States is not something we can afford. We could face serious sanctions and other consequences," explained Federico.

"The last two years have been the best of my life. The education I received here has opened my eyes. Yes, I will go back; but only temporarily. I'm much stronger now and won't be controlled with the same ease as the little girl who ran away. I will reapply for immigration as soon as I turn eighteen," she said with pride.

Having previously reviewed her school record, Federico knew that Kristy had followed an education loaded with science, philosophy, and art since her arrival in space.

What would become of her if she went back home and was forced into marriage? Would her father use physical coercion to make her sign the marriage certificate? What would happen after she turned eighteen and filed for a divorce or an annulment? A custody battle? Federico felt miserable.

"Maybe there's something we can do together to get out of this mess. Will you work with me?"

After mulling over the question for a few seconds, Kristy nodded.

"I need a detailed profile of your father. What's he like? His tastes, habits, beliefs—anything you can tell me. Also, about your mother and the kind of relationship they have at home. The more details, the better," said Federico.

"Why? What are you going to do to him?"

"I promise he will not be harmed in any way, but we need to find anything that can be used as leverage. Is there anything you can think of? This won't be easy for you, I'm sure," he said.

She kept quiet and pensive for a short while and finally added, "It feels like it's the only way out of this. But I honestly don't think there's anything...suspicious about him."

"Maybe not to you or to me. We need to focus on things he's not comfortable with. I will record our conversation from this moment on." At that point, his mobile device on the table automatically lit up, indicating a recording session in progress.

"I love my father very much but don't want to be under his authoritarian rule again. He's not a bad person...just unyielding...set like concrete in his beliefs. He blindly follows his own interpretation of scripture. At home, we were told what to wear, what to eat, and what to think. He met my mother at church in our hometown..."

The son of a pastor himself, Luke Hamilton was born and raised in Columbia, Missouri. As a teenager, he prowled the neighborhood looking for a fight or to challenge his classmates into risky competitions, such as swimming in icy-cold water during the winter. With an athletic build and taller than other boys his age, his short fuse made him prone to frequent fits of rage for which he was physically punished by his father or forced to work long hours while praying for repentance. He accepted the punishments quietly, and, eventually, working hard became second nature. He took random jobs from chopping trees for firewood to cleaning the school premises.

A sudden change in behavior, shortly before finishing high school, showed him to be withdrawn and quiet. He stopped terrorizing his peers and later spoke of a revelation to his father. Delighted, the pastor compelled Luke to obey the higher calling and promised to shape him into the leader he was born to be. Just like his father, he had a sense for making money and did well in his affairs.

Involved in his church's activities now, he immersed himself into the works of the Reverend Billy Graham and others. He followed his father's commands, word for word, even marrying the woman the pastor had chosen for him.

Finally ordained as a pastor, he became a wealthy one. The salary was great and included many allowances paid by the church, such as housing, travel, and personal expenses, plus the large monetary gifts he received from the community.

Consecrating his life to preaching the word of God gave him purpose.

After his daughter went missing, Luke consulted missing persons specialists. Under their advice, he allocated most of his funds to search in the smallest perimeter around Columbia and neighboring towns. He didn't think of including Chicago, which was assigned the lowest probability—sure that his daughter wouldn't have the guts to run that far away. He kept a watchful eye on her credit report, expecting she would need money and probably try to open a bank account. He even consulted psychics. But, as days turned into months, years went by without results.

In a commercial for the Space Initiative, a girl who looked very much like Kristy briefly flashed before his eyes. Luke promptly paused and replayed the commercial over and over again. It was definitely his daughter, and she was holding a toddler! Although Anne, his wife, wasn't entirely sure, he was. That had to be his grandson! All the money spent and all the people he hired had failed because Kristy wasn't on Earth.

Using his church contributions again, he retained the best law firm in the state and immediately filed a suit against the Space Initiative. A few days later, they got a video call from Kristy, holding their grandson.

"Mother! Father!" she said, joyfully.

No longer a redhead, Kristy had reverted to her old hairstyle and natural color. Her glasses were gone, and the light blond mane was tied in an impeccable bun behind her neck. She didn't put any makeup on to avoid displeasing her father.

"Kristy! How are you dear?" asked Anne in tears about six seconds later.

"I'm very well, mother! I've missed you...both, so much! This is Luke," she said turning, so they could see the child. "I named him after you, Father."

"Are they treating you well, my baby?" asked her mother.

"Yes, of course, Mom! I'm well taken care of," said Kristy.

"How did you get into space? It's so far..." inquired her mother.

"It's not hard, Mom Anybody can apply."

"But you're a minor! How did you..." started to ask her mother.

"When are you coming back? That's what I want to know," interrupted her father, annoyed by the back an forth delay.

She dodged a direct answer and said, "I have one request. Will you both come here to get me?"

"Why, dear? You need help with the baby?" asked her mother.

"I knew it! They're holding you!" Luke yelled. His daughter would have never made it into space on her own. Someone else had to be pulling the strings.

"No! No! Father, listen! Nobody is forcing me to do anything. I'm just asking you both to come here and spend a little time with us before we go back. Luke was born here and knows no other place. No child his age, born in space, has gone to Earth yet. Because it'll be a very different place, there might be psychological implications. Let's take it slow and allow him time to get to know his grandparents as part of the adaptation process. It will make the transition to Earth and the trip easier for him. Would you be willing to do this for me?" she asked.

No longer the shy teenager who ran away three years before, she was articulate and mature. They spoke now to a young adult, and it made her mother very happy; their daughter had grown up. It also helped convince Luke.

Visitor visas, physical examinations, and decontamination procedures were expedited by Federico. Hard-to-come-by accommodations were set up, just a short distance from Kristy's quarters.

A month later, she went to the designated access port elevator to welcome her parents.

Visitors from Earth arrived at the Port of Entry after seventy-two hours in space. Because they needed time to readapt to 1G, they were put on a tunnel transport towards their final destination escorted by ground crews to assist them.

Accompanied by a few trusted Space Initiative employees, Luke and his wife made the trip in an empty ship. They coddled and tended to all their needs, making their trip as pleasant as possible.

Kristy was at the waiting area of their designated elevator when they came out in wheelchairs pushed by ground personnel.

"Mom! Dad!" she called, racing towards them with baby Luke in her arms. "Don't try to stand up yet! Believe me, I went through the same thing!"

Hugging and kissing both of them, she then crouched and introduced her son.

"These are your grandparents, Luke!" she said, holding the child for them to touch; their weakened muscles would not allow them to hold the child yet.

"How are you feeling?" Kristy asked.

"Oh, my sweet child!" said Anne. "I'm so happy to see you, but I'm feeling so tired."

"It's all normal, Mom," said Kristy. "The lack of gravity takes a toll on the human body. It was worse when I came because my trip took longer than yours. Fortunately, they are getting shorter as technology improves."

"I'm okay!" said Luke pulling himself halfway up from the wheelchair, prompting the crew to rush to the front in case he fell.

"Very good, Father! Right now, we are going to your quarters for you to recover and readapt to normal gravity. I'll be with you throughout the process. You must rest; we can have breakfast tomorrow morning."

The stress of reuniting with their daughter and acclimating to normal gravity had taken a toll on their bodies. Kristy's parents slept long and peacefully that night.

Luke opened his eyes the next day to find himself lying on an ergonomic bed with his upper body at a comfortable angle. He couldn't remember the last time he had slept that long; it was almost 1100 hours. He tested his strength by pushing himself up. Still feeling a bit weak, he was able to place his feet on the ground. A wheelchair and a pair of crutches were left within reach. He went for the crutches and stood up without too much difficulty.

Lying on a similar bed beside him, his wife was still asleep. Luke headed for the bedroom door. The aroma of eggs, coffee, and freshly baked goods filled his nostrils as he entered the corridor. He followed the smells and noises to the kitchen where Kristy was busy with breakfast.

"Father!" She came to hug him. "You look well! I'm so happy that you're here."

"Thank you. Where is little Luke?"

"I dropped him at school. Mom's still sleeping?"

"Yeah, she seems okay."

"Readjusting to normal gravity is hard and affects everyone differently. Thank you for going through this for me," said Kristy.

"I didn't know you could cook!" he said, a bit surprised.

"I took some courses. I had to get ready before the baby arrived," she said with a smile. "Let's go wake Mom up with a high protein breakfast; it will make you both feel better."

She prepared a breakfast tray, and they went back to the bedroom. He examined the ample space, noticing the impeccable cleanliness and the remarkable comfort and quality of the furniture.

"How much is this costing you?" Luke asked after finishing breakfast.

"Oh! Nothing at all! These quarters are courtesy of the Space Initiative for you and Mom."

"So, you don't live like this?" Luke asked.

"This place is for guests, like a hotel. These are pretty standard quarters and are free for everybody. My place is nicer and bigger; I've got an extra bedroom for Luke."

Completely unprepared for the answer and full of suspicion, he responded, "Free?"

That didn't sound right to him. Granted, the place was nothing like his house in Missouri. But it was quite posh compared to the average apartment a decent job could afford a person on Earth. He was sure Kristy didn't make much for she had no skills. So, how was she paying for all that? It smelled very fishy.

"Yes. Housing, healthcare, and education are covered for everyone living in space. We also get a $20,000 per month allowance—called Universal Basic Income[75]—but only a few people get to spend it all. Most of the food, clothing, and entertainment are free as well."

"Hmm, some sort of communism," Luke said curtly. "Nothing comes free in life."

However, in 2118, that amounted to a lot more than an ever-scarcer member of the upper-middle class could make on Earth.

"It may be so, Father, but close to 120 million people have emigrated to space so far, and I doubt anyone has gone back. In fact, they're coming here faster than new living space is built. I hear there's a wait period now."

"And nobody works?" Luke said, with a distrustful squint.

"Some do. Either they want more than their UBI, their specialty is critical to the Space Initiative, or they're just bored! A few people start businesses, but most don't work. And it is not a requirement to live here. In my case, I'm too busy between school and Luke. My afternoons get pretty full with homework, so my friend Aaisha helps a lot. I never knew learning was...so fulfilling, Father! I have learned so much and still know so little! But I'd like to become a teacher...someday."

Her mother stared at her, eyebrows raised with surprise—proud and incredulous at the same time.

"No sacrifice brings no virtue," quoted Luke. "My father's saying. This easy life brings no devotion, no merit, and no values!"

Kristy yearned to explain that economic freedom gave people the power to say "No", to express thoughts and feelings they would normally keep to themselves; that UBI provided immunity against all forms of abuse because they all had a root cause in economic vulnerability. People wouldn't have to take poor-paying jobs or those with unfair conditions out of necessity; women would be more selective about their romantic partners; and young adults would be secure enough to leave their parents' homes. She would have liked to scream out loud that inequality and ignorance bred crime and exploitation; that a rigged economy without decent living conditions for everyone fostered human trafficking, prostitution, and other forms of slavery; and that UBI was one of the reasons why the crime rate in space was zero.

But, no, it wasn't the time or the place to pick a fight with her judgmental father.

Kristy brought them to the children's playground adjacent to her home for a stroll around her neighborhood. Located in a suburban area, tall buildings from a nearby major city housing millions dominated the background. But the overarching cylindrical architecture made them gasp in awe.

Spreading above their heads were cities, towns, parks, and lakes hung upside down without falling off the sky. The perspective extended for tens of kilometers towards the circular sections on both the left and the right. Unlike anything they'd experienced before, the ground on one end slowly curved, rising above their heads, continuously extending towards the other side.

"I don't think I'll ever understand this abomination of a world," grunted Luke, troubled by the curved horizon.

"What is that other...thing?" her mother inquired from the wheelchair, pointing upward.

A thin, linear structure ran across the sky, six kilometers above the ground. The small cylinder, 200 meters in diameter, traversed the entire rotation axis.

"That's the food production area; it's how we feed the millions living in this habitat," explained Kristy. "By growing our food far away from populated areas—in the zero-gravity zone—we can maximize the use of the drum for human habitation. Production is fully automated and runs 24/7."

The spectacular advances brought by the previous agricultural revolution paled when compared to genetic engineering now pushing the genome to its limits. The new generation of crops included a vast selection of produce tweaked for higher nutritional content, optimized growth cycles, and enhanced flavor that had been adapted to thrive in microgravity.

Image by Katie Lane

Around mid-afternoon, Kristy brought them to her own quarters. After a quick tour of the place, they came to rest on the ample terrace, where a patio dining table with eight comfortable chairs awaited, surrounded by planters overflowing with flowers. Anne was exhausted, but she was fascinated with Kristy's paintings and sculptures. Just as they helped her to a seat, the doorbell rang.

"It's your grandson!"

Kristy ran to open the door. Voices and noises came from the vestibule. Kristy came back holding Luke. Aaisha walked behind with Omar.

"Mom, Father, these are my friends, Aaisha and her son, Omar."

Aaisha walked forward with a friendly smile and gave each of them a warm, two-handed handshake.

"Please, no need to stand up! I know it takes time to recover from zero gravity; take it easy."

Although she still spoke with a foreign accent, her English had improved by leaps and bounds since her arrival, thanks in part to her close friendship with Kristy.

Kristy set baby Luke down, letting the boy walk free.

"Say hello to your grandparents, love!" she said.

Babbling "Want apple," the child twisted both palms at them in a waving gesture.

"He's hungry. Did you hear that, Kristy?" said Luke.

"He's always hungry," replied Kristy, smiling. "I'll get him some juice."

"No, no, no," mumbled the boy.

The child was very outgoing and engaging, quick to warm up to the newcomers. He stumbled forward with extended arms, without shyness or fear, grabbing his grandparents' hands.

"Go get him something to eat. He's hungry!" commanded Luke.

K3+

"It's a bit early yet to feed him, and we're going out for dinner. I don't want to spoil his appetite."

The child stopped beside his grandmother. Fidgeting with the wrinkles on her dress, his tiny index finger felt the fabric with curiosity, and he tapped gently at her thigh. Anne smiled with watery eyes.

"It's really been a pleasure, Mr. and Mrs. Hamilton," said Aaisha, who didn't want to intrude. "Omar has homework to do, and we'll have plenty of time to converse on another occasion."

"Accompany your friend to the door, and bring my grandson something to eat," Luke demanded.

Transformed by the education and freedom she had experienced in space, Aaisha's heart ached to see her dear friend once again subverted to the male dominance imposed on women for ages. She had grown to despise this behavior over recent years, and, although the precious right of equality was granted to her in space, she couldn't stomach her friend having to give it up. Without saying a word, Kristy did as she was told, and Aaisha left the dwelling as fast as she could.

"When is his birthday?" asked her mother, a few minutes later.

"December 10th."

"Who took care of you? And the prenatal exams? How's his health?" asked her mother with a note of anxiety in her voice.

"Relax, Mom, it was all taken care of. Prenatal care is excellent here; the Space Initiative has state-of-the-art medical facilities—better than anything I've seen on Earth. I started my check-ups at their facility in Brazil, before making the trip to Space. Luke is a perfectly healthy, normal boy," Kristy said patiently.

"You've been on your own all this time! My poor child," said Anne.

"We're fine, Mom! I had to work hard to get here, but all my needs have been taken care of since I arrived. I have a great group of friends from school, and my friend Aaisha has been there for me since the beginning."

Knowing her mother would be horrified to know about the time she had spent out of sight at homeless shelters in Chicago, Kristy decided to leave that part out.

"That girl, your friend, is she a Muslim?" asked Luke, reprovingly.

"Father, has it occurred to you that, if you were switched at birth and raised in the Middle East, you would be a Muslim, too?"

Kristy had no doubt her father would be a fundamentalist no matter with which religion he had been raised.

"They're the work of the devil! Worse than atheists! They're waging a holy war against the Lord Jesus Christ and have killed millions of Christians!" he replied, ignoring the question and raising his voice.

"Aaisha and I have not once talked about religion since we've known each other. No one does here," said Kristy.

Until she experienced the outside world, she didn't realize that, even in America, liberty to practice one's own faith had its flaws and that the strict religious indoctrination with which she grew up had deeply affected her personal freedom and scarred her childhood. The day she understood this, Kristy realized she, too, was a refugee from religious persecution, and this fact brought her closer to Aaisha.

"You sound proud of ignoring religion! You've been denying the Lord!" her father yelled.

Kristy remained silent and looked down. The child stared at his grandfather, startled by his thundering voice. No one had ever yelled in his presence.

Well learned, after nearly two decades dealing with Luke, her mother came to the rescue.

"She's not been doing that, Luke. Let's pray together," said Anne, joining hands with both of them and steering the conversation away from the subject.

It was 1900 hours when they headed out to dinner. A network of underground transports traversed the cylinder, allowing anybody to reach their destination within minutes. Kristy ordered a flying transport to make things easier for her parents; her mom had not finished adapting to normal gravity. It took less than ten minutes to reach their destination.

The small, privately owned steakhouse was starting to fill up with customers. The owner doubled as host and sommelier; he ran the place with his brother as chef and a small crew of robots. The man greeted them at the door and walked them to their table; his Southerner's manners and courtesy made Luke feel right at home.

They followed a carnivore diet back home. Kristy had never liked meat, and, after being forced to eat it for years, she hated it with a passion. But it was her father's favorite, and she wanted to please him. Federico had strongly recommended the place and made a reservation for them. The menu offered a variety of beef cuts and, to Kristy's relief, fish choices as well.

"Where do they get their fish from?" asked Anne full of curiosity, lifting her eyes from the menu.

"All food is produced here, Mother, in the micro-gravity section—that thing in the sky you asked me about this morning," explained Kristy. "Not just the crops, but all animal protein, including fish and meat, are grown there too, in vitro. Vegetables are vertically grown using aeroponic irrigation…"

"Aeroponic?" interrupted Luke.

"Yes, Father. Irrigation is done by spraying a solution of nutrients and minerals on the plant's roots which are exposed to the air. It's amazing! Crops grow without soil in a controlled temperature, humidity, and atmospheric environment. They use light outside the human eye's visible spectrum. It wastes no water…"

"Why? Do you have water shortages?" inquired Luke, hoping to find something to criticize.

"Oh, not at all!" she laughed. "This method is just more efficient. But we are a closed ecosystem; air, water, and everything else is recycled. We produce no waste," explained Kristy.

The owner, waiting by the table to take their orders, couldn't help but add more to her explanation.

"Our crops produce yields unheard of a hundred years ago, sir. We can feed millions with a minuscule fraction of the space. And new varieties are introduced all the time to keep up with the evolving tastes of our growing population."

"And this meat you will serve us is also…synthetic?" Luke scoffed, pursing his lips.

"Sir, we can grow any animal or vegetable product," the owner explained enthusiastically, ignoring Luke's rude attitude. "We continuously enhance the DNA templates used to grow our food to be tastier and more nutritious. It's healthy and free of toxins, if that's your concern. I'm pretty sure you'll like it, but I tell you what: If you don't find my food scrumptious, it'll be free," he finished with a friendly wink.

Luke ordered a tomahawk steak, cooked rare. Kristy and her mother ordered fish and a chicken soup for the baby. For a brief moment, Kristy toyed with the idea of ordering a glass of chardonnay, as the drinking age in space was sixteen. She sighed, discarding the thought; better not to make her father angry.

Twenty minutes later, dinner was on the table. Luke asked for God's blessing on the food and attacked his steak. It was elegantly served on a large, dark-wood cutting board, garnished with roasted potatoes and a variety of vegetables and seasonings on the side, and a single sprig of rosemary perfumed the steak with tantalizing aromas.

The serrated knife cut through with little resistance. Seared to perfection, the crispy outside had a smoky, rich flavor, and the meat was juicy inside, slow-cooked and well-seasoned in the Southern style. What blew Luke away was the flavor and tenderness. It was, hands down, the best steak he'd ever had.

Not falling behind, the halibut ordered by Kristy and her mother was fluffy as a pillow, encrusted with a mix of toasted nuts, and served over a bed of butter-laden polenta with savory roasted vegetables on the side.

After such a spectacular meal, Luke wanted to know how the prices in the menu could be so low and started interrogating the owner.

"Everything on the menu is produced locally. My brother and I run the place, and the cooking aides are robots, so our expenses are low. Besides, if our prices were too high, people would stop coming."

Luke glanced around; the place was jam-packed. Some guests ate standing up at a tall counter that ran along a panoramic window with the magnificent city lights as a backdrop. Above their heads, an army of flawlessly coordinated drones delivered items to the patrons without contributing to the loud ambiance.

"If the meat is grown in a petri dish, how do they get the bone in the tomahawk steak?" Luke asked, full of curiosity.

"Oh, I don't know those details," replied the restaurant owner with a friendly smile. As a favor to Federico he had agreed to give Luke and his family special attention that evening. "I suppose they print the bone first and then grow the steak around it? We just need to order it from the farm," he said, pointing at the microgravity section seen through the window. "Always comes out perfect. It's one of our most popular items on the menu."

"How much do you pay in taxes?" asked Luke.

"Taxes? There ain't no taxes in space!" the owner said with a hearty laugh.

"What? You know what they say about death and taxes, right?" chuckled Luke, his mood boosted by the wonderful dinner.

"The Space Initiative is rich enough to satisfy all the needs of its citizens without collecting taxes," explained the owner.

"How's that even possible?"

"Heavy automation, like in this restaurant, combined with unlimited resources," he answered. "There are very few things we need from Earth, but the Space Initiative has plenty of wealth to acquire them. This allows us to do whatever we please, be it sports, arts, science, philosophy...or running a restaurant— anything that makes people happy!"

Luke was completely in disbelief.

"Coffee or tea, on the house?" asked the owner with a smile.

Back in his chambers later that evening, Luke meditated about his first day in space.

'Too much information,' he thought, his head spinning with the ocean of information collected. He sat down and analyzed the entertainment system. It was highly intuitive and easy to learn.

There was a complete channel selection from every country, including the United States, along with a large set of space channels covering sports, education, and news. The space news channels ran incredibly boring news from life in space or coverage of the Earth news.

Full of curiosity, he chose one of the space sports channels, and a racing event was projected in the middle of the room. He didn't have implanted NIs, but a voice-activated AI device allowed switching from multiple views—far, close, and even inside the cockpits. Luke watched the event in awe from any angle he wished by simply pointing at it or with voice commands; he could also zoom into anything he requested. The different views were so detailed and sharp, it felt like he was at the racetrack.

By registering physical reactions, such as the temperature in his hands, heart rate, and pupillary response, and then correlating the information with his verbal instructions, the AI device began narrowing Luke's preferences with its data-driven algorithms. The entertainment system then started streaming recommended channels and personalized shows, including a profusion of interactive content that blew Luke's mind away once again.

During the following weeks, Luke and his wife got to know their grandson and experience the emerging space culture by touring the different towns in neighboring habitats.

One of them was a water town, built in the middle of a massive lake; the main roads were waterways with sidewalks and buildings raised above them. It gave Luke the opportunity to go sailing with his daughter and grandson while his wife, who was afraid of water, visited the nearby shops and a chocolate factory with Aaisha and Omar.

As days went by, it became clear to Luke how much Kristy had grown up. It might pose a challenge to control her when they got back home, but there was nothing a firm hand wouldn't fix. Women were born to be submissive, dependent creatures. Kristy would submit to him and, later, to her husband when she got married. The couple would live at home for him to oversee the child's education. The boy was right at the perfect age for the instruction which would determine the kind of person he became.

Although they still had a week before returning home, Luke knew there were things he would certainly miss from space, like the food. He wished they could grow food like that on Earth. Despite the ongoing criticism for raising and sacrificing animals, they continued to do so, rather than growing their parts in vitro. Nevertheless, he never expected synthetic meat to be so delicious. Luke had never seen anything like it, not even at the upscale grocery stores where his wife shopped. Surely, it would be possible for a smart entrepreneur to develop a savvy business importing some of those steaks to Earth. Perhaps it'd be cheaper than developing the whole infrastructure from scratch? And why not do it himself? He'd have to look into it.

Very pleased with himself for having gotten everything he wanted, Luke felt he was fulfilling the Lord's plan.

Lying on a recliner chair, he turned the fabulous entertainment system on. Having learned his personal preferences and extrapolated his most intimate subconscious desires through many hours of use, the device selected content to please him. Images flew in front of his eyes until he started to doze. Meanwhile, the screen displayed beautiful, highly detailed three-dimensional illusions and abstract art, flowing to the soothing music.

Absently, he started humming a tune, tapping his thigh to the rhythm. The melody evoked a strong reminiscence of his adolescence, though he couldn't pinpoint what it was. Little by little, the display evolved into a pale speckled background until the image revealed shiny tiled walls. Near an open stall, diffuse lighting atoned for the bright glare from the white glazed ceramic, creating a sensual and intimate atmosphere. The back of a naked young man could be seen leaning toward another man, sitting on the toilet lid. Automatically reacting to Luke's interest, the viewing angle changed to a close up. He stared at the two men, gently slipping their tongues into each other's mouth. The one standing up sat on top of the man who was sitting, facing him. Luke took a deep breath and exhaled sharply.

Standing in the doorway behind Luke, Anne had been staring. Tiptoeing, the woman reached for the knob and pulled the door, leaving it just a crack open. She turned around, grim-faced, and left in complete silence.

On the morning of their departure, Kristy's parents waited patiently for her and little Luke by the elevator to the South access port. Kristy showed up thirty minutes late, alone and with no bags.

"Where's my grandson?" Luke asked, puzzled.

"Father, you haven't told me what your plans for me are when we return home," Kristy asked.

"You will have a fresh start..."

"What do you mean by that? I need to know...Will I still have to marry Richard?"

"Well, that's exactly what I mean—starting a real family and being married by the laws of our Lord. You've committed a sin, and your son needs guidance. And a father! As the spiritual leader of our community, I can't allow my daughter to have a son out of wedlock. There are rules; you know that!" he replied, his voice starting to rise.

"But I don't want to marry him, Father!" she protested. "I want to determine my own future."

"A woman's future is not hers to determine!" said Luke, scornfully.

"I don't want to go back under those conditions, Father."

He raised his voice, angered. "You'll do as you're told!"

People around them began to notice the scene.

"This is my home now. I'm not a child anymore..."

"And you're still a minor, you idiot!" he interrupted loudly and scornfully.

"I'm staying!"

"Shut up! You are my daughter and you will do as I say!" Spit came flying from his mouth as he yelled at her.

"I am staying, Father," she repeated calmly.

The blow to Kristy's face made her collapse, as Luke threw his weight behind it. Stepping forward he grabbed the hair behind her neck, clutching it firmly with his right hand, ready to strike again. With her senses still dulled by the impact, time slowed down.

Around them bystanders voiced their outrage.

"Luke, no!" begged Anne, rushing forward.

He pushed hard against her chest with an open palm, knocking his wife aside. He felt powerful, in control of the situation, just like back home. He was amazed by how women forgot their place so often; it was their own fault they needed to be dealt with this way. It was clear to him; force was the only language they understood.

Still on the ground, Anne lay on her side with a hand placed on her chest, coughing and wheezing in pain.

With a strong grip on Kristy's hair, Luke twisted his wrist, forcing her to turn upwards and face him. Every muscle and vein in his neck and arms bulged and throbbed by the sudden rush of blood. He looked down at his daughter's face. A defiant look of utmost hatred shone in her eyes with eyebrows close together, her nostrils swollen, and her teeth bared.

Something woke up inside her—a powerful wave of ire she had not experienced in her short life—years of abuse and subjugation crowding her memory. She thought of her child and felt ready to fight to the death if need be. Uttering a war cry and ignoring the increasing pain on her scalp, she launched against Luke with all her might. Although she was in no position to inflict damage, she pushed and kicked him.

"How dare you? You ungrateful brat!" howled Luke, pulling her closer and raising his hand to strike again.

Just then, two strong pairs of arms restrained Luke from behind, while another man expertly selected a pressure point on Luke's wrist and forced him to let go of his daughter's hair.

Lightheaded and weak, Kristy felt her shaky legs give away and crouched to rest, placing a hand flat on the ground for balance. Her heart still pounding, she made a conscious effort to slow down her breathing, sighing deeply from time to time.

A wiry old man with a slightly bent back gently squeezed himself through the crowd of onlookers around the scene and faced Luke.

"Mr. Hamilton, this behavior is unacceptable. You've attacked one of our citizens. It will not be tolerated," said Federico in his most peaceful tone.

"She is my daughter and a minor! You're holding a US cit..."

"We are not holding anybody. Your daughter sought asylum running away from you, and, after what we just witnessed, it's very clear why," interrupted Federico.

One of the guards called the paramedics and helped the women to get up, then herded the crowd some distance away; soon, the multitude began to disperse.

Luke twisted violently, trying to break free from his captors, but, despite his imposing height and strength, he found himself downright immobilized into a nelson. He was no match for the three hand-to-hand combat-trained security volunteers.

"You will drop your lawsuit against the Space Initiative, or I'll make sure a video of what happened here is broadcast—prime time—in your hometown," added Federico.

"Go to hell!" yelled Luke, still trying to break free.

"Calm yourself down! You have nothing to gain from this fight and much to lose. Think! Will your congregation still respect you and keep you as their leader when they see how you treated your daughter and wife?" Federico tried to reason.

"That's none of your business. They've followed me for years and will continue to do so! You hear me? I know they w..."

Federico cut him off. Steely-eyed, he asked dryly, "Sir, do you remember Martin Constantino?"

He signaled the guards to release Luke. They stayed close by, ready to restrain him again if need be.

"What? How do you..."

"We tracked him down. We have means to find information about people. He gave us a recorded declaration with details of...the incident. I don't think you want that to come out."

"What is he talking about, Luke?" asked his wife.

The man huffed and puffed but remained silent. Unable to look her in the eye, he finally turned his gaze to the ground.

"I...I would like to request asylum," added Mrs. Hamilton, turning to Federico.

"You betray me, too? I don't care! But Kristy, she's a minor. I will see this all the way through..."

Federico interrupted again to reply to Anne.

"Of course, Mrs. Hamilton, you are welcome to stay, immediately, if you wish," he said kindly.

"Did you hear that, sir? Now you don't even have a legal case. As her mother, she won't have any trouble obtaining Kristy's custody. We will provide her with legal and financial backing. After what happened here today, Kristy's age is irrelevant, but her rights aren't. The custody battle won't last long. Still, she will turn eighteen before that happens. You have already lost her."

Luke stepped forward, fists clenching.

"I will make you pay for this!" he yelled.

Federico nodded at the guards; one of them pulled out a hypospray, sedating Luke instantly, while the other two grabbed him before he collapsed.

A team of emergency responders arrived and picked up Luke, placing him gently on a stretcher. Kristy was glad to see that they immediately went over to check on her mother.

Federico approached the paramedic in charge, inquiring about Anne's physical status.

"Her elbows and right forearm have a bloody scrape from the fall, but no broken bones. She seems to be okay but complains about chest pain. Could be just a consequence of the strike. But I'd rather do some tests and keep her in observation in the care unit, just for a bit," said the medic.

"Kristy is hurt; she needs medical attention, too," said Federico, pointing at her bloody, swollen lips and left cheek.

"I'm okay," Kristy blurted out valiantly, dabbing at her lip with a sleeve. "I got worse back home. I'm glad my son wasn't here to see this. Where are they taking him?"

"Back home. I'm sorry it has to be like this, but we couldn't put him on a ship back to Earth in his current state. He could become a danger to himself and the ship. We'll keep him sedated until he wakes up, safe and sound on the ground. We will not proceed against him, now that your mother is on your side," said Federico.

"Who was that guy you mentioned...Constan...?" she asked.

"While in high school, your father had a sexual encounter in a shower room with another boy," said Federico.

Kristy's expression of disbelief made him explain.

"Many heterosexual people, men and women, experiment with someone of their same sex at some point in their lifetime. It was just teenage curiosity triggered by hormones. I'm sure you understand."

"But...yes...of course I do!"

She was at a loss for words but after a few seconds regained her composure.

"Having friended people of multiple sexual orientations, I've come to understand that sex is not a binary characteristic but a spectrum, and not even static...it can change with time. But my father? I'd never expect it...I mean, if you heard him speaking of *homosexuality*! How did you find this out?"

"We have enormous resources at our disposal. We tracked down most of his former classmates and other relations, looking for information we could use as leverage. Mr. Constantino happens to be a valued scientist and a Space Initiative citizen. He came forward."

"I never thought my mom would come to my defense!"

"I'm not surprised. I had a private conversation with her ten days ago about Mr. Constantino, but she denied knowing anything about it. I don't think she even believed me. Nevertheless, she confided a secret to me. Have you ever wondered why you have no siblings?"

"Maybe. I think I did, when I was very young. But I never spoke to her about it. Father said she was *defective.* I wondered...wait! What was her secret?" Her brain was overwhelmed by all the information being fed to it.

"Your mother has been using contraceptives for years—at great risk, I'm sure. Obviously, your father would have never allowed it, and things would have gotten very unpleasant had she been discovered. But I doubt he ever suspected."

"I can't believe it!"

"The hormones were detected in her bloodstream during the physical exams on Earth. When I learned this, I decided to approach her. The opportunity presented itself on the day you went sailing with your father; your mother was alone with your friend, Aaisha. She felt terrible about not being able to properly educate you about sex."

"Were you...planning to use this information to push her to my side?" Kristy asked.

"I did explain that requesting asylum would be the best way to set you free; that she would be able to live here, close to you, if she desired. In the end, it was your father's brutality that convinced her."

She nodded, pensively.

"Go on with your life, Kristy. Make it a great one for you and your son. Continue your education and make sure young Luke does, too," he said with a smile.

She hugged and kissed him on the cheek before leaving.

Federico wandered a good while around the access port elevator, analyzing the events. He was glad Kristy hadn't asked why he didn't instruct the guards to intervene immediately or send drones in before Luke laid a hand on them. The truth was, he needed Luke to go that far to build enough leverage on him...and maybe her mother would come forward. It all worked out just fine.

Federico's team of psychologists had predicted Luke's temperament and reactions, helping him draw a plan of action. Although he very much regretted that the women had to suffer yet more physical violence at the hands of that savage, it would pass. He would have to live with the guilt, but that, too, would pass.

"Time erases everything, good and bad!" he said to himself.

A few days later, at the office, Enzo broke the news: the lawsuit had been dropped.

"I also have improved the background-check rules, as you requested. I'm finishing the setup for the fingerprint matching," he added.

"Ah, about that...," Federico said. "Better to archive them, just in case. Let's just keep things as they are for the time being."

"Alright then. But I thought that the goal was to completely shut the door to any other similar..."

Federico snorted softly and smiled.

Enzo looked at him, puzzled for an instant, and then nodded in understanding.

"Got it. You're the boss, Boss. And I love working for you," he said, beaming an amused smile back at Federico.

"Since we don't pay you, I'll take that as a compliment," he replied with a smile.

"Shouldn't every human being be given the opportunity to escape oppression, an opportunity to grow and thrive, a chance for happiness?" Federico asked himself.

"My dear Enzo, I just remembered a poem. It was inscribed at the pedestal of a statue, written by Emma Lazarus; and I liked it so much that I learned it by heart, over a hundred years ago! It goes like this:

> *Give me your tired, your poor, your huddled*
> *masses yearning to breathe free,*
> *The wretched refuse of your teeming shore.*
> *Send these, the homeless, tempest-tost to me,*
> *I lift my lamp beside the golden door!*

Misty-eyed, Enzo blinked repeatedly. He cleared his throat and swallowed before saying in a whisper, "That is beautiful."

"Now, we only need to find a way to explain all this to the chairman!" said Federico.

Chapter 4: War

A LARGE PROJECTION FLOATED IN FRONT OF FEDERICO displaying medical graphs and tables in real time. Blood panels, along with urine and stool samples, had become obsolete decades ago. In 2216, swarms of nanobots collected all the data as they circulated through to the very last capillary in the bloodstream.

Standing by the display, his physician went through the readings. When he referred to a specific chart or table, it popped out from the panel filling most of the projection.

"Everything looks as good as you can expect for a person in your condition. No noticeable changes in the last ten years."

No surprise there. His physical exams had shown a stable condition for the last two decades.

"So that's it, then. Can I go back to work...?" he started, but the doctor's expression told him it wouldn't work this time.

"Federico, how much longer will you put this off? We've been discussing this for the last twenty years!"

"No, you have been discussing it. Me, I never want to hear about it."

"The rest of the human race has moved forward but, oh no, not you! You're stuck in time, like a living dinosaur. What will it take for you to consider it? Your disease puts you at a disadvantage in every aspect of your life, not the least, your job."

After a brief pause, Federico responded.

"I guess I'm just afraid about its safety. If it...damages my body, I've got nowhere else to go. I don't see why I can't perpetuate my current situation indefinitely."

"Eventually, your body will wear itself out beyond repair. And, in the meantime, you isolate yourself, missing all the benefits that come with the procedure. It is as safe as we can make it; we've had no negative outcomes in the last thirty years."

"Really? And how many of them were performed in that period?" asked Federico.

"Less than a hundred, but yours is a rare disease, one that has been eradicated for nearly a century."

Unable to divide or perform their functions, senescent cells still emitted chemical signals, becoming deleterious to cellular physiology. Removing them and fixing accumulated cellular damage was the start to reverting aging and age-related diseases.

Formally classified as a disease in the late twenty-first century, aging was cured at the turn of the twenty-second century. Science first found ways to slow it down and, later, to stop it. Then there was the matter of dealing with the billions who were already affected by it.

There had been deaths and less than desirable outcomes in the beginning, most of them due to mistakes made by both patients and physicians. But a few thousand well-documented cases of the age-reversal procedure gone wrong made Federico wary of going through with it himself.

"In your particular case, we have run simulations of all the possible outcomes and are very confident it will go by the book. But let me give you another incentive: we've identified a set of DNA enhancements to improve the human body. First, we optimized the genome by removing the evolutionary junk, genetic drifting, and aberrations in the genetic code. Did you know that 75 percent of it is crap? The enhancements will give you better multitasking abilities, increased reflexes, better brain wiring, an improved immune system—smart enough to fight new diseases and adaptive enough to avoid allergies—better muscle tone, and bone strength; the list is extensive. I'll spare the details; you can review them at your leisure."

"Is there a new generation of NIs to match?" asked Federico hopefully.

He had finally mustered the guts to get his NIs implanted a few years ago but was slightly disappointed with their limited functionality and applications.

"The next generation of NIs is made from a fiber of carbon nanotubes, which blends natively with nerve tissue. Combined with the new DNA enhancements, they allow for thought exchange without words, even if the parties don't speak the same language," explained the doctor.

"How will that work?" inquired a baffled Federico.

"When we communicate, there's a continuous translation back and forth between thoughts and words. But language is a crude and often inadequate representation of what's in our minds. Because it's like trying to identify a 3D object just by looking at its shadow, I cannot fully describe thought exchange using words. People often have trouble finding the right words, and we don't always mean what we say, leading to so many misunderstandings. But now a thought in my mind can be transmitted to your mind without translation. Just imagine how much communication will improve if we can truly understand each other without relying on the crudeness of language."

"Are you talking about telepathy?" Federico was blown away. For far too long, telepathy had been the monopoly of quacks and charlatans. But it would be for science to finally make the long-cherished dream a reality.

"It will take a couple more generations of genetic enhancements and NIs to get there, but this will be a leap forward. I, too, envision a future in which people will start dropping the spoken language in favor of thought exchange!"

"That's incredible!" said Federico excitedly. "It'd be a blessing not having to carefully choose our words to avoid offending others. How many people have you...?"

"We've done trials on nearly ten million people so far. I'm one of the volunteer subjects. By the way, Enzo, is also one. How does it feel having a subordinate who's far more capable than yourself?"

Federico was at a loss for words.

"Listen, we are on the verge of a historic milestone for human beings. The first generation of genetic enhancements will usher in a true renaissance for our species. People will no longer be stuck with the cards that nature deals them. But you won't be able to take advantage of these enhancements unless you revert to a younger age first. Your severely shortened telomeres are letting the DNA in your cells unravel, making it very hard to take care of your health. You keep getting cancer, heart disease, diabetes, Alzheimer's, and organ failures..." the doctor explained patiently.

Still concerned about the procedure, Federico didn't say a thing.

"You should know, Federico, that it's always easier and cheaper to fully replace an old piece of technology than continue fixing the parts. I strongly encourage you to take this option. Please?"

Still not a word from Federico.

"You'll be able to have sex again! Can you even remember your last time?" insisted the doctor softly, but relentlessly, in his effort to sway him.

"Okay, yes. I'll do it! You could have started there," said Federico, surrendering with a guilty smile.

The doctor beamed with a sigh of relief and used his enhanced NIs to summon what he needed next.

"Excellent! You won't regret it, and your quality of life will make giant strides! Now please lie down on the table."

The doctor stood up as the door opened, allowing a cube-shaped medical drone to wheel in. The device positioned itself by the doctor, and the top of the unit opened to make way for a tray with multiple cylindrical glass containers to rise from inside. Haze from the cooling system drifted upward, as the doctor grabbed the first vial and plugged it into a hypospray.

"Now, we've gone over the procedure multiple times. I will inject you with a set of compounds and will reprogram your nanobots. The compounds will be used by the nanobots to reconfigure your epigenome[76], triggering a repair of damage caused by age. You will revert about two years for every month until you reach the physiological age of 29.7 years."

"Why that exact number?"

"The human brain continues to grow until the age of thirty (29.7 in your case), and the cranial plates keep expanding to make room for it before fusing together. Because the brain contains the essence of who you are, we don't want to take risks. You may go back to your earlier twenties later if you desire, but not on the first step," explained the doctor.

However, thirty was a dream come true for Federico, who was 250 years old, even if he looked like he was in his seventies.

"So, the complete treatment will be done in a little over a year?"

"Based on your current physiological age of sixty-seven, it will take about seventeen months, give or take. We will closely monitor you remotely, but I still want you to come for weekly visits during the first month."

Developed a hundred years earlier, the carbyne manufacturing technique allowed for the development of anything, from carbon nanotube fibers to hyper-resistant aircraft hulls, all sorts of ultra-light tools, and non-rotating skyhooks.

With a large enough Statite cloud, star lifting had at last become faster and cheaper than mining Mercury. The sun was now churning out enough carbon and metals to outpace human population growth. Just like agriculture, 15,000 years earlier, star lifting revolutionized human civilization forever.

Living in a true post-scarcity society of virtually unlimited resources, triggered a never-before-seen baby boom across the space population. Many people were having eight children or more for they had no economic constraints and lived forever with the health and stamina they had in their early twenties. The space population was now much larger than that of the home planet: roughly seventeen billion compared to less than three.

Sitting upright in his new chair, Federico changed its settings and the height of his also brand-new desk. He was able to control his entire workspace, including the furniture, through his NIs, and it would put itself back in place after he left at the end of the day.

Image by Katie Lane

"This ergonomic chair is ridiculously adaptable," commented Federico to Enzo. He marveled like a kid while they both watched Earth's news.

The Space Initiative's headquarters at the Port of Entry had just been redesigned and redecorated. Absorbed with the nuts and bolts of the Dyson swarm project, Federico designated Enzo to team up with other board members and take care of everything.

Considering how much time they all spent working, they aimed for the healthiest balance of work and quality of life; the results were awesome.

His office area was not much bigger than before, but it was no longer a static room. The cutting-edge design included office space, a meeting room, and a food and beverage station. There was also a relaxation and play area.

"There's so much tension right now! People are leaving the home planet in droves, abandoning jobs, homes, mortgages, and other obligations," Enzo reflected.

"A hundred years ago, it was the poor and destitute, or refugees, who sought to live in space. Now it's...everybody! Impoverished middle-class families, tired of living paycheck to paycheck in backbreaking poverty-trap jobs, are flocking to space and seeking a piece of the post-scarcity society...just as people like me once flocked to the United States in search of the American Dream, I guess," Federico responded.

The truth was he could no longer remember his life in Colombia or his early years in America, but he assumed he had emigrated to the United States in search of a better life like countless others.

The United States population dipped below a hundred million, to a level last seen in 1910, threatening another economic crisis. The inhabitants of Tornado Alley[77] fled after a series of supercells merged together producing a rash of F5 tornadoes.

All across the country, entire cities were deserted, as only the super wealthy lived there a few months per year in their fortified estates. For centuries, they feared the poor would one day come with pitchforks, but now there was no one left to raise.

The homeless had been the first to leave, followed by the indigent and the middle class; while in the heartland, the least gregarious, who loved farmlands and pastoral countryside scenery, stayed in rural America.

Now pacing around the office as he spoke, Federico stood by the floor-to-ceiling glass panes, which opened to a courtyard and merged into a wrap-around terrace with lush vegetation and a spectacular view of the city and towns arching across the cylindrical sky. As the cool breeze carried in the scent of flowers, he looked back at Enzo.

"It happened right under their noses," he continued. "The plutocrats, with the complicity of politicians, accumulated obscene amounts of wealth and used it to solidify their control over the government. They lobbied to obtain all thirty-four authorizations required for the first ever Article V Constitutional Convention[78], radically transforming the US Constitution. This allowed them to take even more power away from the masses. Now, they face the consequences!"

"It's hard for me to understand why the people can't see through this," said Enzo confused. "They eliminated Social Security, Medicare, Medicaid, Unemployment Insurance, and all other government safety nets."

The voice of the people had never been so silenced nor economic slavery so pervasive in American life. Labor unions were outlawed; the work week increased to six days with eighty-four hours; and the minimum wage was abolished. Alcoholism, drug abuse, and suicide rates skyrocketed as gag laws and militarized police forced the masses into submission. Born in space, Enzo could not imagine himself living under such conditions.

"This massive exodus is the result of 200 years of failed Trickle-Down Economics. People are finally fed up waiting for the enlightened benevolence of the elites..."

Enzo's quizzical expression made him pause and explain.

"There was this preposterous idea called Trickle-Down Economics, pitched by an American president over two centuries ago. The more money the rich had, the more they would spend on goods and services, producing a trickle-down of wealth towards the middle class…"

"Wishful thinking!" interrupted Enzo, aghast. He just couldn't believe such idiocy. "If you give the poor and the middle-class money, they'll spend it, which means it'll go right back into the economy. The rich will save it instead, benefiting no one but themselves! I can't believe people put up with that shit for 200 years!"

"And instead of trickle-down, they got vague platitudes and cyclical economic crashes that sank them deeper into poverty…"

"Sir, the US Senate session starts soon!" interrupted Enzo, looking at one of the floating displays. The conversation had disgusted him, and he was glad they had to end it.

"Good! Let's go watch," said Federico. "The board?"

Enzo used his new NIs to access the building's logs. "They're in the meeting chamber. Fujino is in the elevator. Waithera and the chairman are also on their way; they should be there in less than five minutes."

As they headed towards the door, the headline news showed a chart on the main display. A reporter voiced over the data.

The population of Vermont has now dipped below 10,000, becoming unable to collect enough revenues to meet its minimum obligations. They are the first to reinstate the draft in order to function. The military will fill, from now on, critical government posts. As you may remember, a merger of states with low population, brought up during the last Senate session, erupted in a brawl. The regular legislative session was suspended...

In desperate need of higher revenues to save their already shrunken defense budget from collapsing, Congress was between a rock and a hard place: to raise taxes on the rich or on the middle class? Facing the prospect of an even bigger exodus, they went for the wealthy, prompting a major revolt of their ultra-rich constituencies. After centuries of political activism, libertarian advocacy groups had become mighty behemoths. Backed by rogue activist trillionaires, they flooded the coffers of challengers in hundreds of House races across the country, triggering a tsunami that replaced all of them.

Russia and China could see themselves in the US situation a few decades down the road, but their position was far less critical. In those countries, economic inequality was not as pronounced, and the Space Initiative supplied them with plenty of carbyne and precious metals to keep quiet and continue protecting their balloon-raised space vehicles.

Free from the overpopulation maladies of the last two centuries, combined with massive amounts of wealth from trading with the Initiative, China aimed to perpetuate the status quo with the side benefit of sticking it to the United States, following multiple trade and economic wars.

Thanks to the exodus, Republicans consolidated a solid majority by stripping everyone living in space of their citizenship, preventing them from voting. Democrats now had fewer seats than Independents in Congress. Gerrymandering and voter suppression tactics were a thing of the distant past with the United States becoming a one-party country.

At 1100 hours sharp, the early September session of the entirely white male US Senate went live on the floating displays around the meeting chamber. All fifty members of the Space Initiative board were already in the room and listening attentively when the chairman walked in. Next to Federico, Enzo registered the minutes of the meeting.

The 17th Amendment[79] had been repealed over a century before. Recently elected by the state legislature—to replace his predecessor who had voted to raise taxes—the ambitious Senator Chavez from California had the floor.

"...this massive exodus of our citizenry threatens the very fabric of our union," he was saying. "This bill will help to curb emigration by making it an act of treason and by enforcing measures like forbidding international travel to the general population. International travel will still be available to authorized individuals. I now submit the bill for your consideration."

Senator Perez, from Florida, raised a hand.

"Who determines authorization?" he asked.

"The Office of Passport Services at the State Department will make the decision. Members of the executive and legislative branches are pre-authorized, as well as individuals with a personal wealth of over 500 billion," explained Chavez.

Senator Walton from Arkansas raised his hand.

"What are the contemplated penalties for breaking this law?" he asked.

"Because it would be an act of treason, lawbreakers will face capital punishment. There's a twenty-year minimum sentence when caught trying to flee the first time. Capital punishment shall be enforced for a second offense."

A loud rumbling of indistinct conversations exploded throughout the chamber like a thunderbolt, as senators conferred with each other and with their aides. Never in the history of the United States had such a law been proposed. Stripping people of their citizenship for leaving was one thing, but the death penalty? A prison sentence was already bad enough; with all correctional institutions privately run, barely anyone got out. Even those in for minor offenses, like public intoxication, were kept for long periods—even for life. Being paid per inmate, it was easy for the prison administrators to find excuses for extending sentences indefinitely.

"These are trying times, my fellow countrymen," yelled Chavez above the noise, energetically waving his arms to bring the chamber back to order. "The exodus is a cancer consuming our nation and will soon kill it. We need to stop it. These penalties will effectively deter people from trying."

Senator Dell from Texas raised a hand.

"I had the opportunity to read the bill. Are you also outlawing international broadcasts and personal communications? This will make us a police state as repressive as North Korea!"

"We have to, as they'll become the primary accessory in aiding people to flee. Make no mistake, this is the worst crisis our nation has ever faced. We will have no country to run unless this bill is passed," urged Chavez.

Senator Bezos from Washington raised a hand.

"I'd like to propose an amendment to the bill, making it an act of war for any nation to give aid or asylum to US citizens breaking this law."

The rumble erupted again. The US economy relied heavily on trade with the Space Initiative. Going to war would end trading and trigger an even faster collapse of the economy. It seemed completely pointless.

Senator Chavez called the chamber to order again.

"I will support the amendment proposed by the senator from Washington," he said.

Hurriedly patched into the bill, without any reviews or validations, the amendment was added, and the bill went up for a vote, passing 98 to 1, with 1 abstention. It would take an hour to go to the House of Representatives, but, with both chambers under solid Republican majority, the outcome would remain the same.

Before the final tally came in, the chairman inquired, "Thoughts?"

Patrice Waithera stood up briefly, shaking with refrained anger.

"Mr. Chairman, they can't wage a war against us. Not only are they at a disadvantage, but it would cripple them economically!"

Maiko Fujino raised her hand.

"Mr. Chairman, the United States has a population of less than 100 million. We will continue bringing people from other countries, but we can't save everybody. True, they can't win a war against us, but they can do us harm. A single missile can destroy multiple habitats, killing hundreds of millions. I strongly advise you to shut the door to US immigration immediately."

"Speaking of which," said Patrice, "I have an asylum request from Senator Perez and members of his staff."

Federico raised his hand.

"Mr. Chairman, I have key personnel from a technology venture we fund who must be evacuated, as well."

"I have to disagree," pressed Fujino. "We cannot risk the well-being of millions to save a few."

"First of all, I don't think it's up to anyone in this room to decide who can't be saved," Federico argued with a cold smile. "Second, my people are not only loyal Space Initiative citizens but individuals who have made an invaluable contribution to the future of the human race. We must stand by them!"

"That reckless attitude creates a risk for everyone living in space. It'll be our undoing!" Fujino lashed out, raising her voice more than seemed necessary.

"If you were looking at the complete picture, you might have a different opinion," said Federico, using his most irritating, condescending tone.

"Mr. Chairman, fellow board members, this is such an irresponsible position! We do not possess offensive weapons! I have reason to believe the United States has space ballistic missile systems (SBMs) that can reach our habitats. Our defenses are designed for space debris. What if we are not able to destroy all the missiles? I strongly advise you to discard this injudicious advice from our fellow board member and stop immigration from the United States immediately!"

A victim of frequent mood swings due to his ongoing age-reversal procedure, Federico stood up, his palms pushing against the table, his arms shaking slightly but enough for those nearby to notice. A few people in the room held their breath, sure that Federico would yell at her. However, he spoke in his usual assertive tone, keeping his calm.

"If you would allow me, I'd like to share information regarding the recent achievement of this group, so you understand why we must rescue them. The information I'm about to disclose is strictly confidential and must not leave this room," he said politely, with the demeanor of a poker player in possession of a royal flush.

"Please stop right there, Federico. You don't have to patronize us," interrupted the chairman, swiftly standing up. "Ladies, gentlemen, thank you all for your input. I will notify you when I have made a decision. Now, please, let us have the room."

Everybody left except Federico.

"I'm very sorry, sir. I didn't mean to...but our people on Earth..."

"That was just an excuse," interrupted the chairman, walking around the table to sit beside him. "Tell me, what was it you were about to disclose?"

"Everyone in the room had the proper clearance, sir."

"I'm aware of that, but I want to be the first to hear. I've known you for almost two centuries. You were about to drop a big one," said the chairman with a brotherly smile. "What do you have?"

"One of our teams on Earth has finally achieved FTL communication!" exclaimed Federico, biting his lower lip and nodding, excitement pouring out of him. "The discovery, based in part on quantum teleportation[80], has been verified. We are certain to develop the technology in ten years, maybe less!"

Completely taken aback by this revelation, the chairman took a few seconds to digest its enormity. Giddy with excitement, his heartbeat raced out of control. Pressing his back against the chair he took several deep, long breaths, trying to calm his heart.

Faster-than-light communication was on everyone's minds, but it seemed so far away they avoided getting their hopes too high. Over the last century, the Space Initiative had spent tens of trillions trying to achieve this insatiable, unattainable dream.

Often raising eyebrows from his fellow board members, many of whom thought he was much too close to the chairman, Federico himself had spent the largest chunk of that money funding universities, individual research, start-ups, and think tanks—some of them outlandish by any stretch of the imagination. He only got away with it because FTL was the last obstacle to a true spacefaring, interstellar, and possibly intergalactic empire.

But now it had at long last paid off. Those scientists on the ground had just become the most valuable assets in the entire human race. They had to do everything in their power to extract them—and immediately—before word of their discovery got out.

The chairman was glad he had stopped Federico from disclosing such enormity to the board, no matter how many security clearances they had. Brilliant as he was, the guy sometimes let gut feelings rule his actions. The release of a discovery of that magnitude had to be carefully controlled. What if the US military or spies from other nations got wind of it? Those scientists would become bargaining chips, hostages, or bounty.

"Shit! I knew it was big, but I never expected this!" said the chairman a bit recovered. "How long have you been sitting on this?" he inquired.

"Less than forty-eight hours, sir. I've been working on the next steps to ensure there's a path forward before bringing it up at our one-on-one later today. I can assure you nobody outside this room knows about it—not even Enzo—and that a full backup of their work is stored on the Space Initiative's secure cloud. All members of the team are under strict confidentiality agreements, and, after learning of the discovery, I personally reminded them to keep their mouths shut."

"Needless to say, do not share this information with anybody else!" said the chairman, his heart still racing.

"Of course not, sir. This will reshape civilization, humanity itself. I trust you agree we must extract my team at all costs? A discovery is far from a practical application. Not only do we need them to work with our engineering teams to develop the technology, but there's no telling what other major achievements these people will still make."

"That is perfectly clear, old friend. Great job! Now I'm glad we let you spend all that money!" said the chairman with a smile, while using his NIs to recall his aides.

When they were back in the room, he addressed them.

"Inform all board members that, effective immediately, immigration from the United States is halted, but I'm open to consider individual cases for high value assets. Inform board member Waithera her request to extract Senator Perez and his staff is granted and to not discuss it with anyone else."

They nodded while taking notes.

"I'm granting board member Tarifa's request to extract his team of scientists with their families—all of them. Until you hear otherwise, this is your top priority. Give him anything and everything he needs to achieve this, spare no expense, leave no stone unturned. From this very instant, you have the authority to act on my behalf to mobilize all resources necessary to accomplish this task!"

None of the aides had ever seen their boss so feverish or received such extraordinary orders before. Curious as they were about what made those people so special to risk World War III, they did not ask. All three of them simply nodded in acknowledgment.

Turning to Federico, the chairman said. "I won't micromanage the situation by asking for daily updates. But I want to be notified of any obstacles you encounter."

"Yes, sir," Federico acknowledged.

As the chairman left the room, Federico used his NIs to quickly summon Enzo. Two of the aides left to notify the other board members. The remaining one, a petite dark-skinned lady with the name of Albia, looked almost too young to be the chairman's senior aide, yet no one would make the foolish mistake of treating her as such. She commanded the utmost respect from anyone in government important enough to deal with her boss.

She gestured them toward the table and all three sat down.

"Which technology venture do your people work for?" asked Albia.

"Schrodinger Research," replied Federico.

"Alright. It's classified by the US government as critical for national security," she said consulting her screen. "Even though it's wholly owned by the Initiative, they will keep a close eye on it."

"But our security measures..." Federico tried to explain.

"That's not what I meant," she interrupted with a friendly smile. "No doubt they're the best. However, we can't have all your researchers stream through an airport with their families without raising suspicions from the US government. How many people are we talking about?"

"Twenty researchers. But I'll need some time to get you an accurate count that includes family members accompanying them," said Federico.

Right at that moment, Enzo accessed and navigated multiple personnel and postal databases through his NIs, correlating the employee data of the twenty key researchers at Schrodinger's and summarizing it in his mind. It all happened in a split second.

"A first estimate puts that number at fifty-one people," said Enzo.

Federico was shocked. It would have taken someone without the new NIs and DNA enhancements at least fifteen minutes to gather and correlate all the data. His dumbfounded look was met by a quick reassuring wink from Enzo.

"That's fine," said Albia. "We can work with this number. However, they can't all travel together or use any kind of mass transportation that requires ID. I'll reach out to our logistics team, but I suspect the best way is to split them into groups so each team member will travel with his or her own family. Don't worry, they'll choreograph the whole thing for us. Even if the United States or any other nation gets wind of what we're up to, they'll have to deal with multiple targets."

Born in Tel Aviv fifty years earlier and emigrating to the United States soon after college, Ariel Ezra pursued his PhDs while working on quantum computing research at Stanford University. Soon he met his wife to be, Chloé—a tall, bubbly blond, the only child of a French-Canadian couple—who worked as a nurse at Stanford Medical. They fell in love immediately and got married a few years later.

After patenting a number of communications algorithms, Ariel showed up on the radar of Schrodinger Research, a quantum computing start-up funded by the Space Initiative. Federico was able to entice him with the promise of virtually unlimited research funding, and Ariel assembled a constellation of brilliant researchers. Very high IQs and a preposterous number of doctorates were the recruiting standards. Their goal was to focus on an area of quantum entanglement[81] that could hypothetically allow instant communication, regardless of distance.

Because quantum entanglement overcame locality but not causality, most establishment scientists believed it would never make FTL communication possible. But Ariel, wielding his triple Stanford PhD in quantum mechanics, networking, and computer sciences, disregarded their opinions and approached the problem from the communications point of view.

Following twenty years of tireless work, they found a way to overcome causality by using quantum teleportation and were finally able to transmit a mega q-bit of data between Earth and a research station located six light-minutes away then send it back and verify the data was still the same.

By the time Ariel reported the discovery to the Space Initiative, his team had been able to repeat the experiment using different sets of equipment, data, and locations. The discovery was verifiable. The data traveled instantaneously regardless of the distance, maintaining its integrity. It also seemed possible they'd be able to develop practical applications. Interfacing with existing technologies would be one of the challenges but nowhere near impossible.

An urgent video call from Federico came soon after Congress passed the ban on emigration.

"How are you doing, Ariel? Are you aware of the law just passed by Congress?"

They still had a five-plus-second delay between Earth and the closest cylinders. One of the techniques to deal with it was to pack multiple sentences together.

"I'm good, sir! Thank you for asking. Yes, I am aware."

"The bill was signed into law by the president immediately after passing the House, less than ten minutes ago."

What's to become of our research, of our lives? Can you help us? We all want to come to space," said Ariel. The distress in his voice was audible.

"Are you alone?"

"Go ahead," Ariel nodded.

"Yes, we can help. I've been authorized to extract all of you, but we need to act fast. I'm not sure how much time we have before the communications blackout is carried out. I understand your entire team, families included, is around fifty-one?"

"I'll verify the number but that seems right, sir."

"We can't move all of you together. Instructions will be sent to each of you, separately. You will travel with your families to your corresponding extraction points. You must not communicate with the others while in route or share your extraction points. Pack only clothes and small items of value. Leave everything else behind. Destroy all local copies of any work product, even notes on the back of napkins! Destroy all your testing equipment, as well, so it can't be reconstructed."

"Understood!" Ariel said with a lurch in his stomach.

"Godspeed, Ariel. What you've achieved is amazing. Know that the Space Initiative will stop at nothing to get you all out. I'm very much looking forward to meeting you in person!" said Federico.

"Same here, sir! I'll start right way; there's no time to be wasted. We'll be ready. And thank you."

Within minutes, Ariel had rounded up his team and briefed them. Hardware, software, and documents were to be destroyed, as instructed by Federico. There were no printed copies, but they needed to damage hundreds of storage devices beyond repair.

"And don't forget to wipe all marker boards in the lab!" he added as they started rushing out of the room.

Broken into smaller teams, two scientists pushed service carts while a few others ahead meticulously identified and pulled all the storage units from servers, external drives, and workstations— room after room. They dropped all storage media into the carts while someone else collected tablets and other mobile devices that contained any research data.

Reconvening at the gym, three of them started drilling holes in all the devices. This alone damaged the vacuum-sealed units, but they needed to make sure the equipment could not be forensically reconstructed. Dud, a quantum molecular dynamics scientist with a background in chemistry, took the lead by improvising a corrosive solution that filled a large tub halfway.

"Okay, let's kill this stuff!" he instructed. "Be careful!"

"I brought gloves...thick, PVC ones, chemical resistant," said Katherine, a physicist and mathematician.

"Always thorough, dear Kathy!" chuckled Frank, another physicist. "Hey, what's in there? God, it stinks!" he added.

"A superacid—child's play. Some components inside the storage units are polypropylene and polyethylene coated, so they're quite resistant to acid. But this will melt those suckers! Even carbon nanotubes can be dissolved by this type of acid," Dud said proudly.

Three of the scientists put on the gloves and gently dumped the equipment into the acid bath, avoiding splashing.

"Oh, by the way," added Dud. "There are many factors that can affect these PVC gloves, like the duration of the exposure to the super-acid, the temperature, the specific mixture of chem…"

"Straight to the point, Dud. You're always beating around the bush. Tell us what you mean, now!" interrupted Katherine, impatiently.

"Alright, alright! No need to get bossy! Just that if the gloves start feeling hot…well, take them off and throw them in the tub, ASAP. That was all…" he complained.

"Oh dear!" said Katherine, rolling her eyes.

"Breathe, Kathy, breathe," chuckled Steve.

"I wouldn't recommend that," commented Dud, casually. "The acid vapors are harmless at air concentrations of five parts per million, but when you get a runny nose and start tearing up and coughing, as we will do now, then it means the fumes are around ten to fifty parts per million and…"

"Okay, hurry up, and let's go," said Katherine.

Air bubbles surfaced as the acid penetrated inside the units, corroding the electronics and making the information irretrievable by any means. They threw in the gloves, too.

They joined Ariel and the other researchers in the main lab. Now they needed to disable their highly specialized hardware.

"Ladies and gentlemen, this is a far bigger challenge," began Ariel. "Most of our equipment is too big to move or destroy with an explosion."

"Not even a small one? Does anyone here know about that shit? Sue? Dud? Vera?" questioned Alan, a theoretical physicist and cosmologist.

"I know nothing about explosions, just the Big Bang," Vera giggled softly.

"What if we start a fire with a short-circuit?" commented Maggie, quantum physicist and astronomer. "That should be a feasible 'accident'. But it would attract the Fire Department and the Police—the last thing we need at the moment."

"Come on, guys! Let's keep it simple," jumped in Sue, one of their top computer engineers. "Let's just remove the customized key components that are not industry standard and destroy them mechanically. Cheap and effective."

"Agreed! I'll go grab some good old-fashioned sledgehammers from the hardware store," said Donald, a mathematician and computer scientist.

After smashing the parts, each took small sets of different components and dumped them at random landfills all over the Bay Area. The entire process took them 24 hours, nonstop.

Their escape instructions were sent to their mobile devices. Since they were still dismantling the lab, none of them bothered to check them until they returned home to their families.

Ariel's instructions read:

> *Dear Mr. Ezra,*
>
> *Thank you for doing business with Reality Trips!*
>
> *Your private tour "Historic Route 66" will transport you and your family down memory lane—perfect for exploring some of the main attractions of the area. You'll enjoy beautiful landscapes and picturesque towns frozen in time.*
>
> *In just ten days, this tour allows you to see the richness of our history and diversity of the landscape.*

We recommend bringing sleeping bags and camping gear for the exciting one-night stay in our campground with beautiful places to spend the day and swim, fish, or grill!

Your hotels have all been prepaid; we beg you to stick to the schedule for your best traveling comfort.

Your exciting vacation itinerary is attached.

We hope you'll love the experience and will plan your next vacation with us.

Sincerely,

Reality Trips Vacation Agency.

Opening the attachment, he studied the itinerary: a ten-day road trip, starting in Southern California and culminating at the Totem Pole Park near Foyil, Oklahoma.

But how would they be extracted? Foyil was a long way from the equator. It wasn't even close to the ocean, where they could board a submarine or stealth boat to get out of the country.

"Is this a joke? Hmm…I guess we're in for a very interesting ride," he told himself, but decided not to share his concerns with Chloé.

Over 400 miles away, their first stop was San Bernardino, where they were scheduled to arrive that night, and it was already 1600 hours. He hadn't slept for over thirty-six hours and needed a shower, badly. They packed in a rush and jumped in the car. Chloé reclined in the passenger seat, while in the back seat Ariel cleaned himself, best as he could, with moist wipes.

It was a horrible ride. Exhausted and stressed, he tried to rest to no avail. With the car in self-driving mode, Chloe had closed her eyes, but he couldn't tell if she was actually sleep, just like the first time they met.

Ariel had landed at Stanford Medical for an emergency gallbladder surgery that forced him to stay over a couple of days. He woke up during the wee hours on his last night, after many hours of sleep, and decided to go for a walk pushing the IV pole that held his bag of fluids. On the way back, he noticed someone asleep on a couch in the adjacent hallway. A ponytail of luscious golden hair spilling over a shoulder attracted his attention. He stopped to admire the Greek nose and wide lips, but soon his eyes followed the queue onto her chest, which the scrubs did a shoddy job of concealing. Sure that she was asleep, he allowed his eyes to wander, prying on her figure.

"Can I help you Mr. Ezra?" she asked with a smile on her lips, her eyes still closed.

"Oh!" he said, overwhelmed with guilt. "No...I mean...nothing...I didn't mean to stare...sorry, I thought you were asleep."

She opened her eyes wide, pulled her upper body forward, bent her knees, and put her arms around them, fully alert.

"I was just practicing meditation," she said with an ample smile. "For some silly reason this position works better for me than sitting."

The embarrassment of the situation was almost unbearable for Ariel.

"I'm very sorry!" he apologized and weaseled towards his room, fumbling with the pole's wheels.

With an agile move she stood up and followed him.

"How are you feeling?" she asked in a professional tone.

"Only a bit of pain," he said, trying to be brave.

"Exercise is good for you at this stage."

"Can I go hike the Dish?" he joked, referring to a well-known local hiking trail.

"Love that place!" she smiled, dispensing with the professionalism. "I go there often. You should be well enough to return in a few days."

After leaving the hospital, he frequented the trail as often as he could until finally running into her. Soon, he asked her out to dinner at a cozy Italian trattoria in Sausalito with breathtaking views of San Francisco. They started dating soon after.

"I know you're awake, Ari. You're not fooling me with those closed eyelids, baby. Try to sleep while we can; I'll do the same," Chloé said, bringing him back to the present.

Ariel opened one eye.

"Hey, you just woke me up!" he joked. "Okay, I'll try. Thanks, sweetie," he added with a wink.

Able to sleep only a few minutes at a time, he drifted in and out of consciousness, waking up at the slightest vibration of the vehicle or a small bump in the road. Giving up, he rested with his eyes closed, analyzing every possible angle of their complicated situation.

Although an Israeli immigrant, he would—no doubt—be held to his US citizenship obligations. Even if he wasn't, Chloé was US born. If they wanted to leave the country, it would only be as fugitives. Besides, the Initiative's legal team would have considered every possible aspect already. This had to be their best option.

Bothered by the unusual location of their extraction point, he wondered whether the Space Initiative would leave him to rot on

Earth. No, impossible! Yet, would they go to war to save him? No human life was worth a conflict where billions could die. And what about Federico? After a working relationship of over twenty years, he couldn't imagine being thrown under the bus by him. He must have a plan, a great one, Ariel hoped.

It was close to midnight when they arrived at the Wigwam Motel[82], their first landmark on Route 66. The robot at the front desk checked them in and provided keys and instructions for their teepee. Once inside, they dropped on the bed with their clothes on and slept for six wonderful hours.

The next morning, Ariel got the hot shower his body was screaming for and groomed himself, steam filling the air like in a sauna. His black eyes stared back at him from the foggy mirror. He had barely aged during the twenty-five years since leaving college. Dark, unruly hair and big eyes set in a long and triangular head, and, thanks to their indulging lifestyle and frequent culinary adventures, his face looked fuller. He touched the freshly shaved, smooth skin of his cheeks and chin.

"Is all this worth it?" he asked the face in the mirror.

The world seemed vividly complicated that morning. It would be jail forever if caught fleeing. They both had great jobs and a wonderful life together on Earth. He could surely find other opportunities if his line of research came to an end. Was it worth it to risk all that, including their lives, just to escape to continue his work and live on a rotating habitat in space?

Humanity's future belonged in space, he was sure. Human beings would go on and conquer the universe. His discovery would contribute to maintaining a unified civilization that wouldn't fragment into multiple factions, leading to wars and death.

Quantum computers had been available for over a hundred years, and they had gotten incredibly powerful. But now that they would be able to communicate across any distance without time delay, people would be able to talk to each other across the vastness of space.

In the future, colonists would be able to converse with people back home from Alpha Centauri, 4.5 light-years away, as they did among themselves today.

"This process would be replicated across every star in the Milky Way and who knows how many galaxies across the universe!" Ariel mused.

Coalescing into some sort of universal supercomputer, all these linked quantum-nodes across the cosmos would store the entirety of humanity's knowledge. But none of it would happen unless they pushed forward.

The yearning to continue his work was almost painful. The answer was clear. They had to get out or die trying. He wanted to be in the first interstellar ship to Alpha Centauri, dyson it, and move on to the next star. He hadn't discussed this with Chloé, but he didn't have to. Their souls were akin; he knew she'd join him, but there would be plenty of time to ask her.

Recovered and clean, he considered leaving their dirty clothes behind, as they wouldn't bring them in whatever vehicle was used to extract them. In the end, he thought better of it; their vacation cover would be more believable. They filled up a laundry bag, got dressed, and left.

While on an economic mission to strengthen ties with Asian nations along the Pacific rim, Senator Perez and his staff left their hotel in Singapore under the cover of night with the complicity of their security detail. Boarding a supersonic jet chartered by the Space Initiative, they landed on the island of Ambon less than an hour later.

Part of the Maluku province of Indonesia, Ambon was close enough to the equator for a spaceport. Joined by their Secret Service escort, they all boarded the ascension vehicle cradled between hydrogen balloons towards the skyhook fifty kilometers above. They reached the Port of Entry before their absence was noticed at breakfast the next morning.

Pictures and videos of the president of the United States (POTUS), posted by the media during a press conference the next day, showed a man smoldering with rage, bulging veins on his temples, a tight frown, and glittering with sweat.

'A US senator! Defectors, traitors! But their Secret Service...?' the president thought. Alone, back in the Oval Office, he treaded and pounded over the thick carpet—his fists clenched and the tight skin over his knuckles white.

He couldn't hold Singapore accountable, as they were not even aware of the incident.

In a blind bout of rage, he lost control of himself; his foot smashed through a side of the historic Teddy Roosevelt desk in the Oval Office when he kicked it with all his might. If they couldn't even rely on the patriotism of the Secret Service, they were knee-deep in very stinky fecal matter!

Demanding they go through additional extensive psychological evaluations, he ordered an immediate review of the entire organization to determine which agents were most likely to crack and to have them dismissed immediately.

After instructing his ambassador to log a complaint against the Space Initiative at the UN Security Council, POTUS signed an executive order banning international travel for the entire legislative branch amidst a flurry of complaints from both chambers. Then, during a national address a few days later, he issued an ultimatum to the Space Initiative.

"Cease taking our citizens, or we will take military action!" And later in the address, "In these uncertain times, when the well-being of our nation is in peril, it has been deemed crucial to our survival that we reinstate the draft. Effective immediately, all able-bodied men and women, ages seventeen and up, will be conscripted into the armed forces until this crisis subsides."

Watching the address live, the chairman promptly reached out to the leaders of China and Russia to secure their support in case of a unilateral US aggression. He hoped for a peaceful resolution, but, if they faced the might of the US military, the other two superpowers would help balance the engagement.

Rotating habitats in space weren't all too vulnerable; they were equipped with powerful lasers to destroy asteroids and comets that got close by. A missile launched from Earth would have to first escape the planet's gravity-well, and they would be able to track it long before it became a threat.

However, the rotational speed of the cylinder itself packed enough energy to destroy it, if a single missile got through their defenses. The stress on the structure created by the centripetal force, added to the weight of everything inside, would make it tear itself apart with a strong enough impact, like a nuclear warhead.

Flying in all directions, debris would impact neighboring habitats only a kilometer apart. One lucky shot could trigger a chain reaction that would destroy all cylinders. Although this was a low probability scenario, it had to be taken very seriously with over seventeen billion people living in space.

The chairman decided it was now time to acquiesce to the multiple requests from his military strategists and take the necessary steps to prepare for a US preemptive strike.

"Bastards!" yelled Federico. "I don't remember them complaining when it was their rejects—the scorned and the scapegoats that we took! The poor..." He didn't finish the phrase; his chest heaved, and he opened his mouth repeatedly, gasping for air.

A coughing fit shook him spreading through his entire body. Flashes of tiny lights popped in front of his eyes. He covered his mouth, feeling suddenly weak and queasy. Enduring the urge to throw up, he made a vague gesture of apology and rushed to the bathroom.

Patrice was not a doctor but recognized the signs elicited from Federico's ongoing age-reversal procedure. Having gone through it over seventy years earlier, she was looking younger than Federico ever knew her. She had tossed away the reading glasses she once depended on so much, and her skin was as smooth as that of any thirty-year-old.

He came back into the office, grabbing a handful of white napkins, tears blurring his dark eyes.

Looking weaker than before, he dragged his thin body through the office and dropped heavily onto the couch.

"I picked the worst time to go through with the age-reversal procedure,' he thought, hurting.

Pacing around the room, she glanced at him. Patrice continued the dialog without transition, as if he had never left the room, hiding her concern.

"It was a big mistake to belittle and neglect them!"

He wiped his teary eyes and nodded in agreement, still gasping for air.

"I feel like having a cup of tea. I'll bring you some coffee," she said, skillfully avoiding the risk of hurting Federico's pride with any remark about his health. She fixed and brought the beverages and sat beside him, patting his back gently. She still remembered how weakened and diminished she felt during that period and wished Federico would slow down.

"What about your program for buying nonviolent offenders out of their prison sentences...what was it...Funds for Freedom?" asked Federico, clearing his throat.

Most people in prison had committed minor offenses but were still left to rot in jail. A few years back, Patrice came up with the idea of offering prisons twice the total amount of money they expected to make off a prisoner in exchange for their immediate release after the original sentence was served. The Initiative would then offer asylum, which was accepted 75 percent of the time. A few years later, it was formalized into the FxF Program.

It soon became a success. Eager to participate, prisons shared their inmate rosters with the FxF program manager because, in addition to making more money off each inmate, it allowed them to free up more room for new ones.

"The program was frozen after the chairman issued the order to stop immigration from the United States."

"Well, they'll be throwing lots of would-be defectors in jail. And, as usual, we could buy their sentences out. Maybe pay them even more to keep their mouths shut."

"Funny, I never thought it was that obvious! I had the same thought, but I'm afraid if I run it by the chairman, he'll say no," said Patrice.

"What about people from other countries?"

He rested the fingertips of his left hand lightly over his forehead and ran them slowly back and forth.

"Oh, they keep coming in hordes! All the skyhooks are working at full capacity."

Instead of the mess of synchronized rotating skyhooks a century earlier, they now had just three of them, each 30,000 kilometers long, made of carbyne, non-rotating, and hung at geostationary orbit above equatorial points. This cut the trip to the Port of Entry from seventy-two hours down to between seven and eight. Getting to space was now comparable to a commercial flight. Even though each could only be used for a short window of time per day, they were capable of carrying a load of thousands of transports going up and down simultaneously with each transport able to carry hundreds of people.

"I'm a bit worried," he confessed. "I'm extracting my top research team. There's twenty of them, but, adding their families, the number seems to climb each time I check. It's up to fifty-three now."

She raised an eyebrow.

"Oh, don't worry! It's been cleared by the chairman," he rushed to explain. He started to feel queasy again but continued talking. "I broke them down into groups, so each team member travels separately with their own family on a different route."

"I'm sure they planned each and every extraction carefully," she said.

"Yes. But there's twenty different things that can go wrong. I might need your help and expertise to extricate some from prison if they are caught," he said.

"I'm surprised at the large number."

"It's not that big. How many people did you get out with Perez, twenty-five?"

"How do you know...? Oh, I remember now. Of course! The chairman cut you off and dismissed that meeting. I wondered what it was really all about. Tell me, what were you about to disclose? And why is he keeping such a tight lid on it?" she asked.

Federico peered at her with sharp intensity, half-amused and half-desperate to tell her all about it.

"You do want my help, don't you?" she insisted with a mischievous smile.

Overwhelmed by an avalanche of requests, the underfunded US Office of Passport Services made a major screwup, clearing millions to leave the country before the State Department realized the bungle and shut them down.

Meanwhile, Canada and Mexico closed their respective border crossings. Neither country had enough agents to patrol their entire US border but offered to detain and deport any illegal US immigrants.

Trying to make it to Varadero, Cuba, tens of thousands swarmed to the beaches of south Florida. Windsurfs, wave runners, sailboats, body boards—any type of watercraft—seemed good enough to give it a try. Even long-distance swimmers and scuba divers with underwater scooters made the attempt. Cuba, which still had no diplomatic relationships with the United States, kept rescuing them from the sea and facilitating passages out.

When the Space Initiative started turning down asylum requests from US citizens, people ditched their US passports, purchasing fake documents from other countries on the black market and even marrying for legalized status.

The border wall was as useless at keeping people in as it was at keeping people from Mexico out centuries earlier. People climbed it, flew over it, and dug tunnels underneath it with retail power tools. Hardware stores and equipment rental companies saw their best month in ten years.

More than three million people made it to Russia and China where they were granted asylum. The Space Initiative allowed them in as citizens of those nations, despite US protests.

Checkpoint ahead!" warned Chloé, scouting ahead with a pair of binoculars.

Almost at Albuquerque, New Mexico, Chloé and Ariel had started taking turns behind the wheel since the announcement of the draft; one of them spotted the road ahead while the other drove.

Swerving out of the interstate, Ariel crossed over the solid white lines and barely made it to the exit on the right. Hoping the police didn't catch the maneuver from that far away, he continued through town, stopping the car near an ancient walking trail by the Rio Grande. Surrounded by the burbling sounds of the river, they waited in silence for the swirling lights of a police cruiser to show up.

"I can't believe they're setting up conscripting posts right in the middle of the interstate!" whispered Ariel, disheartened.

They were both over fifty, but physically in their mid-twenties. Age wouldn't matter if a person was fit; they would be conscripted if caught.

"What now?" asked Chloé exhausted.

Having missed their last two hotel stops, they had driven for seventy-two hours straight. Their next hotel stop was 150 miles away in Montoya; but with the constant stopping and roundabout detours, Ariel was sure they'd never make it.

"We can't drive anymore. Let's find a place to crash here," he said, trying hard not to sound discouraged.

Hard-hit by the exodus like many other cities, there was not a soul on the streets of Albuquerque. Amidst empty and dusty storefronts, falling-apart signs, and overall neglect, few businesses remained open. None of them was a motel.

Browsing online, they found a bed and breakfast still open near the riverbank, operated by the owner.

"Let's walk to it, baby," said Ariel. "The car draws too much attention."

Leaving the vehicle behind, they grabbed their backpacks and headed out to the deserted street for a few miles walk, as the sun approached the horizon.

An ancient colonial-style manor, the inn was owned by an older couple. Like most people on Earth, they were far too poor to afford the age-reverting procedure that was easily available to everyone living in space.

The elderly woman greeted them and asked to be paid in advance. Ariel paid cash, no questions asked. After checking-in with fake names on the guest book, using an actual pen, they were offered a frugal dinner meal. Ariel bought two small cans of sardines and a bag of crackers.

Arched doorways in the thick stucco walls led to one room after another. Discolored patches of mold and raw adobe mottled the once white walls. Ancient wooden benches lined the corridors around the courtyard. Taking over the stone-tiled ground, weeds grew at will through the cracks. Empty terracotta flower planters stood by each of the columns supporting the heavy wood beams of the roof. A dry and stained fountain in the center of the enclosed yard was surrounded by a few rusty cast-iron tables.

The place had somehow kept its old-world charm, and Chloé thought how beautiful it must have been in better times. Under the poor lighting, they glanced at the few other guests scattered around the yard, discreetly chatting or having dinner. Ariel noticed that everyone appeared to be fit for the draft and wondered what all those people were doing there but had no luck catching fragments of conversation.

The lady led them to their room, one of the many doors facing the inner court. There were no surprises there: an ancient bed with stained, grayish sheets, warped paint on the walls, and greenish bathroom floor tiles that smelled of mold.

A small table and two plastic folding chairs by the window became the dining area, and, after eating hurriedly, they sat on the bed. Ariel's legs were sore from the long walk; the extra weight of the backpack and his lack of exercise during the last years were taking a toll. Lying on the bed holding hands, they passed out almost immediately, their clothes still on.

Seconds later, or so it seemed to Ariel, they awoke abruptly to what sounded like shots fired. They jumped off the bed as someone behind their door yelled.

"Draft! Draft!"

Rushing toward the door, he cracked it open while accessing his mobile device. Using his NIs, he checked the time: 0530 hours. Out in the corridor, the old lady kicked on the neighboring doors yelling, "Draft!"

Ariel was glad they had fallen asleep wearing their clothes.

"Grab your pack! Time to run!" he said.

People were running in all directions as they left their rooms. Ariel overheard a man's voice among the chaos. His instructions were systematic and disciplined; a group of people moved on what appeared to be a well-practiced drill toward an exit.

"This way, everyone! Follow me!"

As they came out of the room, a big commotion—which sounded like a fight—was taking place nearby, but they couldn't see the source.

Following a rocky trail from the back of the house, the runners headed into the woods, scrambling behind their leader—a short, very agile guy who ran as if escaping a zombie apocalypse. Men and women climbed and jumped over the obstacles in the irregular path, vaulting over fallen trees and rocks, while he constantly encouraged the group to go faster. Once inside the woods, the group disappeared from their sight. Ariel and Chloé trailed behind, rushing to catch up.

Behind them were the dimming noises from the inn, but they couldn't tell if they'd been followed into the forest. They couldn't see the others, as the winding trail continued to climb.

Weighing on Ariel like lead, his backpack held him behind. After running for a few minutes, they saw the trees thinning out but still could not see the group ahead.

"Go! Don't lose them!" he said, breathless.

With Chloé already a good fifty meters ahead, Ariel used his NIs to send her a message.

"Try to find out where we're headed. I'll be just a couple of minutes behind."

Although the technology had vastly improved in over a century, it was still a clumsy form of communication. His message was relayed to Chloé's NIs from her mobile. The words echoed inside her head, as if she were wearing a headset.

Ariel lost sight of her before her mobile transmitted a receipt back to him. Then something pulled him from behind.

"I got a dodger right here!" screamed the man holding his backpack.

Consumed by abject terror, Ariel didn't think to unbuckle the backpack and run. Instead he shook, pulled, kicked, and tried to swing at his unreachable captor but was unable to break free.

That was it. He was done! Hopefully, Chloé would be able to continue to their extraction point, as he had shared the instructions with her in case they got separated.

"Let go of me!"

A sudden bump propelled both him and his captor forward, allowing Ariel to break free. He tripped but managed to stop the fall with his hands. Still close to the ground, he struggled with the extra weight to regain his balance.

"Run!" screamed the young fella sporting a bloody lip, as he helped Ariel pull himself up.

He didn't need to be told twice. Ignoring the protests from his racing heart and aching muscles, Ariel ran faster than he ever thought possible.

Moments later he looked around but couldn't see the boy. He risked a peek behind and through the trees saw a group of drafters struggling with the boy, who was putting up a valiant fight.

Despite the adrenaline rush that made his heart beat out of control, the shame and pain nearly overwhelmed him. Nevertheless, Ariel kept up the pace.

Chloé had finally reached the last member of the improvised platoon and asked where they were going.

"To the barge! Keep moving, keep moving!" the man replied harshly.

The trail opened and became wider. The leader stopped for a second, pointing at a gray-green patch by a riverbank, then continued running down the path. Ariel still lagged behind, but at least he could see a few people trickling behind the main group. Chloé turned her head, and he waved at her. He couldn't distinguish her features, but, when she waved back, he knew in his heart she was smiling at him.

Chloé spotted a flat-bottomed boat, hidden under a group of large bushes and trees. An oversize canvas covered the metallic structure on its exposed side. The leader, with the few men that arrived first, quickly removed the cover and jumped on.

A chill ran up Ariel's spine. They could be heading straight into a trap. Were they all guests from the inn? He seemed to recognize some of the faces from the courtyard the previous night. Their choices were limited, so he continued.

In the twilight, he estimated about thirty people on the deck. Chloé had been patiently waiting for him by the barge.

He finally made it, and, holding hands, the couple jumped onto the boat. They were the last to hop on.

The slow revving of the engine rumbled under their feet. They were moving, heading north on the river. A little girl sat in a corner, wrapping her knees with her arms. Soaking wet and weeping quietly, blood trickled from her elbow.

"Hi!" Chloé said, crouching in front of the child. "My name is Chloé. What's your name?"

"Maya," she whimpered.

"May I have a look, Maya? I'm a nurse. I promise to take good care of you," she said with a friendly smile.

Maya nodded, and Chloé put her heavy backpack on the deck before checking the girl's elbow. It was just a scrape, but it kept bleeding. Chloé opened the top of the bag and reached for the tiny First Aid kit.

"How old are you?"

The girl slowly lifted her tiny fists and displayed six fingers.

"A young lady! Well, this won't hurt a bit," Chloé said.

She pulled out a little package and unwrapped it, revealing a standard gauze designed to clean and soothe wounds. Chloe applied it to the wound and pressed a little bit over it. Maya gasped as if she was going to scream but stopped as the drugs on the gauze subdued the pain. She smiled in relief instead.

"See? The worst is over, sweetie."

After a few seconds, Chloé reached for a skin regeneration patch and opened it; then lifted the gauze and used it to wipe clean the area outside the wound before extracting the patch and covering the injury with it..

"Done!" beamed Chloé. "It'll be like new in no time! Where are your parents?"

Maya remained silent, but her eyes teared up.

"Has anybody seen this little girl's parents?" Chloé asked out loud.

None of the bystanders replied. Concerned with their own problems, most of them simply kept an eye on the horizon, scanning for additional signs of danger. Chloé gave Maya a thorough look. Her clothes were dirty, surely worn for a few days, at least.

"Let's get you out of those wet clothes, first of all."

"Maya, can you tell us anything about your parents?" Chloé spoke while she changed the girl's wet clothes with a pair of leggings and a tee shirt of her own. She rolled up the bottom of the leggings and folded down the waist until they fit the girl, more or less. The top looked big, but at least it was dry.

"I don't know," Maya shrugged, tears rolling down her cheeks. Chloé tried a different approach.

"Who's taking care of you?"

"My brother, Tommy" she said sniffling.

"Do you see him on the boat?" asked Chloé.

"He's not on the boat. He was fighting, back at the inn," the girl whispered.

Overwhelmed with guilt and remorse, Ariel struggled to swallow. The kid who helped him escape the snatchers did have a bloody lip, like he was in a fight before meeting him. Could it be...was it possible? Had he cost Maya her brother and guardian, the only person taking care of her? How would he live with himself from now on?

"What happened, sweetie?" asked Chloé, unaware of Ariel's struggle.

"Tommy yelled at me! Said he was older, and I had to obey him." Then, pointing with her index at the guy at the helm, she added. "Said I had to follow that man no matter what, or he would spank me," sobbed the girl.

"Come on, let's talk to him," said Ariel.

The leader of the group, a shaggy looking guy named Rob, turned out be the son of the old couple at the inn. He did this frequently to dodge the draft himself and help others along the way.

"Where are you guys headed?" asked the captain.

"My father's farm, near Tulsa," lied Chloé. "We'll be able to lie low over there."

"You need to be careful; the drafters are all over town," said Rob, shaking his head.

"We found this little girl alone on the barge. She and her brother were guests at the inn. He didn't make it onboard. What's going happen to him?" asked Ariel, with a knot in his chest.

"Most likely, he'll get drafted or jailed for resisting. It's unlikely we'll see him anytime soon. Listen guys, your best bet to get to Tulsa is to get off at Bernalillo and leave the girl at a social services office. Take a bus on I-25 North to Trinidad, then head East—avoid Texas—until you hit I-35 south towards Tulsa," said the captain.

"Oh! We'll never make it..." said Chloé in anguish.

"Look, I know a guy in Bernalillo...I can't promise anything, but he might be able to help you."

"Instead of leaving Maya at Bernalillo, will you take her back to the inn?" asked Chloé. "She'll have a better chance to be reunited with her brother."

"I could. Yes, of course. But I'll still have to call social services," said the captain.

"No! No!" cried Maya, clutching at Chloé's wrist with both hands. "Tommy said it was not safe. The man said he's not coming back. Take me with you, please," the girl pleaded.

Chloé looked at Ariel and sighed. On rare occasions they had discussed kids, having plenty of time ahead and a busy lifestyle that children were a burden to. Nevertheless, they both saw one or two in their distant future. But everything was about to change now—there might even be a war—and she really liked Maya. The girl had unleashed Chloé's maternal instincts with her dark eyes and curly hair that reminded her so much of Ariel's.

"Look at her! She could pass for our daughter!" she added, placing the girl close in front of her and laying a hand, protectively, on each of the girl's shoulders.

Filled with contrition, Ariel knelt down to face Maya and wiped the tears from her eyes.

"Are you sure you want to come with us? We don't know what's ahead; things can get tough," he said gently.

The child nodded, wrapping one arm around his neck and the other around Chloé's waist.

As Ariel hugged the child, tears of grief overcame him.

"We will take care of you. I promise."

Off the boat at Bernalillo, the newly created family walked towards the address provided by Rob. It suited them that the streets were even more deserted than Albuquerque. At their destination, they encountered a small general store built on the side of a centuries-old, weathered power-supply station. The owner, a middle-aged guy named Pete, had little by little transformed the station into a auto repair garage. Over the years he had acquired and fixed a couple of cars.

Ariel introduced himself, making sure to mention he was sent by Rob.

"Follow me," said Pete.

They walked to the yard. Maya and Chloé stayed at the store, stuffing themselves with stale pastries.

Pete asked a ridiculously high price for the ruin of a car he offered him, but Ariel was happy to take the deal; the clunker would not attract attention, and, in their situation, that was priceless. Besides, Ariel noticed the balance on their bank account was much higher. Most likely, the Space Initiative transferred all that money to his account to help him get out of an unforeseen situation. He just hoped the battered rust bucket wouldn't break down before getting to the end of their journey.

Foyil had become a ghost town long before the exodus; no one had lived there for the last hundred years. The rotting away Top Hat store and Tin Foil Cafe were among the few standing structures that were still identifiable.

After six days of eating energy snacks and driving and sleeping in the car without a shower, the thought that it would be over soon should have provided some comfort. But it didn't. Continuing on Highway 28 toward Totem Park, Ariel's fears about their extraction point resurfaced.

Around the park, construction platforms and tall scaffolding blocked the view from outside. Leaving the car off the rough road, they searched for an entrance to the site. Not a soul in sight. At the gate, a robot granted them access after Ariel identified himself. The Space Initiative leased the area, including the park and all encircling land for kilometers around, through a mesh of companies and shell corporations.

Decayed and crumbled half a century earlier, the park museum was now cordoned with plenty of danger signs. The only standing structure in the park was the derelict totem.

"What the hell are we doing here, Ari? The place is dead; there's nothing here. All this rushing, for what? Do you think they'll send a helicopter to pick us up?"

"You said the H-word," laughed Maya.

"What? Ah, no. Um, I asked what the *heck* are we doing here?" lied Chloé.

"Honestly, I have no idea," replied Ariel. "But I doubt it'll be a helicopter."

"Maybe we missed something?" she asked anxiously.

"I've been following the instructions to the letter. They're simple; it's not quantum science. There's nothing else, just a small history capsule on the monument. I'll show you."

He pulled out his mobile device and read the instructions out loud.

"Ed Galloway developed the park as a monument to the Native American...Pole was built between 1937 and 1948. Now follows a description of the building materials. Twenty-seven meters tall... more blah-blah on the materials. Galloway used sturdier building materials that were not available to original American Indian artisans..."

Ariel stopped abruptly and looked up at the totem pole with curiosity.

"Wait a minute. This thing is way taller than twenty-seven meters!"

They approached the totem pole. The entrance door was caved in on the side; its hinges seemed to be almost separating from the frame. The whole thing seemed ready to fall apart.

"Girls, keep a distance. I fear the door will plummet on us."

He shook and pulled on the door, trying to open it. The door came off the upper hinges, collapsing to the side and revealing a smooth, metallic surface. Ariel finished ripping the door away to find himself facing a retinal scanner.

"I can't believe this!" he said, taken aback.

He stared at it, focusing on studying the device.

"If the object under this totem pole is a vehicle, it could only be rocket," he said, dumbfounded.

"What? Those have not been in use for over a hundred years. That's even more ancient than our car!" she said, worried.

However, the polished surface looked anything but ancient. It appeared to continue below the surface, but it was impossible to tell how much deeper.

"But if this is a rocket, it's too small!" he said with a broken voice, fear now replacing his initial excitement.

"What is it then?" inquired Chloé.

"We'll soon find out!"

He leaned forward, presenting his right eye to the scanner. A door slid open immediately allowing them to walk inside.

Over a century ago, rockets had been replaced by the more convenient combination of ascension vehicles and skyhooks, which carried much larger payloads and required little fuel for course corrections.

"Have you ever seen anything like this?" asked Chloé.

"Nope, other than in photos and videos from my history courses. But if my memory is accurate, this rocket couldn't be enough to accommodate a single person, let alone the three of us."

"How do you figure?" asked Chloé.

"Baby, the destination is the Port of Entry, twice the distance from the Moon. A rocket this size can't make it."

What if there wasn't room for Maya? She wasn't included in the original count. They were only expecting him and Chloé. What if this rocket, or whatever it was, couldn't carry the extra weight?

Over the past few days, the little girl had imprinted on them. He realized how deeply her situation had affected him personally. He'd no idea what to do, if faced with a choice between leaving Maya behind and not getting off the planet at all. He could not, would not! Additional information provided by the child unequivocally confirmed Tommy was the boy who helped him escape the drafters back in the woods. Even worse, he hadn't had the guts to confide this to Chloé.

Because rockets had minuscule payloads compared to the total size of the ship, even a little extra weight would doom it to failure. He pushed those feelings out of his mind and tried to focus.

Lights went on as the door closed behind them. They stood in a claustrophobic service area with little room for all three of them. Embedded rungs in the wall started blinking in sequence, indicating a way up.

"I think we have to climb up there. You go first, Clo." Then he turned to Maya. "Come here, sweetie."

He lifted the child, putting her on the rung in front of his head.

"I'll be right behind you. Don't be afraid. I won't let you fall."

"Okay!" said Maya, clearly excited about the adventure.

Climbing toward what he expected would be the cockpit, Ariel followed Maya less than a foot behind, shielding her with his body so she wouldn't fall if she tripped. As they moved up, lights kept turning on, and the rungs continued pointing upwards. After fifteen minutes and a couple of resting breaks, they reached the top, some 180 steps up.

Interior lights slowly illuminated the area, allowing travelers to comfortably adjust their eyes to the cramped surroundings. In the shape of a truncated cone, the cockpit went as far as a meter and a half tall at its highest point. Laid horizontally, at 90-degree angles and meeting at the center, were four pods, each big enough for a human. Curved screens along the circular wall faced each pod. No controls, dials, keys, or any other kind of instrument was discernible.

Ariel's fears lightened.

The cabin was tall enough for Maya to walk standing, but the grownups had to crawl. Running towards the closest pod, Maya laid an exploring hand on its milky surface. Lit up on contact, the top slowly swung open, while the screen on the wall across it displayed instructions.

"We have to undress and lie inside," said Chloé reading the screen.

"I think the tremendous acceleration of—whatever this thing is—generates G-forces too high for the human body. I expect the pods will protect us from the shock," said Ariel.

About to crack a joke on having to undress, Chloé noticed a thin tracheal tube inside the open pod. Quite familiar with the process, she gasped in terror at the prospect of being intubated by a machine.

"Relax, baby. I don't think we'll be awake," said Ariel, as if he could read her mind.

"Yeah? How sure are you?" she challenged.

"Hey! Careful," he pointed at Maya discreetly.

"Right. Sorry," said Chloé. Then she motioned to the girl. "Come here sweetie, we have to get undressed."

They helped Maya inside the pod. A viscous, high density sort of foam lined the pod bottom and gave way with her body.

"How are you feeling?" asked Chloé. "Are you comfortable?"

Maya nodded.

"Now we are all going for a nap, alright? Close your eyes; that's it. Sweet dreams, Maya."

Chloé gave her a kiss and pulled away from the pod.

"Wait!" said Ariel. He leaned and whispered in Maya's ear. "Dream about your new mama and papa. See you soon, baby girl!"

Chloé rolled her eyes and mouthed at Ariel, trying not to laugh. "So cheesy!"

He managed a shy smile.

Maya's pod closed itself after a few seconds, and a friendly mechanical voice echoed throughout the cockpit.

"Please relax, and breathe normally."

The air inside the pod seemed to thin out, and the girl fell into a relaxed sleep. Self-attaching mini-electrodes and sensors detached from the inner surface of the pod and connected to specific points all over her body. After confirming the occupant was sedated, the breathing tube became alive and routed itself towards the child's mouth, delicately penetrating through her trachea. Once the intubation was complete, the foam inside the pod began expanding, slowly, covering every inch of her body.

Feeling a bit silly, Chloé smiled with a sigh of relief.

With Maya sedated, Ariel at last found the courage to confide the secret that had been eating at him for the past days. With a hand on her shoulder but incapable of holding her gaze, he told Chloé everything he knew about Tommy.

"Oh, Ari! I'm so sorry!" she said while hugging him tightly. "Now, I understand. But guilty as you feel, there's nothing you could have done. This is horrible and selfish of me, but I'm rather glad you didn't turn back to help the boy."

They cried in each other arms for several minutes before breaking apart and starting to undress.

"As soon as we get to the Port of Entry, I'll ask Federico to do anything possible to rescue Tommy. The Space Initiative massive resources. We owe it to him," said Ariel.

"Whatever happens, we will do our best for Maya. We owe it to her, as well," said Chloé, wiping her tears one last time before getting into the pod.

As she reclined, her body slowly sank halfway into the warm foam, snuggling her body from every angle. It surprised her how enjoyable it was.

"Do you think we can get a bed made of this material?" she asked in a feeble attempt at a joke.

"I promise," he said, leaning forward to kiss her.

"I love you," she said.

He pulled back, and the pod started to close itself, while the message repeated throughout the cabin.

"I love you, too," said Ariel.

Once the pod latched itself, she began to feel drowsy but managed to giggle and say, "Baby! It *was* rocket science!" and passed out seconds later.

Ariel finished undressing and rushed inside his pod without delay. As the lid closed, he could still see into the cockpit and heard the voice repeat the message. He then breathed in the sedative, falling asleep in seconds.

With the precious cargo secured, the activation process initiated. All over the ship, software and hardware components began waking up. A few minutes later, with all systems active, the main ignition sequence started, and the rocket blasted off with the force of a small nuclear bomb, incinerating Totem Park and everything else within a hundred-meter radius.

Shooting upward, it pushed the unconscious occupants to accelerations of up to 20 Gs until reaching Mach 35. Once outside Earth's atmosphere, it continued accelerating to reach a speed close to a million kilometers per hour.

Deep underneath the White House, the bunker in which Dick Cheney and Condoleezza Rice took shelter during the infamous 9/11 attacks over two centuries before had experienced multiple expansions and modernizations to nothing less than a state-of-the-art facility, suitable for long-term lodging. POTUS and his closest advisors were joined by his chief of staff, the secretary of defense, and the joint chiefs.

As they waited, the president reflected on the current situation.

Deterred by the threat of making it an act of war to provide asylum to fleeing US citizens, most countries deported tens of thousands to face capital punishment. Hundreds of thousands more were caught trying to flee and sent to jail.

Taking into account the jailed, the executed, and the departed, the US GDP shrank at an even faster pace than before. If the exodus continued, the country faced collapse due to underpopulation.

Unequivocally stating they would have no choice but to defend the Space Initiative if the United States initiated a unilateral offensive, Russia and China chose sides.

Meeting with POTUS at the United Nations, the chairman pleaded for a peaceful resolution, stating they had no offensive weapons and no military—only unarmed security volunteers and not a single firearm in the entire population. Attacking one of their rotating habitats could trigger a chain reaction that might destroy all of them, killing billions of civilians. Both statements had been confirmed by his intelligence services and military strategists.

Taking military action against the Initiative would collapse their economy even faster for it was the United States' biggest trading partner. They would also have to face the other two superpowers, and gone were the days when their military superiority was a powerful enough deterrent.

Blinded by his ever-increasing madness and enraged for being backed into a corner of his own making, POTUS was left with no option other than to retaliate with a preemptive strike. He would show the rest of the world their might and resolution. The duplicitous cowards deserved to be slaughtered like animals!

Both action and inaction would lead to the same outcome, he reasoned. In addition, the president was also a believer. Even though the date of the Apocalypse had been guessed wrong so many times over the past two hundred years, he was sure this time humanity was headed for the Second Coming.

It was time for him to come to a decision, and the secretary of defense stood by for an answer.

"We have pursued all the options. All our questions have been answered. It's our move now," POTUS began. "After careful consideration, I have come to the conclusion that we must act decisively to protect our way of life."

He stepped in front of the portrait of one of his predecessors, the forty-fifth POTUS, his personal hero and source of inspiration, whom he believed had been misunderstood in his own time. He had laid the foundation for the world they lived in today. There was no doubt in his mind how he would act in the current situation.

After a brief pause, he turned away from the portrait to face everybody and said, "Give them fire and fury like they've never seen!"

"Yes, Mr. President."

Despite the existence of the Outer Space Treaty[83]—which forbade any nation putting weapons of mass destruction in space, on the Moon, or any other celestial body—the Lunar Missile Station (LUMIS) on the US section of the Moon had been secretly built twenty years earlier and now housed a thousand space ballistic missiles. Like a massive machine gun, it was capable of firing ten SBMs every five seconds by taking advantage of the lower gravity of the Moon.

Each SBM had a rocket engine capable of accelerating to millions of kilometers per hour with enough fuel for complex evasive actions and fifty nuclear warheads, twenty kilotons each.

With the United States at DEFCON 2, LUMIS was already on high alert, all its SBMs hot and ready, when POTUS gave the order to go to war. It took less than ten minutes to fire all its missiles towards the first rotating habitat, where the Port of Entry was located.

Pointing at the Moon, the Space Initiative's telescopes detected the launch. Their laser cannons immediately tried to acquire targets to no avail. The SBMs used an evasive random pattern in their approach vector, making targeting at that distance impossible.

Except for Federico and the chairman, the board had been moved to a secure location at the L3 point weeks ago. But because of the 24-minute communication delay, they were unaware war had already started.

Alerted by the Space Initiative, Russia and China retaliated against the United States at once with joint cyberattacks bringing down every power grid and communication network exposed to the internet. All over the country lights went off, paralyzing businesses, factories, utilities, trains, airports, and all other forms of transportation. Airtight military networks were also crippled when spies deployed computer viruses onsite, immobilizing 80 percent of their ICBMs and conventional weapons.

Now within range of their targeting system, the SBMs continued their approach. Built to defend against space debris approaching in a straight trajectory rather than AI controlled missiles, the Initiative's lasers still proved to have a good striking average.

Able to sneak through the Port of Entry's perimeter, ten missiles deployed all their warheads towards the habitat. Even though they had no propulsion and were easier to target, hundreds of them at such close range made it impossible to eliminate them all. One directly impacted the cylinder and another detonated close enough to penetrate the hull.

Seconds behind, the remaining missiles retargeted toward the second rotating habitat, maintaining evasive patterns. When they showered the cylinder with warheads, most of them were taken off. However, one detonated close enough to its target, causing the outward push to rupture it.

Soon after the impacts, both habitats began to disintegrate when their rotation speed finished the job started by the nuclear detonations. Cameras in neighboring habitats captured the catastrophe. Chunks of metal, glass, dirt, water turned into ice, and human bodies were expelled into space. The catastrophe was broadcast to Earth without delay.

Expecting a sneak attack for months, the Space Initiative had increased the separation between their O'Neill cylinders, from one kilometer to a hundred. The objective was to decrease the chance that debris propelled by the angular velocity of a destroyed habitat would impact another, allowing the laser targeting system to easily destroy any shrapnel on a collision course.

News outlets all over the world screamed of genocide and cold-blooded murder. Still running on their backup power generators and hack-proof communication networks, stock markets crashed, leading to a halt of all trading after the DOW, S&P 500, NASDAQ, and all other major indexes lost 75 percent of their valuations within a single session. Confused, high frequency trading algorithms compounded the problem before someone remembered to shut them off, but the damage was already done. The crash later extended to European and Asian markets.

The reaction of world leaders was immediate. Many reached out to POTUS begging him to stop the attack, advocating peace. The leaders of China and Russia together reached out on the hotline, but he did not answer the call.

An official communiqué from the Space Initiative confirmed that two rotating habitats had been destroyed but the remaining habitats were intact. It didn't disclose the number of casualties.

But it was common knowledge that well over twenty million people lived at the Port of Entry and that the next habitat was nearly as densely populated. The message ended with a direct plea from the chairman to break the hostilities and initiate peace talks.

Unable to open his eyes, Ariel's eyelids felt like lead. His head was about to explode. A weird taste filled his mouth, and his entire body was numb and aching. It was like recovering from an epic beating. As his vision struggled to come into focus, he distinguished the blurry image of his beautiful Chloé. She was speaking to a man in a lab coat.

"He's awake!" exclaimed Maya.

Chloé turned around and slowly made it towards the bed, grabbing his hand. She appeared to be in some pain.

"How are you feeling?" she asked.

"Horrible," he mumbled, struggling to focus his vision. "What happened?"

"You're in good hands, Mr. Ezra," the doctor said. "Your vitals look good, and your recovery is normal. Be patient."

He looked at Chloé and Maya, who appeared to be in much better shape.

"Women have more resilient bodies. Their recovery is faster, as it is for children," explained the doctor. "I want you out of bed and on physical therapy as soon as you can stand up," advised the doctor before leaving the room.

Ariel looked at Chloé. "Tell me everything, baby."

"We spent twenty-seven days unconscious," she began.

"Whoa! No wonder!"

After almost a month hibernating in zero gravity, he had lost a good measure of bone and muscle tissue. He pictured his diminished heart, struggling to pump enough blood to his brain. The accumulated fluid in his head explained his vision impairment and everything else he was experiencing.

"Due to an imminent attack from the United States, all government functions and critical personnel were moved from the Port of Entry to this habitat at the L3 Lagrangian point. That's why our trip took so long!"

"So, is the chairman here?"

"No, he's at an undisclosed location closer to Earth. By the way, we are inside the first McKendree cylinder! You won't believe the size of this thing! There are oceans, mountains, and entire continents hanging upside down. It's a gargantuan beast of 600 kilometers radius by 6,000 kilometers long with a surface of over 22 million squared kilometers," she said excitedly.

Ariel was speechless. That was about the size of the entire North American continent, from Panama all the way to Greenland!

"How many people..." he started to ask, dumbfounded by what he'd just heard.

"They say it'll house five billion! But it's mostly empty right now. Only people who were evacuated, including the board of the Space Initiative, are here. A few thousand."

It was a lot to digest. Then he remembered something burning in his mind.

"What kind of vehicle was that?"

"A metallic hydrogen rocket!" she explained. "We reached 995,000 kilometers per hour after escaping Earth's gravity and still had enough fuel to decelerate before reaching the new Port of

Entry. You were right about the G-forces, by the way; we survived over 20 Gs."

Ariel was blown away. Since he could remember, there were always rumors that someone was on the brink of producing hydrogen in its metallic form, but the breakthrough never seemed to materialize.

"Are we at war?" he inquired.

"Not yet, but it looks like we are headed for one. There's no way to travel between habitats right now because they've been spread 100 kilometers apart. Reaction ships are in short supply and only available for emergencies. The chairman went to meet with POTUS at the United Nations."

"And what have you been up to while I've been unconscious, fighting for my life?" he joked.

"Adoption papers," she said with the most adorable smile. "Maya is being granted space citizenship, and we'll be able to raise her. That is, if you want to be a dad."

Ariel looked at Maya who was holding his other hand, imitating Chloé.

"Nothing would make me happier. Did you find out about Tommy?"

"I spoke to your boss's aide, a funny guy named Enzo, and explained the situation. He promised to put all available resources on it."

He looked at Maya who was looking at him with adoration, unaware of the seriousness of the situation. He smiled back at her.

"I have some more news that will definitely cheer you up," she said.

"My team?"

"Exactly! All accounted for. They caught ascension vehicles from different spaceports and linked with their skyhooks. They reached the old Port of Entry and were moved to safer locations," said Chloé.

"That is excellent news, baby," he said cheerfully, despite the waves of pain running throughout his body with every single movement.

"Try not to move, Ari. Your mobile is within reach, and I bet you've got tons of messages. Katherine and Dud are here, too; they came by earlier to check on you.

Through his NIs, he accessed the device which was now connected to the Space Initiative's secure network. He was glad to see everybody was accounted for, even though a few of them had inexplicably escaped from prison.

There was also a message from Federico.

> *Dear Ariel,*
>
> *I've been informed by your doctor that you are in perfect health, so I won't wish you a speedy recovery. I truly am immensely relieved that we got you and your entire team out without casualties. Please, take a few days off before going back to work while you can. Soon you'll all be working insane hours, advising our engineering teams in developing the first generation of FTL Communication Technology!*
>
> *We are calling it "Ansible Communication v1.0," in honor of the twentieth century writer, Ursula Le Guin.*

I'm looking forward to meeting you in person very soon.

With kind regards,

Federico.

Having just returned from Earth, the chairman met with Federico at their temporary headquarters, set in a habitat close enough to Earth to maintain a six-second communication delay, but far enough from the first cylinders which were most at risk in case of an attack.

"The man was radically uncompromising, Federico. I literally begged him, publicly and privately, for a peaceful resolution to the conflict. I'm afraid he wants war."

"We knew that beforehand, sir. We still had to try," said Federico.

"I know but...I guess I had hoped..."

The alert of the LUMIS SBMs launch interrupted him.

"What should we do now?" asked Federico.

"It's in the hands of our defenses now. All the necessary precautions have been taken. We are perfectly safe here. None of their missiles will be able to make it to this habitat. Let us wait."

A few minutes later they witnessed the destruction of the first two habitats.

"Make sure all news services receive copy of the footage," requested the chairman in a calm voice, as he started preparing official statements with his staff.

K3+

A cold sweat ran down Federico's spine. The Port of Entry had been destroyed! Even with all the evacuations there must have still been over twenty million people on each habitat, he thought, aghast at the brutal reality of what had just happened. Fighting the constant pain and fatigue, questioning whether they had done enough to prevent the tragedy, he managed to publish the content on the Space Initiative's official news channel and started reaching out to all major news organizations through his back channels. Soon everybody, including social media, were talking about it.

Forty-eight hours later, the United States had still not made a statement, and the president remained unreachable.

An oval office replica with all the bells and whistles was set up for POTUS at the underground bunker. Alone at his desk with a glass of Glenfiddich 1937, the president meditated on the current situation.

They had begged for mercy, but he had inflicted a crippling blow to the Space Initiative! Both habitats had been heavily populated. His strategists estimated over forty-six million casualties, and he relished this fact. He felt an almost god-like power coursing through his veins, followed by a deep resolve.

The US retaliation cyberattack against China and Russia was far less effective, causing only minor interruptions. Most of the spies, who were supposed to plant the viruses inside the enemy's airtight military networks, had abandoned their posts and sought space asylum. Others refused to carry out their orders or got captured.

With 80 percent of his nuclear arsenal grounded, he could not win an exchange against the other two superpowers whose arsenals were mostly untouched. It would be a very different world from now on, with the United States no longer a superpower. He had crossed the Rubicon with the first strike; there was no turning back, and no one could stop him.

"This isn't about winning but about the Apocalypse preceding the second coming of Jesus Christ to cleanse the Earth, judge the righteous, and destroy the wicked. I am the chosen instrument of the Lord, and I will have a place by His side, ascending from Earth's ashes in a chariot of fire, driven by the archangel Gabriel," he told himself.

A knock on the door interrupted his thoughts.

"Come in."

"Mr. President?" asked the chairman of the Joint Chiefs of Staff.

"Launch all available missiles towards their targets inside Russia and China."

"Immediately, sir."

As the chairman was discussing the situation with the leaders of China and Russia, they all were alerted that the United States had launched its remaining arsenal against the superpowers. Both leaders dropped off the call.

Federico, whose face was white as chalk, turned to the chairman. Although the answer was evident, he had to ask the question.

"What...what will happen now?" he asked in a broken voice.

"I realize this is hardly the time for a history lesson, but the first war took place right after the invention of agriculture over 15,000 years ago, probably when a tribe's crop went bad and they tried stealing from their neighbor. Ever since then, ambitious, volatile, and often inexperienced leaders—driven by aggressive instincts and selfish motives—have been herding their people into wars," said the chairman.

"Yes, and because humans are wired by evolution to follow their leaders and obey authority, those they led into battle paid the ultimate price," Federico acknowledged.

"Idolizing historians immortalized them, inspiring new generations of leaders to emerge as impulsive, ruthless, power-hungry, obsessed with treasure, and filled with bloodlust—each of them eager to take over in the quest for personal glory," the chairman continued. "Conflicts became deadlier as technology provided the means to unleash unprecedented levels of destruction. Nevertheless, aggressive and belligerent alpha males continued to wage war, regardless of the price."

"Are you arguing that war is inevitable because it's older than civilization itself?" Federico inquired, confused.

"In part. Please hear me out. Over the last two centuries, we had many flirtations with Armageddon at the push of a button, but somehow the Apocalypse never materialized. For example, in 1983, Stanislav Petrov[84], a lieutenant in the Soviet air force, singlehandedly saved Earth from a nuclear cataclysm when a computer malfunction indicated a first strike attack by the United States. The guy kept his cool and, disobeying protocol, did not initiate the retaliatory strike that would have triggered World War..."

"I think I understand your point, sir," interrupted Federico. "Having never learned the history lesson, not even the threat of mutual assured destruction was enough to prevent Armageddon this time."

"Correct! Even with a significant portion of its nuclear arsenal disabled, the United States still has enough firepower to destroy the planet, many times over. I expect Russia and China will be able to destroy some of the incoming missiles, but the radioactive material will still fall down to Earth. They will have no option but to retaliate against strategic targets in the United States, and the planet will fall into a radioactive nuclear winter."

"The survivors...we will be able to rescue survivors." Federico was clearly shaken. "We have plenty of room available."

"Yes, and we can also treat the wounded," said the chairman. "I had hoped he had had enough after he destroyed two of our habitats...that his thirst for blood would be quenched, and, with most of his ICBM's grounded, he wouldn't trigger a nuclear holocaust."

"Even with all the evacuations, we must have lost over forty-five million people when our habitats got destroyed. Those two cylinders were more densely populated than the average!" Federico felt about to faint. He dropped on the nearest chair and covered his face with both hands.

The chairman looked at him, pondering the best answer for a few seconds. It was time to let the cat out of the bag.

"Actually, we did not. Relax, old friend."

Federico stared at him with a quizzical look while struggling to get up.

"We've been concerned with a sneak attack long before this crisis and took preventive measures devised by our strategists. Instead of shipping close to ninety million people through vacuum tunnels, we moved the habitats themselves. Prior to increasing the separation between cylinders, we replaced the first four cylinders, the ones closer to Earth, with empty ones."

Federico uttered a cry of delight.

"But the bodies!"

"Dummies, wearing clothing. At such a distance, the resolution won't allow enough detail. Besides, we deliberately placed additional debris to make it look real," said the chairman.

"You saved millions of lives! That was a brilliant move."

"Well it's always a team effort, you know this. No single person can take all the credit," smiled the chairman.

"But I still don't understand how you managed to do the replacement without everybody noticing! I mean, an O'Neill cylinder is not an easy thing to move around!"

"With over 3,400 cylinders, we've been at it for a few of years. We needed to place four empty cylinders filled with dummies at the beginning of the line where they'd be closest to Earth. We swapped them one at a time from back at the end of the line so the maneuver wouldn't be noticed from the planet. By the time the current crisis started, the dummy cylinders were already within the first ten. After the last couple of swaps were completed, we detached all cylinders from their vacuum tunnels and spread them a hundred kilometers apart."

So simple! Not even the people living inside the habitats themselves would notice the swaps. At most, a few individuals might have been temporarily inconvenienced by vacuum tunnels becoming unavailable for a few hours while a single swapping was taking place. Most likely they did it late at night, and the whole thing would have easily been explained as maintenance and repairs.

Image by Katie Lane

"I noticed you didn't mention casualties in your communiqués," said Federico.

"Secrets can't be kept these days. People will soon figure out the truth when they realize nobody's missing."

"Sir...aren't we somehow responsible for this conflict? We kept accepting people from the United States, alienating the president even further. Didn't we precipitate his actions?" Federico asked.

With a sigh, the chairman mulled his answer once more.

"They made it an act of war for any country to offer asylum to US citizens. Many, including Russia and China, still welcomed the refugees granting them citizenship so they could apply for living in space. We just allowed citizens of those other nations to join us. But the big bully didn't pick a fight with them; instead, he attacked the weakest and defenseless first. Make no mistake, old friend, this was an act of cowardice like no other in human history! Had we not been proactive and swift, over forty million innocent civilians would have been slaughtered."

Had the chairman let those missiles through on purpose? Federico wondered, but didn't ask. He preferred not to know the answer.

Chapter 5: Fedrix

Extinguishing over a billion lives, World War III was the ultimate genocide. Ravaging the planet, atomic detonations sent climate change spiraling out of control. A nuclear hell broke loose when polar caps and permafrost melted altogether, releasing deadly diseases frozen for eons and triggering a complete disruption of the ocean currents that regulated the climate. Sea levels rose to devastate 30 percent of the land.

Scorching temperatures and radiation poisoning accelerated the collapse of food chains. Even worse than the detonations themselves, nuclear fallout precipitated the annihilation of 98 percent of all species. However, there were survivors.

Deploying a cloud of solar collectors to beam power down to the surface as low-energy radio waves, the Space Initiative helped stop temperatures from rising. Along with carbon sequestration technologies, these measures allowed the planet to cool down and restore the climate, while decontamination and reconstruction work took place.

Polar ice caps and all, Earth was cleaned and restored to its pristine glory just a hundred years later. Pre-war DNA banks made it possible to bring many extinct species back to life and restore some ecosystems. Greater life diversity would continue to evolve throughout the eons, but countless species were lost forever.

Survivors emigrated to space as soon as they got treated at medical facilities deployed by the Initiative around the world. In time, the home planet became a vacation destination. The nostalgic few who remained did so to safeguard the facilities and prevent tourists from hurting themselves. Most of the population was born in space, and, having never set foot on a planet, it was easy for them to get in trouble.

Little by little, all the O'Neill habitats were replaced by the new McKendree cylinders. Around the year 2400, a new milestone was reached: a trillion souls now lived in space in the first partial ring, made of 200 rotating habitats.

Skipping millennia ahead of evolution, genetic enhancements produced a breed of super humans capable of extraordinary physical and intellectual prowess. People looked good and felt good, no longer susceptible to weight gain or having to exercise to stay in shape.

Medical technology had been repairing any damage and curing all illnesses; and now the genetically enhanced population didn't suffer from either. In addition, it was possible to grow or to 3D print any organ, system, or tissue from the patient's own DNA; a person had to suffer a pretty bad accident to die.

The biggest enemy in this post-scarcity utopia was boredom. People no longer needed to work for a living, but the Space Initiative needed loads of workers in construction—mostly overseeing the work of robots and creating new designs—as well as in R&D, healthcare, maintenance, and government. Anyone who wanted to work got a job.

"Have I worked so hard I've forgotten to live? Forgotten to live and forgotten everything? Maybe what I need is a change of job? It looks like yet another long night ahead," a gloomy Federico lamented.

Surrounded by small trees and shrubs, he lay alone on his rooftop terrace bathed in glimmering hues of light as the day period approached its end. Thousands of kilometers away, megalopolises[85]—that he could see only with an optical instrument during daytime—came alive all around him in the night sky, forming magical gleaming patterns.

Listening to the whisper of leaves stirred by the gentle breeze, a byproduct of the strict climate control system, Federico sat with a glass of wine in one hand and a notebook in the other. A carved timber box rested open on the black-walnut driftwood coffee table. Centuries earlier, Federico helped a Turkish family smuggle the table into space after the war, and they had allowed him to print a replica.

After 470 years of new memories replacing older ones, Federico felt empty, left with fragmented and blurry recollections of his last years on Earth.

"Lights on," he thought.

Relayed to the UKB by his NIs, the command activated the rooftop lighting system. The floor, vegetation, and furniture lit up with a soothing faint glow.

In a desperate attempt to cling to his crumbling past, he began making notes. He had uploaded digital copies to the UKB centuries ago, but holding the now frail notebook in his hands made it feel more real and comforted him. He flipped through the pages, landing on a note that he had scribbled over 200 years earlier.

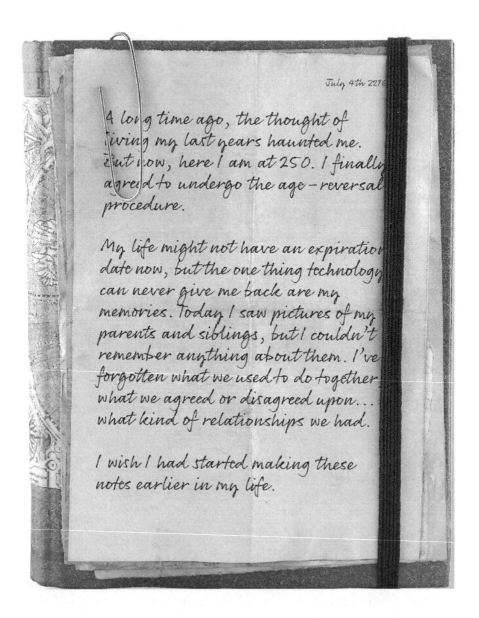

July 4th 227?

A long time ago, the thought of living my last years haunted me. But now, here I am at 250. I finally agreed to undergo the age-reversal procedure.

My life might not have an expiration date now, but the one thing technology can never give me back are my memories. Today I saw pictures of my parents and siblings, but I couldn't remember anything about them. I've forgotten what we used to do together, what we agreed or disagreed upon... what kind of relationships we had.

I wish I had started making these notes earlier in my life.

"I have always been proud of my awesome memory but look at me now. Forgetting is such a piercing wound!" he thought.

At his command, the UKB brought up pictures of his closest relatives. He could see the resemblance with his parents and siblings, but they were now strangers to him. He had tracked down many of their living descendants over the years but had never met them in person. Childhood in his hometown, his last New Year's Eve in Colombia, his life in California, his closest friends, and Yasmin—all had washed away, like water through his cupped hands.

"Ariel is at the front door," announced the UKB.

Federico didn't want to see or talk to anyone, much less to get up even to refill his glass of wine. The thought made him feel guilty. After their escape from Earth, gratitude turned into friendship, and Ariel and Chloé had made him part of the family. So Federico swallowed his feelings and welcomed Ariel as spontaneously as he could possibly pretend.

The UKB allowed him access when Federico sent a message to Ariel: "Come up! I'm upstairs." He stood up to meet his friend by the glowing terrace bar; Ariel showed up a short while later.

"May I treat you to a drink? A bite to eat?" offered Federico.

"Sure! You know me: always hungry! But it's you who needs food. You're skinnier than ever."

"Don't remind me again! As the UKB takes on more and more functions, it tells me constantly. It's like having the damn doctor living with me!" he retorted with disdain.

Ariel grabbed a beer and walked away from the bar, wandering through the terrace. He finally stopped by the inviting lounge furniture, admiring the sweeping view of the cylinder. He sat on a large, plush, beanbag-like piece of furniture that automatically reshaped to provide maximum support to every part of his body.

Federico grabbed a tray loaded with small appetizers and snacks delivered by a flying kitchen drone.

"Man, this place is so relaxing; I could hang out here every day!" Ariel joked.

Federico's look made him laugh out loud.

"So, how come we haven't seen you in almost six months. What have you been up to?"

"Ah, not much. Putting away stuff," replied Federico pointing absently to the box. "A preservation society is asking people for old objects to archive, so I decided to hold them in my hands before donating them. They'll create templates in the UKB so anyone can print copies on demand, but the originals will become human heritage."

"May I?" asked Ariel with curiosity.

He pulled the box toward him and rummaged through its contents.

"Wow! Printed books? I don't think I've ever seen one. You've kept them in mint shape," he said, delighted.

Inside, there was *Ringworld*, *Foundation*, *Star Wars*, *Rendezvous with Rama*, and a few others. Federico had read the digital versions many times throughout his life and remembered them well; but he couldn't recall reading his printed versions. If any of them had been a present, he couldn't tell; there were no inscriptions. Centuries ago, he had them coated with an atom-thick, protective film to safeguard them from the ravages of time.

"Did you know Maya is a member of the Larry Niven Society?" asked Ariel, respectfully holding the book in his hands. "They've created a *Ringworld* Virtual Reality that goes far beyond the original stories. You can explore the many cities at different stages of civilization's decay and become part of the storyline; it's a huge success!"

"I could lose myself in it for years!" chuckled Federico.

"Not me," smiled Ariel. "I prefer VRs based on historical events so I can experience reconstructions of humanity's past."

In addition to an extensive archive with billions of items consumable thru NIs, billions of VR worlds allowed anyone to immerse themselves in all sorts of adventures and fantasies, themed or mixed, where imagination ran boundlessly. One could be any gender, any animal, real or fantasy, and become a hero or work in the shadows in an almost infinite variety of worlds that made one forget real life existed. You could insert yourself into any situation—from space wars to medieval cities and dungeons—wield an ancient sword, or blast away with ray guns while wearing *Alice in Wonderland* clothes, a samurai's kimono, or Batman's suit. It was your choice whether to quest alone or with others—side by side with Super Mario, Kassandra, or Geralt of Rivia. Anyone could design a VR and immerse themselves in it; some spent most of their time in virtual worlds.

Ariel went back to the contents of the box. Unwrapping a protective cloth revealed a wine glass with the inscription "Chateau Montelena." Federico loved their wine but couldn't remember ever being at the winery, which was destroyed during the war and never rebuilt.

"I brought a few things to Terminus almost four centuries ago. I pampered them more than myself," replied Federico.

Ariel then unwrapped a champagne cork from a blue cloth dinner napkin. The image of a steamboat and the words "New Year's Eve 2016" were delicately embroidered in a sharp golden thread.

"Ah, yes. I have a video related to those. Well, at least the dates coincide, but I can't remember any details," he confessed, trying not to sound too gloomy. "I wish I could recognize the voice of the woman on the video. I think we were in love," he added in an undertone, now unable to hide his sadness.

Ariel wrapped the cork carefully, then placed it back in the box.

"Are you okay, my friend?"

Federico nodded. "Just tired. I haven't been sleeping too well lately. And thirsty. I'll get some more wine. You want another beer?"

"Sure."

Now feeling a nice buzz from the alcohol, Federico stood up, letting out a low groan. He rubbed his lower back lazily and went to the bar.

In his mind were myriads of photos and videos from his personal UKB storage. The oldest ones, over 500 years old, depicting his parents and older family members, had been digitized from old printed originals that were now gone forever. But most of his individual archive was made of photos and videos captured by digital cameras and mobile devices. He could recognize himself as an old man but not others.

He came back with the drinks and sat again beside Ariel.

"Take it easy, Federico. It must be hard not being able to remember important people and moments of our lives; it was too long ago."

"I can't remember my pet either," he said.

A matrix made of pictures of Federico and his cat was displayed in the air between them. Fascinated, Ariel used his NIs to shuffle through, chose one, and made it expand. The furry, dark-slate feline looked very affectionate. He read the tag around the cat's neck.

"You named your cat Darwin?" asked Ariel, amused.

"That's the only thing I know about him; but I must have loved him very much to have this many pictures and videos of him."

Overwhelmed with pity, Ariel commented pensively after a short silence, "I've never thought about it before. You've prompted me to reflect on my own life. I'm lucky to have my family close and that our lives are well-documented—even the scary memories, like those dreadful days of our escape from Earth."

"Young and wise. I'm glad for you!" said Federico affectionately, tapping Ariel's knee. "I never realized memories could be so important as time went by. What bothers me the most is being able to almost feel something, but when I try to recall the moment, it fades away. It's frustrating. A part of me died when my oldest memories slipped away. That's why I uploaded every single thing I could still remember—even the hazy, blurry memories and these humble, handwritten notes—to the UKB when it became operational to preserve them for eternity! But enough about me. What's going on with you?"

"We recently went to one of the big parties," said Ariel.

Partying around the clock helped many to escape boredom. Elaborate ceremonies and costumes matched every holiday on the calendar. Each day of the year shared multiple celebrations so there were always many ongoing parties. A random date, such as January 8, was Space Day, Hawking's Birthday, Alfred Wallace's Birthday, State of the Union Day, K1 Day, and many others—anything to keep people happily entertained.

"How was it?"

"It was tons of fun! We slipped from one party to the next until we had enough. Went home after two weeks," Ariel chuckled. "It's a great way to meet new people and escape monotony."

"I'm not exactly bored. But you're right; I should try to get out of the hole I've dug myself into," smiled Federico.

"Now, that's the right attitude! Time to create better and happier new memories, dear friend! You might also want to try sports."

There was no such thing as traditional sports anymore, as all kinds of new competitive games evolved with varying degrees of protection to the participants. Certain combat and racing sports were no-holds barred; the participants tried to kill each other, drawing billions of spectators.

"Sports? Hmm, not a bad idea. Maybe I could try something along the lines of gravity-free sports," said a pensive Federico.

A brand-new genre of zero-gravity sports had emerged. Many were variations on a common theme, such as catching balls and/or scoring with them; also, different combat styles were devised. Millions of leagues, championships, tournaments, and competitions went on and on, all year round.

"Well, there's plenty to choose from. But we won't let you become a stranger, so don't plan on disappearing on us again for so long. Chloé wants you to come for dinner tomorrow. Don't break her heart. I'll be attending a symposium on space colonization during the day. Want to come with me?"

'Not really,' he thought. But he knew Ariel wouldn't let go.

"Alright, yes," he replied with a shy smile.

The squinted eye of a waking dragon, the oval-shaped building hosting the convention center, stared from right across Promethean Square, where Federico and Ariel met the next morning. Two razor-sharp edges on the curved elliptical exterior, each facade was designed as sides of a diamond reflecting bright sparkly flashes, its silky surface smooth as liquid mercury. Translucent glass panels embedded at strategic angles allowed the light in. A thick, semiarch-shaped entrance was at the center with the whole structure balanced on top of three wide, semicircular stairs, ascending as thin layers which completely surrounded the building.

Having been a speaker at several symposiums and a hardcore fan of this type of event, Ariel rarely missed these venues, and lots of people came to say hello to him. They spent a few minutes picking and choosing a number of sessions to attend. Federico became excited by "Shields: The Final Frontier" by Dr. Reshni Chandra. According to the abstract, the speaker would go over the challenges and technologies to meet them. The bio indicated Chandra was an accomplished physicist, doing research on force fields for the last twenty years with many discoveries credited to her.

Federico had a fantastic day going from one session to another with Ariel and running into people he hadn't seen in decades. Chandra's session took place at the end of the day. Once in the conference room, Federico chose a couple of seats at the front.

The session started with Chandra explaining the obstacles shields faced on a ship traveling at relativistic speeds.

"She's amazing!" whispered Federico in Ariel's ear.

"Oh, yes! Such eyes! So smart, too."

"That's what I meant, not the eyes. But yes, that too."

Ariel glanced at him and said with a mocking tone, "Hey! So, you're not blind after all."

"Shhh! May I listen to the talk, please?" replied Federico, a guilty smile written on his face.

"Okay, okay, sorry!" replied Ariel, smiling naughtily.

Right after Chandra finished her speech and left the stage, Ariel stood up.

"Let's catch her before she leaves."

"So, you know her?" asked Federico.

"No. She a physicist, like me, but on the brink of overcoming a major challenge with starship shielding, which makes the Space Initiative lose sleep. Why would I know her?"

Federico stood up with a dumbfounded look.

"Of course, I know her, Federico! She's always busy and in a rush. Follow me, hurry!"

Ariel crossed the corridor to the exit in long strides with Federico on his heels. They walked quickly toward the exit from the main stage.

She had already reached the first step of the stairs leading down.

"Reshni!"

She turned around.

Federico's eyes were nailed to her thin lips and perfect white teeth offering a warm, inviting smile.

"It's so good to see you, Ariel!"

"Same here!" he said, smiling and kissing her on the cheek. "This is Federico Tarifa, a friend of mine, a workaholic, and as elusive as you are."

Federico shook her small hand, feeling a bit nervous for no rational motive. Maybe because her flawless, tan skin was so smooth and delicate! A Nubian nose and the most expressive dark eyes complemented her beautiful Indo-Oriental features. Their outer corners curled up slightly toward her temples, giving a dreamy look to those big eyes. Federico made a conscious effort to avoid sneaking a peek at her curvaceous body.

"Any friend of Ariel is a friend of mine! Nice to meet you."

"I'm not good at compliments, but I must say I could listen to you all day," Federico said sincerely.

He approached her with a truckload of questions and comments. Shielding had become the final roadblock to humanity's interstellar ambitions. But they had not yet been able to produce a force field strong enough to survive a collision with a pebble while traveling at 0.2c.

"Colonizing Alpha Centauri has been on my mind longer than I can remember. You're getting us closer to achieving that. Your interim solution, as you called it, is so ingenious, yet so simple: ice! I am impressed," he said.

"Thank you! Honestly, it all seemed logical to me. A layer of ice, tens of meters thick covering the outside of the drum, will absorb direct micro-meteor impacts, and a three-kilometer-tall cone on the ship's bow will minimize impacts from objects in its direct path by deflecting them."

Rotating habitats made ideal spaceships: they already had the infrastructure and comfort for long-term human habitation. They only required minor adaptations, such as power generators, thrusters for maneuvering and slowing down at the destination, and shields.

"The ship will still be protected by an outer force field as strong as we can build, absorbing part of the energy from impacts, but the ice will stop anything from getting through," Ariel added.

"Well, it will look like a giant white pencil in space, but who's shooting for style?" she laughed.

"Why don't we continue this conversation at home? Chloé expects us for dinner. There's enough food to feed an army, and she will be so happy to see you!"

He then turned to Federico. "I've been told this lady often doesn't bother to go home and sleeps in her lab, babysitting her experiments. We must do something about this!" joked Ariel.

Federico laughed. "I'll give it a try! Reshni, you'll need to have dinner at some point tonight. You're going to waste time deciding where and what to eat. You're elegantly dressed, and it would be a shame if you went straight back to the lab. Besides, I would be honored with your company, and your presence will make it bearable to be alone with Ariel and Chloé, who act like they are still on their honeymoon, even after three centuries together. Is any one of these arguments good enough?" asked Federico.

He offered his arm to her, elbow bent, like a true gentleman. She hesitated for an instant.

"You had me when you said, 'I could listen to you all day,'" said Reshni, with a broad smile and in a good mood.

She delicately placed her hand under Federico's arm, curled it back over it, and said, "Gentlemen, let's go. I'm starving!"

Chloé had prepared such a lavish dinner an extra guest made no difference whatsoever. The design of new dishes, safe mind-altering drugs, and inebriating beverages had become a form of art. Billions were dedicated to it. Anyone could sample them through their NIs or in a VR before consuming them.

With so many ways collagen crosslinks could be arranged to bind protein, food development was taken a step beyond DNA enhancement. Engineered protein derivates that weren't purely animal or vegetable anymore, but with irresistible taste and texture, had been created.

His lack of appetite evaporated at the smell of delicious cooking and wonderful company. Federico ate his way through an incredible amount of food to his friends' delight.

"So, what's stopping us from a dry run?" Federico asked.

Still in love with his job and visibly infatuated with Reshni, he couldn't stop talking. They had just finished dessert and were lounging on their hosts' ample terrace, chilled under a myriad of city lights arching along the sky.

"Nothing at all! We're just years away from finishing our probe: a small O'Neill cylinder made of carbyne, identical to the real thing but filled with sensors instead of people. Once the technology is deemed safe, it'll be time for the first manned interstellar trip," Reshni answered.

Carbyne was so much cheaper and stronger than the old Kevlar composite used to build the first generation of rotating habitats; they wouldn't think of using anything else.

Chloé raised her hand.

"It's not school, dear," said Reshni with her cute smile. "Go ahead."

"How do they stop the ship?" Chloé asked, uncertain of using the correct terminology.

"Oh! A huge magnetic field that acts as a sail is deployed in front of the ship for the initial slowdown. Then the fusion reactors will take it down to orbital speed and maneuver it around Proxima, the first star in the α Cen system," she explained.

"But won't the ice melt?" Chloé asked.

"Of course, but the ship will need to shed the ice covers upon entering orbit in order to harvest power from Proxima instead of its own fusion reactors, which will be almost out of hydrogen."

"We want to go!" said Chloé with the excitement of a child.

"I assume you'll be able to fit twenty million, like in the old O'Neill habitats?" asked Federico.

"Quite a bit less because the ship's systems, storage, and other stuff will eat into the living space. But I expect at least ten million people can enjoy the doubtful privilege of the first manned interstellar trip," Reshni chuckled.

"Why do you say that?" Ariel asked.

"Where to start? The forward acceleration, though gentle, will make it feel as if the floor is slightly tilted, 2.9 degrees to be precise. It doesn't sound like a lot, but trust me; it's enough to make you trip when you're not paying attention." She smirked, imagining a variety of funny scenarios.

Then, pointing upward, "This beautiful sky won't be there either. The rotation axis will be buried under layer after layer of equipment, materials, and other stuff necessary to kickstart our swarm at α Cen. And that's the only thing you'll see when looking up for the next twenty-five years."

"A lot longer," said Federico. "I suppose it'll be a few decades before the first rotating habitat is ready to accommodate people."

"And finally, can you imagine being stuck with only ten million people to develop a social circle? It'd be like living in a small town for decades!"

"I wonder what they'll call the ship?" murmured Ariel pensively.

"Oh, I'm sure it will be something grandiose. Space Cruiser Hope? The Long Shot? Or maybe a great name from history! Perhaps Magellan!" said Federico excitedly.

Minutes later, a slightly inebriated Reshni stumbled to get up.

"Thank you for a lovely evening, my dears," she said hugging Ariel and Chloé.

"I don't think you should walk home alone," said Federico, courteously offering his arm again.

"Oh, I don't intend to!" she said, holding on to it and kissing him on the cheek. "You're such a gentleman! How old are you?"

After such an unexpected and improvised date, Reshni and Federico were still together thirty years later, as humanity prepared for the first manned interstellar voyage.

Joining Ariel and Chloé, along with ten million other people, Federico signed up for the adventure. Intending to help dyson the sun's closest neighbors before moving on to the next destination and unsure if they would ever return to the solar system—much less to Earth—they planned an unforgettable two-month vacation trip.

Not having a great amount of nostalgia for the home planet nor having set foot on it since leaving for Terminus, Federico wasn't keen on the idea, but Ariel still managed to convince him. Federico resigned his post at the Space Initiative, and Reshni agreed to accompany him on their "Farewell to Earth" vacation.

"It's beautiful! You lived here 400 years ago?" Reshni was blown away.

Profoundly moved by their first stop, they contemplated the quaint little cottage shoring a peaceful lake. Federico had asked his friends for a brief detour to visit one of the very few places on Earth he could still remember.

"Space Initiative records confirm this was my last address. Four hundred twenty years is a long time, and things change. But my blurry recollections in the UKB appear to match this area. I think I was...happy...living here," said Federico, leading them through the backyard.

After him, the property had had multiple owners in the 170 years preceding the war; but was it possible that anything belonging to Federico had survived? They followed him inside, exploring the tiny house. Then, in the living room, something jogged his memory. Browsing through his pictures of the period, he found an image of Darwin, comfortably lying on a pillow by the fire with a peaceful, loving expression, like a ghostly presence from the past, staring at them across the unconquerable chasm of time.

The walls were a different color, but the brick fireplace looked exactly as in the photograph! Sharing the image with the group, he knelt in front of it with a flooding rush of tears rolling down his cheeks. Reshni hugged him, profoundly affected by the moment. There was nothing she could say.

"This alone makes the trip worth it," sobbed Federico, finally standing up and wiping his eyes. Taking his time to record every single detail, he uploaded the memory to the UKB in real time, where it would remain forever.

Visiting major cities, monuments, and natural preserves allowed him to create a fresh new load of memories from Earth. They climbed Devil's Tower, hiked the Half Dome, glided over the Angel Falls, visited the restored Taj Mahal, Easter Island, the Great Wall, and many other places before arriving in Bali. There they would spend their last three days surfing and enjoying the beach before celebrating Federico's 500th birthday.

On the southern tip of the Bukit Peninsula, Uluwatu had been a popular vacation destination for centuries. From the transparent cabin of the aerial vehicle, Federico marveled at the steep coastline, home to numerous coves and beaches and crowded with surfers. High limestone cliffs, risen from the ocean floor during the Tertiary period, bordered the shoreline in hues of yellow and orange under the glowing light of sunset.

Having no surfing experience whatsoever, Federico downloaded the skill into his brain from the UKB, and, although the muscle memory wasn't part of it, his genetic enhancements gave him increased balance and reflexes, allowing him to develop it within the first session. He wasn't very impressed, but surfing all day wasn't a requirement, and he could always go back to the boat after a couple of hours and chill on the deck with Reshni.

Catching waves on the morning of his birthday, they paddled over the swells as the sun warmed their tanned backs. An avid surf aficionado, Ariel stood up to catch a rising wave, and Federico imitated him. Federico's board started torqueing over the wave as he positioned himself in the sweet spot of the barrel with great ease. Gliding along the smooth, crystal-clear, emerald surface, he focused his balance and physical strength on the task. His skills honed wave after wave. Riding their powerful energy at full speed with the wind on his face and the ever-changing colors of the water became a most exhilarating feeling. His spirits lifted, and he began to understand why so many people liked surfing so much as to make a lifestyle of it.

Freed in his body and soul, he faced another wave full of joy, while skimming the foam with his board. Without warning, the green face grew into a towering wall that cornered him in a few seconds, making his self-confidence evaporate. The wall started curving into a tunnel, drowning all noises but the roaring ocean, isolating him from the world. Time slowed down, and he felt alone and scared. Ariel had managed to get ahead of the wave. Joy turned to terror when the exit of the tunnel began getting farther and farther away.

"I swear this will be my last wave!" he screamed, suddenly desperate to be on shore and walking on his two feet, just before the tunnel collapsed over him.

He woke up at a medical facility hours later, his left arm immobilized, his chest hurting like hell, and his traveling companions around the bed.

"Fuck! What happened to me?"

"Well, you drowned, dislocated your shoulder...and had to be resuscitated," answered Reshni. "Otherwise, you're as good as can be expected for a refurbished item!" she finished with a naughty smirk that cracked them all up.

"I got goosebumps when I heard you scream, right before that wave swallowed you," said Chloé.

"Where were you?" he asked. "I thought you were right behind me."

"I was. But I had a hunch and chickened out. I called for help when I saw what you were up against," she said, looking so ashamed it made them chuckle again.

"I screwed up my party, didn't I? All those people coming down to Earth for my birthday..."

"Not really. You'll be out soon," explained Reshni.

"In three hours, twenty minutes. Your arm will be in a sling for two days for complete recovery," added the UKB.

"See? We can still go ahead with your 500th birthday celebration, my dear," said Reshni.

At the edge of a seventy-meter-high cliff, the party was held at the Uluwatu Temple, joined by a large group of Federico's friends and family descendants who came for the occasion and to bid him farewell. The pain in his arm was under control with drugs, making the situation bearable, and Reshni stood by ready to help him.

Federico was in the middle of an animated chat with some relatives from his sister's line, when a tall dark man with Asian features walked up to him, holding hands with a beautiful blond lady. The couple was followed by identical twin girls.

"Federico! My name is Tae-Won Tarifa! It's very nice to finally meet you," he said, smiling.

The last name Tarifa had been adopted by others. However, Tae-Won wouldn't have made the trip from space if they weren't related. Overwhelmed with excitement, Federico shook hands.

"This is my wife Antonia," said Tae-Won. "And our kids, Kari and Rika."

"Very nice to meet you, too! This is my girlfriend, Reshni." He then stooped down, addressing the twins with "Hello, ladies!" making the girls half-hide behind their parents, giggling.

"I come from your brother's line. His oldest child, Andrés, also had a son named Federico. He emigrated from Colombia to South Korea. He's my ancestor!" Tae-Won explained.

Federico recalled images of his brother and nephew from the UKB. Tae-Won sure looked Asian, but, after analyzing his physiognomy in detail, some of his features could be construed as Hispanic. He also shared the dimpled chin common to both Federico and his brother. The public UKB profile had detailed information about Tae-Won's parents and ancestors, all the way back to Federico's brother.

Giving him a big hug, Federico said wistfully and with a slight tremor in his lips, "Wow! Your presence is such a wonderful gift! I don't have enough words to thank you for being here today. Please, come share my table. There are so many things I would like to know about your family, Tae-Won," he said, leading the group to a nearby large, round table. A drone visited the table from time to time offering beverages and party food.

The chairman of the Space Initiative suddenly dropped by to see them.

"Happy Birthday, old friend! Reshni, dear, you're dazzling, as usual."

"Thank you, sir! This night is full of surprises and good friends. I didn't know you would come," said Federico, standing up. "Allow me to introduce some of my relatives and their families."

"Oh, I wouldn't have missed it for the world. It's a true honor to meet you all! You must be so happy!" the chairman said, shaking hands with everybody.

Tae-Won turned out to be a superb storyteller and regaled the group with anecdotes from the Korean branch of the family and their migration to space. Federico was fascinated by the stories, enjoying every single detail. Some of his other relatives sitting at the table didn't remember Federico's siblings, and the group started thinning out as they went to check out the rest of the party.

"I realize we've been monopolizing the guest of honor and bored my children to sleep!" Tae-Won said with a smile. "Time for us to put the twins to bed. It's very nice to have met you, uncle."

They hugged and exchanged good-byes, promising to keep in touch.

Reshni, the chairman, and Federico remained at the table. Ariel and Chloé joined them after a short while.

"How's that arm, Federico? I heard about your accident," the chairman asked.

"Oh, it's nothing, sir! It's almost over, just a bit of pain now. How are things?"

"A lot of things have happened since you left. To start with, we have a new name: the Space Colonization Initiative. All government functions were spun off and placed in the hands of the people, where they belong. Now that everyone can instantly vote on any issue with their NIs and having most of the government functions executed and safeguarded by the UKB, there's little for us to do. I've been offered to continue as chairman of the new government until the next election but turned it down."

"Sir?" Federico was puzzled.

"Yep! I'm joining the first colony ship to Alpha Centauri! I will continue as a board member and will chair the Council while we build the new set of Dyson swarms over there. But most likely, I will continue on to the next destination when they're done."

"That's great news! A toast to that decision and welcome to the club, sir!" said Ariel. "Federico also plans to continue beyond Alpha Centauri. Chloé and I decided to accompany our mentor, as well."

"I can't think of better company than the four of you!" said the chairman with a wide smile.

"Three, sir. I'm staying," said Reshni.

"Oh, I'm sorry to hear that. For once, I don't know what to say," he said.

An awkward silence settled in.

"By the way, we've known each other for centuries. Let's dispense with formality. It's time you guys call me by my name," he added with a smile.

"Feels strange to call you "Leonard," sir. Sorry, sir. I mean, Leonard," laughed Ariel.

"Leonard? I didn't even know your name." Chloé said.

"Please, call me Len! I never liked Leonard," he chuckled.

Reshni kept silent and was moody the rest of the evening. After Federico's accident, they had all moved to one of the hotels on the coast. Back in their room, she felt restless and decided to go for a walk along the beach to clear her thoughts. Federico's body still ached and tiredness slowed him further. After a few minutes, however, he couldn't bear the uncertainty of her attitude and went to find her.

He saw the unmistakable silhouette of her body sitting on the sand, knees bent to the chest, her arms wrapped around them. He sat down in silence beside her.

She didn't acknowledge his presence but kept looking at the ocean, disappearing into the dark horizon.

His chest was hurting but not from the accident.

"Do you want to have a baby with me?" she blurted out.

Caught off guard, he mulled the answer for a few seconds.

"So you're coming to Alpha Centauri with me?" he asked with high hopes.

Four hundred fifty years in the past, memories of Yasmin had turned into dust long ago. For Federico, Reshni felt like the first love of his life. She was gorgeous, cerebral, assertive, pragmatic, and supportive—qualities he very much appreciated in a woman. What more could he possibly desire in a partner? He felt lucky to have attracted such a woman.

"I need to stay here to continue my work," she said. "I meant combining our DNA to have a baby."

"Who will raise the child?" he asked.

"Our baby will live here with me while you go colonizing the stars, or, even better, we can have identical twins and take one each. You haven't had children yet, which is a terrible waste for such a remarkable individual."

"Remarkable, yet not good enough for you to come with me. Flattery will get you nowhere," Federico chuckled. He didn't mean to, but the laughter came out hollow and sarcastic.

"I'm serious, babe! I really want to have a child with you. But I want to stay in the solar system to continue my research. And…I know I won't enjoy interstellar travel; I like it here. You're 500 years old; what are you waiting for?"

Fragile, noisy, and unpredictable, children scared Federico to death. And contrary to Reshni's assessment, he never thought there was anything remarkable about himself or worth passing onto the next generation. But watching Maya grow up and seeing Tae-Won's twins earlier made him sense he could be missing out on something wonderful.

Like an epiphany, he suddenly realized there wasn't one good reason not to.

"Okay, let's have a baby," said Federico cautiously but with increasing excitement in his heart.

"But in the old fashion way, without UKB intervention. I want to conceive it ourselves. You will get me pregnant, and then we'll transfer the embryo from my body to the artificial womb at the nursery," she said.

"Whoa! No UKB? Are you sure?" asked Federico, a bit alarmed.

"I don't mind the UKB stepping in and fixing the baby's DNA at the nursery, if necessary. But I don't want the heartless AI deciding what blend of our traits we pass onto our child. I want it to be as natural and random as possible," she argued.

At the dawn of humanity, newborns needed to be small and flexible enough to pass through the birth canal. A smaller skull meant a more vulnerable baby because of a less-developed brain. Finding that precise balance for a neonate to survive and thrive in the African savanna, as well as being able to pass their genes to the next generation, was the most amazing balancing act ever achieved by evolution.

But now that technology had taken humankind so much further, it seemed silly—even careless—to leave things to Mother Nature. Federico pondered the risks. Even a major chromosome defect would be easy to fix in the artificial womb. Their genetic enhancements extended the gestation period beyond a year, allowing newborns to be better developed with fewer vulnerabilities; birth was no longer a traumatic experience. Controlled down to the millisecond, artificial womb conditions were adjusted for fetus development, making the term "infant mortality" obsolete.

After brief consideration and happier than he was ready to admit, he acquiesced to Reshni's request.

Sex with Reshni had always been spectacular and seemed to get even better over time, which was one of the reasons their relationship was still going strong after so many years. Looking at him, not only with desire but with love as their entangled bodies created a vacuum, she smiled and pushed her sensations onto him at the climax through their NIs, so he could experience sex her way combined with his own sensations. For some reason, it seemed even better this time. They were at it for three days.

A few weeks later, his possessions packed and sent to the ship, they walked hand in hand to the access port elevator. They had known this was coming for a while and had had plenty of time to say goodbye. Nevertheless, Reshni had tears in her eyes. It was the first time he had ever seen her cry, and he loathed himself for it.

"I'm so sorry," he said, mortified, gently wiping the tears rolling down her cheeks.

"Don't be, dear. We've given each other these wonderful years. We'll keep in touch through Ansible and will never forget each other," she replied.

"Alpha Centauri is not too far away. If you ever change your mind, you'll be able to get there in twenty-five years; even faster, I'm sure, when shields improve," he said sweetly.

"You know you won't be staying in that system. As soon as those stars are dysoned, you'll move on to the next destination. Exploring the universe has always been your dream. This is goodbye for us, baby," she said, tears flowing again.

He placed a hand over her flat belly and gently moved it across. "Please, don't stop sending me news every day."

She nodded.

"I love you," he said, giving her a last passionate kiss. He then held her in a loving hug for a long time. They broke apart only when the doors opened.

The elevator inside a McKendree cylinder was more of a train. After luggage was secured and the passengers strapped to their acceleration couches, it left the station towards a soft curve turning ninety degrees up and accelerated towards the access port 600 kilometers away, reaching its destination in less than twenty-five minutes.

To Federico's utter disappointment, the first manned interstellar ship was artlessly named Interstellar-1.

"Seriously? So many great names to choose from, and this is what they came up with? What a failure of imagination! Why use such a pedestrian name when there were so many great ones in history to choose from?" he said out loud, triggering an outburst of giggles from the people around him.

Docked between two McKendree cylinders, on the opposite side of their south vacuum tunnel and tilted at an angle, the Interstellar-1 waited for passengers and remaining equipment to be loaded. The transport delivered them from the vacuum tube to the rotation axis where elevators then carried them in smaller groups to the normal gravity section.

Stepping out, Federico looked around. Somehow Reshni's warning didn't adequately prepare him for the ugliness of the Interstellar-1. The food production area along the rotation axis was buried under so many layers of machinery, equipment, and storage that the sky was barely a kilometer high. It was impossible to see anything on the opposite side.

Strictly functional, the ship was nowhere near as pleasant as the old O'Neill cylinders. No lakes, rivers, parks, not even a tree. Just austere, Spartan dwellings and facilities. No wonder Reshni didn't like interstellar travel! Luckily, they weren't mandated to have roommates!

After deploying the aft shield, a massive array of solar-powered lasers fired on it, slowly accelerating the Interstellar-1 half a meter per second every second towards the α Cen system. It would spend the first 3.8 years (3 years, 9 months, 18 days) accelerating to 0.2c. Then, 3.8 years before reaching Alpha Centauri, the mag-sail and fusion thrusters on the bow would engage, producing a similar thrust, slowing down to orbital speed around Proxima. It would take a little under twenty-five years to traverse the distance separating the sun from its closest neighbor.

A diverse bunch, Alpha Centauri was a triple star system. About 1.1 times the mass of the sun, α Cen A had 1.5 times its luminosity.

Slightly smaller, at 0.9 times the sun's mass, α Cen B had only one half of its visual luminosity. And orbiting the two main stars at a distance of one-fifth light-year, α Cen C (a red dwarf known as Proxima Centauri) had one-eighth the mass of the sun and less than one-five-hundredth of its luminosity.

Getting back to work as Len's adviser made Federico's life busier than ever—not that there was any lack of talent on the ship. Top experts from many fields and disciplines had joined the trip to help seed the Dyson swarms on our closest neighbor. But his 450 years of experience in the Space Initiative made him still useful.

He also signed up for ship duties, managing dozens of processes and helping test equipment. The thought of the mag-sail failing to deploy and not being able to stop the ship at Proxima terrified him. The Interstellar-1 would wander through space for eternity, but they wouldn't last that long. Running out of hydrogen and unable to power the life support systems, they would die of asphyxiation. However, it was a silly concern; everything in the ship had a ridiculous number of redundant backups, not to mention enough spare parts to rebuild it many times over.

After working sixteen hours straight for days, Len and Federico crashed at a bar one evening, drinking beer and gorging on raw chunks of Hamachi belly over rice.

"I'm making a statement: this is my favorite fish," announced Federico, holding the perfectly cut piece of nigiri between his chopsticks. "So delicious I can't stop chewing it!"

Leaps and bounds beyond the original yellowtail species that once roamed Earth's oceans, the extraordinary texture and complex flavors of this engineered version, paired with the aromatic hops of a delicate red ale, lifted Federico's spirits.

"Lucky for us, the SCI didn't cut back on culinary choices or recreational facilities. I'd be going insane otherwise!" chortled Len.

"Speaking of insanity, the baby's in an artificial womb. Amazing. I'm lucky, when you think of it," slurred Federico.

"It's been over two years since she's out of the artificial womb! You're drunk," said Len, sipping some more beer.

"No, no! I wasn't talking about my daughter but babies in general. I meant...back in our time...we were born the natural way...and yet, we turned out alright. Aren't we lucky? Let's toast to that!" added Federico.

"If you think you turned out alright, you have something else going on!" exclaimed Len with a hearty belly laugh.

However, Federico's matter of fact expression made him realize something else was going on.

"You talked to her?" Len inquired.

"To whom? Reshni or my daughter?"

"Zhanna."

"Every day since she got her NIs! My baby girl is doing so well!" replied Federico, proudly.

Like all children, NIs had been implanted in Federico's daughter later in her maturing cycle, allowing the child to start learning and parents to communicate with their baby before birth. Federico had joined Reshni through Ansible, every single day, talking to their beloved child.

"But Reshni...Ansible was okay, I guess," continued Federico. "A year ago, we were still in touch. Sex was still amazing but became more and more random. She moved on, met someone."

"You kept that a secret all this time? Why?"

"It's a tough subject. I miss her very much," confided Federico.

"You both knew this would happen," said Len, using an "I told you so" tone. "You should move on, too."

Federico nodded with his mind occupied almost a light-year away, concerned with how Reshni's new mate would shape his daughter's development. He was there for his child every day, but, as good as Ansible was, it couldn't make up for constant personal interaction, especially during early development.

"I've been meaning to ask you," Len said, changing subjects with the obvious intent of distracting him. "What do you make of the second planet on α Cen B?"

There was nothing alive on the only planet around Proxima's habitable zone. Its proximity to the star bathed the alien world in deadly radiation. Tidally locked[86] as well, one side of the planet was roasted in perpetual daylight while the other was frozen in eternal darkness. Furthermore, tidally locked planets didn't have a strong magnetic field, causing their atmospheres to be stripped away by the stellar wind.

In a different turn of events, the second planet of α Cen B had evolved complex multicellular life. About 1.3 times the mass of Earth, probes had revealed great life diversity, roamed by millions of species, but nothing on the path towards intelligence.

Back on Earth, there wasn't a call to make because they couldn't allow the home planet to be impacted by comets or asteroids. Rotating habitats formed protective rings beyond Earth's orbit, shielding it from outer space debris with their laser defenses. However, doing the same at α Cen B would fetter evolution because comets and asteroids were major game changers, like the dinosaur-killer asteroid that trashed Earth sixty-six million years earlier proved.

"I know this might sound ugly, but I'm firmly in the controlled evolution camp," said Federico. "I don't want another civilization to evolve and challenge us. Competing for resources will no doubt lead to future wars. No matter how much humanity has learned, our basic instincts still remain. A species shaped by natural selection will be as violent as we are. It's like sending two aggressive individuals with loaded weapons into a dark room. Sooner or later, the shooting will start."

Gulping half a pitcher, he continued.

"Furthermore, I strongly believe we must establish manned research stations to monitor the course of life on the surface of each and every single habitable planet and moon around a colonized star, so we can shape evolution away from intelligence."

"Wow!" exclaimed Len. "You don't want to take any risks, do you?"

"No, I don't! I don't care how evolved we think humanity has become. Just look at what we've done to each other throughout history and imagine what we would do to a completely different species with no kinship to us, whatsoever. And they would do the same or worse to us if they achieved technology!"

"You're right. The prospect is terrifying," agreed Len.

"I expect in the next billion years that we might finally encounter another civilization."

"You really believe that? I know that's a long time, but I think we're alone," Len said.

"I hope we are! But if we're not, I wouldn't like the responsibility of dealing with it. Meanwhile, we must eliminate every possibility for a species on a planet under our control to develop intelligence," Federico said.

"How do you plan to achieve your macabre plan?"

"Oh, nothing evil! Evolutionarily speaking, big brains are almost a disadvantage, requiring lots of energy. It'll be easy to manipulate selective pressures with minor tweaks to their environment, like varying the global temperature by a couple of degrees at the right time to mess with the energy budget of a species…something that will make it harder for specimens with larger brains to reproduce. Over thousands of generations, the genes for larger brains will lose the competition and disappear from the population, without the need for killing a single specimen."

"Some would still consider your point of view merciless," replied Len.

"We are imperfect beings shaped by a ruthless competitive process, vulnerable to illusions, selective perception, self-centeredness, self-sabotaging, self-inflicted wounds, and supine stupidity."

Unable to contain his laughter, Len banged on the table a couple times.

"I think you're playing the victim, the accused, the jury, and the judge of humanity! No more beer for you!"

"I know how it sounds. But make no mistake, my friend. A technologically capable alien species will be shaped by the same process, creating beings very much like us in order to cross the ultimate great filter. The lessons from World War III have already been forgotten and will not help us prevent a future clash between spacefaring civilizations."

Len found this impossible to argue, yet satisfied with achieving his objective, he ordered two more beers and switched subjects once more.

"I understand the reasons Proxima was chosen as the starting point. But given the proximity of the other two stars in the system,

I was wondering if there's a way we can work on all three stars at the same time."

Although it would be easier to start with the yellow dwarfs because of their similarity to the sun, at least ninety percent of stars within a twenty-light-year radius—along with the vast majority of stars in the Milky Way—were tiny red dwarfs akin to Proxima. So, it made sense to start with it to develop and tune the process.

"Funny you ask. There's actually a dissertation on the subject by one of our passengers, Dr. Bev Dijkstra," answered Federico. "She developed a method to colonize double stars in parallel. In a nutshell, we ship equipment to the second star and operate it remotely through our own UKB node and people with VR interfaces. Alpha Centauri is a triple system, but the same principles obviously apply."

The Interstellar-1 was carrying a nano UKB node with plenty of capacity and computing power to run their operations until the Proxima node was built.

"I saw it, too!" said Len. "I was wondering if we could recruit more people for the task. Teams from back home to do the work through Ansible? Would something like that work?"

Most of the construction and mining tasks for building a Dyson swarm were automated, requiring minor human intervention. But with millions of these running in parallel, they needed millions of people. Multiply by three stars and the number would easily go over the ten million people onboard, assuming everyone on the ship was qualified and willing to work.

"You mean getting bored people back home to do the additional work, multiplying our capacity?" he laughed.

"Now, seriously, Federico. Put that beer down! Do you really think it's feasible?"

"It's a brilliant idea! Our engineers use either VR or any other kind of interface to do their jobs. We just plug in additional help from the solar system into whatever interface is needed through Ansible. We'll have no shortage of workers and all three Dyson clouds could have critical mass, perhaps in less than 500 years!" said Federico excitedly.

That was close to a third of the original projection, calculated for working on the stars one at a time with the added benefit of giving their full attention to the red dwarf.

"And perhaps sooner, since we don't have to wait for the other two stars to have critical mass in order to engage towards our next destination. Once we have a UKB node on Proxima and the first habitats are remotely built on A & B, people can travel from Proxima to occupy them," said Len with enthusiasm.

"A lot of stars are double and triple systems. We have to get Dijkstra to advise us on this project. We'll need her to fill in a lot of details! Lots of stuff will come up that she hasn't foreseen in her dissertation. Do you think we can recruit her?" asked Federico.

"How many people can say 'no' to me?" Len joked. "I'll make it my top priority! She hasn't signed up for ship duties yet, but I don't think she joined the trip for leisure."

A quite intoxicated Federico pulled himself up a few pints later. A little too fast for his impaired brain, which miscalculated the center of mass necessary to remain straight compensating for the ship's acceleration, he fell forward and instinctively raised his arms to regain balance.

His hands landed on a firm pair of breasts, poorly hidden under a minuscule V-neck tee shirt. In the struggle, their arms had collided, spilling her icy-cold drink over her face and chest leaving a distinct foamy mustache on her upper lip.

Now translucent, the thin rose fabric revealed her nipples brushing lightly against his fingers. Beer drops continued to race over the bronzed skin into the cleaved crack between her breasts, pushing tightly against each other.

Frozen into complete incoherence, the feeling of her chest still burning through his fingers, Federico removed his hands as if electrocuted and took one step back with his gaze still down. The scent of beer mixed with her perfume continued to fill the air around them.

"Well, it's nice to meet you, too!" said the woman, annoyed and wiping her upper lip.

"I am absolutely sorry!" he responded, almost crying. He regained his wits and straightened up with his brain now properly compensating for the acceleration.

Embarrassment written all over his face turned the woman's aggravation into sympathy.

"It's alright. Now be a good sport and grab me another IPA#8 while I go clean up," she said.

A few minutes later, she came back wearing a clean tee shirt. They both got up to greet her. Federico pulled a chair from a neighboring table and placed it in front of her new beer.

"I'm Olena," she said, sitting down.

"I'm Len. And the stumbling boy here is Feder...hicks," he hiccupped. "Feder-hicks, oh, sorry!" he hiccupped again.

"Isn't that original! Fedrix?" she asked with a mischievous smile.

"Federico!" said Len, laying both hands on his shoulders and giving him a friendly shake before going back to their seats.

"Too bad! Fedrix had a nice ring to it. Cheers, boys! You're not drinking?" she said, taking a good sip of her ale.

"Cheers! Enjoy! We've had enough for the night, as you may have noticed," chuckled Len.

Federico glanced at her UKB profile: born in Ukraine 325 years ago, emigrated to space at the age of nineteen. A child developmental technician with five kids of her own, her youngest with her on the ship.

"Zhanna is a beautiful girl!" said Olena, who was looking at his UKB profile, too.

"Thank you! She's my only first...I mean, my first and only child," he explained, trying to focus.

"Is this your first acceleration stumble, too?" she smirked.

"No, but it's the most unforgettable," Federico said, and they all laughed.

"You're 503 years old and only have one child?" she asked full of curiosity.

"That he knows of!" joked Len.

"What made you join the trip to Alpha Centauri?" asked Federico, eager to get the focus off himself.

It was the most frequently asked question on the ship, but she still pondered her answer a couple of seconds.

"I believe the first interstellar voyage will be our last chance to add our names to the history records. No other interstellar journey will be as relevant as this. No matter how hard you try, it'll be almost impossible to catch the first intergalactic trip: we don't know yet when or from where it will depart. Chances of being on that ship are close to zero."

She was right. The Space Colonization Initiative was putting all its efforts into developing better and faster ships which they would start sending out to colonize other neighboring stars, even before the Proxima swarm reached critical mass. By the time they were ready to move on to their next destination, there might be tens of ships leaving the solar system for other neighboring stars.

Based on Michael Hart's prediction, back in 1975, each colonized star would also start sending ships to colonize its neighbors, and, even before the entire Milky Way disappeared under humanity's expansion wave, there would be ships traveling towards Canis Major, the Magellanic clouds, Andromeda, and many other neighboring galaxies. The human race would become an intergalactic civilization long before reaching K3 status.

"That's an interesting point!" said Federico. "I never considered that angle."

"That's because you're too busy groping women in bars," she snickered.

"I think I'm going to change my name, lock myself in my quarters, and spend the next hundred years trying to disappear," said Federico mortified.

"Consider Fedrix for the name change. It's very cool!" said Olena.

"Granted. But only if I have your forgiveness."

"What's the upside of forgiving you? I'll tell you what, Fedrix, take me to your quarters for a last drink, and maybe I'll consider it," said Olena with a flirtatious smirk.

"And this is me, saying good night," said Len, rushing to get up. "It was a pleasure meeting you, Olena. Have fun, Fedrix."

"Look, Daddy, it's Vega!" said Kaira excitedly, pointing at the window.

Like every three-year-old child, Kaira had mastered the use of her NIs to the point it was not easy to ignore her.

"Yes, pumpkin. That little yellow dot is Vega," said Fedrix, his mind engaged somewhere else, as he walked with the child perched on his shoulders.

At less than half a light-year ahead, the star was the easiest identifiable object in their field of vision. Every morning, they detoured on the way to school, passing through the ship's viewport to look at their destination.

Improvements in shield technology did away with ice layers ages ago, and these viewports were now standard on the bow of all ships. Enclosed by a dark corridor, windows made of a transparent alloy running along the ship's circumference allowed passengers to enjoy a fully detailed view of the space ahead. Thousands around them were also enjoying the view or just hanging around. Their current ship, Endeavor, reached 20 kilometers in radius by 100 kilometers long, with a living surface of over 12,500 squared kilometers (or about the surface of Puerto Rico) and carried over eighty million people, at a speed of .25c.

"Did you see it, Mommy?"

Breaking the silence, Nova said out loud, "Now, now, Kaira. What did Mommy say? Words, please!"

People around them smiled with sympathy and understanding. Like most young children these days, Kaira didn't like "using words" and preferred thought exchange. One of her teachers explained that Kaira was averse to speaking in school and that the girl needed to be encouraged to practice. People who couldn't speak were labeled inarticulate, and, although it wasn't as bad as being illiterate a few millennia earlier, no parent wanted their child to grow up with such disadvantage.

Early thought exchange required a controlled effort and didn't feel natural to most people, so they continued to use the spoken language in the presence of others. But long before the time Kaira was born, continuous improvements on NIs and additional genetic enhancements made it so much easier for people to communicate, they didn't bother with words anymore.

Nova and Fedrix did their best to follow the teacher's advice and spoke to their daughter often in ways that felt natural to the child.

"Did you see Vega, Mommy?" Kaira obliged in a fit of giggles, conscious of people around looking at her.

Bystanders cheered at her effort, making her blush.

Fedrix stopped by the window for Kaira to point at Vega.

"Of course, I did, my precious!" said Nova with a smile, ignoring the extra attention.

The ship's deceleration, combined with stage fright, made Nova lose her balance for an instant. Fedrix leaned and grabbed her by the waist, pulling her gently against his body. Nova lifted her jade eyes at him and, getting on her toes, stretched up to kiss him on the cheek, smiling.

"Thanks, love," she whispered to Fedrix in thought exchange, then asked the girl. "And what are we doing when we get there?"

"I dunno. I don't know," the girl corrected herself before her mother did, shrugging her little shoulders.

"We are building a new home!" said Nova.

"Building a home!" said Kaira, nodding and pushing a strand of shiny auburn hair behind her ear, imitating her mother's demeanor. She had the same dimpled chin as her father. Nova was a redhead with curly hair, too, but she was short and curvy and quite athletic.

"Shall we go?" said Fedrix, now holding Nova's hand as they walked.

At twenty-seven, Nova was part of the vast majority who didn't need or want a job to be happy. He suspected it was due to her young age and not having chosen a specialty yet. With plenty of time ahead, Nova was enjoying every minute of raising their daughter and losing herself in VR games and adventures while their child was at school.

Jumping off his shoulders, Kaira rushed toward her playmates once they arrived at her school. Nova hugged and kissed Fedrix before walking back to their quarters; he continued on his way towards the Space Colonization Initiative's headquarters where, for the last hour, he had been remotely participating in a meeting through his NIs.

He wasn't the only one; most of the participants were attending from star systems across colonized space. These once-a-year meetings allowed the representatives of each colony ship to present their status to the SCI board.

Len was sharing:

"...you've all been briefed on the challenges of MZ28UF9K. We're less concerned with its variability than with its low metallicity."

MZ28UF9K was the official designation of Vega in the universal catalog. With less than a fifth of the sun's metallicity, it posed a minor challenge because it would be five times harder and longer to lift enough carbon to build rotating habitats and rare metals for components like quantum processors.

Kevin Perry, the board member representing the Solar System, commented on the subject.

"The variability of the star is quite low, compared to a red dwarf, and shouldn't pose a challenge. I'm more concerned with its size because Vega is twice the mass of the sun and will become a red giant much sooner. You'll need to aggressively reduce its mass by removing anything heavier than hydrogen from it."

The more massive a star, the sooner it would die. Stars like the sun and Vega became red giants in their final years. Even more massive stars died in catastrophic supernova[87] explosions, wreaking havoc hundreds or even thousands of light-years away. In either case, the death of a star would make it unsuitable for colonization. Star lifting not only provided the materials they needed for construction but reduced the mass of the star, extending its life.

"The plan is to return hydrogen to the star and keep the heavier elements. We will deploy particle accelerators in orbit to fuse helium into heavier elements, compensating for its low metallicity," answered Len.

Particle accelerators in space were greatly simplified, requiring something essential that was in abundance: vacuum. The Endeavor carried prefabricated sections to build linear accelerators hundreds of kilometers long and capable of accelerating particles close to the speed of light.

"Your brief didn't mention anything about life on the habitable planets and moons of the system," remarked Indah Mactaru, the board member from α Cen B.

"It's a chaotic system," answered Len. "There are massive rings of debris and no rocky planets in the habitable zone. It's also one-tenth the age of the sun, so there wouldn't have been enough time for complex life forms to evolve yet. The best candidates are the frozen moons around its huge gas giant. The tidal friction might melt the ice inside, creating underground oceans that could harbor life, but none of our probes has penetrated deep enough into the system to make such a determination."

He paused briefly to allow for questions before continuing.

"This leads to my next point. The rings of debris are far out, starting at 8 AU. But the inner orbit, where we have selected to build our swarm, is a shooting gallery with a deluge of comets and asteroids continuously flung inward. We will need to clear the system of debris before we can start laying out habitats."

"How will you clear the perimeter?" asked Perry.

"The only idea on the table so far is to deploy a ring of lasers orbiting the star on the same plane as the asteroid belt. It will take over a hundred years to build them and clear the orbit, but it's a safe bet," answered Len.

"Looks like you have your work cut out for you," said Terry Mattos, the board member from the Barnard system[88].

There were no more questions, so Len stopped sharing. At the same time, Fedrix walked into the room.

"What do you think?" asked Len.

"I think you have your work cut out for you," joked Fedrix, mimicking Mattos's pompous demeanor.

Len gazed at him with a gloomy expression.

"You're not in the best mood, I see. This should cheer you up: I've been brainstorming with some Dyson architects back at Sol, and they've come up with an ingenious idea. We'll start the first ring of rotating habitats perpendicular, rather than parallel, to belt plane. Comets and asteroids are being swung into the inner orbit where we want to build our swarm—that is, along the same plane of the asteroid belt. The habitats will only be in the line of fire when crossing the plane at two intercepting points. That way, we can use a slightly reinforced array of shared lasers on each ring to protect our habitats..."

"Yes!" interrupted Len excitedly. "The next ring will also be perpendicular to the belt but intercepting it at two different points. By the time all the rings in the swarm are finished, we'll have a complete defensive system covering the entire orbit!"

"Precisely," said Fedrix. "And without deploying extra laser units to sanitize the entire orbit before we start. It'll save us over a hundred years."

"The best news I've gotten, so far!" said Len, with a smile of relief. "But it concerns me where to find the first chunks of materials to start," he continued. "If the star is low on metals, you can bet planets and asteroids in the system are too. I feel like I'm back on Earth before the space era, trying to figure out where to get metals to build the foundation."

"Asteroids should have plenty of carbon, a key element for building rotating habitats and everything else in our Dyson swarm. Our equipment includes a prefab particle accelerator. We just have to assemble the sections and load it with helium. Between that and what we mine from the star, we'll move forward," said Fedrix.

"Now, that will be painfully slow! To think I was starting to cheer up. I'm afraid we'll be here for 1,000 years before the cloud reaches critical mass, and we can move to our next destination," complained Len.

"What's the rush, old friend? This is the fun part. The techniques we pioneered at Proxima are being used all over to dyson red dwarfs and double stars. We have an opportunity to break new ground again! Besides, as we continue towards the galactic center, stars are packed closer together, and interstellar trips will start getting shorter," said Fedrix trying to cheer him up.

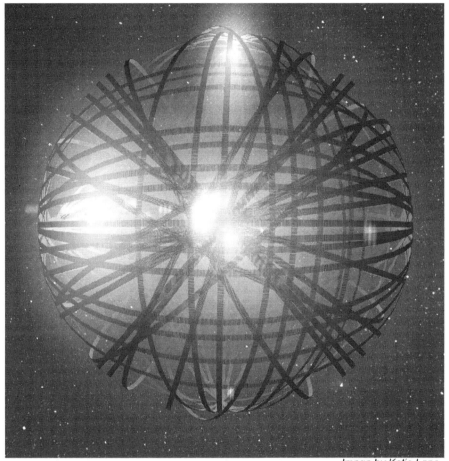

Image by Katie Lane

Over 2,000 years since the first interstellar voyage, humanity had now successfully colonized all the stars within twenty light-years from the sun. Less than forty of them—including the sun, α

Cen, and a few others close to the home star—had complete Dyson swarms. The rest of them were getting along, thanks to a fast-growing population.

As human beings ventured outside that twenty-light-year sphere toward the galactic core, their expansion could now be seen within 2,000 light-years from the sun, as stars disappeared from the visible spectrum forming an expanding void from the home star, like a drop of ink on paper.

Having lived in space thirty times longer than on Earth, Fedrix had only two children but hundreds of descendants from his first daughter, Zhanna. Following in his footsteps, she became a space colonization engineer and was currently assigned to the swarm on Wolf 1055. Although they had never met in person, they were close in their hearts and had gotten to know each other really well through Ansible. He knew all her children and grandchildren. But beyond them, it was complicated to keep track of the family, and he often needed to look them up in the UKB when they sent birthday and holiday greetings.

During the times when human survival depended on attaining food and shelter, tedium was uncommon. However, in the space era, boredom continued to be a voracious predator. Intense personalities, having a strong need for variety and emotion, were more susceptible. The latest frenzy had started over the last 1,000 years with something of utmost importance to humans: pets.

With a lot of thought given to choosing their physical characteristics and preconditioning them to be loving companions, pet engineering emerged as a viral trend. A vast DNA database now existed in the UKB, as designers continued to create new templates for monkeys, birds, dogs, and other pets. People then added their own tweaks to produce a new pet in real life or just to admire it in a VR before making a commitment. Anyone could browse through the database or seek assistance from a pet designer for a perfect match.

Millions of new species had been designed, including miniature dinosaurs, unicorns, and trilobites, but, inextricably linked to human evolution, cats and dogs remained among the all-time favorites. For months, Kaira had been begging for "a kitty" and they had finally acquiesced, promising her to meet with a pet designer.

When Nova and Fedrix went to pick up their daughter at school, they found her petting her playmate's arctic fox. The animal was lying on a large pillow, enjoying the attention of a group of children.

Artistically enhanced by an asymmetric blue streak ascending from the left paw all the way to the tip of the tail, the tantalizing specimen was the size of a Great Dane with flawless, snowy fur. Drawn by the animal's charm, they knelt among the children, feeling the rich, fluffy coat through their fingers. In a movement that made a pair of sizable ears flap, the animal turned up, presenting Fedrix its white tummy to be rubbed.

"He loves you!" said Nova, delighted, as Fedrix caressed the fox's belly.

Giving the fox a hug, Kaira placed her cheek on its chest, prompting the animal to open its mouth and utter a high-pitched howl of happiness. Through their child's NIs, they experienced an outburst of delight, pleasure, and excitement that made Fedrix wonder if their daughter had a change of heart about her pet choice.

Sitting together in their living room later that evening, Kaira wedged herself between her mom's crossed legs. Fedrix initiated an Ansible session with the pet designer at the scheduled time and opened it to Nova and Kaira.

"I want a kitty!" exclaimed Kaira, as soon as the session was established.

"Anything you wish! We have many different kinds," said Elton with a smile, catering to the child.

"This was my cat, a long time ago. I was wondering if you could use it as a baseline," said Fedrix sharing UKB photos and videos of Darwin.

The designer couldn't hide his astonishment at Fedrix's age.

"I would recommend starting with this design," he said, sharing a simulation of the base species, tweaking it on the fly to give it Darwin's looks.

"It's a template developed from the original domestic cat species you just shared. It has been improved to be four times the original size and to have an IQ of fifty. And best of all, its unpleasant reflexes––like scratching, biting, and hissing––have been erased. I've made it like the one you showed me but can make it smaller if you prefer..."

"No, please don't!" interrupted Fedrix. "I love the size! Can you give it an outgoing personality and make it engaging and playful? I'd like to bring it when we go out."

"Certainly! I have access to your personality profiles and will tune it to respond to you. They're very good with kids. You may select the specific features you prefer, like the shape and size of the skull, eyes, ear length and style, snout, paws, claws, whiskers, tail, etc. Just for the fur alone, there are thousands of shades and texture choices! Take your time," said Elton.

It took three long hours to go through every single characteristic. Inspired by the fox at school, Nova came up with the idea of giving their pet an asymmetric purple-blue highlight, tilted on the left side of its head.

"It'll make its amber eyes even more striking," she said.

The final design looked like a dark slate panther with the highlight going up diagonally from the left cheek, interrupted by his eye and continuing all the way to the tip of the right ear.

When they finished, the designer updated the simulation for them to admire.

Nova gasped in awe; it was nothing less than gorgeous. The simulation wasn't purely visual. Fedrix reached forward and ran his fingers through the rich coat on the back of the animal, experiencing the flawless silky fur. It was warm and welcoming to the touch, and Fedrix's hands glided through unimpeded. Searching his memories in the UKB, he couldn't recall experiencing anything like it before.

"I love it, Mommy!" exclaimed Kaira, gripping the fur on the neck. "Can we print it?"

They both laughed, and Nova gave the child a hug, while kissing her loudly on the cheek.

"They can't be printed, sweetie; it takes five months to grow one from the template I'm making for you. But you'll be able to see it grow in an incubator at your local nursery," the designer explained.

"Do you have a preference for the sex?"

"Let's make it male, like Darwin," requested Fedrix. Nova nodded.

"Perfect!" Elton said. "We'll implant NIs in your pet, allowing you to control it. If you're unable to, the UKB can take over if ever necessary," explained the designer.

"What do they eat?" asked Nova.

"You'll be provided with a nutritional ration tailored to your pet. Its appetite and instincts will be regulated by the UKB. Just one portion per day. If it needs more, you'll be notified. You can have an automatic feeder, but it'll create a stronger bond if one of you feeds him," Elton explained

They all seemed happy.

"How old do you want it to be when he comes home?" asked the Designer.

"What are the choices?" inquired Nova.

"Well, animals—especially cats—could be raucous and require patience to control them, even with NIs implanted. Many adults choose grown up animals, but, since you have a little one, she might be happier..." He stopped to avoid making the choice for them. Kaira was too young to understand what he was talking about.

"Yes," said Nova. "We'll get a kitten."

Kaira repeated her mother's words.

Reclined against a tree with Darwin's large head and upper torso arched over his extended legs like a furry bridge, Fedrix was thoroughly relaxed. Rolling down ahead, lime and shamrock strokes colored the hills, adorned by random patches of kaleidoscopic wildflowers. Far below, city lights would start turning on in a few hours, as the daylight period neared its end. Soothing sounds from the crystalline brook began to make him doze, contemplating the intertwined coontails rising from the white sands at the bottom of the never-ending stream.

Darwin's paws started kneading the grass in a rhythmic fashion; he appeared to be in the middle of a pleasant dream. But before Fedrix could look inside his pet's mind to investigate what the dream was about, an overexcited Len burst onto the stage of his own mind.

"You won't believe what I'm about to share with you, old buddy!"

"Whatever it is, can wait till tomorrow! I'm exhausted," he pushed back, trying to dismiss him.

Having worked fourteen-hour days for the last few weeks, he had decided to take the afternoon off.

"Our team has been chosen for the first intergalactic mission!" said Len ignoring him.

Shifting into gear, Fedrix forgot all about his exhaustion and jumped into the conversation with undivided attention.

"Are you hammered?"

But Fedrix knew it wasn't possible, for he would have detected drunkenness or other kinds of impairment in the thought exchange; like slurred words, thoughts and feelings became fuzzy when a person was woozy. Besides, Len was on the SCI Council; he was probably telling the truth!

With the exception of Ariel and a few others who'd been assigned to different missions, most of the original crew from Alpha Centauri had remained together. With such an accumulation of experience and knowledge, they were assigned groundbreaking missions. This would be no less challenging.

"Almost! But with my own endorphins! Canis Major is closer to us than the galactic core; that's why the SCI decided to send us there now. Our next mission is a yellow dwarf in intergalactic space, 856 light-years away!" replied Len, unable to curb his excitement.

Frequent galaxy collisions led to a messy consolidation process. By the time things settled down, billions of stars were flung out to intergalactic space. The expanse between galaxies was littered with stars, and the voyage to Canis Major would have multiple stops in order to colonize some of them, creating a path of outposts—like stepping-stones in the vast intergalactic void.

"Have we learned enough? Have we reached that milestone that prepares us to colonize other galaxies, having barely reached thirty light-years away from the sun?"

"...asked Fedrix, the philosopher! What does it matter? Canis Major is just 25,000 light-years from here; not a big distance compared to the size of our own galaxy! Besides, we are at the edge of the Milky Way. It's an ideal location to reach out for neighboring ones," said Len.

"But, at 0.25c, it will take us..."

"Three-thousand-four-hundred-thirty years to reach the first target, including the acceleration and deceleration periods of 3.17 years at 0.75 meter per second squared, when the ship will be traveling below its maximum speed," replied the UKB.

"Shit! Can you imagine yourself living on a ship for over 3,400 years?" asked Fedrix.

Being just 3,203 years old, it was hard to come to terms with a single journey taking longer than his entire life, so far.

"That's one of the reasons our new ship is so large and comfortable. And guess its name..." said Len, with a challenge in his voice.

"Intergalactic-1?" replied Fedrix with gloom.

"Hawking!"

"Wow!"

Although a name had not been chosen yet, they had all been briefed on their upcoming ship's specs: 50 kilometers radius by 500 kilometers length, yielding a habitable surface of 157,000 squared kilometers (or about the size of Tunisia). It would be capable of housing over 100 million people comfortably.

Carrying more fuel and equipment than any ship in history, it was also more spacious and featured a lot of entertaining options designed to make life comfortable: beaches, rivers, lakes, and even mountain scenery, providing passengers with no lack of choices for recreation and adventure.

At thirty kilometers high above the ground, the low gravity area where food was grown and the equipment stored was made invisible to the human eye by a new, revolutionary, cloaking technology. Based on a metamaterial that bent the light appearing to pass through an object, it rendered the entire rotation axis completely invisible from the infrared to the ultraviolet of the light spectrum.

However, another concern popped into Fedrix's mind. Until then, all their ships had been single voyage, as the fast-paced human civilization made a lot of the technology they carried obsolete. So, it made sense to build a brand-new one from scratch. As soon as the ship was no longer necessary, they sank it into the star to recycle it—with the exception of The Interstellar-1, which became a museum.

"Aren't we flying into obsolescence?" asked Fedrix, concerned.

With this voyage being a hundred times longer than average, they would be stuck in time for 3,430 years, while humanity continued to make technological advances.

"Yes, we are, but not so much that they'll develop a faster ship that will beat us there. Besides, due to the distance, we will be the only ship going to Canis. Anyway, how much has the maximum speed of our ships increased in the last 3,000 years?"

"Right. But that's not the only thing we'll miss. To me, it seems a bit premature to reach for intergalactic space when we have colonized less than 300 stars within our own galaxy."

"Does that mean you're not coming? I understand some people lose interest in making history or chicken out."

It was clear Len was patronizing him, but it worked.

"When has a small thing like obsolescence stopped me? Of course, we're coming!" said Fedrix, feeling silly.

"Cheer up, my friend. There are other perks! Don't you want to be among the first humans to see what the Milky Way actually looks like? The slanted, spiral arms around the bulging core, its gas clouds..." listed Len with growing excitement.

Suddenly, a few millennia of obsolescence seemed to Fedrix a very cheap price to pay.

"Yes, I would! All this time, it has been pretty much like being inside a forest jumping from tree to tree, preventing us from appreciating it in all its glory from a distance. We will know how many arms it has, produce the first accurate map...and besides...Hawking! Now that's a name for a ship!" said Fedrix with a hearty laugh.

"That's the spirit!" said Len, joining in the laughter.

Still in the Vega system, barely 700 years since their arrival, the first two rings of rotating habitats around the star had already been completed. Improvements in star lifting and particle accelerators had helped them to speed up the progress.

With the Hawking almost completed, passengers and crew would start moving in over the next few years. Most of the population would be born during the voyage. The period of three and a half millennia was a long time.

Fedrix sent a memory of his conversation with Len to Nova, who nowadays spent her time at school helping to educate young children, but her reaction cut his excitement short.

"I understand that living on the Hawking will be more comfortable than on the Endeavor, where I was born, but not as much as the habitat we live in. And I don't like the isolation of space. In the beginning, with less than a million people onboard, it will feel deserted. I also like the freedom of jumping on a transport and visiting other habitats to see my family and friends. To be honest, I haven't decided yet if I want to go."

Nevertheless, her response made him feel as if she had already decided.

"Don't be sad, love," she said, following his thoughts. "Although I've been thinking about your next step for a while, I haven't decided yet."

This was a major blow. They had been together for over 700 years—longer than any partner he ever had. And they had gotten to know each other so intimately! How had he not anticipated this?

Out to dinner that evening, Fedrix opened a bottle of Nova's favorite wine made from an arctic blue grape. The rare varietal, locally engineered, produced a crisp light blue wine with a slight green hue, rivaling with the best he ever tried from Earth. Making small talk all night and avoiding what they feared discussing, Nova finally broached the subject.

"Please give me time to consider the situation, love. I'll give you an answer soon."

A little window of hope opened in his heart. Besides, it would be a few years before the Hawking was ready to travel, and he didn't want to put pressure on her.

Weeks later, Kaira visited in person with the youngest of her seven children, a rebellious twenty-one-year-old named Aaron. She had moved on her own at twenty and currently worked for the city council. She had inherited Nova's beautiful almond eyes and was as tall as Fedrix.

Tall and blue-haired, Aaron had the dimpled chin and brown skin of his grandfather. He had just moved in with his boyfriend, and they were thrilled about having their first child together (already at the nursery) and brimming with plans for the future. Genetic manipulation and artificial wombs allowed same-sex couples to procreate with the same ease as their heterosexual counterparts, without the need for surrogates.

Darwin galloped to his mistress, placing his paws on Kaira's belly. He uttered a loud and deep meow, almost like a cry, stating how much he missed her. She hugged him and pulled his fur affectionately before embracing her dad.

"So, you're going!" said Kaira. Her eyes immediately became tearful.

"It's not like you're losing me, pumpkin," he said, holding her tight.

"I'm used to coming and hugging my dad whenever I want to. Ansible can't replace that," she said with profound sadness.

Nova embraced the pair of them.

"You'll always have Mommy, my precious!" she said.

They broke apart and sat down.

"So, Canis Major is 25,000 light-years away but you're stopping every 1,000 light-years to colonize stars in intergalactic space. That means you'll reach Canis in...?" Kaira asked.

"The complete trajectory is mapped. With twenty-seven stops to colonize stars and based on their metallicity, each should take an average of 300 years for the swarm to reach critical mass. Assuming no shield improvements or course corrections, the trip to Canis Major would be roughly 108,500 years," said the UKB.

A thought vacuum filled the room. Only a handful of people, as far out as Vega, were near 1,000 years of age. Talk of a hundred thousand years was not something that happened at a regular dinner table.

"I know it seems like a long time..." Fedrix started.

"But you're not coming back, right?" interrupted Nova. "After reaching the edge of Canis Major, you'll continue to settle other stars there before moving onto Andromeda or whatever destination you get assigned to next."

"Please, understand. This has been my life, even on the home planet before the space era..."

"How can you know that? You have no memories of that period," interrupted Kaira, overwhelmed with emotion.

"Don't be mean to your dad," said Nova.

"It's okay," said Fedrix. "I have fragmented recollections and notes I wrote before the UKB was built. Also, historic records show I was hired by the Space Initiative..."

"Hired?" interrupted Nova.

"Before the space era, people on the home planet had to work for a living," explained the UKB. "Individuals were remunerated for work they did in a currency that could be exchanged for goods and services like food, clothing, and entertain..."

"Pre-UKB records show I started working for the Space Initiative, a precursor to the SCI, when I was fifty-five," interrupted Fedrix. "There's also mention of me working with scientists to educate the public about space colonization in the early twenty-first century. I helped refugees escape the home planet to settle in space. I was a witness to the last great war. My whole life has been dedicated to space colonization. I was on the first interstellar ship from the home star over 2,000 years ago. This is who I am. Please, understand."

"I think we should respect Grandpa's decision," interjected Aaron, aiming to lower the tension.

Nova found the courage to ask the question still burning in her mind.

"Honey, tell us. Were you a slave?" she asked, hiding her face in his neck.

Like everyone else, Nova had studied the dark pages of human history in basic education. But having been born into a post-scarcity society, so far removed from it, she couldn't grasp the difference between employment and slavery.

"I...don't believe so. I think I was born after slavery was abolished," said Fedrix, unsure.

"Over 200 years after," clarified the UKB. "Furthermore, slaves had no choice but to obey their masters, while free individuals had a choice of employers who paid for their work."

"Still feels like slavery to me," added Kaira uncomfortably. "I can't imagine being forced to work to satisfy my needs."

"A job was considered a privilege. For most people, it was not an option but the only way to survive. In most cases, individuals had to compete for it and work harder every year in order..." the

UKB promptly stopped the explanation as their uneasiness mounted.

"I understand your point, sweetie. But this is the way society was before the space era. It was much worse before my time," said Fedrix.

"After the first colonies were established, the Space Initiative began providing for all the basic needs of its citizenry, regardless of whether they worked or not. They also received a stipend known as Universal Basic Income to allow them to purchase goods and services that were only available from the home planet," explained the UKB.

"It's so strange not remembering key parts of your life," said Aaron, full of curiosity. "How does it affect you?"

Fedrix had had this conversation with his grandson when the boy was younger, but Aaron continued to be aghast at the prospect of forgetting key experiences from one's existence.

"All I have are my written notes and visual content. I've forgotten how to read, but the UKB translates for me. I recognize myself in the videos and still images but not the other people in them. Otherwise, I feel fine."

He could download the reading skill into his brain again, but it would only be useful for a couple of hours every few centuries, when he decided to peek at his notes. So, he just let the UKB translate them into words for him.

Fedrix put an arm around his grandson's shoulder and hugged him, feeling a rush of love. Then he addressed Kaira.

"We are eternal beings, pumpkin. Some future day, you may want to jump on a ship and visit other stars or even come to see your dad again. We will never lose touch. I only have two children, and although I never met your sister in person, I love you both the same."

"Will you ever return home?" Kaira asked.

"It's not impossible. There's a limit to what humanity can colonize before the expansion of the universe puts the rest of space beyond our reach. We won't be able to colonize new stars beyond that point."

"When? Where is that?" asked Aaron, visibly interested.

Realizing how deeply ingrained the juxtaposition of space and time continued to be in human brains made Fedrix smile. "There's no easy answer. Different regions of space are moving at different speeds. Galaxies closer to us are retreating at slower speeds than galaxies farther away. Everything within a billion light-years of us is moving away at 0.15c, but our ships can currently reach 0.25c. So, we might catch up with them. However, our ships are getting faster as we develop better shielding technology and one day might be able to reach 0.99c. But the speed of the expansion is accelerating, too, so that sphere—a billion light-years in radius—will grow in size as it retreats at even higher speeds."

Fedrix stopped for a second, but Aaron didn't interrupt, his attention fixated and wanting to know more.

"So, the answer is: we don't know, yet. Future colonized galaxies that are moving away will become unreachable in the very distant future as the expansion exceeds the maximum speed of our ships. However, we'll still be able to communicate with them through Ansible. It's a challenge that future generations will face," he finished.

Aaron listened in amazement with a curious eye on the magic of reality.

"I think you've just given him a subject of interest to continue his education," said Kaira with a smile.

Ten years later, Nova accompanied Fedrix to the elevator of his access port. It was strange knowing their relationship had an expiration date, inexorably approaching day after day. Eternal life had changed the way people perceived the passage of time; ten years wasn't considered long anymore. Fedrix had taken as much time as possible to say goodbye to friends and family and to spend more time in person with Kaira.

There was nothing he needed to carry; his few belongings had already been shipped to the Hawking. Nova held Fedrix's hand, Darwin heeling on his other side. The scene eerily reminded him of that day he said good-bye to Reshni over 2,700 years ago.

"Are you sure you won't change your mind? There's nobody I would rather spend eternity with," he said, invaded by a profound melancholy.

"I would be miserable in space, love. Please try to understand," she said.

As the train arrived and the doors opened for its passengers, Nova knelt and hugged Darwin, who returned the gesture with an affectionate nibble. She then stood up to embrace Fedrix, one last time.

With his heart smashed to pieces, they broke apart, the taste of their last kiss lingering on his lips. An unhindered thought lit his mind: this was the pinnacle of a long learning period. He was now complete; humanity was now complete and ready to face the unknowable challenges of the cosmos.

Much more than just grabbing a few neighboring stars, this was the end of childhood, the culmination of the beginning of humankind's space era. It was their first step towards colonizing the universe.

It became clear beyond doubt why they were reaching for intergalactic space now. The learning process wouldn't stop there—on the contrary. Humanity's future was wide open, bright, and eternal. The universe was waiting for them.

His chest still ached, but, with this thought warming his heart, he walked decisively toward the door, followed by Darwin, to start yet another chapter of his life.

Chapter 6: Civilization

THE TINY, SUFFOCATING COCKPIT FELT EVEN TIGHTER under the stress. Despite nearly 360-degree visibility, there was barely enough space for Fedrix to turn his head or move his body. His agonizing muscles—especially those of his legs—were cramping under the torture.

Faced with a myriad of dizzying instruments, power switches, and dials, Fedrix rechecked the flight deck. His gloved right hand clung slippery and mushy onto the stick, swimming in its own sweat after ten hours of uninterrupted combat. The jumpsuit squeezed tight to prevent a blackout, and he found himself making a conscious effort to get enough air into his lungs. Chasing Stralk through the rocky twisting canyon, the remains of an ancient river, they flew identical Raptor-X fighter planes at frantic speeds through the maze-like canyon.

Pathways of rock formations opened and closed before Fedrix's eyes. Suddenly, a bulging rock outcropping came at him out of nowhere. With no choice but to bank hard, his peripheral vision popped in little bright spots as the centrifugal acceleration pushed the blood flow away from his brain. The darkness of tunnel vision began to envelop him, and a buzzing noise filled his ears. Nauseated, he shook his head, struggling to remain conscious. The jumpsuit squeezed him harder, and Fedrix corrected the course to continue the chase. The light-headedness dwindled after he exited the turn.

"I've got him! He's dead!" Fedrix exclaimed, victorious.

Now close enough to Stralk, the targeting system lit up. Feverishly, he fired all the remaining rounds in his cannons. Stralk got hit, but the ship took only minor damage and continued to fly.

They had started with sixteen ships, eight on each team; now just the two of them remained. The others had been shot down, ejected, or had bailed. Now that they were both out of weapons, it made no sense to continue.

"I'm out!" yelled Fedrix, using words, so the microphone in his helmet would relay the message to Stralk.

"Me, too!"

"Should we call it a tie?" asked Fedrix, aching and anxious to get it over with. It had been a lot of fun, but he'd had enough of it.

Luck had brought him this far, but Stralk was a much better pilot. Combined with his extraordinary agility and reflexes, Fedrix would never stand a chance with just the two of them alone if they decided to reload and keep going. A tie was as good as victory.

"Sure thing!" yelled Stralk, glad Fedrix couldn't access his thoughts. His body was getting numb. They had never gone this long in combat, and he was beginning to make mistakes.

With their minds closed to members of the opposite team to avoid them getting wind of their maneuvers—otherwise it would be a tedious and pointless exercise—they used the ship's radios to communicate.

A message from Len suddenly came up in their minds.

"I'm terribly sorry to interrupt the fun, but we have an emergency."

Completely caught by surprise, Fedrix's attention wandered for a fraction of a second. Unable to keep up with the challenging canyon geography, his plane crashed against the rock wall in a spectacular ball of fire. He didn't even have time to eject.

As he was pulled out of the virtual reality and opened his eyes, Fedrix perceived the noise from the room they were in. Cheering and booing filled his ears as everyone screamed and laughed at him.

The cramps throughout his body started to dissipate. The sensations were just a figment created by the VR, but he couldn't help shaking his head, joggling his right hand, and flexing his legs multiple times, trying to stimulate the blood flow. This game was one of Stralk's favorites, and they got together often to play.

"What the hell happened!? This is the closest we've ever come to a tie! I can't believe you blew it like that!" said one of Fedrix's teammates, cracking up on the couch.

Completely recovered, Fedrix stood up in a rush.

"Let's go people! We have an emergency, whatever that means!" he said.

"Do not share with anybody!" urged Len. "We are having an in-person meeting to discuss. Please, get here as soon as possible!"

Only then he realized that he and Stralk were the only ones to get the message from Len.

"An emergency? What's an emergency?" their dumbfounded friends around the room started asking.

Fedrix promptly closed his mind again; they would have to rely on the UKB to understand what an emergency was.

"Sorry guys, we've been asked not to share," said Stralk, politely closing his mind too, as they rushed out of the room amidst torrents of complaints from their bewildered friends.

Fedrix summoned a transport. They both normally walked and used public transportation. But, if this was an actual emergency, they'd better get there fast. Meanwhile, his mind raced, wondering what it could possibly be. Were they heading straight into a black hole? About to get fried by a gamma-ray burst? Did they miss a nearby star about to turn supernova? The only emergency they had ever had was having to fill in for Len at an SCI status meeting a long time ago.

Fifteen minutes later, they walked into Len's office. There were other people in the room already with a few more rushing behind them, all senior members of Len's team. As soon as they entered, Len shared telemetry data from the ship's sensor array and, without giving them time to digest it, made the following announcement.

"We've detected an alien civilization."

The thought exploded in their minds like antimatter fireworks. A rush of adrenaline struck Fedrix's chest, knocking every wisp of air from his lungs—much like the VR game he just left behind. His mind spun out of control, and felt like a block of ice materialized in his chest.

Whatever he had speculated the emergency could be wasn't this. In over a billion years of space colonization, they had found no sentient species, no intelligence, no technosignatures, and no civilization—not even ruins of an extinct one. Life in space was incredibly dull, and he hoped the future would bring surprises. But this?

He gathered himself and dove into the telemetry, which included atmospheric readings and images from the planet's surface, as Len continued addressing those assembled.

"The Council has reviewed this information, and I've been authorized to share it only with the people in this room. We understand it will leak out, sooner than later, but for now we are insisting that none of you share it outside this room."

They were just outside M87, still in route towards VCC1281. The Eternity had just entered orbit around this yellow dwarf, their second star in intergalactic space, over a week ago.

Fedrix instructed the UKB to do a comparative analysis, sharing it with everyone in the room. A yellow dwarf of the same size, mass, and brightness—the star was a twin to the Earth's sun, a billion years ago. The ratio of elements made its chemical composition eerily similar, and even the spectrum was identical. The six-planet inner system had a massive gas giant, no asteroid belts, and a slim cometary cloud[89].

Had they found this star inside the Milky Way, before the space age, they would have inferred it had formed from the same nebula cloud as the sun. Of course, out there in the Virgo cluster, that was an impossible hypothesis.

"If it took this long to discover them, their technology footprint has to be nanoscopic," ventured Fedrix. "An advanced civilization, especially one building Dyson swarms, would be visible from millions of light-years away."

"They have not developed advanced technology yet. No space capability, radio, laser, or any kind of transmission. The carbon and methane footprints in their atmosphere aren't from artificial sources. The amount of heat irradiated from the planet confirms this as well," explained Len.

"How was that even possible?" wondered Fedrix. A civilization should go from preindustrial to spacefaring in 1,000 years or so. It took humans less than 600 years to go from the Middle Ages to launching the first satellite. Considering the size and age of the universe, the probability that they had arrived here in that precise sliver of time, after a billion years of space colonization, was staggeringly small.

"Is this a joke?" he asked Len. As he hadn't reopened his mind, no one else could follow his train of thought.

"It's not a joke," said Len. "I've been wondering that myself. But look at the sensor data. You can't make up stuff like that. This shit is for real! Besides, have you ever known the UKB to tell a joke?"

A few people chuckled but some glanced at Stralk, who sported a mischievous smile. His ability to pull pranks was legendary, but not even he could have gotten away with a practical joke of that magnitude, or could he?

"I'm not so sure of anything anymore," said Fedrix, giving Stralk a baleful look.

A few years ago, Stralk somehow got Darwin to jump on Fedrix while he was having sex with a girlfriend and shared the whole scene with their closest friends, live from his cat's NIs. How did Stralk manage to bypass the UKB safety protocols that governed the behavior of pets? He would never know.

"It wasn't me, bud!" said Stralk with a sheepish face.

Fedrix nodded, accepting his explanation but then came up with another objection.

"We have millions of telescopes on M87! This wouldn't be an easy thing to miss!" He said, still hoping the whole thing was a fluke.

"I suppose sometimes even the UKB misses things," said Len. "The closest telescope is 50,000 light-years away; it confirms the settlement lights on the planet."

A few seconds passed.

"No, that's impossible! There must be a mistake! Somehow, we must be looking at two copies of the same feed! Those lights couldn't possibly have been there 50,000 years ago; it would mean that they haven't developed advanced technology in all that time," said Stralk completely baffled.

The gravitational lensing telescope on M87 was receiving images of the alien planet that were 50,000 years in the past and transmitting them to The Eternity through Ansible.

"The feeds from the telescope and the ship differ. Today, lights form different patterns from those of 50,000 years ago. Furthermore, the telescope is unable to image The Eternity at our present coordinates, which also confirms we are not looking at the same feed," said the UKB sharing both feeds, side by side.

The UKB was right, of course. It was a mark of the severity of the situation that even Stralk would rather consider the possibility of the UKB making a mistake.

"I wonder, what could have possibly prevented them from developing an advanced technology in such a long time?" asked Len, completely disconcerted.

"Let's just add it to the unsolved mysteries bucket," said Fedrix. "I was thinking exactly the same thing, but it might not last much longer. We have no time to waste!"

He turned back to the telemetry. The alien planet was a super Earth[90], 2.3 times bigger than the home planet with almost 1.8 times the gravity and an oxygen content slightly higher than what humans were accustomed to.

It would be challenging to visit the planet. Even with all their genetic enhancements, humans would need to wear exoskeletons[91] to help them cope with almost twice their weight. However, the Council might not allow anyone to go down to the planet yet.

"We've launched low orbit probes," said Len. "Soon, we'll be able to see what the aliens look like. It'll also help us create detailed maps and identify possible landing sites. Our top priority is to build a skyhook down to seventy-five kilometers above a chosen landing point and to use buoyancy vehicles to go up and down the surface."

"What? Why not build a space elevator all the way down to the planet?" someone asked.

"Too much of a risk. If the aliens capture our base, they might get access to space," said Stralk.

"If these beings evolved through natural selection, they will be violent and cunning. We can't risk anyone being captured. Watching from a safe distance is the smart thing to do," offered Fedrix. "Anyway, a balloon ship will only add a few hours to the trip."

"We also don't want them getting hold of any samples of our technology," added Len. "Our base on the ground will be just a landing site, built using their available construction materials, so they will learn nothing by capturing the structure. The ascension vehicles will not remain on the surface long for obvious reasons."

"Do we have a directive from the Council yet?" inquired Fedrix.

"No humans will be allowed on the planet's surface, and the presence of The Eternity must remain concealed from the aliens. That means every single piece of technology we send to the planet must be cloaked. That includes the skyhook as well," explained Len. "We'll start by building whatever infrastructure is needed to study the aliens. Dysoning this star has been put on hold."

Thought exchanges among the people in the room flooded the air, becoming almost audible.

"We'll still need a cloud of Statites, as I presume some of the options will involve moving their star system," said Stralk.

Statites could also be used to move a star by turning it into a stellar engine, slowly accelerating it, and dragging planets, asteroid belts, and cometary cloud. Compounded over thousands of years, the momentum would move a star across its galaxy.

"What about research facilities, including isolation containers, where we can keep live specimens?" asked Fedrix.

"Yes, to both," acknowledged Len. "We plan to build a small station where we can keep all the different species isolated."

"Why are we bringing in multiple species?" someone asked.

"Isn't that obvious?" asked SueLing, who was a late arrival. "We'll have to feed our subjects; they most likely eat other species."

After a billion years of feeding on engineered vegetables and synthetic derivatives of animal protein grown in-vitro, stomachs throughout the room churned at the thought of an animal slaughtering another to eat it.

"Suck it up, guys!" said SueLing. "We are on our way to witness extremely unpleasant things. Those who can't take it should instruct the UKB to put a filter on what is shared with you."

"That's going to ruin some appetites," joked Stralk, while instructing the UKB to place a content filter for himself.

"I think the Council should consider lifting the secrecy order," said Fedrix. "The more people working on this, the more ideas will come in. Besides, our society is founded on the principle of equal privilege. Keeping this discovery secret could be a violation."

"Agreed," said Len. "I will argue the point."

"The feeds from the first probe are arriving," reported the UKB.

The announcement extinguished all thoughts as they turned their attention to the images of dwelling units in small clusters along an orange-colored riverbank. A large pyramidal structure stood farther inland, adjoined by roads and what appeared to be crop fields.

A wheel was spinning down a street, probably ejected from a crash between two wheeled vehicles, rolling away from the scene due to the inertia.

Zooming in revealed not an object, but an eight-legged creature, each leg ending in a sort of pod. An eerie eye at the center spun along with the rest of the body.

"What the...?" started Stralk.

"Stereoscopic vision!" exclaimed SueLing, when another creature rolled by from the opposite direction revealing an identical eye on the other side.

No one was surprised; it was a forgone conclusion that stereoscopic vision must be a standard feature of sentient beings.

Expecting something humanoid or at least bipedal, the images shocked Fedrix to his core. The surprise was greater than anything he had ever experienced. The aliens were clearly sentient; but, of the countless species humans had encountered, how were these funny looking beings the ones who managed to get across the ultimate great filter? So many assumptions were about to be thrown away today!

With his mind still closed to others, he breathed a sigh of relief knowing no one could notice the chill that had gripped his soul.

Thousands of satellite probes deployed around the planet allowed humans to get a closer look at the alien civilization. With their limbs converging into a disk-shaped body, SueLing christened the first alien sentient beings *Echinopods*, reminiscent of an ancient starfish species from Earth—Echinoderms.

With their bodies averaging 2.5 meters in diameter, the creatures' movement was achieved by spinning their entire body, propelled by short jumps from each pod, pushing away from the ground. Covered in hundreds of suction cups and tactile sensors, their limbs doubled as legs and arms. Tool-manipulating appendages remained safely folded inside their pods while rotating.

Light and powerfully built, the echinopods were capable of sprinting to speeds of nearly fifty kilometers per hour in their 1.8g environment. The lack of a skeleton made their limbs and fingers flexible enough for omnidirectional movements to handle tools and weapons. It was astonishing they'd not developed advanced technology yet.

Far away from populated continents, a remote island was chosen as the landing site. Although not ideally located along the equatorial line, it appeared to be unknown to the aliens. After close to a hundred years, the crew of The Eternity had managed to build a cloaked skyhook, ascension vehicles, and a research station for the alien specimens.

SueLing walked into the meeting room where all her team leaders were gathered.

"We expect our lab expansion to be ready in a few weeks. Where do we stand with the specimens, Lou?" she asked.

Lou, the head of the molecular biology team, said, "We've launched multiple expeditions from our base of operations into nearby landmasses and managed to capture some of their primitives. We've completed their genome sequencing, but we don't know how much it will differ from the higher-functioning sentient aliens. However, it's evident they share a common evolutionary path."

Their first specimens came from plants and animals collected from their landing site. The encoding molecule carrying the genetic instructions of all the scrutinized species was made of six unique base pairs, producing a greater tissue diversity than DNA and giving incredible resilience to all life on the planet. They dubbed the molecule HNC (Hexa Nucleic Code).

"We now need sentient specimens to examine," finished Lou.

"Good point, but we can't just abduct a sentient being without sedating it first," SueLing argued.

"We're just beginning to understand their biochemistry but managed to figure out the recipe of the concoction they use to get drugged. We synthesized it ourselves and tested it on their primitives."

Lagging very far behind in medical technology, the aliens had no knowledge of anesthesia. Surgical procedures were nothing less than gruesome to watch. Barely drugged with a cocktail from a mixture of plants and soil compounds, patients remained conscious. Unaccustomed to pain and suffering, very few humans could stomach watching them and usually had to purge the memory from their minds to avoid suffering from PTSD.

"After a few tweaks, we produced a much stronger version, a true sedative that puts our current primitive specimens completely under," finished Lou.

"Can you share with the group what can possibly compel you to call their primates *primitives*?" inquired SueLing amusedly.

"Well...after lengthy discussions on the subject, I just wanted to avoid any confusion. Because we use primate to designate our own evolutionary cousins, people outside this room might be dumbfounded," said Lou ashamed, provoking a few cackles from his colleagues.

Communicating in thought exchange, the word *primate* didn't even form in their minds, as the set of characteristics it represented was clear to everybody without the need for articulating the word. Back on Earth, primates were meant to designate the top rank of apes, including humans and other hominids that shared a common ancestor. By analogy, the alien primates were closely related as well—they wouldn't know how much until sequencing their HNC—deserving the same qualification. It was clear a decision needed to be made, and SueLing took the lead.

"Let's start calling them primates, okay? Anyone who gets confused can look it up in the UKB."

With some smirks directed at Lou, everyone agreed.

"Excellent! So, are we ready to try the sedative on the alien beings? How are you planning to deliver it?"

"The survey team devised a variety of drones, all cloaked, a few of which can be used for our purposes. We can deploy flying or land-based ones on sparsely populated areas to track and shoot individuals with the sedative when they wander away on their own and observe the results," said Lou.

"Okay. I know it's unlikely, but what will happen if they capture a land-based drone or manage to shoot a flying one?" SueLing inquired.

"They've done their homework! The drone will decompose into a pile of silicates before the aliens can figure out there was anything there. Because the chemical analysis necessary to examine the residue is beyond their capabilities, they'll think they're looking at a pile of common sand."

"And the delivery vehicle, will it decay too?"

"Better. The sedative will be stored frozen in the shape of a tiny spike that quickly dissolves after penetration. They will feel a mild sting, but the echinopods have demonstrated a much higher pain threshold. It leaves no other traces," Lou smiled.

"So, the first subject to drop completely sedated, we will abduct! After we sequence their genome, we will perfect the sedative and capture more of them! Fantastic job, Lou!"

"Once we've mapped their entire anatomy and developed the technology to repair their bodies, we can keep our subjects in full health," Lou smiled, feeling redeemed.

"How far do you want to go?"

"This might require approval from the Council, but we feel abducting them is already bad enough and don't want to cause additional suffering. We want to go all the way, including age reversal," said Lou.

"I'll get you an answer. Who's next?"

Marie, the leader of the alien-anatomy team, spoke up.

"By studying their primates, we've learned their brains have a fast-compensating mechanism—making up for the rotation—which allows them to see a stable view. They can see just like us, even while their bodies rotate."

Everyone in the room was blown away. The echinopods didn't get dizzy!

"I don't think we've ever found another alien species with such adaptation," said SueLing baffled.

"That is correct," intervened the UKB. "However, back on the home planet, in the twentieth century, psychologist George Stratton performed an inverted glasses experiment in which subjects wore glasses that showed them an upside-down view.

After a few days of wearing them, their brains developed the necessary connections to adapt to the inversion."

"But the echinopods are able to do it on the fly as they rotate their bodies to move forward or backwards. Remarkable!" SueLing was still astounded.

"We've also learned they require three types of individuals with slightly different physiology for breeding. Their mating acts are just barbaric. The process of extracting the gametes is brutal, resulting in the death of the weaker gender. The third sex just carries the offspring to term, a litter of individuals of all three genders, and has the primary function of nursing and raising them. The strong sex dominates society while the other two are relegated to reproduction and caring for the offspring," Marie continued.

Max, the sociology expert, added to her explanation.

"Breeding is not the only barbaric thing about our aliens. Multiple factions are constantly at war, decimating their population. The victorious kill or enslave all remaining members of the strong sex and capture the others for reproduction. After each conflict, their numbers dip so low, it triggers a procreation boom to replenish the population. Because the winners are the strongest and most violent, these are the dominant traits passing onto the next generation, making their species increasingly violent. In my opinion, this is the main cause their civilization has stagnated."

SueLing did not like that assessment at all. They might be stuck now, but it was conceivable they might somehow continue to grow as a civilization, develop advanced technology, conquer space, and become a super-predator.

Some in the room shivered, following her train of thought.

"Let's not panic yet, please!" she reprimanded. "Nobody can predict the future. I will reach out to Fedrix for the risk and feasibility analysis. Meanwhile, let's focus on our jobs!"

The level of apprehension in the room went down by a couple notches.

"With the first holding facilities a few weeks away, I expect everyone to be ready. Lou, this is your go ahead!"

Image by Katie Lane

Spinning to produce 1.8g, the 1.5-kilometers-in-radius-by-4-kilometers-wide toroid, dubbed Attenborough—in honor of Earth's famous naturalist—was near completion. Coated with a self-healing and highly resistant-to-impact metamaterial that replaced solar panels, long before the first intergalactic voyage, it was capable of harvesting stellar power with 100 percent efficiency. Traversing spokes intersected at the access point to the station and served as conduits to reduce travel time between the farthest points.

Operational already, the effort now continued toward completing holding facilities comfortable enough for sentient beings. It would house thousands of echinopods, along with millions of plant and animal specimens to feed them, allowing humans to closely study their species.

"The wheels are in motion," said Lou.

After a few months of trial and error, their first subject finally dropped to the ground completely sedated and was promptly abducted.

Once onboard the Attenborough, a scan revealed details of its brain and other vital organs. All the different systems and tissues in its body were meticulously cataloged and analyzed. Mapping of the alien brain got underway.

With the first echinopod in captivity, things progressed much faster. The sedative was perfected, and the team started developing advanced medical technology to repair the alien bodies. Soon they were ready for more specimens.

A dedicated scientist from the Akmaar protectorate, Odan specialized in optics and had worked on lenses for most of his life. Extremely useful in war, telescopes allowed a peek into the enemy's movements from afar. Being a master at building them made him a privileged citizen of the kingdom.

Having demonstrated an exceptional aptitude for science and especially math, he was nurtured by his teachers and given extra tutoring very early in life. He later became part of a tiny elite allowed to attend university, where he was immediately captivated by lenses and their magnification properties. Soon, he was taken under the wing of Akmaar's master crafter, who was in charge of making lenses for telescopes and taught classes at the educational institution.

Odan's skills and dedication allowed him to surpass the achievements and knowledge of his mentor, taking over after his retirement. By discovering new ways to craft sharper lenses with higher amplification and by extending his research into telescope design, he gave Akmaar's military a clear advantage.

But scrutinizing the evening sky became his true passion. Besides their moons, five dots of light stood out, slowly wandering back and forth, night after night. When he first pointed his telescope at them, Odan encountered fuzzy spheroids orbited by moons, not unlike the ones orbiting his own world.

"Why do they have moons?" he asked himself. He was intrigued. "Does it mean they're actually worlds, like our own?"

It led him to an unsettling realization.

"Does that mean our own world is spherical too? If it is, it would have to be gigantic to look this flat!"

To find the answer, he designed an experiment. Two days later he summoned his teaching assistant, Peiden.

"I have a crucial mission to entrust to you. Travel East to Shivlobiv. There you'll stay for ten consecutive days. Exactly at the turn of the sixteen period on your timekeeper, precisely measure the length of the shadow cast by the commemorative pillar at the main square. You must do this for the ten days without failure."

"Yes, professor," he said and rolled out of the room.

Without telling anyone else, Odan left for another village with an identical pillar, a few days of travel in the opposite direction. If the world was flat, both pillars would cast identical shadows.

They did not.

With the measurements on hand, knowing the height of both pillars and the distance between them, Odan was able to determine that their world was in fact spherical, and he could calculate its size. Peiden had faithfully measured as instructed, for his calculations using all ten pairs of measurements confirmed their world's shape and size with a small margin of error that could be attributed to their instruments.

Rattled by his discovery, Odan kept it to himself but didn't stop his research. Painstakingly analyzing the positions of the other worlds, night after night, he reached the unassailable conclusion: they rotated around the Glorious One, what they often called their sun, explaining their apparent back and forth wandering. It was clear their world must rotate around the sun as well.

But, according to their Common Doctrine, the world was flat and placed at the center of the universe with the sun, moons, stars, and everything else in the sky revolving around it. A universe created by the supreme being, solely for his people. These, among other teachings, were considered sacred and had been compiled into multiple volumes generations ago.

One third of their night sky was occupied by a massive ellipse full of stars. Odan didn't understand why so many stars clumped together inside the ellipse but speculated it was very far away.

His telescopes allowed him to discover other star clumps, invisible to the naked eye—some shaped like spirals, others elliptical as well—but he couldn't tell if they were just smaller or looked faint because they were so far away.

"Why do most stars clump together, but only a few are isolated in space? Were they expelled as some sort of punishment?" he chuckled. The most likely explanation was that some sort of process caused them to get ejected.

Finding ever-mounting contradictions to the Common Doctrine, Odan could not retreat from the conclusions his carefully gathered data led him to formulate. They proved beyond doubt that at least some of its teachings were wrong.

He also knew better than to challenge it. He had a comfortable life that allowed him to teach and do research at the university, where he was admired and respected by his students and colleagues. Furthermore, there was no doubt in his mind the supreme leader, a devout believer, wouldn't think twice to sentence him to death for heresy against doctrine if he ever dared to speak—no matter how high his value as a scientist was.

He couldn't understand why or how a third of the ellipse was missing. It looked like some kind of disease that slowly consumed the stars one by one. For many years, he had observed some of the stars right at the terminator line between light and darkness, and they appeared to be getting dimmer.

Other clumps he could see through his telescope did not appear to be affected by the disease. However, he could not see any behind the ellipse, only on the opposite side of it. Were they all dead?

Concerned for his own safety, Odan kept hidden hundreds of pages with his discoveries and conclusions. Bound into a volume and concealed among hundreds of books at his place of residence on the university grounds, they were safe.

The now-burning questions in his mind—the ones he longed the most to know the answers to—were: "Are we alone in the universe?" "Are there other people on the other worlds around our sun?" "Is our sun another star?"

With these thoughts on his mind, Odan rolled uphill toward the stronghold. He had been summoned to the palace of government, to the supreme leader's chamber, where he held audiences and discussed matters of war and security with his military.

Built on the blood from generations of slaves, the walloping fifty-meter-tall citadel was an extraordinary piece of military engineering. Completed by the previous ruler, it rested on an elevated plain, surrounded by a pair of outermost stone walls encircling a moat filled with muddy waters diverted from a nearby river. At the bottom, sharp spikes and swimming predators spelled martyrdom for any invading army.

Once inside, with an already shaken morale, aggressors faced an uphill killing field crowned by a third wall with seventy-five-meter-tall towers along it. Fearless elite legionary forces, attacking from within its safety, made the palace an impregnable fortress.

Shivering at the sight, Odan thought of the ones who built such a leviathan: a lifetime in captivity, filled with abuse, cruelty, sweat, and misery all the way to the grave. He pushed these thoughts out of his mind as he rolled across the bridge over the canal.

Past the courtyard and into the gardens, he entered the main residence and rolled into the hall. Lavishly decorated with works of art and war trophies plundered from conquered kingdoms, it was crowded by guards, the supreme leader's court, those summoned for an audience, and a few power-hungry schemers who stood there ready to take advantage of any opportunity.

On the far end of the room, away from prying eyes and permanently guarded by professional soldiers, a large situation table allowed the supreme leader to track the locations of his armies and ships. Behind it, a wall covered in maps displayed the regions of Akmaar and other territories.

Odan was greeted coldly by a guard and then waited patiently in line. After reaching the front of the row, he stood by until he was spoken to.

A true alpha, descending from a long line of leaders, the supreme leader had been nurtured from birth to command. Under his despotic, strong-minded rule, millions had lost their lives, as the Akmaar protectorate grew beyond the boundaries of his predecessor. Imbued with legacy, dreaded by most, admired by very few, he had conquered and plundered many kingdoms, annexing them with little resistance.

"Master crafter. Approach."

Standing on two of his limbs, Odan approached slowly. It felt awkward and rather uncomfortable to move around this way, but rolling was forbidden in the presence of the supreme leader.

"Your highness," he said with utter submission.

"All essential subjects are mandated to conceive descendants. Your role makes you essential," said the supreme leader without preamble.

Indispensable to the kingdom, Odan enjoyed a privileged status with plenty of perks, reserved for a select group. Throughout years of war, his life had been spared over and over again. Whether his side won or lost didn't matter; his value as a scientist had been enough to keep him alive, along with a few others.

"Supreme leader, I cannot bear being responsible for the death of a fellow Nakkhal being..." Odan started to say.

"Your weakness is shameful. We need a strong relay generation, and you will procreate," interrupted the supreme leader with a demeanor that made it clear he did not care for Odan's feelings at all.

Odan had been dreading this moment for a very long time. Traumatized when he first learned of what went on during their reproduction act, he had tried to come to terms with it for most of his adult life. In the end, he decided never to mate.

"With all due respect, your highness, I teach at the university and have passed my trade to hundreds of students. Surely, many of them..." he tried to argue.

'Cowardly whimpering pacifists!' thought the supreme leader with profound disdain. Pointing an extended limb at Odan, he said.

"You will comply or face punishment."

"Exalted one, I implore you! Consider my contributions to the protectorate," he begged.

"Your final answer, NOW!"

"I have no choice but to face punishment," sobbed Odan, accepting his fate.

A deep silence settled in the room.

What a waste! But it would be foolish to sentence him to death, no matter how much he'd like to do it himself. However, like many tyrants, the supreme leader regarded himself as a merciful ruler.

And, perhaps, after spending time in the dungeons, the weakling idiot would reconsider.

"Very well! You will spend the rest of your life as a slave. Now, take this scum out of my sight."

The guards immediately shackled Odan's top limbs.

'A slave!' After his padded, cushy existence, he surely wouldn't last long at a labor camp. 'A quick death would have been preferable', thought Odan. His cry for mercy did not elicit the compassionate response he had hoped from the supreme leader, who, once his mind was made up, never reversed himself.

As Odan was rushed out of the chamber and dragged down to the dungeons, he wondered what possibly could have led to his current predicament. He had done well by the kingdom and could ensure a fine replacement to take over when he got older. Was it that the supreme leader knew he'd refuse, or someone at the court had it in for him for some stupid reason he couldn't fathom? There were abundant rumors of a secret society where members of his same gender carried out forbidden sex acts with each other. Perhaps someone close to the supreme leader thought he might be a member?

Put into a transport along with tens of other prisoners, days later, he didn't know their final destination. Odan glanced at his city for the last time, the place he grew up, and thought of the dear friends and students he was leaving behind. And his beloved books and other possessions—what would happen to them? No doubt the university would replace him and take over what he left behind. Were his discoveries lost forever, or would someone find and read his book?

A last glance at the shrinking university tower brought back a conversation with one of his most promising students, years earlier.

"Professor, have you ever tried looking at objects in the night sky with a telescope?"

He felt an overwhelming desire to share his findings with him, but the pupil was much too young to share such a burden.

"That would be purposeless. There's nothing to be gained from the experience," Odan answered instead.

"I'm very curious," said the student excitedly. "There must be better applications for telescopes than war. Maybe we can learn new things about our world. I beseech you to try! I will volunteer to help."

Hoping to keep his young and excitable student out of trouble, he had courteously shut down the idea before rolling away towards the courtyard with the excuse of being late for his next class.

Now a castaway from his own world, Odan felt a profound regret and an asphyxiating sense of loss, sinking deeper and deeper into depression.

The transport delivered the prisoners to the port of Akmaar. Gossip among the other captives was that they would be sent to work in construction at one of the recently conquered territories.

As they got out of the transport, a terrified prisoner jumped off and rolled away in a desperate attempt to escape. One of the guards reached for a dagger and, in a calm well-practiced maneuver, swung it with deadly precision, stabbing the panicked runaway in the brain and right through his eye when he was already twenty meters away.

The guard then rolled without rushing to retrieve his blade and, with contempt, tossed the still-twitching body into the murky waters, where a school of creatures started dismembering it and squabbled over the pieces.

"Anyone else want to roll away?" yelled another guard defiantly.

For a moment, Odan thought of it—a quick death rather than spending the rest of his life as a slave—but soon the opportunity was gone.

The supreme leader was right! He was such a coward.

They were shoved onto a ship below the main deck in the rowing area. The sailboat was propelled by the wind, but the slaves supplied additional power. He hated the dark, always damp and humid compartment and grew increasingly terrified of the guards who didn't think twice to maul those they perceived to be slacking.

Odan soon lost all track of time. Life as a slave was a hard and wretched existence, much worse than anything he ever imagined. Underfed and thirsty, he lived in constant pain and anxiety. Becoming weaker day after day, he dreaded the other slaves who bullied him at mealtimes.

Late one night, dozing over his rowing post, his monotonous existence was disrupted by a loud commotion. Living in a constant state of terror, he woke up fully alert, prepared for the usual blow or whiplash to fall on him. Instead, screams were coming from the deck above. Were they under attack?

The skipper's vociferating orders to coordinate the fighters cleared any doubt. A few guards fell through from the main deck. Cuffed down to the floor on his post, he glanced at other inmates who seemed as confused as he was.

"We are all doomed!" screamed a nearby prisoner, unleashing a wave of panic.

They all let go of their oars and struggled with their shackles in a futile attempt to free themselves. Screams of terror from the others filled the room.

Was this the way he would die, bound to the floor of a ship? Would he still be alive when they sank? He couldn't imagine a more horrible way to die than drowning. How long would the horror last?

Once again, he found himself hoping for a quick and painless death at the hands of the enemy when, suddenly, he felt the sting. Turning instinctively to locate his attacker, he didn't see anything in the dimly lit lower deck. He felt for the wound with a limb while checking his surroundings again, but a sudden light-headedness made him extremely weak, and he fainted.

As the anesthetic dissipated, Odan started coming around. It felt so peaceful and tranquil that he thought the whole episode had been a dream. His body rested over a warm and pleasant bed, just like back home, but opening his eyes revealed the strangest room he'd ever seen.

With no discernible junctions, the white wall before him arched and continued turning above his head to become the wall behind him. Made of the same material, the floor and most of the furniture were a perfect white like nothing he'd seen before. It had plenty of the comfort he was accustomed to but, with no doors or windows, he felt like a prisoner. Many times, he had read about and heard others talk of the afterlife. Was this it?

But the strange objects and devices spread throughout the room reminded him of the biology lab at the university where they studied plants and animals. A different kind of fear electrified his body.

He realized, however, he would not be in such a room if they wanted him dead, so he focused on remaining calm and waited. If he had been captured by an enemy kingdom, he surely was more valuable to them alive. But the technology around was beyond his understanding. How did they get him into this room without a door?

The wounds inflicted by the guards and the shackles appeared to be a few days old and were almost healed. How was this possible? Had he been unconscious for a long period of time? His captors did not intend immediate physical harm and obviously wanted him to be comfortable. Why?

A slice of the wall in front of him vanished in front of his eyes and a curious being carrying what appeared to be a tray came in the room. Odan's first impulse was to attack—not that he knew how to fight—but the smell of food reminded him of how weak he felt. Besides, it didn't seem threatening in any way, so he decided to remain still and study the strange creature instead.

With only four limbs, the upper two being significantly short, it didn't have eyes and still it moved around without difficulty, stepping on the two longer limbs. The smooth and shiny surface of the thing spoke of a craftsmanship Odan couldn't even imagine. He was unable to recognize the material—metal or maybe glass? Pure metal or alloy? When was this technology developed? As far as he knew, no one in Akmaar had been able to produce anything so masterly shaped and polished.

Odan tried to roll toward the opening, but the creature reacted swiftly to match his movement and, with unparalleled agility, blocked the way out—without things falling off the tray it was carrying.

As it was both bringing him food and preventing his escape, Odan concluded the visitor could only be a prison guard.

"Who are you? What do you want from me? Why am I your prisoner?"

For an answer, the guard put the food down on a table and retreated. The opening disappeared after it.

Odan voraciously attacked the food. After being famished and thirsty for so long, having enough food and water to satisfy himself raised his spirits. The food was delicious, too, in contrast to the horrible scraps fed to slaves.

Feeling his strength return as he continued to eat and drink, he wondered. "Why would my captors go to such an extent for a prisoner? Do I have any scientific value to them?" He couldn't fathom what such powerful beings could possibly want from him.

The bipedal returned after Odan stopped eating, this time carrying a squared, thin piece of glass. Placing it on the table facing Odan, it then proceeded to clear the leftover food.

The perfectly flat and polished surface was superior to any mirror, but it was transparent. As he approached, puzzled by staring at his own reflection, it suddenly illuminated, displaying the image of a boat in bright colors.

"A boat?" asked Odan.

The screen then repeated in his exact same voice and inflection. "A boat?"

The idea burst into his brain like a bolt of lightning from the sky. His captors were not of this world and were trying to learn his language! Stumbling back, he lost his balance and collapsed on the floor. The guard stopped cleaning and approached to help him up. A few moments passed before he could overcome the shock and return to the table. Yet his captor did not appear to be in a rush.

With a new understanding of the situation, Odan controlled his shaky voice and tried to say with perfect enunciation. "Boat."

The screen repeated the word, and Odan made an affirmative gesture with one of his upward-facing pods. The screen then displayed the next image.

SueLing and Len watched the exchange from The Eternity with mounting excitement. Of the hundreds of alien beings they had abducted so far, this was the only one who didn't attack the drone. Destroying the equipment or wildly trying to escape, his peers displayed extremely aggressive instincts. This one, instead, was willing to teach them their language, which was paramount for humans to learn more about the echinopods.

"That has to be their equivalent of a nod!" exclaimed SueLing.

Each time the UKB repeated a word through the screen, the echinopod made that gesture. Len instructed it to mispronounce the next word. This time, the alien repeated the word and waited for the UKB's turn. Only when the word was properly pronounced, did the alien make the gesture again.

"It certainly is!" smiled Len, imitating the gesture with his right hand.

Back at the Attenborough, the apparent ability of the screen to progress from single words to simple sentences in a matter of hours had Odan astonished. The UKB continued to query him on ordinary objects and actions common to life, developing a base vocabulary, and worked its way up towards small sentences. Odan worked tirelessly, feeding the UKB with words and phrases in order to achieve communication with his captors as soon as possible.

Overwhelmed by such technology, he laughed and cried and then laughed again. When he dared to touch the screen with one of his tool-manipulating appendages, trying to point at something, Odan discovered he could draw on it as well. A low howl of surprise escaped him. He then started sharing even more information, accelerating the exchange. He later started writing descriptions so the aliens could assimilate their writing as well.

"Hungry," he said, pointing at his mouth after many hours of work.

When the drone returned to the room with another tray of food and beverages, Odan pointed at it and asked:

"Alive?"

"No. Machine," said the screen.

He was amazed! How could his guard not be alive and yet have such incredible mobility to carry things around, and agility to prevent his escape?

Odan pointed at the screen and asked. "You alive?"

"No. Machine," the UKB answered through the screen.

"Others...alive?" he asked, knowing their vocabulary was still limited.

Since none of the other echinopods had been as forthcoming, Len decided their alien's willingness to help deserved a kind gesture in return. With SueLing standing beside him, he instructed the UKB to display their image on the screen.

The shock made Odan forget the food.

"We are alive," said Len. Then, with his hand, he made the nod gesture he had learned from Odan a few hours earlier.

Of all the possible shapes Odan imagined alien beings could have, bipedal wasn't one he had considered. Often hunted for food, many bipedal animals in his world were considered inferior and weak. And what was it with both eyes in the front when that made them so prone to being attacked from behind? They didn't look particularly strong either. Odan was sure none of them would stand a chance in combat against a Nakkhal warrior. But then, looking at their technology, he realized they probably didn't need to.

The drone placed a larger display on the wall, allowing Odan to rest comfortably on his bed or a chair while continuing to make progress.

The UKB made exponential advances by identifying the meaning of new words by their context, occasionally confirming with Odan. But it was the alien's willingness to work almost around the clock that allowed the UKB to completely assimilate the alien language and writing in a matter of days. Len and SueLing had multiple face-to-face conversations with him, during this period.

"Are you from one of the other worlds around our sun?" Odan inquired.

"No. We come from very far away," said Len.

"From the ellipse?"

Thinking this must be the way the aliens referred to the M87 galaxy, Len instructed the UKB to display its image on the screen.

"Is this what you call the ellipse?" he asked.

Odan made an affirmative gesture with a pod.

"Our star clump is very far away from the ellipse," explained Len, making SueLing smile. Although the UKB could translate their thoughts into alien words, Len had chosen to speak using the alien word for galaxy.

He instructed the UKB to display the route from the solar system, inside the Milky Way, to the M87 galaxy. Their star clump was much farther than any Odan had identified through his telescopes—so far and immersed in such a vast space! It left the Echinopod breathless and motionless with wonder, struggling to clear his thoughts.

"How many clumps have you visited?"

"Our kind has visited thousands of clumps," said Len.

"Is the ellipse dying?" asked Odan.

"What?" Len was confused. "Sorry, I don't understand the question."

"Stars inside the ellipse are going dark. I've watched the disease advance for many years," explained Odan.

This made them realize that, from the echinopod's perspective, the human expansion wave throughout M87 would appear as if the galaxy was being consumed by an advancing black blob, akin to some kind of disease.

"Be very careful how you answer that question! You could alter the course of their civilization," SueLing warned Len privately so the UKB wouldn't translate to the alien.

"I understand. But this information will not get out to his peers," said Len.

"The ellipse is not dying," Len said.

"Why are you turning off the stars?" asked Odan.

"He's such a remarkable individual!" SueLing said to Len.

She was full of admiration for the echinopod's powers of deduction. With the limited information he had and without the genetic enhancements to augment their intellect that humans benefited from, the alien blew her mind by connecting them to the darkening of the stars in M87.

"We are not turning them off. We simply harvest the light that doesn't fall on the other worlds and use it to feed our people. The worlds around the stars are unaffected by our presence," simplified Len.

However, this reminded Odan about one of the questions burning in his mind.

"Is our sun a star, too?"

"Yes, it is," said Len.

A sense of elation invaded Odan. He had hoped their sun was just another star in the universe. He wondered if the people living on worlds around other stars coexisted peacefully and harmoniously.

"Will our star join the ellipse? Will it go dark too?"

"No. Your star will continue to orbit around the ellipse for millions of your years. We will not colonize it," replied Len.

After a brief pause, Odan continued firing questions. Nothing seemed to quench his thirst for knowledge.

"Are there many other beings like us, in the universe?"

"No. We have found no other intelligent beings. Your people are the first we've encountered," said Len.

This was an incredible revelation. Although Odan wasn't even sure their sun was a star until moments ago nor knew if other stars had worlds, he was certain the universe must be teeming with other civilizations.

"So, nobody lives on the other worlds around our star or other stars?"

"There is life! Many of them are inhabited by countless species, but none of them are intelligent like your kind," answered SueLing.

"I wonder why we are so rare," Odan said, thoughtfully. "Do you know?"

"When individuals reproduce, they pass their characteristics onto their descendants. If that makes them stronger and better prepared to survive, they have a better chance to reproduce. As the cycle repeats over many thousands of generations, new and better species may develop. I'm sure you've noticed the similarities between your kind and other species on your world," said SueLing.

Odan nodded.

"I always wondered about the smaller animals that look like us, almost physically identical, but with no understanding and limited learning capacity."

"Thousands of generations ago, your species diverged from a common ancestor. But we haven't had an opportunity to learn enough about your evolution. Our kind evolved in a smaller but very similar world to yours, around an identical star. They colonized a diversity of challenging environments, including deserts, tropical rainforests, high-altitude plains, mountains, and the polar caps. At some point, there were multiple species similar to us, but only we survived."

"What happened to those species?" Odan asked.

"We don't know for sure, but it's possible our ancestors killed the males and enslaved the females for reproduction because we all carry some of their characteristics. Although our kind lives in peace now, we have a very violent history," said SueLing.

"Like we do in my world," said Odan. "What is it that makes us so...similar?"

"It's your large brains that makes your kind intelligent, allowing you to build a civilization. We don't know what prompted your species to evolve. In our case, we suspect a sudden change in our world's climate threatened the survival of our early ancestors, favoring the evolution of problem-solving abilities. Little by little it made our kind smarter, helping our ancestors figure out answers to challenges, increasing their chances for survival, finally leading to us," she explained.

"How big is the universe?" asked Odan.

"About 200 billion of your light-years," said Len.

"Light-years?" asked Odan confused.

"Light is the fastest thing in the universe. Nothing can travel at the same speed or faster. It can traverse the land you came from, thousands of times, in the blink of an eye. But the universe is vast. It takes light thousands of years to go from your sun to the closest star."

Odan was just blown away. He couldn't visualize the explanation in his mind.

"Is there a supreme being?" he felt compelled to ask.

"All our ancient scriptures speak of different supreme beings, but, as science allowed us to surpass their purported achievements, we started discarding them. Although we have not visited enough of the universe to say there isn't a supreme being, our people don't believe there is one," said Len.

'They have limits, too!' thought Odan. 'They just have incredible technology but they're not supreme beings.'

"What is this miraculous machine that translates our conversations?"

The words from his captives came to Odan in his own voice with the monotone inflection he used to feed them words. It almost felt like speaking to his twin. Because the screens in his room used the same voice when they were learning Odan's language, he assumed they were part of some contraption translating their conversations.

Len stood up and advanced towards the device carrying their image to the screen in Odan's room.

"We can't speak your tongue because it's beyond our vocalization capability. Our technology allows us to exchange thoughts with each other and with the machine translating to your language."

He used actual words and instructed the UKB to carry his voice to the alien, instead of translating, and to display the words in the echinopod's writing on the screen.

The incomprehensible noise of their language reminded Odan of the guttural sounds made by a flying species discovered in a remote region of high-altitude mountains. He had come across them a few years back when a specimen was displayed at the university.

So very far beyond Odan's vocalization capability, the language of his captors would be impossible for any of his kind to try to pronounce. Even a single word.

It was a moment of realization for Odan, who, now for the first time, understood the enormous challenges to bridge the differences between their species, making communication possible. He could now appreciate how far they'd come with the help of their miraculous technology. It was mind-boggling what they had achieved in the short period of his captivity.

Of all the things that astonished and fascinated him about his bipedal hosts, this was the greatest achievement of their civilization, by far. If Odan's people could learn to communicate the way they did, understanding each other beyond words, there would be no wars. He was in awe and inspired by imagining his own kind one day, united and reaching out for the stars.

The exchange also gave SueLing an idea.

"Can we fit the alien with NIs?" the question was addressed to the UKB, but she included Len in the conversation, so he could get the answer as well.

"Based on what is known so far, we will be able to reengineer the current NIs to work on the echinopods, after completing mapping of their brains and anatomy," said the UKB.

Len was blown away by this information and temporarily interrupted the session. It had never occurred to him that they could communicate with the alien, just like they did with each other, experiencing his thoughts and emotions. The alien memories could be uploaded to the UKB for all humankind to experience, allowing people to better understand them. It would be an unprecedented experience and a unique opportunity not to be missed!

"I suppose you want to put it on a leash and parade it around the ship!" said Fedrix beyond furious.

Fedrix was prone to drama sometimes, and Len had to make a serious effort to keep a straight face.

"Oh, lighten up!" hissed SueLing.

She had never gotten into an argument with Fedrix. As far as she could tell, Fedrix had never gotten into an argument with anybody. But ever since news of the alien civilization broke, he had closed his mind so no one could tell how he felt or what he was thinking. These days, he just shared his work thoughts as required by his job but nothing else. SueLing missed the gentle person she had known all her life. Her beloved friend, mentor, and confidant had been ripped away from her.

"Let's take the excitement down a notch, please," intervened Len to break up the argument.

He had been holding periodic meetings since they captured the first specimens, and it was clear that emotions had been running higher; but Len had never witnessed an argument between colleagues or had to reprimand anybody working for him before.

News of the alien civilization was now widespread throughout colonized space. Some people were excited, some were terrified, but the overall curiosity was overwhelming. Feeds from the probes were made immediately available to the public after Len argued the point with the Council. He had also continued to make all his memories available without limitations, as he had done for the last billion years, including his interactions with the alien being. SueLing and most people on the team did the same, except for Fedrix, Stralk, and a few others who had also declined to interact with the alien.

Conversations about the echinopods were now happening in every home, street, school, park, and workplace. The most paranoid wanted to turn the Statites around the alien star into a Nicoll-Dyson beam, focusing enough light on the planet to disintegrate it in an instant. The most peace-loving wanted to help the aliens, giving them technology, and ushering them into space as humanity's equals.

However, Fedrix knew these were the two most extreme points of view. The solution would fall somewhere in the middle. His conversation with Len on the first interstellar trip, over a billion years ago, continued to replay in his mind.

"With their star in intergalactic space and a few others scattered thousands of light-years apart, M87 is the closest galaxy. But relocating our entire population is a tough sell," said Stralk. "The aliens will have to travel millions of light-years away from our space in order to find the first non-dwarf galaxy with billions of stars to colonize."

"Stopping all expansion towards alien space is unthinkable. The Virgo cluster is a thousand times richer in stars and galaxies than the Local Group and much closer than other galactic clusters of similar size," replied one of Len's team members.

With most colonized stars fully populated already—taking much less than a thousand years these days—humanity had been forced to adopt a "one child per couple" policy, millions of years before. The only option nowadays was conceiving their children remotely, on ships or newly colonized stars, raising them through Ansible without ever meeting them in person. Many waited a million years for the privilege.

Even with so many abstaining from procreation, there was already talk of who would be the last generation of humans to have children. It was inconceivable to picture a time when not a single child would be born again. Humanity needed the stars in the Virgo cluster to continue growing.

"Let's assume for a moment we're willing to stop our expansion in this region of space," said Stralk. "We missed the microscopic footprint of the aliens, and, even though we've reprogrammed all our telescopes to scan for micro-technosignatures, we could miss another preindustrial civilization, and another. If we give up at each and every turn, humanity's expansion will soon be choked and cut off completely!"

Most people in the room agreed with him.

The crew of The Eternity was tasked with evaluating all options, and they had enlisted the help of experts and scientists from all over colonized space.

A team of digital scientists from the Matrioshka brain wrote a software component for the redesigned nanoprobes to target the alien reproductive system, curbing their offspring numbers with each generation. Cloning themselves, the nanoprobes would jump onto the aliens' progeny, eventually reaching the entire species. In a few hundred generations, the echinopods would become extinct, without having to kill a single individual or causing them any pain or suffering. Humans would then quarantine their star system, redirecting evolution to prevent primates or any other species from ever becoming sentient.

Another option was moving their star system so far away from the human expansion wave that they would never be able to meet again. However, this idea was less favored. Based on the size of their star, it would take many millions of years to get them to a safe distance, and the aliens could develop advanced technology before that happened.

Although the elevated gravity of their planet would make it extremely difficult for the echinopods to get into space using chemical rockets, it was not impossible. They could develop a space program and turn the star around. Revenge was a powerful motive.

Therefore, the modified nanoprobes were the most attractive option until SueLing came up with a new idea.

"SueLing has a new proposal. I want everybody to give her their full attention," said Len, interrupting all thought in the room.

"My proposal is to uplift the aliens. We have enough specimens to isolate the HNC segments that code for their violent and aggressive behaviors. We can program the new nanoprobes to rewrite those segments and deploy them into their drinking sources, reaching the entire population. They will alter the HNC of all individuals, and these changes will be passed to their offspring, eliminating these traits and reshaping their society. Over time there should be fewer wars, which will allow scientific research, arts, and philosophy to thrive," SueLing explained.

"We can't code our way out of this mess! Just look at the way they reproduce!" said an angry Stralk.

She and Stralk had grown apart a long time ago but continued to be friendly to each other. It made her wonder if Fedrix was influencing him.

"I'm not being influenced by anybody!" said Stralk, following her thoughts. "But I am very concerned about a future clash between spacefaring civilizations with highly advanced technology."

"We will be able to modify their reproductive mechanism to eradicate the killing of their weaker sex. Because they're rarely out in the open, it'll be more challenging to abduct specimens of the other two sexes, but not impossible. After sequencing their HNC, we'll understand the process and find a way to redesign it. We can deploy the changes using the nanoprobes," explained SueLing in a conciliatory way.

Thought exchanges across the room indicated most were not in favor of her idea.

"I know this is a radical proposal. We will genetically reengineer an entire species, tens of millions of individuals, without their knowledge. It won't be easy or ethical, but it is well within our capabilities. This is a better option than euthanizing them or allowing them to evolve into a super-predator that will threaten our survival," she argued in an effort to sway the team.

"I think you're being too cavalier with the super-predator scenario, not giving enough thought to the dire consequences it poses," said Fedrix.

He was certain if the aliens continued on their current path, they would develop advanced technology, even if it took a million years. Being so violent and given the dynamics of the HNC molecule, they had the potential for evolving into a hyper-aggressive, highly resilient species that would stop at nothing to obtain the necessary resources to expand through their region of space.

Without a doubt, humans would be considered a threat. The aliens would hunt them to profit from their technology and to take away their stars—even for fun—given their current level of cruelty. As peaceful as human beings had become, they would not pose a challenge.

Faced with imminent extermination, humanity would eventually react, prompting a resurgence of their alphas, who would go from playing games and sports into leadership positions, militarizing their entire civilization and leading to an all-out genocidal war between two species capable of weaponizing the most powerful energy sources in the universe.

"We believe uplifting will prevent that scenario from happening," SueLing argued.

"You cannot be sure; there's still a huge risk. I personally don't think we should gamble with humanity's future. Our analysis shows 'progressive extinction' to have the lowest risk, without killing a single alien or causing them additional pain," said Fedrix.

"Imagine they enjoy violence so much that, even though you remove it from their HNC, they later find a way to put it back in, along with additional genetic improvements that turn them into the ultimate super-predator. Make no mistake. Just as we control our own genetic code today, so will they in the future," warned Stralk.

Thoughts across the room made it clear SueLing had the losing end of the argument. Even with their minds under lockdown, Fedrix and Stralk had made a very powerful case. Furthermore, with all their meetings also open to the general population, countless people across colonized space were tuning in and probably taking sides. Len decided to intervene.

"I'd like to remind everybody it's not in our power to make such a decision. Therefore, I want SueLing's proposal fully studied and evaluated and its execution plan developed. We must keep all options open and viable for the Council to consider. Because this comes late in the game, it'll require extra work to catch up. I want you all to support SueLing's team in developing the plan," he said, looking at Fedrix.

As a risk specialist, it would fall on him and his team to develop the implementation plan. He couldn't refuse an order from Len. But he knew he could not and would not do his best on the assignment.

"Understood," he indicated noncommittally.

"In the meantime, we will proceed with implanting NIs in our alien. This will allow everybody to experience his memories, thoughts, and emotions, which will be uploaded to the UKB. Direct communication with the alien will be restricted to the Council and senior members of the team," said Len.

Fedrix and others had plenty of objections but didn't bring them forward. They had lost this round; Len had chosen a course of action.

The easiest part was to convince the alien. First, he was given a crash course on science and technology by the UKB, explaining the fundamentals of the microscope, the cell, the atom, and highlights of the echinopod physiology—unknown to themselves but unearthed by human technology—including their brains and nervous systems.

It felt odd to Odan being a student again, but his insatiable intellectual curiosity and hardworking attitude drove him to learn as much as possible.

They had a session to discuss their plan with the alien.

"These technological bridges," asked Odan, "what do they look like?"

Len instructed the UKB to display the prototype NIs redesigned for his species. A single interface looked like a long and smooth tubular surface wrapped around a nerve. Then the UKB showed all the points in his alien body where the NI's would be implanted.

"It looks just like a piece of metal," said Odan.

The UKB then magnified the device to show millions of microscopic devices and molecular circuits. Scrolling within a single nanometer, Odan glanced at a complex array of quantum components passing by at dizzying speeds. The prototype was then slowly returned to its actual size.

He was astonished by the miniaturization and the levels of complexity that human technology had achieved.

"And you get these implanted before you're born?" he asked.

Len pondered his answer for a second. But if the alien was to be allowed access to their society, he would figure things out sooner or later.

"Everybody does. I was born before they were invented, so they had to be surgically implanted in me, as well."

"How old are you?" inquired Odan, full of curiosity. But it was obvious he must be older than anything he imagined.

"I was born roughly 830 million of your years ago," said Len.

Odan had to sit down after this revelation.

"How...how long do you live?" asked Odan, knowing what the answer would be.

"Our technology allows us to live forever," said Len.

"And we'll be able to understand each other without your machine speaking to me on your behalf?" inquired Odan, anxious to change subjects.

"All our communications go through the machine. When we communicate with each other, our thoughts are delivered without translation because our brains work the same way," explained SueLing. "Your brain is quite different, though. Translation will be performed at the lower-level brain functions establishing an equivalence layer, but results will be the same: we will experience each other's memories, thoughts, and emotions. It'll be more intimate and detailed than speech. At the beginning, the machine might ask you for more information in order to make a better translation."

"Your machine explained what anesthesia is. There's no pain during the procedure. I wish my people had this technology! Would you be willing to share it with us?" asked the alien hopefully.

"We need time to get to know each other better. You've been the only one of your species who's been...nonviolent and willing to communicate with us," said Len, instructing the UKB to display other captives.

The UKB then played video feeds of some of the captives before sedation. The screen showed them trying to destroy everything in the room and attacking the drone which didn't even try to defend itself.

"I'm sorry," Odan said, ashamed.

"You've helped us to bridge the abyss between our species. None of this would have been possible without your selfless, tireless effort. We are very thankful," said SueLing.

"Will you allow me to leave my room and see you and your ship with my own eyes?" inquired Odan.

"Yes," said Len after verifying with the UKB that exposure to 1G would not harm the alien.

"I am ready," said Odan. "You may perform the procedure."

A drone entered the room with a beverage.

"This is a first stage anesthetic. Deeper sedatives will be administered prior and during the surgery. You won't feel or remember anything. Time won't pass for you." said SueLing.

Odan nodded with one of his limbs, drank the beverage, and reclined on his bed. A few seconds later he felt sleepy and passed out.

"Is it a good idea to let him out of confinement?" asked SueLing, a bit concerned.

"Of course! The UKB will be able to rein him in if he gets out of control. Security protocols that govern our behavior apply to him as well. No worries," said Len casually.

Nevertheless, this was a shocking revelation to SueLing.

"What?" she asked in disbelief.

She never thought the UKB could have that amount of power over people, nor that it should be allowed. "Are you implying the UKB can control us, like pets?"

"Well, not like pets," said Stralk. "The UKB is our servant. Because it's a non-sentient AI, we fully control it. But long ago, we also put safeguards in place designed to protect ourselves. Have you ever tried to hit someone in anger?"

"Of course not! Have you?" asked SueLing, intrigued by the idea.

Outside of sports and games, violence was unheard of.

"I have," volunteered Len, to everyone's surprise. "A very long time ago. Before I did, all of a sudden my ire vanished, and I calmed down instantly. It wasn't until a few hours later that I realized what must have happened and asked the UKB if it reshaped my emotions. It answered that it was necessary at the moment to prevent harm to myself and others."

SueLing continued to be aghast.

"Think of it as a handrail, a very smart one, that'll prevent you from falling if you lost your balance and were about to get hurt. Otherwise, you won't even know it's there," explained Fedrix.

He was still angry with SueLing—jealous of her friendship with the alien and upset by the proposal to uplift their species. But he loved her too much to leave her in the dark. Nevertheless, he decided to follow the events up close. Being there at a critical moment might allow him to shape the outcome, maybe even prevent something from happening.

"I'm less concerned with safety than with the knowledge it can gain of our civilization," commented Stralk.

"He's just one individual," said Len. "Besides, consider the benefit of having his memories added to the UKB, allowing everyone to experience them. Because he's an outlier echinopod, I suspect they will be amazing. Letting him out of the cage is a very small price to pay."

"What about his right to privacy?" argued SueLing. "Shouldn't he have a say in whether his memories become public domain for humans to peruse?"

"Most people wave that right when they choose to have no filter on their minds. The echinopod hasn't been given that right, but, since the contents of his mind could help sway the final decision we make for his entire species, I believe it merits that his rights be waived for the time being. So does the Council," said Len.

"That is horrible!" SueLing was still appalled.

"Unfortunately, this is one of those situations we never planned for. We may grant him equal rights someday. I'll advocate in his favor, I promise. But for now, we need things to stay this way," said Len.

Understanding that people might be less afraid of the echinopods if they got a closer look at the alien's memories made SueLing drop the matter.

Odan started opening his eyes and pulled himself up as the anesthetic wore off. A thought materialized in his mind.

"How are you feeling, my friend?" asked Len.

He could tell the difference between his own thoughts and the thoughts coming from Len. But he wondered if he would have trouble later remembering which thoughts were his own.

"Your own thoughts are tagged differently than those coming from outside," explained the UKB. "You'll always be able to determine a thought's origin when you examine your individual recollections."

"I'm feeling...good!" said Odan.

Although the UKB seamlessly translated for the humans, Odan had used words.

"Don't try to speak. You only need to think of what you want to communicate," said the UKB.

"I'm feeling good!" he repeated, after struggling for a few seconds.

"Excellent!" said Len. "It took me much longer to make my NIs work properly. When they're implanted before birth, you don't need to worry about mastering them."

Odan was able to understand not only the message but the mood and demeanor of his interlocutor. He smiled. Technology like this would definitely get him in trouble in front of the supreme leader.

"You have complete control over what you share. Focus if you want to keep feelings, thoughts, or ideas private. You may also close your mind and limit what you share," explained the UKB.

"I understand."

"You're still articulating words in your mind. Practice will give you complete control over your NIs to achieve pure thought exchange," added the UKB.

"I'm Len, the leader of this group. I'm honored to meet you."

Due to his unpronounceable name, in the past Odan had recognized Len by his physical appearance—mostly his face—and the weird human writing characters that made his name. But now, thought exchange allowed him to perceive Len's signature.

Impossible to translate into words, it gave Odan an unmistakable sense of Len as an individual, making him realize names were unnecessary. He could access a wealth of information about Len, not just his physical appearance but his memories, friends, family, accomplishments, and every single piece of information about him in the UKB.

"I'm Odan, a scientist from the Akmaar protectorate on my world. I'm proud and humbled to represent my people. We are known as Nakkhal," he imitated Len, hoping the UKB would transmit his own signature.

"Your individual signature is always transmitted with every thought you share. A profile containing all your individual characteristics and memories has already been created. The receiver of the message can understand who you are," explained the UKB.

The familiar slice reappeared, as a portion of the wall vanished, revealing a drone on the other side.

"If you follow the drone, it will lead you to a transport that will bring you to our ship."

Odan rolled through the door and followed the drone, which didn't attempt to stop him this time. He had already seen the rest of the Attenborough through images and videos displayed by the UKB. He followed the drone toward the closest spoke, leaving behind the compartments where other Nakkhals were kept comfortably sedated.

The UKB had explained the effects of low gravity, including the disorientation and weightlessness that he would probably experience due to his physiology. Now, as Odan climbed the stairs inside the spoke toward the station's entrance, he started to feel lighter.

"You're currently experiencing 1G. This is what it will feel like inside The Eternity," explained the UKB minutes later.

It wasn't uncomfortable at all. On the contrary, he felt he could easily get used to it.

"Will it cause any permanent damage to my body?" he paused to ask.

"No. The long-term effects caused by exposure to low gravity will be prevented by our technology. Nanoprobes in your bloodstream are repairing your cells, adjusting your blood flow, and will supplement your oxygen levels, once you enter The Eternity. Just breathe normally."

As they approached the rotation axis, rolling became increasingly harder as each push from his pods made him jump higher and higher until finally drifting freely in midair, clumsily floating and happy as a child

"It's like a dream!"

It was an exhilarating experience until the disorientation feeling made him realize he no longer had control of his movements, and instinct crept into his brain, alerting him of an imminent fall. Just when he started wondering how to get back down, the drone extended one arm and pulled him down gently.

A small reaction ship was waiting at the docking port to take him from the Attenborough to The Eternity. The drone helped him through the hatch, securing him to a seat tailored to his anatomy. Minutes later, the transport docked, and the echinopod was helped into an elevator car with another seat specially built for him. Feeling comfortable and pleased with all the attention he had been subject to, Odan waited patiently as the gravity slowly increased, while the elevator continued toward the drum.

He had been shown live feeds from the ship, but experiencing the full view would have been terrifying to anyone without his experience and understanding of the humans. He felt excited thinking that his people would one day be able to build megastructures like this, to live and travel throughout the universe.

A large crowd, kept at a distance by a line of drones, encircled the exit as Odan rolled out of the elevator. Standing by closer, Len and his team were there too. He still found the humans, with their bipedal anatomy, quite odd, but the random thoughts he caught from the crowd made him understand they found him just as strange.

In a swift effort to break from the awkwardness of the moment, Len advanced to face Odan and made the standard greeting of Akmaar with his right hand.

"These are the senior members of my staff," he said, gesturing towards his people.

One after another, they each identified themselves and saluted him in the same way.

"I'm honored to meet you all," said Odan, a little conscious of the crowd behind them.

"Don't worry about them. They are just very curious and wanted to see you with their own eyes," said Len, following his thoughts.

This was true. Their thoughts were peaceful, but why were the drones needed to keep them away?

"Just a precaution to give you space," said Len. "Come with us on a brief tour of our home."

"You live on this ship permanently?" inquired Odan.

"Most people live in rotating habitats, much larger than this ship. Only a few of us spend most of their lives on ships. I was born here," explained SueLing, walking close to Odan with the rest of the team as they advanced through the crowd.

"Our ships are smaller versions of our habitats. You wouldn't know the difference unless we pointed them out to you," said another member of the team.

Odan looked around. A full view of the titanic scale of The Eternity's 400-kilometer diameter extended in front of his eyes. Cities, mountains, rivers, lakes, and even a small sea along the ever-curving wall of the drum...

"A sea? You have an entire sea inside a ship!" asked Odan, between baffled and amused.

"Trips between stars can take thousands of years. It's important that we are comfortable. We surround ourselves with nature and things that are dear to us," explained SueLing.

"How fast is this ship?" inquired Odan.

"We can reach a speed of .6c," said Len.

Sixty percent of light-speed! Incredibly fast and yet incredibly slow. But if the Glorious One was thousands of light-years away from the ellipse, it must have taken them...

"This is only the second star we visited since we left M87 behind," said Len. "Taking into account the time we stayed on the previous one to colonize it, the total number comes to..."

"Four thousand, one hundred seventy Nakkhal years," the UKB filled in.

"What do you do during all that time?" asked Odan. He was baffled.

"Yes, boredom is an issue," said SueLing. "But we do have plenty of things to entertain ourselves and keep us occupied. A few of us work, but most of the population just goes about their lives like they would in a regular habitat."

"And, in over a billion human years, you haven't figured out a way to travel faster than light?" Odan asked bewildered.

He didn't mean to criticize the humans, but it seemed quite a long time to not be able to figure out a way around such a critical barrier.

"We keep trying," said Len. "But the speed of light seems woven into the fabric of reality. We haven't found anything that can travel faster, with the exception of space itself. We could reach 99 percent of light speed, but we haven't developed powerful enough shields to protect us against collisions with space debris. Right now, it is a balancing act between force fields, lasers, and antimatter canons."

The exchange continued for hours while they wandered around The Eternity, until Odan asked the inevitable question.

"What are your plans for my people? If you leave us alone, we will eventually develop technology and conquer space like you have. If we are the only civilizations in this corner of the universe, shouldn't we work together?"

The changes that had taken place in the alien just with his brief mixed education were evident to the humans. Len finally broke the expectant thought vacuum.

"We've been here for less than a hundred Nakkhal years. We don't know enough about your civilization and haven't decided how to proceed yet," replied Len.

In the few hours Odan had been exchanging thoughts with the humans, he'd gotten accustomed to the additional sensory information that indicated, among other things, how his interlocutor felt. However, the last thought from Len was missing that. Flat, or lacking depth, would be the best way to describe it. It felt like a fog that let him understand their ideas but not to look inside the other party's mind. Had he just caught Len in a lie?

Ashamed, noticing Odan's train of thought, Len reopened his mind.

"Please understand that the Nakkhal is the first civilization we've encountered after a billion of our years. We have no previous experience, no frame of reference to deal with this. Our leaders are considering a wide range of options. But whatever they decide, we will not harm any of your kind."

"So, what comes next?" asked Odan.

"You're our guest. We've assigned you living quarters here, but you are free to return to the Attenborough, if you prefer. Whatever you decide to do, many of our leaders wish to communicate with you over Ansible. I encourage you to accept their invitations. They speak for our people, and you can help shape their perception of the Nakkhal. You're in a unique position to help them make up their minds on how to move forward," said Len.

When they arrived at Odan's temporary quarters, the humans left, allowing him to get comfortable and rest. He contemplated the place in awe. Dark semicircular steps with a scaly pattern gave way to a whitish structure. Shaped like a tridimensional spiral, the building had a wide oval mouth for entrance.

As the door vanished to allow him inside, he stepped in, full of curiosity. The first turn of the spiral revealed a main chamber—a large and lavish space, blending together living and dining areas. One of his pods gently caressed the smooth curved walls, trying to get a feeling of the strange material. Stretching over twice his height to a strangely lit ceiling, large skylights allowed the warm light to flood the room.

The width of the spiral decreased progressively as he rolled upwards to explore the higher levels. As he passed by the alcove, he noticed that the spiral pattern wasn't tight, but loosely coiled around itself. The space among the turns was decorated with beautiful Nakkhal plants, weaving and flowing around the structure until blending discreetly at the center of the spiral, where a lounging deck met the lush green central garden. Ship views sneaked in through large windows on the outer side of the spiral walls.

The whole area was bigger than anything he was accustomed to back home. It made Odan wonder if everyone's quarters were as luxurious.

"Everyone designs their own living quarters. Given the constraints imposed by interstellar travel, it's important that people feel comfortable. In your case, we designed them for you based on your personality and needs. However, anything can be modified to your liking," said the UKB.

"May I see other people's quarters?"

"Yes. Most people have unfiltered minds and will allow it," said the UKB.

"May I see Len's?" thought Odan.

In a split second, his surroundings morphed into Len's quarters, a VR based on live feeds projected into his mind by the UKB. After the initial surprise, Odan wandered inside Len's living room. A bent sofa followed the wall curvature with a table made of a stone-like material in front. A panoramic view of the cylindrical sea through a window across the room was partially obstructed by a couple of armchairs. The monochromatic color scheme and monastic austerity extended to the bedroom, where a large and empty bed was situated.

"This is it? I thought the leader's quarters would be bigger, more luxurious. They seem even smaller than mine."

"Len designed his living space according to his own needs and desires. Human homes have evolved over the eons. Today's living quarters are smaller, as most people prefer to eat with their peers in common areas or have food brought to them if they don't feel like going out," said the UKB.

Odan found it extremely boring, even depressing.

"May I see SueLing's?"

The VR transitioned into SueLing's quarters. Considerably larger, her receiving area alone appeared bigger than Len's entire quarters. Hexagonal in shape with walls painted bright gold, it had no partitions; yet a joyful, cozy atmosphere colored the large, multipurpose space. A sumptuous seating bench, upholstered in golden fabric-like material, matched the walls and enhanced a sleek transparent alloy table. Several large windows displayed sweeping views of the city.

Multicolored couches, matched by hexagonal chairs, surrounded a large sphere almost as tall as Odan at the center of the home. His sensitive heat receptors detected a pleasant warmth emanating from the mystifying object. Not knowing what it was, he approached for a closer look. Incomprehensible noises filled his ears, reminding Odan of human voices. He walked around the sphere to find SueLing and a male he hadn't encounter before, lying on the floor. Their naked bodies were entangled, wiggling rhythmically.

Rather than coherent thoughts, random images and flashes of recollections rushed through his brain, as he accessed SueLing's mind. It was filled with wonderful and pleasurable sensations like he had never experienced before. Contractions all over her body and a sudden sense of weightlessness—almost like being in low gravity—SueLing's brain was lit up with pleasure and delight.

"What is happening?" Odan asked in complete bewilderment.

"Sex is no longer used for reproduction. However, humans derive great pleasure from it and do it quite often," explained the UKB.

Odan was so taken aback by an overwhelming outsider's guilt, the UKB promptly ended the VR. Like missing a step, the abrupt transition forced Odan to rebalance himself when his own quarters reappeared around him.

"SueLing, like most humans, has no filter on her mind. Unfiltered people don't mind being watched during intimacy, because everybody has sex. It makes no sense for them to be ashamed," explained the UKB.

But letting others watch...

"Humans live in a society where all their needs are tended to. Free from fear, the most valuable possessions individuals with unfiltered minds have are their memories. Because they are safeguarded for eternity, they share them freely," explained the UKB.

He tried to imagine any of his kind, like the supreme leader, allowing others to watch while he reproduced. Unthinkable!

"Human beings used to feel the same way about sex eons ago. Many ancient cults saw it as a morals-lacking shameful act and tried to curtail and penalize it. In some early human cultures, sex was only allowed for reproduction and in a restricted fashion. But for human bodies, sex is healthy, stress-relieving, and increases their happiness."

"What about Fedrix's quarters? May I see those?" Odan asked with profound embarrassment, wanting to move forward.

"He closed his mind eighty-three Nakkhal years ago, so I can't grant you access. However, I can let you see his quarters from any moment before that point in time."

So that was the reason his thoughts felt flat. He wasn't sharing with anybody.

"He blocked outside access to his thoughts when the Nakkhal civilization was discovered. There was an order not to share that information outside Len's team. However, after the order was revoked, he did not reopen his mind," said the UKB, showing Odan the original meeting where Len made the announcement.

Odan couldn't help flipping through Fedrix's public memories in the UKB, which dated back to over 830 million of his years.

Woven into a tree, each individual's memories were indexed by common topics, and timestamps. It made it easy to follow a single thread to witness an entire chain of events or jump between related threads, which were folded into a branch of the tree. It also simplified following memories sequentially or doing a search for a specific event or point in time.

With insatiable curiosity, he delved through one of Fedrix's threads in reverse order. Hours went by as Odan traversed the branch, glancing through some memories while entirely skipping others. The least communicative human he had met taught him more about humankind than anything he had learned or done so far.

Diving back in time, he saw many of the stars and galaxies human beings had colonized. Although most lifeforms in the universe were single-celled organisms, there were still countless worlds where multicellular life had evolved. It was so hard to grasp that there were so many species in the universe but none of them sentient! The unfathomable fact they had encountered no other civilization until now made both species exceptionally rare.

Human technology had become impressive in over a billion years of continuous development. The pace of new discoveries had slowed down, despite their dedicating more and more resources to research. Nevertheless, they could do things that would seem like magic to Odan's peers: building planets, healing stars, living forever, and even moving entire galaxies. Things only the gods could do...

It made Odan wonder if the supreme being was just a figment of his people's imagination, created by fear of death and empirical reasoning. But, during one of their conversations, Len had said they couldn't ascertain the nonexistence of a supreme being. However, it was now clear to Odan that if such a powerful being existed, it had to be even greater and more complex than everything the Nakkhal imagined. It definitely wasn't the being who answered their individual invocations for victory in battle against a much stronger army, plentiful crops, or good health. And they would not find any proof of its existence in the Common Doctrine sacred writings, which Odan now knew were wrong in every respect and full of wishful thinking.

Human beginnings were as humble as Odan's people. The Nakkhal, too, had the potential to evolve and grow, achieving as much as humans had. Perhaps working together, both species could find answers to things they hadn't figured out yet? But Odan's dream was shattered when he found the conversation between Fedrix and Len discussing the creation of research stations back on the maiden interstellar voyage.

"So that's what they're planning to do with us? Slowly drive us to extinction?" thought Odan.

The UKB couldn't answer, but a message from Len came into his mind.

"That is one of the options that has been proposed. Countless— myself included—strongly oppose it and are lobbying the Council to rule against it. Fedrix is not a bad person; he and others are just terrified of a future war between our species over resources. As you have seen, the space behind our expansion wave is fully colonized. Over 10^{30} of our people already live in the M87 ellipse. You'll have a tough time expanding in the other direction because there are few stars and dwarf galaxies. The closest normal size galaxy is millions of light-years away. This is an exceedingly complex situation with many variables and outcomes. But I want to assure you we're fighting hard to win the hearts and minds of our people," finished Len.

Len's mind was open, so Odan could see he was being honest or, at least, he meant what he said. What would he do in Len's position?

"If our roles were reversed, you might have acted the same way to protect yourselves and preserve your species' way of life," said Len, following his thoughts. "It's very important you respond to invitations from members of the Council and help them understand your people better. The fact that a peaceful individual such as yourself exists proves our species can coexist in harmony."

A star enclosed by layer after layer of quantum processors, each made by billions of rings, the Matrioshka brain project started in the 30,000th century. With no energy waste, the heat irradiated from the first layer was turned into power to feed the second layer, and so on, until the heat released by the outermost layer was close to the average temperature of the universe.

With an off-the-charts amount of computing power, a large portion of the Brain was applied to research in theoretical physics, quantum mathematics, and other fields of study requiring mind-boggling, number-crunching capabilities.

A billion times more people than a standard Dyson swarm lived in the Big Brain, which measured as a K2.1 civilization itself. All of its inhabitants were digital minds, either uploaded from living individuals or born inside the Brain. This was a result of an algorithm that combined existing minds adding random variations, similar to the way the UKB combined DNA when humans procreated.

When the project was established, there was a call for volunteers to donate a copy of their minds to inhabit the Brain. Even though most were afraid of being trapped in a VR for eternity, people from all over colonized space came forward providing a high diversity mind-pool. Fedrix was among them.

Even though his digital self had diverged from Fedrix eons ago, it was closer to him than his two daughters or any other human being. Like the elder brother Fedrix never had or the father he couldn't remember and as close to a spiritual guide as was possible in a highly rational era, it was an ever-calming presence in his mind. He trusted no one else so completely and blindly.

Although humanity had evolved into a fact-based logical society—favoring reason over gut-feelings—the inhabitants of the Big Brain took it to the extreme, making it the cornerstone of their society. By purging all emotions from their digital selves, they had built a community entirely based on logic.

It was customary for clones to change their names, differentiating themselves from their original donors. Fedrix's digital self reverted to his original human name, Federico.

"Why have you kept your mind closed all these years?" Federico inquired.

Although Fedrix's mind had been closed for everyone else, it wasn't the case for Federico. They often communed with each other and followed each other's memories.

"I suppose I'm afraid others can see my fears and prejudices towards the aliens. I wish this was one of those problems we could make disappear in an instant and go on with our lives. I hate the complexity and contradiction that has plagued my existence since we encountered them," answered Fedrix.

"'The only thing we have to fear is fear itself', said an Earth president a long time ago, before the space era," replied Federico warmly.

"Oh, come on! We are nothing like them! We're so much...better. How is this at all relevant to our current predicament?" asked Fedrix, exhaling in short, angry puffs.

"Despite all your genetic enhancements and technology, you are still like them: emotional," said Federico in a soothing demeanor.

"Even today, humans continue to be ruled—albeit in smaller measure—by emotions, and fear is a very powerful one. People do unconventional things out of fear. It made you behave in an irrational way. You lose so much by allowing it to rule your existence! Take SueLing, for example. You know how much she misses you."

With people all around colonized space conceiving children through Ansible, there was a diverse gene pool to seed new Dyson swarms. However, the bureau of DNA management—an organization mandated to prevent humanity from branching into multiple species—instructed the UKB to mix DNA from the general population to produce additional children. This added even greater diversity to the population and helped homogenize the gene pool throughout the cosmos. SueLing was one of those children.

Without parents, they were raised by educators, aided by androids, and lived together until ready to be on their own. Although their "families" were unconventional, there were no differences between them and children raised by their biological parents—either in person or through Ansible; they were as well adjusted and educated. They shared the same schools, many of the same experiences, and the same access to information.

Although Fedrix had other partners after Nova, he did not have another child. He, among many others, often visited the local nursery to spend time with parentless children and share experiences with them.

A funny little girl, SueLing stole his heart the first time they met, and a very special bond grew between them over the years. He watched her grow and helped her through the difficult times everyone experiences on the road to adulthood. After growing up and moving on her own, she had taken to visiting the nursery herself and doing for others what Fedrix had done for her.

He loved her like his own children and mentored her in many subjects, encouraging her to grow intellectually and later to specialize in her favorite subject—biology—becoming the top field expert she was today.

"You should offer both her and Len an apology," said Federico, following his thoughts.

"Yes, I'll make peace with them," said Fedrix, acknowledging his own stupidity.

"The Nakkhal are a burden too large for you to shoulder alone. This is a challenge for all humanity and will only be met by all our minds working together."

At last they were getting to the subject he wanted to discuss!

"There's more than one solution to our conundrum, but I think we've come up with the best possible scenario. We're approaching what's being called the cosmic horizon of humanity. This is how far we can go before the expansion of the universe prevents us from going back. With every colonized galactic cluster moving farther away from the Local Group at an increasing speed, the time has come to take measures to keep our civilization together," said Federico.

Painfully aware of the situation, Fedrix had tried to ignore it his entire life, hoping someone else would come up with a solution. As the universe continued to expand at an ever-faster pace, it would exceed the maximum speed of their ships, making everything outside the Local Group unreachable.

"We must start moving all our colonized stars towards the Milky Way and assemble them into a galaxy, millions of times bigger than anything in the observable universe. Closely held together, when the Laniakea super-cluster gets torn apart, our hyper-structure will remain whole," said Federico.

"I can't believe that after a billion years we haven't figured out how to break the light-speed barrier! I always hoped you guys would solve this," said Fedrix disheartened.

"We need more computing power."

"Really? I thought you had more than you'd ever need!" said Fedrix surprised.

"There are almost three octillion minds living inside the Brain. It takes so much computing power to keep us all alive, one half of us go into storage for years at a time to free up processing cycles to do research. But, even adding spare cycles from all UKB nodes at nighttime, we still come up short. However, it will change soon. We've gotten approval from the Council to build two additional brains; only these will be slave processors—with no one living in them—for us to run pure research. Hopefully, that will give us some of the computing power we need to help us find answers."

"How does that feel, being in storage?" asked Fedrix, full of curiosity, the aliens temporarily pushed out of his mind.

"Just like taking a nap. We don't need to sleep since we don't have physical bodies to regenerate. But sometimes we have to go into storage during hardware maintenance, so we also started doing it to free-up processing cycles."

"How much computing power does it take to make new discoveries?" questioned Fedrix. This wasn't an issue he encountered often.

"The pace of discovery began slowing down over a billion years ago, although we didn't notice until much later. Even before the space age, increasingly larger teams of people were necessary to make new discoveries. Today the complexity of research is such that, rather than biological minds, we need raw computing power. But, even with all the available cycles from our entire civilization, the process has slowed to a crawl. Thousands of years go by between minor discoveries. With two dedicated extra brains, we will quadruple the amount of processing power available for pure research," said Federico.

"And that would accelerate the pace of discovery to what...once every few hundred years?"

"Not exactly, but definitely faster than anything we have now," said Federico.

"So, what about the aliens?"

"What do you think about Odan's memories?"

The alien's memory tree had become the most accessed item in the UKB. Over 99.9 percent of all humanity had accessed it. Nothing had ever been in such demand since the UKB became operational. Powerful as it was, it just didn't have enough bandwidth, so it pushed copies of it to trillions of local nodes to eliminate bottlenecks and prevent access jams.

"Although we have the largest UKB node in existence, we were not immune to the bandwidth problem. We took our copy and cloned it a million times to keep up with demand," said Federico.

Despite translation, the quality was excellent. The emotional content allowed people to experience Odan's thoughts and feelings: fear of the inevitable consequences of his discoveries; his courage and moral values in challenging the supreme leader by accepting punishment for refusing to mate; and the deep sense of loss and humiliation after being dragged like a convict from the city where he grew up. Reactions varied, but there was a general feeling of sympathy towards him.

"They were...touching, to say the least," acknowledged Fedrix.

"Our conclusion supports SueLing's argument that the Nakkhal can be biologically reengineered into a species that can partner with humankind," replied Federico.

"Partner?" snorted Fedrix.

"Of course! But we first must stop further colonization of M87 and withdraw from it by moving the stars we've already taken, using stellar engines, back to our side of space. While Odan's species is being reengineered, we will move their star towards what's left of the ellipse, where they will have over 600 billion stars to colonize, plenty of room for their initial expansion."

Fedrix was now beginning to put some of the pieces together. Humans would withdraw from Nakkhal space, allowing them to start their own colonization wave. In time, the expansion of the universe would isolate the two civilizations from each other, making it impossible to come into physical contact. The uplifted aliens would not pose a threat, and the two civilizations would coexist peacefully.

"Will we give them our technology?"

"We will provide them as much help as they request, including technology," answered Federico.

"What will prevent the Nakkhal from reengineering themselves into a super-predator species after we uplift them?"

"The same thing that prevented humans from following that path. If the majority are peace-loving individuals, living in a scarcity-free civilization where everyone's happy, their alphas will be kept at bay by the same safeguards we built into our society," said Federico.

It was crystal clear and so simple! The human expansion would continue away from the Virgo cluster, allowing the Nakkhal room to grow. But what would happen if humans encountered other alien civilizations while expanding through the other galactic clusters?

"As time goes by, it'll be more likely for new civilizations to emerge, but, given we are approaching our own cosmic horizon, it won't matter. We'll colonize as many stars as possible until then and help any new civilizations we come upon."

With all his questions answered and fears reined in, Fedrix breathed a sigh of relief. As the huge load came off his shoulders, he reopened his mind, groomed himself, and put on fresh clothes.

Darwin trotted up to him, stood on his hind legs, and wrapped his front paws around his human's neck, begging for love. Fedrix hugged the cat, pulling and scratching its silky fur—something he hadn't done in a long while. Resting his head against the cat's, cheek to cheek, he was flooded with unconditional healing love from his purring feline friend.

As the door vanished on his way out, something tackled him with a loud cry. A mane of dark burgundy hair with bright yellow streaks obstructed his vision. SueLing had launched herself at him with a hug that made him stumble, nearly knocking the wind out of him. He realized what was happening and, recovering from the shock, hugged the girl tightly while making an effort to regain balance. For a few seconds they remained in each other's arms, tears washing over the scars of their long separation. Although a hundred years wasn't a long time, Fedrix felt an incredible sorrow for keeping his mind closed to her for so long.

"I'm so sorry!" he whispered, with tears rushing down his face.

"No apology is necessary between us!"

Time seemed to slow down as memories of the two of them together ran through her mind...like the day they entered a father-child sand sculpture competition and dethroned the local champions, or the time she and a friend dyed Darwin's fur green. As she grew up, his arms became smaller, but they were still the most comfortable place in the universe.

"I remember," he said, touched by her memories. "Better stop it, or I'll start crying again."

After a few minutes, the door vanished again, and Len walked in.

"Welcome back, old friend! It has been too long," he said walking in to hug him.

"A conspiracy, I see," said Fedrix, wiping away his tears and smiling.

SueLing made room, and they got entangled in a three-way embrace. Fedrix shared the recent conversation with his digital self.

"We know!" said SueLing, "Federico was sharing it with us, live."

"That sneaky traitor! Can't even trust one's digital self," exclaimed Fedrix, and they all laughed again.

"Amazing how he knows you better than yourself," smirked Len.

"You do know we used to be the same person, right?" Fedrix said, continuing the banter.

"What now?" asked SueLing.

"First, I owe Odan an apology. Second, we need to start working on your implementation strategy. I expect the Big Brain will be unified in its collective proposal to the Council. We need to make sure all the contingencies are covered, and the project plan is flawless," said Fedrix.

"It's so good to have you back, old friend!" smiled Len.

A bad habit caught in his early university years—while waiting for the result of a particularly difficult test and, later on, while waiting for the outcome of a crucial experiment—made Odan roll back and forth in erratic patterns, like a tumbling wheel. It didn't escape him that he was doing it much more often since arriving on The Eternity.

"Could you please stop rolling? You're driving me crazy!" nagged Fedrix, oddly reminding Odan of how rolling was forbidden in the presence of the supreme leader.

Fedrix followed his train of thought and, having traversed his memory tree many times, felt ashamed. Decades of tireless work together had made Odan and Fedrix great friends.

"Some people are easily bothered when environmental distractions disrupt their concentration. He didn't mean to be rude," explained SueLing with kindness.

"Of course not! I'm very sorry!" said a sheepish Fedrix.

"There's nothing to regret, dear friend," said Odan with a smile.

"Our species has plenty of quirks, too. I hope none of them is making you lose your mind," she smirked.

"If the vote comes against us, will you upload a copy of my mind to the Big Brain and euthanize my body?" Odan asked a few minutes later.

"Why would we do that?" asked Len. "In that unlikely scenario, you'll be able to remain here with us."

"That's a very nice offer, but I feel lonely with no others of my kind here. Besides, this is not my natural environment. I kind of miss our own gravity, and breathing at this low oxygen level is not the most pleasant sensation. Besides, the lower atmospheric pressure affects my balance. But, if I were transferred to the Brain, at least I'd have other minds to interact with as peers. It would be closer to home for me," said Odan.

Since an individual was the sum of all his or her memories, Odan would effectively cease to exist in the physical world, transitioning into the virtual one inside the Big Brain with no discontinuity, Fedrix thought intrigued.

"It has been done before," said the UKB. "Some of the original donors to the Matrioshka brain requested their bodies to be disposed of after being uploaded."

"This is a premature discussion. Although the vote is not yet in, we are positive public opinion has been swayed by our continued engagement with the help of Odan's memories. Nevertheless, we would very much welcome you to upload a copy of your mind, regardless of the outcome of the vote. We have much room for newcomers, and you'll be able to procreate with other digital brains," said Federico.

They were all at the SCI's headquarters in the Asimov tower, waiting for the final announcement from the Council. Over the last fifty years, they had identified and tested the genetic changes to entirely reengineer the Nakkhal. During that period, the team had also worked on the implementation plan and risk analysis, covering all possible scenarios. They had also determined many HNC enhancements to significantly improve the aliens' physical and mental abilities and had developed the technology to reverse aging in their bodies. Odan himself volunteered to test most of them.

Busier than ever before in his short life, Odan completed basic education and specialized in astrophysics, quantum theory, and the biology of his own species. He also helped make the case for uplifting the Nakkhal to members of the Council and influential thinkers.

His memory tree had greatly contributed to shaping public opinion and had a transformative influence on humanity's culture and creativity. Inspired by his life struggle, music, stories, and many other kinds of artwork were crafted by the human mind. From the banality of having his image printed on their bodies or clothing to becoming a scholarly icon, Odan's image was everywhere. In many intellectual circles, he was compared to notable human scientists persecuted during the dark ages. Some even called for naming humanity's next age group the "Odan Generation" in his honor.

SueLing and Stralk were sitting together holding hands, her head resting on his shoulder. They were not back together as a couple but remained close friends. With so many people around to choose from—whether locals or Ansible acquaintances—and given the possibility of manufacturing the perfect partner inside a VR, there were no broken hearts, and unsatisfied sexual desire was unheard of. Friendship had stronger ties and sometimes lasted forever.

A legislative body made of representatives from each colonized galaxy, the Council ensured that all voices were heard equally. With a vote proportional to the size of the population they represented, each galaxy had its own local council and were organized in different ways. Dwarf galaxies with less than a billion stars had a representative for every single one, but large galaxies were broken down in smaller units with the representatives of each star reporting to their local unit. The result was the same: one person, one vote.

Rather than making the decision themselves, the Council had decided to put the matter of the Nakkhal to a vote, and they were now waiting for their citizens to decide. For the first time in millions of years, every single human being made their voice heard on one specific issue.

Throughout the vastness of colonized space, UKB nodes tallied the votes of their local swarms and reported them to their regional governments. When the final count arrived, the president of the Council made the announcement using words. The UKB translated it into thoughts for anyone who preferred it.

"Today, for the first time in eons, humanity has spoken with one voice. A long time ago, we miraculously left our technological adolescence behind and avoided self-annihilation, emerging united from the shadows of war. In over a billion years of history, humanity has risen from its evolutionary cradle, taking the first steps into the cosmos.

We thought we were alone in the universe, but we found a fellow civilization struggling to rise. The lessons learned from first contact in the dark pages of human history have not been forgotten. This time we will do the right thing to help our fellow sentient beings, like we do with our young when they need to stand up, to become citizens of the universe. With this vote, humankind comes together lending a hand of friendship to our younger sibling, to walk and to take its first steps into the cosmos as our equals."

It was a bit grandiose, but, after the announcement ended, it took a few seconds before any of them could elaborate a thought. This was the decision they had hoped for, and they were ecstatic.

"Wow! That was even more long-winded than one of your speeches!" Stralk said, clapping Fedrix on the back and making them all laugh.

Odan, who had carefully studied the dark pages of human history in an effort to learn from their mistakes, thought that his own species had been spared for not having to go through the technological adolescence that caused so much death, suffering, and destruction to humanity. It would save so many lives and untold misery for his people! How fortunate for them...

SueLing, who was following his thoughts, said with a kind smile. "We are happy to help."

"Okay, everybody! Let's get to it. We have plenty of work ahead of us," said Len.

Epilogue

IT TOOK 5,000 YEARS TO UPLIFT THE NAKKHAL. AS THE crew of The Eternity engineered their evolution towards a smarter and less violent species, progress took over, leading to a fast-forward development in sciences, arts, philosophy, and culture.

Odan and the others remained on board and, from specimens in captivity, became ambassadors to their own species. With their assistance, contact between the two civilizations was made possible for the first time in history.

With the help of humans and their technology, the Nakkhal were now taking their first steps into space. It would still take a while to finish moving their star back into M87 but, in the meantime, they were hard at work dysoning their home star. The Eternity remained in their system for the duration of the entire project and was now waiting for enough lasers to be completed so it could be accelerated back toward M87.

Meanwhile, humanity started pulling back towards the Local Group. On trillions of stars in galaxies across colonized space, UKB nodes realigned their Statite clouds turning them into stellar engines, and headed back home. Like so many other Earth native species before them, humans were returning to their place of birth.

"What kind of hyper-structure will it be?" asked Fedrix, while conversing with his digital self.

"We designed a hyper-cube held together by the mutual gravity of the stars, which the expansion of the cosmos will not be able to unravel. It will be visible in the infrared spectrum across the entire universe before it tears itself apart," answered Federico.

"Have you figured out how long it will last?"

"Right now, we scoop helium and heavier elements from our suns. What's not needed for construction we break down into hydrogen and inject it back into the stars. This way, they will continue burning for many trillions of years."

Something wasn't right. If Federico had a body, Fedrix would say he was nervously fidgeting with his fingers.

"And they lived happily ever after...for trillions of years? Elaborate, please!"

"Well...the process is inefficient; there's waste in it. As we start running low on elements, our stars will get dimmer. Unless we find a solution in about a quadrillion years, all our stars will die and humanity with them. We are stardust and into dust will turn."

That was kind of poetic for a being without emotion, thought Fedrix amused. His digital self smiled broadly, something that Fedrix had never thought a non-corporeal being capable of.

"The truth is we need more data," continued Federico. "Our two new brains are starting to produce answers, but we are finding we still need more computing power. We got approval from the Council for twenty more. Once they're completed, we will be able to run more calculations. Perhaps..."

Humans were not the eternal beings he once told his daughter Kaira they were over a billion years in the past. Eternity was a myth. Sooner or later, the universe would end, get torn apart, or something else.

"That's very likely," said Federico, following his thoughts. "Our ancestors were mortal. Our life span may be trillions of times longer, but, in the end, we are mortal as well. Our time in the cosmos is finite, and we should make the most of it."

"I wonder what will happen to us now?"

The Eternity was too far away to join remaining colonization efforts that would continue for a while on other galactic clusters before they too were forced to turn back. Humanity's colonization era was approaching its sunset.

"I'm afraid your jobs will no longer be necessary," said Federico, smiling again and using real words.

"What's funny about that?"

"That's what they used to tell people back on the home planet when they lost their jobs before the space era."

"I still don't find it amusing, but I'm pretty sure I'll find something else to do," said Fedrix confidently.

"I think you should consider taking time off; you have all worked so hard."

He then shared a video that Fedrix recognized immediately: the New Year's Eve fireworks that made his friends emotional on the night of his billionth year birthday. Barely ten thousand years ago, it felt like a million to Fedrix.

"You tracked the woman in the video!" Fedrix said with sudden realization.

"Indeed! Her name was Yasmin Shehzad. She passed away thirty years after the video was recorded. She did have a daughter, still alive back at the home star. Her name is Amanda...Tarifa."

Humans had stopped using last names eons ago, but they both remembered theirs. "Is...is she...my daughter?" asked Fedrix with choking anxiety.

He had a daughter from before the space era! Someone who might know things about himself, forgotten eons ago!

"Our daughter, Amanda, escaped the home planet before the last great war. Yasmin shared many things about you with her daughter, most of which she wrote in a diary. When the UKB became operational, she uploaded them, just like you did."

Like most people born before the UKB, Amanda had hundreds of thousands of stills and videos uploaded from her mobile device. Federico started sharing a few of her images, giving Fedrix a serious case of butterflies in his stomach. She had his eyes and dimpled chin, just like Kaira and Zhanna.

"But how in the universe did you find her?"

Federico shared a picture, timestamped May 2016. Fedrix recognized himself next to a woman. She was quite beautiful, and Amanda looked very much like her. He looked so old and frail, holding hands with the woman in front of a vineyard. Their faces were illuminated with love and happiness, as they raised their glasses. Federico then zoomed onto their glasses to reveal the inscription, *Chateau Montelena*.

"Oh!"

Those glasses! He quickly looked up the objects he had donated to humankind's heritage museum and found it. It was the same one he brought with him to Terminus!

"That's how I was able to find her," revealed Federico.

"But how come I was unable to track her with so many pictures and videos?"

"The UKB couldn't share them with you because they were marked private. Amanda only decided to make those pictures and videos public when moved by Odan's memories. An impulsive, empathic reaction, I suppose," Federico explained.

Fedrix was at a loss for thoughts.

"You know, Amanda is quite lovely despite having half your DNA," joked Federico.

"Poetry and jokes?" asked Fedrix, surprised and amused. "This is so unlike you!"

Instead of answering, Federico shared one of Amanda's videos. For a moment, Fedrix thought it was a still photo, showing a bedroom, but Yasmin walked in from behind the camera with a newborn baby in her arms. Amanda had to be days or weeks old; the video was dated early 2017.

"Hello Fedri joon. This is your daughter, Amanda. I hope you're happy and safe in Oregon. I know that your economic situation isn't perfect, so I decided to raise Amanda on my own. She is the product of our love and will transcend us. I hope you can meet each other someday. She looks so much like you!"

What economic situation? Fedrix couldn't understand what she was talking about.

"Amanda and I were able to make sense of her notes. Back then, people needed to work to cover their..."

"Yes, I know," Fedrix interrupted impatiently. "Please continue!"

"Apparently you lost your job and decided to move far away to live on your own, according to your diminished means. Yasmin decided not to burden you with raising Amanda, since your resources were limited and you had already left," explained Federico.

It broke Fedrix's heart. Even though it couldn't be compared to the darkest pages in the history of humanity, his was a cruel and ruthless era, nonetheless. A tear rolled down his cheek, moved by this forgotten piece of his past, rescued from the eons of time.

"According to Amanda's notes, her mother never forgot you and always spoke of you with great love and admiration," said Federico. "Would you like to meet her?"

Fedrix nodded and the UKB placed him in a VR with Amanda. She was the very image of her alluring mother with many of the imperfections of her father.

"Hello..." he started to say. But without giving him time to react, Amanda flung herself into his arms.

Acknowledgments

As I expressed before, no one raises themselves purely on their own; it's always a team effort. I therefore would like to thank the following people for their contributions to this novel:

To my dear friend Gala Stevenson, whom I've not seen in over twenty-five years, for her invaluable help in rewriting key parts of the novel and for teaching me many tricks of the trade.

To Seth Shostak from whom I've learned so much over the last decade for allowing me to use him as a character.

To my editor Leah Rubin for her supreme patience in dealing with my insecurities as a writer and guiding me through to the final completion of the manuscript.

To Katie Lane for the outstanding graphics illustrating the story.

To Charlie McKee, my proofreader, who made sure we got it "just right."

To Sharon Miller, my formatter, who put the whole thing together so we could make it available to the readers for whom it was written.

To Anand Giridharadas whose teachings in his book *Winners Take All* shaped many of the ideas in the story.

References

In order of appearance:

1. The Fermi Paradox: The Dyson Dilemma v2.0 by Isaac Arthur
   *https://www.youtube.com/watch?v=QfuK8la0y6s&feature=yo
   utu.be*

2. Science & Futurism with Isaac Arthur (Facebook Group) -
   https://www.facebook.com/groups/isaacarthur

3. Free Fall - *https://en.wikipedia.org/wiki/Free_fall*

4. Anthocyanin - *https://en.wikipedia.org/wiki/Anthocyanin*

5. Galaxy - *https://en.wikipedia.org/wiki/Galaxy*

6. Yellow Dwarf - *https://en.wikipedia.org/wiki/G-type_main-
   sequence_star*

7. M87 - *https://en.wikipedia.org/wiki/Messier_87*

8. Milky Way - *https://en.wikipedia.org/wiki/Milky_Way*

9. Virgo Cluster - *https://en.wikipedia.org/wiki/Virgo_Cluster*

10. AI (Artificial Intelligence) -
    https://en.wikipedia.org/wiki/Artificial_intelligence

11. Dyson Swarm -
    https://en.wikipedia.org/wiki/Dyson_sphere#Dyson_swarm

12. Terminal Velocity -
    https://en.wikipedia.org/wiki/Terminal_velocity

13. Graphene - *https://en.wikipedia.org/wiki/Graphene*

14. Metamaterial - *https://en.wikipedia.org/wiki/Metamaterial*

15. Reaction Engine - *https://en.wikipedia.org/wiki/Reaction_engine*

16. Neural Interface (NI) - *https://en.wikipedia.org/wiki/Brain%E2%80%93computer_interface*

17. Metallicity - *https://en.wikipedia.org/wiki/Metallicity*

18. Alpha Centauri - *https://en.wikipedia.org/wiki/Alpha_Centauri*

19. G-Force (1G/Earth's Gravity) - *https://en.wikipedia.org/wiki/G-force*

20. Andromeda Galaxy - *https://en.wikipedia.org/wiki/Andromeda_Galaxy*

21. Triangulum Galaxy - *https://en.wikipedia.org/wiki/Triangulum_Galaxy*

22. Local Group Galaxy Group - *https://en.wikipedia.org/wiki/Local_Group*

23. Galactic Cluster - *https://en.wikipedia.org/wiki/Galaxy_cluster*

24. Laniakea Supercluster - *https://en.wikipedia.org/wiki/Laniakea_Supercluster*

25. Micro-G environment - *https://en.wikipedia.org/wiki/Micro-g_environment*

26. Plate tectonics - *https://en.m.wikipedia.org/wiki/Plate_tectonics*

27. Astrobiology - *https://en.wikipedia.org/wiki/Astrobiology*

28. Ansible - *https://en.wikipedia.org/wiki/Ansible*

29. "Auld Lang Syne" - *https://en.wikipedia.org/wiki/Auld_Lang_Syne*

30. Ringworld - *https://en.wikipedia.org/wiki/Ringworld*

31. Matrioshka Brain - *https://en.wikipedia.org/wiki/Matrioshka_brain*

32. Speed of Light - *https://en.m.wikipedia.org/wiki/Speed_of_light*

33. Fermi Paradox - *https://en.m.wikipedia.org/wiki/Fermi_paradox*

34. Faster-Than-Light (FTL) - *https://en.wikipedia.org/wiki/Faster-than-light*

35. Cyanobacteria - *https://en.wikipedia.org/wiki/Cyanobacteria*

36. Gravitational Lensing Telescopes (FOCAL Spacecraft) - *https://en.m.wikipedia.org/wiki/FOCAL_(spacecraft)*

37. H-1B Visa - *https://en.wikipedia.org/wiki/H-1B_visa*

38. Enrico Fermi - *https://en.wikipedia.org/wiki/Enrico_Fermi*

39. Dyson Sphere - *https://en.wikipedia.org/wiki/Dyson_sphere*

40. Freeman Dyson - *https://en.wikipedia.org/wiki/Freeman_Dyson*

41. Michael Hart - *http://adsabs.harvard.edu/full/1975QJRAS..16..128H*

42. Exoplanet - *https://en.m.wikipedia.org/wiki/Exoplanet*

43. Habitable Zones (Circumstellar) - *https://en.m.wikipedia.org/wiki/Circumstellar_habitable_zone*

44. Breakthrough Starshot - *https://en.wikipedia.org/wiki/Breakthrough_Starshot*

45. Gamma-Ray Burst - *https://en.wikipedia.org/wiki/Gamma-ray_burst*

46. Black Hole - *https://en.wikipedia.org/wiki/Black_hole*

47. Great Filter - *https://en.wikipedia.org/wiki/Great_Filter*

48. Perimeter of Ignorance - *https://www.haydenplanetarium.org/tyson/essays/2005-11-the-perimeter-of-ignorance.php*

49. Isaac Asimov - *https://en.wikipedia.org/wiki/Isaac_Asimov*

50. Seth Shostak - *http://sethshostak.com/*

51. O'Neill Cylinder - *https://en.wikipedia.org/wiki/O'Neill_cylinder*

52. James Webb Space Telescope - *https://en.wikipedia.org/wiki/James_Webb_Space_Telescope*

53. Space Elevator - *https://en.wikipedia.org/wiki/Space_elevator*

54. Star Tram - *https://en.wikipedia.org/wiki/StarTram*

55. Skyhook - *https://en.wikipedia.org/wiki/Skyhook_(structure)*

56. CRISPR - *https://en.m.wikipedia.org/wiki/CRISPR*

57. Near-Earth Asteroids (NEAs) - *https://en.wikipedia.org/wiki/Near-Earth_object#Near-Earth_asteroids_NEAs*

58. Star lifting - *https://en.m.wikipedia.org/wiki/Star_lifting*

59. Kardashev Scale - *https://en.wikipedia.org/wiki/Kardashev_scale*

60. Planetary Chauvinism - *https://en.m.wikipedia.org/wiki/Planetary_chauvinism*

61. Roundtable TV Interview - *https://www.youtube.com/watch?v=DM88sUBTTRM&feature=youtu.be*

62. Gerard K. O'Neill - *https://en.m.wikipedia.org/wiki/Gerard_K._O'Neill*

63. Carrying Capacity - *https://en.wikipedia.org/wiki/Carrying_capacity*

64. Burj Khalifa - *https://en.wikipedia.org/wiki/Burj_Khalifa*

65. Kessler syndrome - *https://en.wikipedia.org/wiki/Kessler_syndrome*

66. Static Satellites (Statites) - *https://en.m.wikipedia.org/wiki/Statite*

67. Mass Driver - *https://en.wikipedia.org/wiki/Mass_driver*

68. Virtual Reality - *https://en.wikipedia.org/wiki/Virtual_reality*

69. McKendree cylinder - *https://en.wikipedia.org/wiki/McKendree_cylinder*

70. Carbyne - *https://en.wikipedia.org/wiki/Linear_acetylenic_carbon*

71. Lagrange Point - *https://en.wikipedia.org/wiki/Lagrangian_point*

72. Astronomical Unit (AU) - *https://en.wikipedia.org/wiki/Astronomical_unit*

73. Maglev - *https://en.m.wikipedia.org/wiki/Maglev*

74. Roe vs. Wade - *https://en.m.wikipedia.org/wiki/Roe_v._Wade*

75. Universal Basic Income (UBI) - *https://en.wikipedia.org/wiki/Basic_income*

76. Epigenome - *https://en.wikipedia.org/wiki/Epigenome*

77. Tornado Alley - *https://en.wikipedia.org/wiki/Tornado_Alley*

78. Article V Constitutional Convention - *https://en.wikipedia.org/wiki/Convention_to_propose_amend ments_to_the_United_States_Constitution*

79. 17th Ammendment - *https://en.wikipedia.org/wiki/Seventeenth_Amendment_to_the _United_States_Constitution*

80. Quantum Teleportation - *https://en.wikipedia.org/wiki/Quantum_teleportation*

81. Quantum Entanglement - *https://en.wikipedia.org/wiki/Quantum_entanglement*

82. Wigwam Motel - *https://en.wikipedia.org/wiki/Wigwam_Motel*

83. Outer Space Treaty - *https://en.wikipedia.org/wiki/Outer_Space_Treaty*

84. Stanislav Petrov - *https://en.wikipedia.org/wiki/Stanislav_Petrov*

85. Megalopolis - *https://en.wikipedia.org/wiki/Megalopolis*

86. Tidal Locking - *https://en.wikipedia.org/wiki/Tidal_locking*

87. Supernova - *https://en.wikipedia.org/wiki/Supernova*

88. Barnard's Star (Barnard System) - *https://en.wikipedia.org/wiki/Barnard's_Star*

89. Cometary Cloud (Oort Cloud) - *https://en.wikipedia.org/wiki/Oort_cloud*

90. Super Earth - *https://en.wikipedia.org/wiki/Super-Earth*

91. Exoskeletons - *https://en.wikipedia.org/wiki/Powered_exoskeleton*

About the Author

 Erasmo Acosta was born in Cantura, Venezuela, and moved to the United States in 1996 to pursue a software engineering career, sponsored by a small Silicon Valley company. He retired to Portland, Oregon, in 2020 after achieving 32 successful years in the industry.

In 2015, Acosta became interested in the implications of the Fermi Paradox as it relates to the prospects of finding another civilization in the universe. Further research into Futurism, upcoming technologies, and the works of American physicist Gerard O'Neill led him to write *K3+*. The dystopian novel explores human migration, triggered by inequality and climate change, to rotating habitats in space, based on many currently available technologies. Acosta tells the story of how humanity moved past the unsettling times we live in, to a post-scarcity and egalitarian society – absent of fear, uncertainty, inequality, and despair.

Join the Mission

Learn more about space colonization, how it's possible, and why it's the future of humanity. Read it on Medium: *https://medium.com/@erasmix*

Follow Erasmo on Facebook: *https://www.facebook.com/erasmix*

Want even more of K3+? Check out the book page to get the audiobook and share with your space-loving friends: *https://erasmixbooks.blogspot.com*

Thank You!

Thanks so much for reading *K3+*! If you enjoyed this book, please leave an honest review on the book page in the platform where you purchased it. I would very much appreciate your time and input.

Apple: *http://books.apple.com/us/book/id1507830631*

Google: *https://play.google.com/store/books/details/?id=zvj3DwAAQBAJ*

Amazon: *https://www.amazon.com/dp/B086YLNZMQ*

Made in the USA
Monee, IL
24 May 2022

b43d60c4-bb0b-4656-aec3-05a02110f43fR02